The Octopus
A Story Of California
Book II

by

Frank Norris

Double 9
BOOKS

The octopus
A story of california
Book II
by Frank Norris

Copyright © 2024

All Rights reserved.

ISBN: 978-93-64284-88-2

Published by

DOUBLE 9 BOOKS

2/13-B, Ansari Road
Daryaganj, New Delhi – 110002
info@double9books.com
www.double9books.com
Tel. 011-40042856

This book is under public domain

ABOUT THE AUTHOR

Frank Norris (1870-1902) was an American novelist and journalist known for his realistic and naturalistic writing style. He was born in Chicago, Illinois, and raised in a family with a strong literary background. Norris studied at the University of California, Berkeley, and later attended Harvard University. Norris is best remembered for his novels that depicted the social issues and struggles of his time. His most notable work is "The Octopus: A Story of California" (1901), a sprawling epic that explores the conflicts between wheat farmers and the powerful railroad monopolies in California. The novel is considered a classic of American literature and is often associated with the naturalist literary movement. Tragically, Norris's writing career was cut short when he died at the age of 32 due to complications from appendicitis. Despite his short life, he left a lasting impact on American literature, influencing later writers such as Upton Sinclair and Theodore Dreiser. His works continue to be celebrated for their realism, vivid portrayals of the human condition, and insightful social commentary.

CONTENTS

CHAPTER I

In his office at San Francisco, seated before a massive desk of polished redwood, very ornate, Lyman Derrick sat dictating letters to his typewriter, on a certain morning early in the spring of the year. The subdued monotone of his voice proceeded evenly from sentence to sentence, regular, precise, businesslike.

"I have the honour to acknowledge herewith your favour of the 14th instant, and in reply would state— —"

"Please find enclosed draft upon New Orleans to be applied as per our understanding— —"

"In answer to your favour No. 1107, referring to the case of the City and County of San Francisco against Excelsior Warehouse & Storage Co., I would say— —"

His voice continued, expressionless, measured, distinct. While he spoke, he swung slowly back and forth in his leather swivel chair, his elbows resting on the arms, his pop eyes fixed vaguely upon the calendar on the opposite wall, winking at intervals when he paused, searching for a word.

"That's all for the present," he said at length.

Without reply, the typewriter rose and withdrew, thrusting her pencil into the coil of her hair, closing the door behind her, softly, discreetly.

When she had gone, Lyman rose, stretching himself putting up three fingers to hide his yawn. To further loosen his muscles, he took a couple of turns the length of he room, noting with satisfaction its fine appointments, the padded red carpet, the dull olive green tint of the walls, the few choice engravings—portraits of Marshall, Taney, Field, and a coloured lithograph—excellently done—of the Grand Canyon of the Colorado—the deep-seated leather chairs, the large and crowded bookcase (topped with a bust of James Lick, and a huge greenish globe), the waste basket of woven coloured grass, made by Navajo Indians, the massive silver inkstand on the desk, the elaborate filing cabinet, complete in every particular, and the shelves of tin boxes, padlocked, impressive, grave, bearing the names of clients, cases and estates.

He was between thirty-one and thirty-five years of age. Unlike Harran, he resembled his mother, but he was much darker than Annie Derrick and his eyes were much fuller, the eyeball protruding, giving him a pop-eyed, foreign expression, quite unusual and unexpected. His hair was black, and he wore a small, tight, pointed mustache, which he was in the habit of pushing delicately upward from the corners of his lips with the ball of his thumb, the little finger extended. As often as he made this gesture, he prefaced it with a little twisting gesture of the forearm in order to bring his cuff into view, and, in fact, this movement by itself was habitual.

He was dressed carefully, his trousers creased, a pink rose in his lapel. His shoes were of patent leather, his cutaway coat was of very rough black cheviot, his double-breasted waistcoat of tan covered cloth with buttons of smoked pearl. An Ascot scarf—a great puff of heavy black silk—was at his neck, the knot transfixed by a tiny golden pin set off with an opal and four small diamonds.

At one end of the room were two great windows of plate glass, and pausing at length before one of these, Lyman selected a cigarette from his curved box of oxydized silver, lit it and stood looking down and out, willing to be idle for a moment, amused and interested in the view.

His office was on the tenth floor of the EXCHANGE BUILDING, a beautiful, tower-like affair of white stone, that stood on the corner of Market Street near its intersection with Kearney, the most imposing office building of the city.

Below him the city swarmed tumultuous through its grooves, the cable-cars starting and stopping with a gay jangling of bells and a strident whirring of jostled glass windows. Drays and carts clattered over the cobbles, and an incessant shuffling of thousands of feet rose from the pavement. Around Lotta's fountain the baskets of the flower sellers, crammed with chrysanthemums, violets, pinks, roses, lilies, hyacinths, set a brisk note of colour in the grey of the street.

But to Lyman's notion the general impression of this centre of the city's life was not one of strenuous business activity. It was a continuous interest in small things, a people ever willing to be amused at trifles, refusing to consider serious matters—good-natured, allowing themselves to be imposed upon, taking life easily—generous, companionable, enthusiastic; living, as it were, from day to day, in a place where the luxuries of life were had without effort; in a city that offered to consideration the restlessness of a New York, without its earnestness; the serenity of a Naples, without its languor; the romance of a Seville, without its picturesqueness.

As Lyman turned from the window, about to resume his work, the office boy appeared at the door.

"The man from the lithograph company, sir," announced the boy.

"Well, what does he want?" demanded Lyman, adding, however, upon the instant: "Show him in."

A young man entered, carrying a great bundle, which he deposited on a chair, with a gasp of relief, exclaiming, all out of breath:

"From the Standard Lithograph Company."

"What is?"

"Don't know," replied the other. "Maps, I guess."

"I don't want any maps. Who sent them? I guess you're mistaken." Lyman tore the cover from the top of the package, drawing out one of a great many huge sheets of white paper, folded eight times. Suddenly, he uttered an exclamation:

"Ah, I see. They ARE maps. But these should not have come here. They are to go to the regular office for distribution." He wrote a new direction on the label of the package: "Take them to that address," he went on. "I'll keep this one here. The others go to that address. If you see Mr. Darrell, tell him that Mr. Derrick—you get the name—Mr. Derrick may not be able to get around this afternoon, but to go ahead with any business just the same."

The young man departed with the package and Lyman, spreading out the map upon the table, remained for some time studying it thoughtfully.

It was a commissioner's official railway map of the State of California, completed to March 30th of that year. Upon it the different railways of the State were accurately plotted in various colours, blue, green, yellow. However, the blue, the yellow, and the green were but brief traceries, very short, isolated, unimportant. At a little distance these could hardly be seen. The whole map was gridironed by a vast, complicated network of red lines marked P. and S. W. R. R. These centralised at San Francisco and thence ramified and spread north, east, and south, to every quarter of the State. From Coles, in the topmost corner of the map, to Yuma in the lowest, from

Reno on one side to San Francisco on the other, ran the plexus of red, a veritable system of blood circulation, complicated, dividing, and reuniting, branching, splitting, extending, throwing out feelers, off-shoots, tap roots, feeders—diminutive little blood suckers that shot out from the main jugular and went twisting up into some remote county, laying hold upon some forgotten village or town, involving it in one of a myriad branching coils, one of a hundred tentacles, drawing it, as it were, toward that centre from which all this system sprang.

The map was white, and it seemed as if all the colour which should have gone to vivify the various counties, towns, and cities marked upon it had been absorbed by that huge, sprawling organism, with its ruddy arteries converging to a central point. It was as though the State had been sucked white and colourless, and against this pallid background the red arteries of the monster stood out, swollen with life-blood, reaching out to infinity, gorged to bursting; an excrescence, a gigantic parasite fattening upon the life-blood of an entire commonwealth.

However, in an upper corner of the map appeared the names of the three new commissioners: Jones McNish for the first district, Lyman Derrick for the second, and James Darrell for the third.

Nominated in the Democratic State convention in the fall of the preceding year, Lyman, backed by the coteries of San Francisco bosses in the pay of his father's political committee of ranchers, had been elected together with Darrell, the candidate of the Pueblo and Mojave road, and McNish, the avowed candidate of the Pacific and Southwestern. Darrell was rabidly against the P. and S. W., McNish rabidly for it. Lyman was supposed to be the conservative member of the board, the ranchers' candidate, it was true, and faithful to their interests, but a calm man, deliberate, swayed by no such violent emotions as his colleagues.

Osterman's dexterity had at last succeeded in entangling Magnus inextricably in the new politics. The famous League, organised in the heat of passion the night of Annixter's barn dance, had been consolidated all through the winter months. Its executive committee, of which Magnus was chairman, had been, through Osterman's manipulation, merged into the old committee composed of Broderson, Annixter, and himself. Promptly thereat he had resigned the chairmanship of this committee, thus leaving Magnus at its head. Precisely as Osterman had planned, Magnus was now one of them. The new committee accordingly had two objects in view: to resist the attempted grabbing of their lands by the Railroad, and to push forward their own secret scheme of electing a board of railroad commissioners who should regulate wheat rates so as to favour the ranchers of the San Joaquin. The land cases were promptly taken to the courts and the new grading—fixing the price of the lands at twenty and thirty dollars an acre instead of two—bitterly and stubbornly fought. But delays occurred, the process of the law was interminable, and in the intervals the committee addressed itself to the work of seating the "Ranchers' Commission," as the projected Board of Commissioners came to be called.

It was Harran who first suggested that his brother, Lyman, be put forward as the candidate for this district. At once the proposition had a great success. Lyman seemed made for the place. While allied by every tie of blood to the ranching interests, he had never been identified with them. He was city-bred. The Railroad would not be over-suspicious of him. He was a good lawyer, a good business man, keen, clear-headed, far-sighted, had already some practical knowledge of politics, having served a term as assistant district attorney, and even at the present moment occupying the position of sheriff's attorney. More than all, he was the son of Magnus Derrick; he could be relied upon, could be trusted implicitly to remain loyal to the ranchers' cause.

The campaign for Railroad Commissioner had been very interesting. At the very outset Magnus's committee found itself involved in corrupt politics. The primaries had to be captured at all costs and by any means, and when the convention assembled it was found necessary to buy outright the votes of certain delegates. The campaign fund raised by contributions from Magnus, Annixter, Broderson, and Osterman was drawn upon to the extent of five thousand dollars.

Only the committee knew of this corruption. The League, ignoring ways and means, supposed as a matter of course that the campaign was honorably conducted.

For a whole week after the consummation of this part of the deal, Magnus had kept to his house, refusing to be seen, alleging that he was ill, which was not far from the truth. The shame of the business, the loathing of what he had done, were to him things unspeakable. He could no longer look Harran in the face. He began a course of deception with his wife. More than once, he had resolved to break with the whole affair, resigning his position, allowing the others to proceed without him. But now it was too late. He was pledged. He had joined the League. He was its chief, and his defection might mean its disintegration at the very time when it needed all its strength to fight the land cases. More than a mere deal in bad politics was involved. There was the land grab. His withdrawal from an unholy cause would mean the weakening, perhaps the collapse, of another cause that he believed to be righteous as truth itself. He was hopelessly caught in the mesh. Wrong seemed indissolubly knitted into the texture of Right. He was blinded, dizzied, overwhelmed, caught in the current of events, and hurried along he knew not where. He resigned himself.

In the end, and after much ostentatious opposition on the part of the railroad heelers, Lyman was nominated and subsequently elected.

When this consummation was reached Magnus, Osterman, Broderson, and Annixter stared at each other. Their wildest hopes had not dared to fix themselves upon so easy a victory as this. It was not believable that the corporation would allow itself to be fooled so easily, would rush open-eyed into the trap. How had it happened?

Osterman, however, threw his hat into the air with wild whoops of delight. Old Broderson permitted himself a feeble cheer. Even Magnus beamed satisfaction. The other members of the League, present at the time, shook hands all around and spoke of opening a few bottles on the strength of the occasion. Annixter alone was recalcitrant.

"It's too easy," he declared. "No, I'm not satisfied. Where's Shelgrim in all this? Why don't he show his hand, damn his soul? The thing is yellow, I tell you. There's a big fish in these waters somewheres. I don't know his name, and I don't know his game, but he's moving round off and on, just out of sight. If you think you've netted him, I DON'T, that's all I've got to say."

But he was jeered down as a croaker. There was the Commission. He couldn't get around that, could he? There was Darrell and Lyman Derrick, both pledged to the ranches. Good Lord, he was never satisfied. He'd be obstinate till the very last gun was fired. Why, if he got drowned in a river he'd float upstream just to be contrary.

In the course of time, the new board was seated. For the first few months of its term, it was occupied in clearing up the business left over by the old board and in the completion of the railway map. But now, the decks were cleared. It was about to address itself to the consideration of a revision of the tariff for the carriage of grain between the San Joaquin Valley and tidewater.

Both Lyman and Darrell were pledged to an average ten per cent. cut of the grain rates throughout the entire State.

The typewriter returned with the letters for Lyman to sign, and he put away the map and took up his morning's routine of business, wondering, the while, what would become of his practice during the time he was involved in the business of the Ranchers' Railroad Commission.

But towards noon, at the moment when Lyman was drawing off a glass of mineral water from the siphon that stood at his elbow, there was an interruption. Some one rapped vigorously upon the door, which was immediately after opened, and Magnus and Harran came in, followed by Presley.

"Hello, hello!" cried Lyman, jumping up, extending his hands, "why, here's a surprise. I didn't expect you all till to-night. Come in, come in and sit down. Have a glass of sizz-water, Governor."

The others explained that they had come up from Bonneville the night before, as the Executive Committee of the League had received a despatch from the lawyers it had retained to fight the Railroad, that the judge of the court in San Francisco, where the test cases were being tried, might be expected to hand down his decision the next day.

Very soon after the announcement of the new grading of the ranchers' lands, the corporation had offered, through S. Behrman, to lease the disputed lands to the ranchers at a nominal figure. The offer had been angrily rejected, and the Railroad had put up the lands for sale at Ruggles's office in Bonneville. At the exorbitant price named, buyers promptly appeared—dummy buyers, beyond shadow of doubt, acting either for the Railroad or for S. Behrman—men hitherto unknown in the county, men without property, without money, adventurers, heelers. Prominent among them, and bidding for the railroad's holdings included on Annixter's ranch, was Delaney.

The farce of deeding the corporation's sections to these fictitious purchasers was solemnly gone through with at Ruggles's office, the Railroad guaranteeing them possession. The League refused to allow the supposed buyers to come upon the land, and the Railroad, faithful to its pledge in the matter of guaranteeing its dummies possession, at once began suits in ejectment in the district court in Visalia, the county seat.

It was the preliminary skirmish, the reconnaisance in force, the combatants feeling each other's strength, willing to proceed with caution, postponing the actual death-grip for a while till each had strengthened its position and organised its forces.

During the time the cases were on trial at Visalia, S. Behrman was much in evidence in and about the courts. The trial itself, after tedious preliminaries, was brief. The ranchers lost. The test cases were immediately carried up to the United States Circuit Court in San Francisco. At the moment the decision of this court was pending.

"Why, this is news," exclaimed Lyman, in response to the Governor's announcement; "I did not expect them to be so prompt. I was in court only last week and there seemed to be no end of business ahead. I suppose you are very anxious?"

Magnus nodded. He had seated himself in one of Lyman's deep chairs, his grey top-hat, with its wide brim, on the floor beside him. His coat of black broad-cloth that had been tightly packed in his valise, was yet wrinkled and creased; his trousers were strapped under his high boots. As he spoke, he stroked the bridge of his hawklike nose with his bent forefinger.

Leaning-back in his chair, he watched his two sons with secret delight. To his eye, both were perfect specimens of their class, intelligent, well-looking, resourceful. He was intensely proud of them. He was never happier, never more nearly jovial, never more erect, more military, more alert, and buoyant than when in the company of his two sons. He honestly believed that no finer examples of young manhood existed throughout the entire nation.

"I think we should win in this court," Harran observed, watching the bubbles break in his glass. "The investigation has been much more complete than in the Visalia trial. Our case this time is too good. It has made too much talk. The court would not dare render a decision for the Railroad. Why, there's the agreement in black and white—and the circulars the Railroad issued. How CAN one get around those?"

"Well, well, we shall know in a few hours now," remarked Magnus.

"Oh," exclaimed Lyman, surprised, "it is for this morning, then. Why aren't you at the court?"

"It seemed undignified, boy," answered the Governor. "We shall know soon enough."

"Good God!" exclaimed Harran abruptly, "when I think of what is involved. Why, Lyman, it's our home, the ranch house itself, nearly all Los Muertos, practically our whole fortune, and just now when there is promise of an enormous crop of wheat. And it is not only us. There are over half a million acres of the San Joaquin involved. In some cases of the smaller ranches, it is the confiscation of the whole of the rancher's land. If this thing goes through, it will absolutely beggar nearly a hundred men. Broderson wouldn't have a thousand acres to his name. Why, it's monstrous."

"But the corporations offered to lease these lands," remarked Lyman. "Are any of the ranchers taking up that offer—or are any of them buying outright?"

"Buying! At the new figure!" exclaimed Harran, "at twenty and thirty an acre! Why, there's not one in ten that CAN. They are land-poor. And as for leasing—leasing land they virtually own—no, there's precious few are doing that, thank God! That would be acknowledging the railroad's ownership right away—forfeiting their rights for good. None of the LEAGUERS are doing it, I know. That would be the rankest treachery."

He paused for a moment, drinking the rest of the mineral water, then interrupting Lyman, who was about to speak to Presley, drawing him into the conversation through politeness, said: "Matters are just romping right along to a crisis these days. It's a make or break for the wheat growers of the State now, no mistake. Here are the land cases and the new grain tariff drawing to a head at about the same time. If we win our land cases, there's your new freight rates to be applied, and then all is beer and skittles. Won't the San Joaquin go wild if we pull it off, and I believe we will."

"How we wheat growers are exploited and trapped and deceived at every turn," observed Magnus sadly. "The courts, the capitalists, the railroads, each of them in turn hoodwinks us into some new and wonderful scheme, only to betray us in the end. Well," he added, turning to Lyman, "one thing at least we can depend on. We will cut their grain rates for them, eh, Lyman?"

Lyman crossed his legs and settled himself in his office chair.

"I have wanted to have a talk with you about that, sir," he said. "Yes, we will cut the rates—an average 10 per cent. cut throughout the State, as we are pledged. But I am going to warn you, Governor, and you, Harran; don't expect too much at first. The man who, even after twenty years' training in the operation of railroads, can draw an equitable, smoothly working schedule of freight rates between shipping point and common point, is capable of governing the United States. What with main lines, and leased lines, and points of transfer, and the laws governing common carriers, and the rulings of the Inter-State Commerce Commission, the whole matter has become so confused that Vanderbilt himself couldn't straighten it out. And how can it be expected that railroad commissions who are chosen—well, let's be frank—as ours was, for instance, from out a number of men who don't know the difference between a switching charge and a differential rate, are going to regulate the whole business in six months' time? Cut rates; yes, any fool can do that; any fool can write one dollar instead of two, but if you cut too low by a fraction of one per cent. and if the railroad can get out an injunction, tie you up and show that your new rate prevents the road being operated at a profit, how are you any better off?"

"Your conscientiousness does you credit, Lyman," said the Governor. "I respect you for it, my son. I know you will be fair to the railroad. That is all we want. Fairness to the corporation is fairness to the farmer, and we won't expect you to readjust the whole matter out of hand. Take your time. We can afford to wait."

"And suppose the next commission is a railroad board, and reverses all our figures?"

The one-time mining king, the most redoubtable poker player of Calaveras County, permitted himself a momentary twinkle of his eyes.

"By then it will be too late. We will, all of us, have made our fortunes by then."

The remark left Presley astonished out of all measure He never could accustom himself to these strange lapses in the Governor's character. Magnus was by nature a public man, judicious, deliberate, standing firm for principle, yet upon rare occasion, by some such remark as this, he would betray the presence of a sub-nature of recklessness, inconsistent, all at variance with his creeds and tenets.

At the very bottom, when all was said and done, Magnus remained the Forty-niner. Deep down in his heart the spirit of the Adventurer yet persisted. "We will all of us have made fortunes by then." That was it precisely. "After us the deluge." For all his public spirit, for all his championship of justice and truth, his respect for law, Magnus remained the gambler, willing to play for colossal stakes, to hazard a fortune on the chance of winning a million. It was the true California spirit that found expression through him, the spirit of the West, unwilling to occupy itself with details, refusing to wait, to be patient, to achieve by legitimate plodding; the miner's instinct of wealth acquired in a single night prevailed, in spite of all. It was in this frame of mind that Magnus and the multitude of other ranchers of whom he was a type, farmed their ranches. They had no love for their land. They were not attached to the soil. They worked their ranches as a quarter of a century before they had worked their mines. To husband the resources of their marvellous San Joaquin, they considered niggardly, petty, Hebraic. To get all there was out of the land, to squeeze it dry, to exhaust it, seemed their policy. When, at last, the land worn out, would refuse to yield, they would invest their money in something else; by then, they would all have made fortunes. They did not care. "After us the deluge."

Lyman, however, was obviously uneasy, willing to change the subject. He rose to his feet, pulling down his cuffs.

"By the way," he observed, "I want you three to lunch with me to-day at my club. It is close by. You can wait there for news of the court's decision as well as anywhere else, and I should like to show you the place. I have just joined."

At the club, when the four men were seated at a small table in the round window of the main room, Lyman's popularity with all classes was very apparent. Hardly a man entered that did not call out a salutation to him, some even coming over to shake his hand. He seemed to be every man's friend, and to all he seemed equally genial. His affability, even to those whom he disliked, was unfailing.

"See that fellow yonder," he said to Magnus, indicating a certain middle-aged man, flamboyantly dressed, who wore his hair long, who was afflicted with sore eyes, and the collar of whose velvet coat was sprinkled with dandruff, "that's Hartrath, the artist, a man absolutely devoid of even the commonest decency. How he got in here is a mystery to me."

Yet, when this Hartrath came across to say "How do you do" to Lyman, Lyman was as eager in his cordiality as his warmest friend could have expected.

"Why the devil are you so chummy with him, then?" observed Harran when Hartrath had gone away.

Lyman's explanation was vague. The truth of the matter was, that Magnus's oldest son was consumed by inordinate ambition. Political preferment was his dream, and to the realisation of this dream popularity was an essential. Every man who could vote, blackguard or gentleman, was to be conciliated, if possible. He made it his study to become known throughout the entire community—to put influential men under obligations to himself. He never forgot a name or a face. With everybody he was the hail-fellow-well-met. His ambition was not trivial. In his disregard for small things, he resembled his father. Municipal office had no attraction for him. His goal was higher. He had planned his life twenty years ahead. Already Sheriff's Attorney, Assistant District Attorney and Railroad Commissioner, he could, if he desired, attain the office of District Attorney itself. Just now, it was a question with him whether or not it would be politic to fill this office. Would it advance or sidetrack him in the career he had outlined for himself? Lyman wanted to be something better than District Attorney, better than Mayor, than State Senator, or even than member of the United States Congress. He wanted to be, in fact, what his father was only in name—to succeed where Magnus had failed. He wanted to be governor of the State. He had put his teeth together, and, deaf to all other considerations, blind to all other issues, he worked with the infinite slowness, the unshakable tenacity of the coral insect to this one end.

After luncheon was over, Lyman ordered cigars and liqueurs, and with the three others returned to the main room of the club. However, their former place in the round window was occupied. A middle-aged man, with iron grey hair and moustache, who wore a frock coat and a white waistcoat, and in some indefinable manner suggested a retired naval officer, was sitting at their table smoking a long, thin cigar. At sight of him, Presley became animated. He uttered a mild exclamation:

"Why, isn't that Mr. Cedarquist?"

"Cedarquist?" repeated Lyman Derrick. "I know him well. Yes, of course, it is," he continued. "Governor, you must know him. He is one of our representative men. You would enjoy talking to him. He was the head of the big Atlas Iron Works. They have shut down recently, you know. Not failed exactly, but just ceased to be a paying investment, and Cedarquist closed them out. He has other interests, though. He's a rich man—a capitalist."

Lyman brought the group up to the gentleman in question and introduced them. "Mr. Magnus Derrick, of course," observed Cedarquist, as he took the Governor's hand. "I've known you by repute for some time, sir. This is a great pleasure, I assure you." Then, turning to Presley, he added: "Hello, Pres, my boy. How is the great, the very great Poem getting on?"

"It's not getting on at all, sir," answered Presley, in some embarrassment, as they all sat down. "In fact, I've about given up the idea. There's so much interest in what you might call 'living issues' down at Los Muertos now, that I'm getting further and further from it every day."

"I should say as much," remarked the manufacturer, turning towards Magnus. "I'm watching your fight with Shelgrim, Mr. Derrick, with every degree of interest." He raised his drink of whiskey and soda. "Here's success to you."

As he replaced his glass, the artist Hartrath joined the group uninvited. As a pretext, he engaged Lyman in conversation. Lyman, he believed, was a man with a "pull" at the City Hall. In connection with a projected Million-Dollar Fair and Flower Festival, which at that moment was the talk of the city, certain statues were to be erected, and Hartrath bespoke Lyman's influence to further the pretensions of a sculptor friend of his, who wished to be Art Director of the affair. In the matter of this Fair and Flower Festival, Hartrath was not lacking in enthusiasm. He addressed the others with extravagant gestures, blinking his inflamed eyelids.

"A million dollars," he exclaimed. "Hey! think of that. Why, do you know that we have five hundred thousand practically pledged already? Talk about public spirit, gentlemen, this is the most public-spirited city on the continent. And the money is not thrown away. We will have Eastern visitors here by the thousands—capitalists—men with money to invest. The million we spend on our fair will be money in our pockets. Ah, you should see how the women of this city are taking hold of the matter. They are giving all kinds of little entertainments, teas, 'Olde Tyme Singing Skules,' amateur theatricals, gingerbread fetes, all for the benefit of the fund, and the business men, too—pouring out their money like water. It is splendid, splendid, to see a community so patriotic."

The manufacturer, Cedarquist, fixed the artist with a glance of melancholy interest.

"And how much," he remarked, "will they contribute—your gingerbread women and public-spirited capitalists, towards the blowing up of the ruins of the Atlas Iron Works?"

"Blowing up? I don't understand," murmured the artist, surprised. "When you get your Eastern capitalists out here with your Million-Dollar Fair," continued Cedarquist, "you don't propose, do you, to let them see a Million-Dollar Iron Foundry standing idle, because of the indifference of San Francisco business men? They might ask pertinent questions, your capitalists, and we should have to answer that our business men preferred to invest their money in corner lots and government bonds, rather than to back up a legitimate, industrial enterprise. We don't want fairs. We want active furnaces. We don't want public statues, and fountains, and park extensions and gingerbread fetes. We want business enterprise. Isn't it like us? Isn't it like us?" he exclaimed sadly. "What a melancholy comment! San Francisco! It is not a city—it is a Midway Plaisance. California likes to be fooled. Do you suppose Shelgrim could convert the whole San Joaquin Valley into his back yard otherwise? Indifference to public affairs—absolute indifference, it stamps us all. Our State is the very paradise of fakirs. You and your Million-Dollar Fair!" He turned to Hartrath with a quiet smile. "It is just such men as you, Mr. Hartrath, that are the ruin of us. You organise a sham of tinsel and pasteboard, put on fool's cap and bells, beat a gong at a street corner, and the crowd cheers you and drops nickels into your hat. Your ginger-bread fete; yes, I saw it in full blast the other night on the grounds of one of your women's places on Sutter Street. I was on my way home from the last board meeting of the Atlas Company. A gingerbread fete, my God! and the Atlas plant shutting down for want of financial backing. A million dollars spent to attract the Eastern investor, in order to show him an abandoned rolling mill, wherein the only activity is the sale of remnant material and scrap steel."

Lyman, however, interfered. The situation was becoming strained. He tried to conciliate the three men—the artist, the manufacturer, and the farmer, the warring elements. But Hartrath, unwilling to face the enmity that he felt accumulating against him, took himself away. A picture of his—"A Study of the Contra Costa Foot-hills"—was to be raffled in the club rooms for the benefit of the Fair. He, himself, was in charge of the matter. He disappeared.

Cedarquist looked after him with contemplative interest. Then, turning to Magnus, excused himself for the acridity of his words.

"He's no worse than many others, and the people of this State and city are, after all, only a little more addle-headed than other Americans." It was his favourite topic. Sure of the interest of his hearers, he unburdened himself.

"If I were to name the one crying evil of American life, Mr. Derrick," he continued, "it would be the indifference of the better people to public affairs. It is so in all our great centres. There are other great trusts, God knows, in the United States besides our own dear P. and S. W. Railroad. Every State has its own grievance. If it is not a railroad trust, it is a sugar trust, or an oil trust, or an industrial trust, that exploits the People, BECAUSE THE PEOPLE ALLOW IT. The indifference of the People is the opportunity of the despot. It is as true as that the whole is greater than the part, and the maxim is so old that it is trite—it is laughable. It is neglected and disused for the sake of some new ingenious and complicated theory, some wonderful scheme of reorganisation, but the fact remains, nevertheless, simple, fundamental, everlasting. The People have but to say 'No,' and not the strongest tyranny, political, religious, or financial, that was ever organised, could survive one week."

The others, absorbed, attentive, approved, nodding their heads in silence as the manufacturer finished.

"That's one reason, Mr. Derrick," the other resumed after a moment, "why I have been so glad to meet you. You and your League are trying to say 'No' to the trust. I hope you will succeed. If your example will rally the People to your cause, you will. Otherwise—" he shook his head.

"One stage of the fight is to be passed this very day," observed Magnus. "My sons and myself are expecting hourly news from the City Hall, a decision in our case is pending."

"We are both of us fighters, it seems, Mr. Derrick," said Cedarquist. "Each with his particular enemy. We are well met, indeed, the farmer and the manufacturer, both in the same grist between the two millstones of the lethargy of the Public and the aggression of the Trust, the two great evils of modern America. Pres, my boy, there is your epic poem ready to hand."

But Cedarquist was full of another idea. Rarely did so favourable an opportunity present itself for explaining his theories, his ambitions. Addressing himself to Magnus, he continued:

"Fortunately for myself, the Atlas Company was not my only investment. I have other interests. The building of ships—steel sailing ships—has been an ambition of mine,—for this purpose, Mr. Derrick, to carry American wheat. For years, I have studied this question of American wheat, and at last, I have arrived at a theory. Let me explain. At present, all our California wheat goes to Liverpool, and from that port is distributed over the world. But a change is coming. I am sure of it. You young men," he turned to Presley, Lyman, and Harran, "will live to see it. Our century is about done. The great word of this nineteenth century has been Production. The great word of the twentieth century will be—listen to me, you youngsters—Markets. As a market for our Production—or let me take a concrete example—as a market for our WHEAT, Europe is played out. Population in Europe is not increasing fast enough to keep up with the rapidity of our production. In some cases, as in France, the population is stationary. WE, however, have gone on producing wheat at a tremendous rate.

"The result is over-production. We supply more than Europe can eat, and down go the prices. The remedy is NOT in the curtailing of our wheat areas, but in this, we MUST HAVE NEW MARKETS, GREATER MARKETS. For years we have been sending our wheat from East to West, from California to Europe. But the time will come when we must send it from West to East. We must march with the course of empire, not against it. I mean, we must look to China. Rice in China is losing its nutritive quality. The Asiatics, though, must be fed; if not on rice, then on wheat. Why, Mr. Derrick, if only one-half the population of China ate a half ounce of flour per man per day all the wheat areas in California could not feed them. Ah, if I could only hammer that into the brains of every rancher of the San Joaquin, yes, and of every owner of every bonanza farm in Dakota and Minnesota. Send your wheat to China; handle it yourselves; do away with the middleman; break up the Chicago wheat pits and elevator rings and mixing houses. When in feeding China you have decreased the European shipments, the effect is instantaneous. Prices go up in Europe without having the least effect upon the prices in China. We hold the key, we have the wheat,—infinitely more than we ourselves can eat. Asia and Europe must look to America to be fed. What fatuous neglect of opportunity to continue to deluge Europe with our surplus food when the East trembles upon the verge of starvation!"

The two men, Cedarquist and Magnus, continued the conversation a little further. The manufacturer's idea was new to the Governor. He was greatly interested. He withdrew from the conversation. Thoughtful, he leaned back in his place, stroking the bridge of his beak-like nose with a crooked forefinger.

Cedarquist turned to Harran and began asking details as to the conditions of the wheat growers of the San Joaquin. Lyman still maintained an attitude of polite aloofness, yawning occasionally behind three fingers, and Presley was left to the company of his own thoughts.

There had been a day when the affairs and grievances of the farmers of his acquaintance—Magnus, Annixter, Osterman, and old Broderson— had filled him only with disgust. His mind full of a great, vague epic poem of the West, he had kept himself apart, disdainful of what he chose to consider their petty squabbles. But the scene in Annixter's harness room had thrilled and uplifted him. He was palpitating with excitement all through the succeeding months. He abandoned the idea of an epic poem. In six months he had not written a single verse. Day after day he trembled with excitement as the relations between the Trust and League became more and more strained. He saw the matter in its true light. It was typical. It was the world-old war between Freedom and Tyranny, and at times his hatred of the railroad shook him like a crisp and withered reed, while the languid indifference of the people of the State to the quarrel filled him with a blind exasperation.

But, as he had once explained to Vanamee, he must find expression. He felt that he would suffocate otherwise. He had begun to keep a journal. As the inclination spurred him, he wrote down his thoughts and ideas in this, sometimes every day, sometimes only three or four times a month.

Also he flung aside his books of poems—Milton, Tennyson, Browning, even Homer—and addressed himself to Mill, Malthus, Young, Poushkin, Henry George, Schopenhauer. He attacked the subject of Social Inequality with unbounded enthusiasm. He devoured, rather than read, and emerged from the affair, his mind a confused jumble of conflicting notions, sick with over-effort, raging against injustice and oppression, and with not one sane suggestion as to remedy or redress.

The butt of his cigarette scorched his fingers and roused him from his brooding. In the act of lighting another, he glanced across the room and was surprised to see two very prettily dressed young women in the company of an older gentleman, in a long frock coat, standing before Hartrath's painting, examining it, their heads upon one side.

Presley uttered a murmur of surprise. He, himself, was a member of the club, and the presence of women within its doors, except on special occasions, was not tolerated. He turned to Lyman Derrick for an explanation, but this other had also seen the women and abruptly exclaimed:

"I declare, I had forgotten about it. Why, this is Ladies' Day, of course."

"Why, yes," interposed Cedarquist, glancing at the women over his shoulder. "Didn't you know? They let 'em in twice a year, you remember, and this is a double occasion. They are going to raffle Hartrath's picture,— for the benefit of the Gingerbread Fair. Why, you are not up to date, Lyman. This is a sacred and religious rite,—an important public event."

"Of course, of course," murmured Lyman. He found means to survey Harran and Magnus. Certainly, neither his father nor his brother were dressed for the function that impended. He had been stupid. Magnus invariably attracted attention, and now with his trousers strapped under his boots, his wrinkled frock coat—Lyman twisted his cuffs into sight with an impatient, nervous movement of his wrists, glancing a second time at his brother's pink face, forward curling, yellow hair and clothes of a country cut. But there was no help for it. He wondered what were the club regulations in the matter of bringing in visitors on Ladies' Day. "Sure enough, Ladies' Day," he remarked, "I am very glad you struck it, Governor. We can sit right where we are. I guess this is as good a place as any to see the crowd. It's a good chance to see all the big guns of the city. Do you expect your people here, Mr. Cedarquist?"

"My wife may come, and my daughters," said the manufacturer.

"Ah," murmured Presley, "so much the better. I was going to give myself the pleasure of calling upon your daughters, Mr. Cedarquist, this afternoon."

"You can save your carfare, Pres," said Cedarquist, "you will see them here."

No doubt, the invitations for the occasion had appointed one o'clock as the time, for between that hour and two, the guests arrived in an almost unbroken stream. From their point of vantage in the round window of the main room, Magnus, his two sons, and Presley looked on very interested. Cedarquist had excused himself, affirming that he must look out for his women folk.

Of every ten of the arrivals, seven, at least, were ladies. They entered the room—this unfamiliar masculine haunt, where their husbands, brothers, and sons spent so much of their time—with a certain show of hesitancy and little, nervous, oblique glances, moving their heads from side to side like a file of hens venturing into a strange barn. They came in groups, ushered by a single member of the club, doing the honours with effusive bows and polite gestures, indicating the various objects of interest, pictures, busts, and the like, that decorated the room.

Fresh from his recollections of Bonneville, Guadalajara, and the dance in Annixter's barn, Presley was astonished at the beauty of these women and the elegance of their toilettes. The crowd thickened rapidly. A murmur of conversation arose, subdued, gracious, mingled with the soft rustle of silk, grenadines, velvet. The scent of delicate perfumes spread in the air, Violet de Parme, Peau d'Espagne. Colours of the most harmonious blends appeared and disappeared at intervals in the slowly moving press, touches of lavender-tinted velvets, pale violet crepes and cream-coloured appliqued laces.

There seemed to be no need of introductions. Everybody appeared to be acquainted. There was no awkwardness, no constraint. The assembly disengaged an impression of refined pleasure. On every hand, innumerable dialogues seemed to go forward easily and naturally, without break or interruption, witty, engaging, the couple never at a loss for repartee. A third party was gracefully included, then a fourth. Little groups were formed,—groups that divided themselves, or melted into other groups, or disintegrated again into isolated pairs, or lost themselves in the background of the mass,—all without friction, without embarrassment,—the whole affair going forward of itself, decorous, tactful, well-bred.

At a distance, and not too loud, a stringed orchestra sent up a pleasing hum. Waiters, with brass buttons on their full dress coats, went from group to group, silent, unobtrusive, serving salads and ices.

But the focus of the assembly was the little space before Hartrath's painting. It was called "A Study of the Contra Costa Foothills," and was set in a frame of natural redwood, the bark still adhering. It was conspicuously displayed on an easel at the right of the entrance to the main room of the club, and was very large. In the foreground, and to the left, under the shade of a live-oak, stood a couple of reddish cows, knee-deep in a patch of yellow poppies, while in the right-hand corner, to balance the composition, was placed a girl in a pink dress and white sunbonnet, in which the shadows were indicated by broad dashes of pale blue paint. The ladies and young girls examined the production with little murmurs of admiration, hazarding remembered phrases, searching for the exact balance between generous praise and critical discrimination, expressing their opinions in the mild technicalities of the Art Books and painting classes. They spoke of atmospheric effects, of middle distance, of "chiaro-oscuro," of fore-shortening, of the decomposition of light, of the subordination of individuality to fidelity of interpretation.

One tall girl, with hair almost white in its blondness, having observed that the handling of the masses reminded her strongly of Corot, her companion, who carried a gold lorgnette by a chain around her neck, answered:

"Ah! Millet, perhaps, but not Corot."

This verdict had an immediate success. It was passed from group to group. It seemed to imply a delicate distinction that carried conviction at once. It was decided formally that the reddish brown cows in the picture were reminiscent of Daubigny, and that the handling of the masses was altogether Millet, but that the general effect was not quite Corot.

Presley, curious to see the painting that was the subject of so much discussion, had left the group in the round window, and stood close by Hartrath, craning his head over the shoulders of the crowd, trying to catch a glimpse of the reddish cows, the milk-maid and the blue painted foothills. He was suddenly aware of Cedarquist's voice in his ear, and, turning about, found himself face to face with the manufacturer, his wife and his two daughters.

There was a meeting. Salutations were exchanged, Presley shaking hands all around, expressing his delight at seeing his old friends once more, for he had known the family from his boyhood, Mrs. Cedarquist being his aunt. Mrs. Cedarquist and her two daughters declared that the air of Los Muertos must certainly have done him a world of good. He was stouter, there could be no doubt of it. A little pale, perhaps. He was fatiguing himself with his writing, no doubt. Ah, he must take care. Health was everything, after all. Had he been writing any more verse? Every month they scanned the magazines, looking for his name.

Mrs. Cedarquist was a fashionable woman, the president or chairman of a score of clubs. She was forever running after fads, appearing continually in the society wherein she moved with new and astounding proteges—fakirs whom she unearthed no one knew where, discovering them long in advance of her companions. Now it was a Russian Countess, with dirty finger nails, who travelled throughout America and borrowed money; now an Aesthete who possessed a wonderful collection of topaz gems, who submitted decorative schemes for the interior arrangement of houses and who "received" in Mrs. Cedarquist's drawing-rooms dressed in a white velvet cassock; now a widow of some Mohammedan of Bengal or Rajputana, who had a blue spot in the middle of her forehead and who solicited contributions for her sisters in affliction; now a certain bearded poet, recently back from the Klondike; now a decayed musician who had been ejected from a young ladies' musical conservatory of Europe because of certain surprising pamphlets on free love, and who had come to San Francisco to introduce the community to the music of Brahms; now a Japanese youth who wore spectacles and a grey flannel shirt and who, at intervals, delivered himself of the most astonishing poems, vague, unrhymed, unmetrical lucubrations, incoherent, bizarre; now a Christian Scientist, a lean, grey woman, whose creed was neither Christian nor scientific; now a university professor, with the bristling beard of an anarchist chief-of-section, and a roaring, guttural voice, whose intenseness left him gasping and apoplectic; now a civilised Cherokee with a mission; now a female elocutionist, whose forte was Byron's Songs of Greece; now a high caste Chinaman; now a miniature painter; now a tenor, a pianiste, a mandolin player, a missionary, a drawing master, a virtuoso, a collector, an Armenian, a botanist with a new flower, a critic with a new theory, a doctor with a new treatment.

And all these people had a veritable mania for declamation and fancy dress. The Russian Countess gave talks on the prisons of Siberia, wearing the headdress and pinchbeck ornaments of a Slav bride; the Aesthete, in his white cassock, gave readings on obscure questions of art and ethics. The widow of India, in the costume of her caste, described the social life of her people at home. The bearded poet, perspiring in furs and boots of reindeer skin, declaimed verses of his own composition about the wild life of the Alaskan mining camps. The Japanese youth, in the silk robes of the Samurai two-sworded nobles, read from his own works—"The flat-bordered earth, nailed down at night, rusting under the darkness," "The brave, upright rains that came down like errands from iron-bodied yore-time." The Christian Scientist, in funereal, impressive black, discussed the contra-will and pan-psychic hylozoism. The university professor put on a full dress suit and lisle thread gloves at three in the afternoon and before literary clubs and circles bellowed extracts from Goethe and Schiler in the German, shaking his fists, purple with vehemence. The Cherokee, arrayed in fringed buckskin and blue beads, rented from a costumer, intoned folk songs of his people in the vernacular. The elocutionist in cheese-cloth toga and tin bracelets, rendered "The Isles of Greece, where burning Sappho loved and sung." The Chinaman, in the robes of a mandarin, lectured on Confucius. The Armenian, in fez and baggy trousers, spoke of the Unspeakable Turk. The mandolin player, dressed like a bull fighter, held musical conversaziones, interpreting the peasant songs of Andalusia.

It was the Fake, the eternal, irrepressible Sham; glib, nimble, ubiquitous, tricked out in all the paraphernalia of imposture, an endless defile of charlatans that passed interminably before the gaze of the city, marshalled by "lady presidents," exploited by clubs of women, by literary societies, reading circles, and culture organisations. The attention the Fake received, the time devoted to it, the money which it absorbed, were incredible. It was all one that impostor after impostor was exposed; it was all one that the clubs, the circles, the societies were proved beyond doubt to have been swindled. The more the Philistine press of the city railed and guyed, the more the women rallied to the defence of their protege of the hour. That their favourite was persecuted, was to them a veritable rapture. Promptly they invested the apostle of culture with the glamour of a martyr.

The fakirs worked the community as shell-game tricksters work a county fair, departing with bursting pocket-books, passing on the word to the next in line, assured that the place was not worked out, knowing well that there was enough for all.

More frequently the public of the city, unable to think of more than one thing at one time, prostrated itself at the feet of a single apostle, but at other moments, such as the present, when a Flower Festival or a Million-Dollar Fair aroused enthusiasm in all quarters, the occasion was one of gala for the entire Fake. The decayed professors, virtuosi, litterateurs, and artists thronged to the place en masse. Their clamour filled all the air. On every hand one heard the scraping of violins, the tinkling of mandolins, the suave accents of "art talks," the incoherencies of poets, the declamation of elocutionists, the inarticulate wanderings of the Japanese, the confused mutterings of the Cherokee, the guttural bellowing of the German university professor, all in the name of the Million-Dollar Fair. Money to the extent of hundreds of thousands was set in motion.

Mrs. Cedarquist was busy from morning until night. One after another, she was introduced to newly arrived fakirs. To each poet, to each litterateur, to each professor she addressed the same question:

"How long have you known you had this power?"

She spent her days in one quiver of excitement and jubilation. She was "in the movement." The people of the city were awakening to a Realisation of the Beautiful, to a sense of the higher needs of life. This was Art, this was Literature, this was Culture and Refinement. The Renaissance had appeared in the West.

She was a short, rather stout, red-faced, very much over-dressed little woman of some fifty years. She was rich in her own name, even before her marriage, being a relative of Shelgrim himself and on familiar terms with the great financier and his family. Her husband, while deploring the policy of the railroad, saw no good reason for quarrelling with Shelgrim, and on more than one occasion had dined at his house. On this occasion, delighted that she had come upon a "minor poet," she insisted upon presenting him to Hartrath.

"You two should have so much in common," she explained.

Presley shook the flaccid hand of the artist, murmuring conventionalities, while Mrs. Cedarquist hastened to say:

"I am sure you know Mr. Presley's verse, Mr. Hartrath. You should, believe me. You two have much in common. I can see so much that is alike in your modes of interpreting nature. In Mr. Presley's sonnet, 'The Better Part,' there is the same note as in your picture, the same sincerity of tone, the same subtlety of touch, the same nuances, —ah."

"Oh, my dear Madame," murmured the artist, interrupting Presley's impatient retort; "I am a mere bungler. You don't mean quite that, I am sure. I am too sensitive. It is my cross. Beauty," he closed his sore eyes with a little expression of pain, "beauty unmans me."

But Mrs. Cedarquist was not listening. Her eyes were fixed on the artist's luxuriant hair, a thick and glossy mane, that all but covered his coat collar.

"Leonine!" she murmured— "leonine! Like Samson of old."

However, abruptly bestirring herself, she exclaimed a second later:

"But I must run away. I am selling tickets for you this afternoon, Mr. Hartrath. I am having such success. Twenty-five already. Mr. Presley, you will take two chances, I am sure, and, oh, by the way, I have such good news. You know I am one of the lady members of the subscription committee for our Fair, and you know we approached Mr. Shelgrim for a donation to help along. Oh, such a liberal patron, a real Lorenzo di' Medici. In the name of the Pacific and Southwestern he has subscribed, think of it, five thousand dollars; and yet they will talk of the meanness of the railroad."

"Possibly it is to his interest," murmured Presley. "The fairs and festivals bring people to the city over his railroad."

But the others turned on him, expostulating.

"Ah, you Philistine," declared Mrs. Cedarquist. "And this from YOU!, Presley; to attribute such base motives——"

"If the poets become materialised, Mr. Presley," declared Hartrath, "what can we say to the people?"

"And Shelgrim encourages your million-dollar fairs and fetes," said a voice at Presley's elbow, "because it is throwing dust in the people's eyes."

The group turned about and saw Cedarquist, who had come up unobserved in time to catch the drift of the talk. But he spoke without bitterness; there was even a good-humoured twinkle in his eyes.

"Yes," he continued, smiling, "our dear Shelgrim promotes your fairs, not only as Pres says, because it is money in his pocket, but because it amuses the people, distracts their attention from the doings of his railroad. When Beatrice was a baby and had little colics, I used to jingle my keys in front of her nose, and it took her attention from the pain in her tummy; so Shelgrim."

The others laughed good-humouredly, protesting, nevertheless, and Mrs. Cedarquist shook her finger in warning at the artist and exclaimed:

"The Philistines be upon thee, Samson!"

"By the way," observed Hartrath, willing to change the subject, "I hear you are on the Famine Relief Committee. Does your work progress?"

"Oh, most famously, I assure you," she said. "Such a movement as we have started. Those poor creatures. The photographs of them are simply dreadful. I had the committee to luncheon the other day and we passed them around. We are getting subscriptions from all over the State, and Mr. Cedarquist is to arrange for the ship."

The Relief Committee in question was one of a great number that had been formed in California—and all over the Union, for the matter of that—to provide relief for the victims of a great famine in Central India. The whole world had been struck with horror at the reports of suffering and mortality in the affected districts, and had hastened to send aid. Certain women of San Francisco, with Mrs. Cedarquist at their head, had organised a number of committees, but the manufacturer's wife turned the meetings of these committees into social affairs—luncheons, teas, where one discussed the ways and means of assisting the starving Asiatics over teacups and plates of salad.

Shortly afterward a mild commotion spread throughout the assemblage of the club's guests. The drawing of the numbers in the raffle was about to be made. Hartrath, in a flurry of agitation, excused himself. Cedarquist took Presley by the arm.

"Pres, let's get out of this," he said. "Come into the wine room and I will shake you for a glass of sherry."

They had some difficulty in extricating themselves. The main room where the drawing was to take place suddenly became densely thronged. All the guests pressed eagerly about the table near the picture, upon which one of the hall boys had just placed a ballot box containing the numbers. The ladies, holding their tickets in their hands, pushed forward. A staccato chatter of excited murmurs arose. "What became of Harran and Lyman and the Governor?" inquired Presley.

Lyman had disappeared, alleging a business engagement, but Magnus and his younger son had retired to the library of the club on the floor above. It was almost deserted. They were deep in earnest conversation.

"Harran," said the Governor, with decision, "there is a deal, there, in what Cedarquist says. Our wheat to China, hey, boy?"

"It is certainly worth thinking of, sir."

"It appeals to me, boy; it appeals to me. It's big and there's a fortune in it. Big chances mean big returns; and I know—your old father isn't a back number yet, Harran—I may not have so wide an outlook as our friend

Cedarquist, but I am quick to see my chance. Boy, the whole East is opening, disintegrating before the Anglo-Saxon. It is time that bread stuffs, as well, should make markets for themselves in the Orient. Just at this moment, too, when Lyman will scale down freight rates so we can haul to tidewater at little cost."

Magnus paused again, his frown beetling, and in the silence the excited murmur from the main room of the club, the soprano chatter of a multitude of women, found its way to the deserted library.

"I believe it's worth looking into, Governor," asserted Harran.

Magnus rose, and, his hands behind him, paced the floor of the library a couple of times, his imagination all stimulated and vivid. The great gambler perceived his Chance, the kaleidoscopic shifting of circumstances that made a Situation. It had come silently, unexpectedly. He had not seen its approach. Abruptly he woke one morning to see the combination realised. But also he saw a vision. A sudden and abrupt revolution in the Wheat. A new world of markets discovered, the matter as important as the discovery of America. The torrent of wheat was to be diverted, flowing back upon itself in a sudden, colossal eddy, stranding the middleman, the ENTRE-PRENEUR, the elevator-and mixing-house men dry and despairing, their occupation gone. He saw the farmer suddenly emancipated, the world's food no longer at the mercy of the speculator, thousands upon thousands of men set free of the grip of Trust and ring and monopoly acting for themselves, selling their own wheat, organising into one gigantic trust, themselves, sending their agents to all the entry ports of China. Himself, Annixter, Broderson and Osterman would pool their issues. He would convince them of the magnificence of the new movement. They would be its pioneers. Harran would be sent to Hong Kong to represent the four. They would charter— probably buy—a ship, perhaps one of Cedarquist's, American built, the nation's flag at the peak, and the sailing of that ship, gorged with the crops from Broderson's and Osterman's ranches, from Quien Sabe and Los Muertos, would be like the sailing of the caravels from Palos. It would mark a new era; it would make an epoch.

With this vision still expanding before the eye of his mind, Magnus, with Harran at his elbow, prepared to depart.

They descended to the lower floor and involved themselves for a moment in the throng of fashionables that blocked the hallway and the entrance to the main room, where the numbers of the raffle were being drawn. Near the head of the stairs they encountered Presley and Cedarquist, who had just come out of the wine room.

Magnus, still on fire with the new idea, pressed a few questions upon the manufacturer before bidding him good-bye. He wished to talk further upon the great subject, interested as to details, but Cedarquist was vague in his replies. He was no farmer, he hardly knew wheat when he saw it, only he knew the trend of the world's affairs; he felt them to be setting inevitably eastward.

However, his very vagueness was a further inspiration to the Governor. He swept details aside. He saw only the grand coup, the huge results, the East conquered, the march of empire rolling westward, finally arriving at its starting point, the vague, mysterious Orient.

He saw his wheat, like the crest of an advancing billow, crossing the Pacific, bursting upon Asia, flooding the Orient in a golden torrent. It was the new era. He had lived to see the death of the old and the birth of the new; first the mine, now the ranch; first gold, now wheat. Once again he became the pioneer, hardy, brilliant, taking colossal chances, blazing the way, grasping a fortune—a million in a single day. All the bigness of his nature leaped up again within him. At the magnitude of the inspiration he felt young again, indomitable, the leader at last, king of his fellows, wresting from fortune at this eleventh hour, before his old age, the place of high command which so long had been denied him. At last he could achieve.

Abruptly Magnus was aware that some one had spoken his name. He looked about and saw behind him, at a little distance, two gentlemen, strangers to him. They had withdrawn from the crowd into a little recess. Evidently having no women to look after, they had lost interest in the afternoon's affair. Magnus realised that they had not seen him. One of them was reading aloud to his companion from an evening edition of that day's newspaper. It was in the course of this reading that Magnus caught the sound of his name. He paused, listening, and Presley, Harran and Cedarquist followed his example. Soon they all understood. They were listening to the report of the judge's decision, for which Magnus was waiting—the decision in the case of the League vs. the Railroad. For the moment, the polite clamour of the raffle hushed itself—the winning number was being drawn. The guests held their breath, and in the ensuing silence Magnus and the others heard these words distinctly:

".... It follows that the title to the lands in question is in the plaintiff—the Pacific and Southwestern Railroad, and the defendants have no title, and their possession is wrongful. There must be findings and judgment for the plaintiff, and it is so ordered."

In spite of himself, Magnus paled. Harran shut his teeth with an oath. Their exaltation of the previous moment collapsed like a pyramid of cards. The vision of the new movement of the wheat, the conquest of the East, the invasion of the Orient, seemed only the flimsiest mockery. With a brusque wrench, they were snatched back to reality. Between them and the vision, between the fecund San Joaquin, reeking with fruitfulness, and the millions of Asia crowding toward the verge of starvation, lay the iron-hearted monster of steel and steam, implacable, insatiable, huge—its entrails gorged with the life blood that it sucked from an entire commonwealth, its ever hungry maw glutted with the harvests that should have fed the famished bellies of the whole world of the Orient.

But abruptly, while the four men stood there, gazing into each other's faces, a vigorous hand-clapping broke out. The raffle of Hartrath's picture was over, and as Presley turned about he saw Mrs. Cedarquist and her two daughters signalling eagerly to the manufacturer, unable to reach him because of the intervening crowd. Then Mrs. Cedarquist raised her voice and cried:

"I've won. I've won."

Unnoticed, and with but a brief word to Cedarquist, Magnus and Harran went down the marble steps leading to the street door, silent, Harran's arm tight around his father's shoulder.

At once the orchestra struck into a lively air. A renewed murmur of conversation broke out, and Cedarquist, as he said good-bye to Presley, looked first at the retreating figures of the ranchers, then at the gayly dressed throng of beautiful women and debonair young men, and indicating the whole scene with a single gesture, said, smiling sadly as he spoke:

"Not a city, Presley, not a city, but a Midway Plaisance."

CHAPTER II

Underneath the Long Trestle where Broderson Creek cut the line of the railroad and the Upper Road, the ground was low and covered with a second growth of grey green willows. Along the borders of the creek were occasional marshy spots, and now and then Hilma Tree came here to gather water-cresses, which she made into salads.

The place was picturesque, secluded, an oasis of green shade in all the limitless, flat monotony of the surrounding wheat lands. The creek had eroded deep into the little gully, and no matter how hot it was on the baking, shimmering levels of the ranches above, down here one always found one's self enveloped in an odorous, moist coolness. From time to time, the incessant murmur of the creek, pouring over and around the larger stones, was interrupted by the thunder of trains roaring out upon the trestle overhead, passing on with the furious gallop of their hundreds of iron wheels, leaving in the air a taint of hot oil, acrid smoke, and reek of escaping steam.

On a certain afternoon, in the spring of the year, Hilma was returning to Quien Sabe from Hooven's by the trail that led from Los Muertos to Annixter's ranch houses, under the trestle. She had spent the afternoon with Minna Hooven, who, for the time being, was kept indoors because of a wrenched ankle. As Hilma descended into the gravel flats and thickets of willows underneath the trestle, she decided that she would gather some cresses for her supper that night. She found a spot around the base of one of the supports of the trestle where the cresses grew thickest, and plucked a couple of handfuls, washing them in the creek and pinning them up in her handkerchief. It made a little, round, cold bundle, and Hilma, warm from her walk, found a delicious enjoyment in pressing the damp ball of it to her cheeks and neck.

For all the change that Annixter had noted in her upon the occasion of the barn dance, Hilma remained in many things a young child. She was never at loss for enjoyment, and could always amuse herself when left alone. Just now, she chose to drink from the creek, lying prone on the ground, her face half-buried in the water, and this, not because she was thirsty, but because it was a new way to drink. She imagined herself a belated traveller, a poor girl, an outcast, quenching her thirst at the wayside brook, her little packet of cresses doing duty for a bundle of clothes. Night was coming on. Perhaps it would storm. She had nowhere to go. She would apply at a hut for shelter.

Abruptly, the temptation to dabble her feet in the creek presented itself to her. Always she had liked to play in the water. What a delight now to take off her shoes and stockings and wade out into the shallows near the bank! She had worn low shoes that afternoon, and the dust of the trail had filtered in above the edges. At times, she felt the grit and grey sand on the soles of her feet, and the sensation had set her teeth on edge. What a delicious alternative the cold, clean water suggested, and how easy it would be to do as she pleased just then, if only she were a little girl. In the end, it was stupid to be grown up.

Sitting upon the bank, one finger tucked into the heel of her shoe, Hilma hesitated. Suppose a train should come! She fancied she could see the engineer leaning from the cab with a great grin on his face, or the brakeman shouting gibes at her from the platform. Abruptly she blushed scarlet. The blood throbbed in her temples. Her heart beat. Since the famous evening of the barn dance, Annixter had spoken to her but twice. Hilma no longer looked after the ranch house these days. The thought of setting foot within Annixter's dining-room and bed-room terrified her, and in the end her mother had taken over that part of her work. Of the two meetings with the master of Quien Sabe, one had been a mere exchange of good mornings as the two happened to meet over by the artesian well; the other, more complicated, had occurred in the dairy-house again, Annixter, pretending to look over the new cheese press, asking about details of her work. When this had happened on that previous occasion, ending with Annixter's attempt to kiss her, Hilma had been talkative enough, chattering on from one subject to another, never at a loss for a theme. But this last time was a veritable ordeal. No sooner had Annixter appeared than her heart leaped and quivered like that of the hound-harried doe. Her speech failed her. Throughout the whole brief interview she had been miserably tongue-tied, stammering monosyllables, confused, horribly awkward, and when Annixter had gone away, she had fled to her little room, and bolting the door, had flung herself face downward on the bed and wept as though her heart were breaking, she did not know why.

That Annixter had been overwhelmed with business all through the winter was an inexpressible relief to Hilma. His affairs took him away from the ranch continually. He was absent sometimes for weeks, making trips to San Francisco, or to Sacramento, or to Bonneville. Perhaps he was forgetting her, overlooking her; and while, at first, she told herself that she asked nothing better, the idea of it began to occupy her mind. She began to wonder if it was really so.

She knew his trouble. Everybody did. The news of the sudden forward movement of the Railroad's forces, inaugurating the campaign, had flared white-hot and blazing all over the country side. To Hilma's notion, Annixter's attitude was heroic beyond all expression. His courage in facing the Railroad, as he had faced Delaney in the barn, seemed to her the pitch of sublimity. She refused to see any auxiliaries aiding him in his fight. To her imagination, the great League, which all the ranchers were joining, was a mere form. Single-handed, Annixter fronted the monster. But for him the corporation would gobble Quien Sabe, as a whale would a minnow. He was a hero who stood between them all and destruction. He was a protector of her family. He was her champion. She began to mention him in her prayers every night, adding a further petition to the effect that he would become a good man, and that he should not swear so much, and that he should never meet Delaney again.

However, as Hilma still debated the idea of bathing her feet in the creek, a train did actually thunder past overhead—the regular evening Overland,—the through express, that never stopped between Bakersfield and Fresno. It stormed by with a deafening clamour, and a swirl of smoke, in a long succession of way-coaches, and chocolate coloured Pullmans, grimy with the dust of the great deserts of the Southwest. The quivering of the trestle's supports set a tremble in the ground underfoot. The thunder of wheels drowned all sound of the flowing of the creek, and also the noise of the buckskin mare's hoofs descending from the trail upon the gravel about the creek, so that Hilma, turning about after the passage of the train, saw Annixter close at hand, with the abruptness of a vision.

He was looking at her, smiling as he rarely did, the firm line of his outthrust lower lip relaxed good-humouredly. He had taken off his campaign hat to her, and though his stiff, yellow hair was twisted into a bristling mop, the little persistent tuft on the crown, usually defiantly erect as an Apache's scalp-lock, was nowhere in sight.

"Hello, it's you, is it, Miss Hilma?" he exclaimed, getting down from the buckskin, and allowing her to drink.

Hilma nodded, scrambling to her feet, dusting her skirt with nervous pats of both hands.

Annixter sat down on a great rock close by and, the loop of the bridle over his arm, lit a cigar, and began to talk. He complained of the heat of the day, the bad condition of the Lower Road, over which he had come on his way from a committee meeting of the League at Los Muertos; of the slowness of the work on the irrigating ditch, and, as a matter of course, of the general hard times.

"Miss Hilma," he said abruptly, "never you marry a ranchman. He's never out of trouble."

Hilma gasped, her eyes widening till the full round of the pupil was disclosed. Instantly, a certain, inexplicable guiltiness overpowered her with incredible confusion. Her hands trembled as she pressed the bundle of cresses into a hard ball between her palms.

Annixter continued to talk. He was disturbed and excited himself at this unexpected meeting. Never through all the past winter months of strenuous activity, the fever of political campaigns, the harrowing delays and ultimate defeat in one law court after another, had he forgotten the look in Hilma's face as he stood with one arm around her on the floor of his barn, in peril of his life from the buster's revolver. That dumb confession of Hilma's wide-open eyes had been enough for him. Yet, somehow, he never had had a chance to act upon it. During the short period when he could be on his ranch Hilma had always managed to avoid him. Once, even, she had spent a month, about Christmas time, with her mother's father, who kept a hotel in San Francisco.

Now, to-day, however, he had her all to himself. He would put an end to the situation that troubled him, and vexed him, day after day, month after month. Beyond question, the moment had come for something definite, he could not say precisely what. Readjusting his cigar between his teeth, he resumed his speech. It suited his humour to take the girl into his confidence, following an instinct which warned him that this would bring about a certain closeness of their relations, a certain intimacy.

"What do you think of this row, anyways, Miss Hilma,—this railroad fuss in general? Think Shelgrim and his rushers are going to jump Quien Sabe—are going to run us off the ranch?"

"Oh, no, sir," protested Hilma, still breathless. "Oh, no, indeed not."

"Well, what then?"

Hilma made a little uncertain movement of ignorance.

"I don't know what."

"Well, the League agreed to-day that if the test cases were lost in the Supreme Court—you know we've appealed to the Supreme Court, at Washington—we'd fight."

"Fight?"

"Yes, fight."

"Fight like—like you and Mr. Delaney that time with—oh, dear—with guns?"

"I don't know," grumbled Annixter vaguely. "What do YOU think?"

Hilma's low-pitched, almost husky voice trembled a little as she replied, "Fighting—with guns—that's so terrible. Oh, those revolvers in the barn! I can hear them yet. Every shot seemed like the explosion of tons of powder."

"Shall we clear out, then? Shall we let Delaney have possession, and S. Behrman, and all that lot? Shall we give in to them?"

"Never, never," she exclaimed, her great eyes flashing.

"YOU wouldn't like to be turned out of your home, would you, Miss Hilma, because Quien Sabe is your home isn't it? You've lived here ever since you were as big as a minute. You wouldn't like to have S. Behrman and the rest of 'em turn you out?"

"N-no," she murmured. "No, I shouldn't like that. There's mamma and——"

"Well, do you think for one second I'm going to let 'em?" cried Annixter, his teeth tightening on his cigar. "You stay right where you are. I'll take care of you, right enough. Look here," he demanded abruptly, "you've no use for that roaring lush, Delaney, have you?" "I think he is a wicked man," she declared. "I know the Railroad has pretended to sell him part of the ranch, and he lets Mr. S. Behrman and Mr. Ruggles just use him."

"Right. I thought you wouldn't be keen on him."

There was a long pause. The buckskin began blowing among the pebbles, nosing for grass, and Annixter shifted his cigar to the other corner of his mouth.

"Pretty place," he muttered, looking around him. Then he added: "Miss Hilma, see here, I want to have a kind of talk with you, if you don't mind. I don't know just how to say these sort of things, and if I get all balled up as I go along, you just set it down to the fact that I've never had any experience in dealing with feemale girls; understand? You see, ever since the barn dance—yes, and long before then—I've been thinking a lot about you. Straight, I have, and I guess you know it. You're about the only girl that I ever knew well, and I guess," he declared deliberately, "you're about the only one I want to know. It's my nature. You didn't say anything that time when we stood there together and Delaney was playing the fool, but, somehow, I got the idea that you didn't want Delaney to do for me one little bit; that if he'd got me then you would have been sorrier than if he'd got any one else. Well, I felt just that way about you. I would rather have had him shoot any other girl in the room than you; yes, or in the whole State. Why, if anything should happen to you, Miss Hilma—well, I wouldn't care to go on with anything. S. Behrman could jump Quien Sabe, and welcome. And Delaney could shoot me full of holes whenever he got good and ready. I'd quit. I'd lay right down. I wouldn't care a whoop about anything any more. You are the only girl for me in the whole world. I didn't think so at first. I didn't want to. But seeing you around every day, and seeing how pretty you were, and how clever, and hearing your voice and all, why, it just got all inside of me somehow, and now I can't think of anything else. I hate to go to San Francisco, or Sacramento, or Visalia, or even Bonneville, for only a day, just because you aren't there, in any of those places, and I just rush what I've got to do so as I can get back here. While you were away that Christmas time, why, I was as lonesome as—oh, you don't know anything about it. I just scratched off the days on the calendar every night, one by one, till you got back. And it just comes to this, I want you with me all the time. I want you should have a home that's my home, too. I want to take care of you, and have you all for myself, you understand. What do you say?"

Hilma, standing up before him, retied a knot in her handkerchief bundle with elaborate precaution, blinking at it through her tears.

"What do you say, Miss Hilma?" Annixter repeated. "How about that? What do you say?"

Just above a whisper, Hilma murmured:

"I—I don't know."

"Don't know what? Don't you think we could hit it off together?"

"I don't know."

"I know we could, Hilma. I don't mean to scare you. What are you crying for?" "I don't know."

Annixter got up, cast away his cigar, and dropping the buckskin's bridle, came and stood beside her, putting a hand on her shoulder. Hilma did not move, and he felt her trembling. She still plucked at the knot of the handkerchief. "I can't do without you, little girl," Annixter continued, "and I want you. I want you bad. I don't get much fun out of life ever. It, sure, isn't my nature, I guess. I'm a hard man. Everybody is trying to down me, and now I'm up against the Railroad. I'm fighting 'em all, Hilma, night and day, lock, stock, and barrel, and I'm fighting now for my home, my land, everything I have in the world. If I win out, I want somebody to be glad with me. If I don't—I want somebody to be sorry for me, sorry with me,— and that somebody is you. I am dog-tired of going it alone. I want some one to back me up. I want to feel you alongside of me, to give me a touch of the shoulder now and then. I'm tired of fighting for THINGS—land, property, money. I want to fight for some PERSON—somebody beside myself. Understand? want to feel that it isn't all selfishness—that there are other interests than mine in the game—that there's some one dependent on me, and that's thinking of me as I'm thinking of them—some one I can come home to at night and put my arm around—like this, and have her put her two arms around me—like—" He paused a second, and once again, as it had been in that moment of imminent peril, when he stood with his arm around her, their eyes met,—"put her two arms around me," prompted Annixter, half smiling, "like—like what, Hilma?"

"I don't know."

"Like what, Hilma?" he insisted.

"Like—like this?" she questioned. With a movement of infinite tenderness and affection she slid her arms around his neck, still crying a little.

The sensation of her warm body in his embrace, the feeling of her smooth, round arm, through the thinness of her sleeve, pressing against his cheek, thrilled Annixter with a delight such as he had never known. He bent his head and kissed her upon the nape of her neck, where the delicate amber tint melted into the thick, sweet smelling mass of her dark brown hair. She shivered a little, holding him closer, ashamed as yet to look up. Without speech, they stood there for a long minute, holding each other close. Then Hilma pulled away from him, mopping her tear-stained cheeks with the little moist ball of her handkerchief.

"What do you say? Is it a go?" demanded Annixter jovially.

"I thought I hated you all the time," she said, and the velvety huskiness of her voice never sounded so sweet to him.

"And I thought it was that crockery smashing goat of a lout of a cow-puncher."

"Delaney? The idea! Oh, dear! I think it must always have been you."

"Since when, Hilma?" he asked, putting his arm around her. "Ah, but it is good to have you, my girl," he exclaimed, delighted beyond words that she permitted this freedom. "Since when? Tell us all about it."

"Oh, since always. It was ever so long before I came to think of you—to, well, to think about—I mean to remember—oh, you know what I mean. But when I did, oh, THEN!"

"Then what?"

"I don't know—I haven't thought—that way long enough to know."

"But you said you thought it must have been me always."

"I know; but that was different—oh, I'm all mixed up. I'm so nervous and trembly now. Oh," she cried suddenly, her face overcast with a look of earnestness and great seriousness, both her hands catching at his wrist, "Oh, you WILL be good to me, now, won't you? I'm only a little, little child in so many ways, and I've given myself to you, all in a minute, and I can't go back of it now, and it's for always. I don't know how it happened or why. Sometimes I think I didn't wish it, but now it's done, and I am glad and happy. But NOW if you weren't good to me—oh, think of how it would be with me. You are strong, and big, and rich, and I am only a servant of yours, a little nobody, but I've given all I had to you—myself—and you must be so good to me now. Always remember that. Be good to me and be gentle and kind to me in LITTLE things,—in everything, or you will break my heart."

Annixter took her in his arms. He was speechless. No words that he had at his command seemed adequate. All he could say was:

"That's all right, little girl. Don't you be frightened. I'll take care of you. That's all right, that's all right."

For a long time they sat there under the shade of the great trestle, their arms about each other, speaking only at intervals. An hour passed. The buckskin, finding no feed to her taste, took the trail stablewards, the bridle dragging. Annixter let her go. Rather than to take his arm from around Hilma's waist he would have lost his whole stable. At last, however, he bestirred himself and began to talk. He thought it time to formulate some plan of action.

"Well, now, Hilma, what are we going to do?"

"Do?" she repeated. "Why, must we do anything? Oh, isn't this enough?"

"There's better ahead," he went on. "I want to fix you up somewhere where you can have a bit of a home all to yourself. Let's see; Bonneville wouldn't do. There's always a lot of yaps about there that know us, and they would begin to cackle first off. How about San Francisco. We might go up next week and have a look around. I would find rooms you could take somewheres, and we would fix 'em up as lovely as how-do-you-do."

"Oh, but why go away from Quien Sabe?" she protested. "And, then, so soon, too. Why must we have a wedding trip, now that you are so busy? Wouldn't it be better—oh, I tell you, we could go to Monterey after we were married, for a little week, where mamma's people live, and then come back here to the ranch house and settle right down where we are and let me keep house for you. I wouldn't even want a single servant."

Annixter heard and his face grew troubled.

"Hum," he said, "I see."

He gathered up a handful of pebbles and began snapping them carefully into the creek. He fell thoughtful. Here was a phase of the affair he had not planned in the least. He had supposed all the time that Hilma took his meaning. His old suspicion that she was trying to get a hold on him stirred again for a moment. There was no good of such talk as that. Always these feemale girls seemed crazy to get married, bent on complicating the situation.

"Isn't that best?" said Hilma, glancing at him.

"I don't know," he muttered gloomily.

"Well, then, let's not. Let's come right back to Quien Sabe without going to Monterey. Anything that you want I want."

"I hadn't thought of it in just that way," he observed.

"In what way, then?"

"Can't we—can't we wait about this marrying business?"

"That's just it," she said gayly. "I said it was too soon. There would be so much to do between whiles. Why not say at the end of the summer?"

"Say what?"

"Our marriage, I mean."

"Why get married, then? What's the good of all that fuss about it? I don't go anything upon a minister puddling round in my affairs. What's the difference, anyhow? We understand each other. Isn't that enough? Pshaw, Hilma, I'M no marrying man."

She looked at him a moment, bewildered, then slowly she took his meaning. She rose to her feet, her eyes wide, her face paling with terror. He did not look at her, but he could hear the catch in her throat.

"Oh!" she exclaimed, with a long, deep breath, and again "Oh!" the back of her hand against her lips.

It was a quick gasp of a veritable physical anguish. Her eyes brimmed over. Annixter rose, looking at her.

"Well?" he said, awkwardly, "Well?"

Hilma leaped back from him with an instinctive recoil of her whole being, throwing out her hands in a gesture of defence, fearing she knew not what. There was as yet no sense of insult in her mind, no outraged modesty. She was only terrified. It was as though searching for wild flowers she had come suddenly upon a snake.

She stood for an instant, spellbound, her eyes wide, her bosom swelling; then, all at once, turned and fled, darting across the plank that served for a foot bridge over the creek, gaining the opposite bank and disappearing with a brisk rustle of underbrush, such as might have been made by the flight of a frightened fawn.

Abruptly Annixter found himself alone. For a moment he did not move, then he picked up his campaign hat, carefully creased its limp crown and put it on his head and stood for a moment, looking vaguely at the ground on both sides of him. He went away without uttering a word, without change of countenance, his hands in his pockets, his feet taking great strides along the trail in the direction of the ranch house.

He had no sight of Hilma again that evening, and the next morning he was up early and did not breakfast at the ranch house. Business of the League called him to Bonneville to confer with Magnus and the firm of lawyers retained by the League to fight the land-grabbing cases. An appeal was to be taken to the Supreme Court at Washington, and it was to be settled that day which of the cases involved should be considered as test cases.

Instead of driving or riding into Bonneville, as he usually did, Annixter took an early morning train, the Bakersfield-Fresno local at Guadalajara, and went to Bonneville by rail, arriving there at twenty minutes after seven and breakfasting by appointment with Magnus Derrick and Osterman at the Yosemite House, on Main Street.

The conference of the committee with the lawyers took place in a front room of the Yosemite, one of the latter bringing with him his clerk, who made a stenographic report of the proceedings and took carbon copies of all letters written. The conference was long and complicated, the business transacted of the utmost moment, and it was not until two o'clock that Annixter found himself at liberty.

However, as he and Magnus descended into the lobby of the hotel, they were aware of an excited and interested group collected about the swing doors that opened from the lobby of the Yosemite into the bar of the same name. Dyke was there—even at a distance they could hear the reverberation of his deep-toned voice, uplifted in wrath and furious expostulation. Magnus and Annixter joined the group wondering, and all at once fell full upon the first scene of a drama.

That same morning Dyke's mother had awakened him according to his instructions at daybreak. A consignment of his hop poles from the north had arrived at the freight office of the P. and S. W. in Bonneville, and he was to drive in on his farm wagon and bring them out. He would have a busy day.

"Hello, hello," he said, as his mother pulled his ear to arouse him; "morning, mamma."

"It's time," she said, "after five already. Your breakfast is on the stove."

He took her hand and kissed it with great affection. He loved his mother devotedly, quite as much as he did the little tad. In their little cottage, in the forest of green hops that surrounded them on every hand, the three led a joyous and secluded life, contented, industrious, happy, asking nothing better. Dyke, himself, was a big-hearted, jovial man who spread an atmosphere of good-humour wherever he went. In the evenings he played with Sidney like a big boy, an older brother, lying on the bed, or the sofa, taking her in his arms. Between them they had invented a great game. The ex-engineer, his boots removed, his huge legs in the air, hoisted the little tad on the soles of his stockinged feet like a circus acrobat, dandling her there, pretending he was about to let her fall. Sidney, choking with delight, held on nervously, with little screams and chirps of excitement, while he shifted her gingerly from one foot to another, and thence, the final act, the great gallery play, to the palm of one great hand. At this point Mrs. Dyke was called in, both father and daughter, children both, crying out that she was to come in and look, look. She arrived out of breath from the kitchen, the potato masher in her hand. "Such children," she murmured, shaking her head at them, amused for all that, tucking the potato masher under her arm and clapping her hands. In the end, it was part of the game that Sidney should tumble down upon Dyke, whereat he invariably vented a great bellow as if in pain, declaring that his ribs were broken. Gasping, his eyes shut, he pretended to be in the extreme of dissolution—perhaps he was dying. Sidney, always a little uncertain, amused but distressed, shook him nervously, tugging at his beard, pushing open his eyelid with one finger, imploring him not to frighten her, to wake up and be good.

On this occasion, while yet he was half-dressed, Dyke tiptoed into his mother's room to look at Sidney fast asleep in her little iron cot, her arm under her head, her lips parted. With infinite precaution he kissed her twice, and then finding one little stocking, hung with its mate very neatly over the back of a chair, dropped into it a dime, rolled up in a wad of paper. He winked all to himself and went out again, closing the door with exaggerated carefulness.

He breakfasted alone, Mrs. Dyke pouring his coffee and handing him his plate of ham and eggs, and half an hour later took himself off in his springless, skeleton wagon, humming a tune behind his beard and cracking the whip over the backs of his staid and solid farm horses.

The morning was fine, the sun just coming up. He left Guadalajara, sleeping and lifeless, on his left, and going across lots, over an angle of Quien Sabe, came out upon the Upper Road, a mile below the Long Trestle. He was in great spirits, looking about him over the brown fields, ruddy with the dawn. Almost directly in front of him, but far off, the gilded dome of the court-house at Bonneville was glinting radiant in the first rays of the sun, while a few miles distant, toward the north, the venerable campanile of the Mission San Juan stood silhouetted in purplish black against the flaming east. As he proceeded, the great farm horses jogging forward, placid, deliberate, the country side waked to another day. Crossing the irrigating ditch further on, he met a gang of Portuguese, with picks and shovels over their shoulders, just going to work. Hooven, already abroad, shouted him a "Goot mornun" from behind the fence of Los Muertos. Far off, toward the southwest, in the bare expanse of the open fields, where a clump of eucalyptus and cypress trees set a dark green note, a thin stream of smoke rose straight into the air from the kitchen of Derrick's ranch houses.

But a mile or so beyond the Long Trestle he was surprised to see Magnus Derrick's protege, the one-time shepherd, Vanamee, coming across Quien Sabe, by a trail from one of Annixter's division houses. Without knowing exactly why, Dyke received the impression that the young man had not been in bed all of that night.

As the two approached each other, Dyke eyed the young fellow. He was distrustful of Vanamee, having the country-bred suspicion of any person he could not understand. Vanamee was, beyond doubt, no part of the life of ranch and country town. He was an alien, a vagabond, a strange fellow who came and went in mysterious fashion, making no friends, keeping to himself. Why did he never wear a hat, why indulge in a fine, black, pointed beard, when either a round beard or a mustache was the invariable custom? Why did he not cut his hair? Above all, why did he prowl about so much at night? As the two passed each other, Dyke, for all his good-nature, was a little blunt in his greeting and looked back at the ex-shepherd over his shoulder.

Dyke was right in his suspicion. Vanamee's bed had not been disturbed for three nights. On the Monday of that week he had passed the entire night in the garden of the Mission, overlooking the Seed ranch, in the little valley. Tuesday evening had found him miles away from that spot, in a deep arroyo in the Sierra foothills to the eastward, while Wednesday he had slept in an abandoned 'dobe on Osterman's stock range, twenty miles from his resting place of the night before.

The fact of the matter was that the old restlessness had once more seized upon Vanamee. Something began tugging at him; the spur of some unseen rider touched his flank. The instinct of the wanderer woke and moved. For some time now he had been a part of the Los Muertos staff. On Quien Sabe, as on the other ranches, the slack season was at hand. While waiting for the wheat to come up no one was doing much of anything. Vanamee had come over to Los Muertos and spent most of his days on horseback, riding the range, rounding up and watching the cattle in the fourth division of the ranch. But if the vagabond instinct now roused itself in the strange fellow's nature, a counter influence had also set in. More and more Vanamee frequented the Mission garden after nightfall, sometimes remaining there till the dawn began to whiten, lying prone on the ground, his chin on his folded arms, his eyes searching the darkness over the little valley of the Seed ranch, watching, watching. As the days went by, he became more reticent than ever. Presley often came to find him on the stock range, a lonely figure in the great wilderness of bare, green hillsides, but Vanamee no longer took him into his confidence. Father Sarria alone heard his strange stories.

Dyke drove on toward Bonneville, thinking over the whole matter. He knew, as every one did in that part of the country, the legend of Vanamee and Angele, the romance of the Mission garden, the mystery of the Other, Vanamee's flight to the deserts of the southwest, his periodic returns, his strange, reticent, solitary character, but, like many another of the country people, he accounted for Vanamee by a short and easy method. No doubt, the fellow's wits were turned. That was the long and short of it.

The ex-engineer reached the Post Office in Bonneville towards eleven o'clock, but he did not at once present his notice of the arrival of his consignment at Ruggles's office. It entertained him to indulge in an hour's lounging about the streets. It was seldom he got into town, and when he did he permitted himself the luxury of enjoying his evident popularity. He met friends everywhere, in the Post Office, in the drug store, in the barber shop and around the court-house. With each one he held a moment's conversation; almost invariably this ended in the same way:

"Come on 'n have a drink."

"Well, I don't care if I do."

And the friends proceeded to the Yosemite bar, pledging each other with punctilious ceremony. Dyke, however, was a strictly temperate man. His life on the engine had trained him well. Alcohol he never touched, drinking instead ginger ale, sarsaparilla-and-iron—soft drinks.

At the drug store, which also kept a stock of miscellaneous stationery, his eye was caught by a "transparent slate," a child's toy, where upon a little pane of frosted glass one could trace with considerable elaboration outline figures of cows, ploughs, bunches of fruit and even rural water mills that were printed on slips of paper underneath.

"Now, there's an idea, Jim," he observed to the boy behind the soda-water fountain; "I know a little tad that would just about jump out of her skin for that. Think I'll have to take it with me."

"How's Sidney getting along?" the other asked, while wrapping up the package.

Dyke's enthusiasm had made of his little girl a celebrity throughout Bonneville.

The ex-engineer promptly became voluble, assertive, doggedly emphatic.

"Smartest little tad in all Tulare County, and more fun! A regular whole show in herself."

"And the hops?" inquired the other.

"Bully," declared Dyke, with the good-natured man's readiness to talk of his private affairs to any one who would listen. "Bully. I'm dead sure of a bonanza crop by now. The rain came JUST right. I actually don't know as I can store the crop in those barns I built, it's going to be so big. That foreman of mine was a daisy. Jim, I'm going to make money in that deal. After I've paid off the mortgage—you know I had to mortgage, yes, crop and homestead both, but I can pay it off and all the interest to boot, lovely,— well, and as I was saying, after all expenses are paid off I'll clear big money, m' son. Yes, sir. I KNEW there was boodle in hops. You know the crop is contracted for already. Sure, the foreman managed that. He's a daisy. Chap in San Francisco will take it all and at the advanced price. I wanted to hang on, to see if it wouldn't go to six cents, but the foreman said, 'No, that's good enough.' So I signed. Ain't it bully, hey?"

"Then what'll you do?"

"Well, I don't know. I'll have a lay-off for a month or so and take the little tad and mother up and show 'em the city—'Frisco—until it's time for the schools to open, and then we'll put Sid in the seminary at Marysville. Catch on?"

"I suppose you'll stay right by hops now?"

"Right you are, m'son. I know a good thing when I see it. There's plenty others going into hops next season. I set 'em the example. Wouldn't be surprised if it came to be a regular industry hereabouts. I'm planning ahead for next year already. I can let the foreman go, now that I've learned the game myself, and I think I'll buy a piece of land off Quien Sabe and get a bigger crop, and build a couple more barns, and, by George, in about five years time I'll have things humming. I'm going to make MONEY, Jim."

He emerged once more into the street and went up the block leisurely, planting his feet squarely. He fancied that he could feel he was considered of more importance nowadays. He was no longer a subordinate, an employee. He was his own man, a proprietor, an owner of land, furthering a successful enterprise. No one had helped him; he had followed no one's lead. He had struck out unaided for himself, and his success was due solely to his own intelligence, industry, and foresight. He squared his great shoulders till the blue gingham of his jumper all but cracked. Of late, his great blond beard had grown and the work in the sun had made his face very red. Under the visor of his cap—relic of his engineering days—his blue eyes twinkled with vast good-nature. He felt that he made a fine figure as he went by a group of young girls in lawns and muslins and garden hats on their way to the Post

Office. He wondered if they looked after him, wondered if they had heard that he was in a fair way to become a rich man.

But the chronometer in the window of the jewelry store warned him that time was passing. He turned about, and, crossing the street, took his way to Ruggles's office, which was the freight as well as the land office of the P. and S. W. Railroad.

As he stood for a moment at the counter in front of the wire partition, waiting for the clerk to make out the order for the freight agent at the depot, Dyke was surprised to see a familiar figure in conference with Ruggles himself, by a desk inside the railing.

The figure was that of a middle-aged man, fat, with a great stomach, which he stroked from time to time. As he turned about, addressing a remark to the clerk, Dyke recognised S. Behrman. The banker, railroad agent, and political manipulator seemed to the ex-engineer's eyes to be more gross than ever. His smooth-shaven jowl stood out big and tremulous on either side of his face; the roll of fat on the nape of his neck, sprinkled with sparse, stiff hairs, bulged out with greater prominence. His great stomach, covered with a light brown linen vest, stamped with innumerable interlocked horseshoes, protruded far in advance, enormous, aggressive. He wore his inevitable round-topped hat of stiff brown straw, varnished so bright that it reflected the light of the office windows like a helmet, and even from where he stood Dyke could hear his loud breathing and the clink of the hollow links of his watch chain upon the vest buttons of imitation pearl, as his stomach rose and fell.

Dyke looked at him with attention. There was the enemy, the representative of the Trust with which Derrick's League was locking horns. The great struggle had begun to invest the combatants with interest. Daily, almost hourly, Dyke was in touch with the ranchers, the wheat-growers. He heard their denunciations, their growls of exasperation and defiance. Here was the other side—this placid, fat man, with a stiff straw hat and linen vest, who never lost his temper, who smiled affably upon his enemies, giving them good advice, commiserating with them in one defeat after another, never ruffled, never excited, sure of his power, conscious that back of him was the Machine, the colossal force, the inexhaustible coffers of a mighty organisation, vomiting millions to the League's thousands.

The League was clamorous, ubiquitous, its objects known to every urchin on the streets, but the Trust was silent, its ways inscrutable, the public saw only results. It worked on in the dark, calm, disciplined, irresistible.

Abruptly Dyke received the impression of the multitudinous ramifications of the colossus. Under his feet the ground seemed mined; down there below him in the dark the huge tentacles went silently twisting and advancing, spreading out in every direction, sapping the strength of all opposition, quiet, gradual, biding the time to reach up and out and grip with a sudden unleashing of gigantic strength.

"I'll be wanting some cars of you people before the summer is out," observed Dyke to the clerk as he folded up and put away the order that the other had handed him. He remembered perfectly well that he had arranged the matter of transporting his crop some months before, but his role of proprietor amused him and he liked to busy himself again and again with the details of his undertaking.

"I suppose," he added, "you'll be able to give 'em to me. There'll be a big wheat crop to move this year and I don't want to be caught in any car famine."

"Oh, you'll get your cars," murmured the other.

"I'll be the means of bringing business your way," Dyke went on; "I've done so well with my hops that there are a lot of others going into the business next season. Suppose," he continued, struck with an idea, "suppose we went into some sort of pool, a sort of shippers' organisation, could you give us special rates, cheaper rates—say a cent and a half?"

The other looked up.

"A cent and a half! Say FOUR cents and a half and maybe I'll talk business with you."

"Four cents and a half," returned Dyke, "I don't see it. Why, the regular rate is only two cents."

"No, it isn't," answered the clerk, looking him gravely in the eye, "it's five cents."

"Well, there's where you are wrong, m'son," Dyke retorted, genially. "You look it up. You'll find the freight on hops from Bonneville to 'Frisco is two cents a pound for car load lots. You told me that yourself last fall."

"That was last fall," observed the clerk. There was a silence. Dyke shot a glance of suspicion at the other. Then, reassured, he remarked:

"You look it up. You'll see I'm right."

S. Behrman came forward and shook hands politely with the ex-engineer.

"Anything I can do for you, Mr. Dyke?"

Dyke explained. When he had done speaking, the clerk turned to S. Behrman and observed, respectfully:

"Our regular rate on hops is five cents."

"Yes," answered S. Behrman, pausing to reflect; "yes, Mr. Dyke, that's right—five cents."

The clerk brought forward a folder of yellow paper and handed it to Dyke. It was inscribed at the top "Tariff Schedule No. 8," and underneath these words, in brackets, was a smaller inscription, "SUPERSEDES NO. 7 OF AUG. 1"

"See for yourself," said S. Behrman. He indicated an item under the head of "Miscellany."

"The following rates for carriage of hops in car load lots," read Dyke, "take effect June 1, and will remain in force until superseded by a later tariff. Those quoted beyond Stockton are subject to changes in traffic arrangements with carriers by water from that point."

In the list that was printed below, Dyke saw that the rate for hops between Bonneville or Guadalajara and San Francisco was five cents.

For a moment Dyke was confused. Then swiftly the matter became clear in his mind. The Railroad had raised the freight on hops from two cents to five.

All his calculations as to a profit on his little investment he had based on a freight rate of two cents a pound. He was under contract to deliver his crop. He could not draw back. The new rate ate up every cent of his gains. He stood there ruined.

"Why, what do you mean?" he burst out. "You promised me a rate of two cents and I went ahead with my business with that understanding. What do you mean?"

S. Behrman and the clerk watched him from the other side of the counter.

"The rate is five cents," declared the clerk doggedly.

"Well, that ruins me," shouted Dyke. "Do you understand? I won't make fifty cents. MAKE! Why, I will OWE,—I'll be—be—That ruins me, do you understand?"

The other, raised a shoulder.

"We don't force you to ship. You can do as you like. The rate is five cents."

"Well—but—damn you, I'm under contract to deliver. What am I going to do? Why, you told me—you promised me a two-cent rate."

"I don't remember it," said the clerk. "I don't know anything about that. But I know this; I know that hops have gone up. I know the German crop was a failure and that the crop in New York wasn't worth the hauling. Hops have gone up to nearly a dollar. You don't suppose we don't know that, do you, Mr. Dyke?"

"What's the price of hops got to do with you?"

"It's got THIS to do with us," returned the other with a sudden aggressiveness, "that the freight rate has gone up to meet the price. We're not doing business for our health. My orders are to raise your rate to five cents, and I think you are getting off easy."

Dyke stared in blank astonishment. For the moment, the audacity of the affair was what most appealed to him. He forgot its personal application.

"Good Lord," he murmured, "good Lord! What will you people do next? Look here. What's your basis of applying freight rates, anyhow?" he suddenly vociferated with furious sarcasm. "What's your rule? What are you guided by?"

But at the words, S. Behrman, who had kept silent during the heat of the discussion, leaned abruptly forward. For the only time in his knowledge, Dyke saw his face inflamed with anger and with the enmity and contempt of all this farming element with whom he was contending.

"Yes, what's your rule? What's your basis?" demanded Dyke, turning swiftly to him.

S. Behrman emphasised each word of his reply with a tap of one forefinger on the counter before him:

"All—the—traffic—will—bear."

The ex-engineer stepped back a pace, his fingers on the ledge of the counter, to steady himself. He felt himself grow pale, his heart became a mere leaden weight in his chest, inert, refusing to beat.

In a second the whole affair, in all its bearings, went speeding before the eye of his imagination like the rapid unrolling of a panorama. Every cent of his earnings was sunk in this hop business of his. More than that, he had borrowed money to carry it on, certain of success—borrowed of S.

Behrman, offering his crop and his little home as security. Once he failed to meet his obligations, S. Behrman would foreclose. Not only would the Railroad devour every morsel of his profits, but also it would take from him his home; at a blow he would be left penniless and without a home. What would then become of his mother—and what would become of the little tad? She, whom he had been planning to educate like a veritable lady. For all that year he had talked of his ambition for his little daughter to every one he met. All Bonneville knew of it. What a mark for gibes he had made of himself. The workingman turned farmer! What a target for jeers—he who had fancied he could elude the Railroad! He remembered he had once said the great Trust had overlooked his little enterprise, disdaining to plunder such small fry. He should have known better than that. How had he ever imagined the Road would permit him to make any money?

Anger was not in him yet; no rousing of the blind, white-hot wrath that leaps to the attack with prehensile fingers, moved him. The blow merely crushed, staggered, confused.

He stepped aside to give place to a coatless man in a pink shirt, who entered, carrying in his hands an automatic door-closing apparatus.

"Where does this go?" inquired the man.

Dyke sat down for a moment on a seat that had been removed from a worn-out railway car to do duty in Ruggles's office. On the back of a yellow envelope he made some vague figures with a stump of blue pencil, multiplying, subtracting, perplexing himself with many errors.

S. Behrman, the clerk, and the man with the door-closing apparatus involved themselves in a long argument, gazing intently at the top panel of the door. The man who had come to fix the apparatus was unwilling to guarantee it, unless a sign was put on the outside of the door, warning incomers that the door was self-closing. This sign would cost fifteen cents extra.

"But you didn't say anything about this when the thing was ordered," declared S. Behrman. "No, I won't pay it, my friend. It's an overcharge."

"You needn't think," observed the clerk, "that just because you are dealing with the Railroad you are going to work us."

Genslinger came in, accompanied by Delaney. S. Behrman and the clerk, abruptly dismissing the man with the door-closing machine, put themselves behind the counter and engaged in conversation with these two. Genslinger introduced Delaney. The buster had a string of horses he was shipping southward. No doubt he had come to make arrangements with the Railroad in the matter of stock cars. The conference of the four men was amicable in the extreme.

Dyke, studying the figures on the back of the envelope, came forward again. Absorbed only in his own distress, he ignored the editor and the cowpuncher.

"Say," he hazarded, "how about this? I make out— —"

"We've told you what our rates are, Mr. Dyke," exclaimed the clerk angrily. "That's all the arrangement we will make. Take it or leave it." He turned again to Genslinger, giving the ex-engineer his back.

Dyke moved away and stood for a moment in the centre of the room, staring at the figures on the envelope.

"I don't see," he muttered, "just what I'm going to do. No, I don't see what I'm going to do at all."

Ruggles came in, bringing with him two other men in whom Dyke recognised dummy buyers of the Los Muertos and Osterman ranchos. They brushed by him, jostling his elbow, and as he went out of the door he heard them exchange jovial greetings with Delaney, Genslinger, and S. Behrman.

Dyke went down the stairs to the street and proceeded onward aimlessly in the direction of the Yosemite House, fingering the yellow envelope and looking vacantly at the sidewalk.

There was a stoop to his massive shoulders. His great arms dangled loosely at his sides, the palms of his hands open.

As he went along, a certain feeling of shame touched him. Surely his predicament must be apparent to every passer-by. No doubt, every one recognised the unsuccessful man in the very way he slouched along. The young girls in lawns, muslins, and garden hats, returning from the Post Office, their hands full of letters, must surely see in him the type of the failure, the bankrupt.

Then brusquely his tardy rage flamed up. By God, NO, it was not his fault; he had made no mistake. His energy, industry, and foresight had been sound. He had been merely the object of a colossal trick, a sordid injustice, a victim of the insatiate greed of the monster, caught and choked by one of those millions of tentacles suddenly reaching up from below, from out the dark beneath his feet, coiling around his throat, throttling him, strangling him, sucking his blood. For a moment he thought of the courts, but instantly laughed at the idea. What court was immune from the power of the monster? Ah, the rage of helplessness, the fury of impotence! No help, no hope,—ruined in a brief instant—he a veritable giant, built of great sinews, powerful, in the full tide of his manhood, having all his health, all his wits. How could he now face his home? How could he tell his mother of this catastrophe? And Sidney—the little tad; how could he explain to her this wretchedness—how soften her disappointment? How keep the tears from out her eyes—how keep alive her confidence in him—her faith in his resources?

Bitter, fierce, ominous, his wrath loomed up in his heart. His fists gripped tight together, his teeth clenched. Oh, for a moment to have his hand upon the throat of S. Behrman, wringing the breath from him, wrenching out the red life of him—staining the street with the blood sucked from the veins of the People!

To the first friend that he met, Dyke told the tale of the tragedy, and to the next, and to the next. The affair went from mouth to mouth, spreading with electrical swiftness, overpassing and running ahead of Dyke himself, so that by the time he reached the lobby of the Yosemite House, he found his story awaiting him. A group formed about him. In his immediate vicinity business for the instant was suspended. The group swelled. One after another of his friends added themselves to it. Magnus Derrick joined it, and Annixter. Again and again, Dyke recounted the matter, beginning with the time when he was discharged from the same corporation's service for refusing to accept an unfair wage. His voice quivered with exasperation; his heavy frame shook with rage; his eyes were injected, bloodshot; his face flamed vermilion, while his deep bass rumbled throughout the running comments of his auditors like the thunderous reverberation of diapason.

From all points of view, the story was discussed by those who listened to him, now in the heat of excitement, now calmly, judicially. One verdict, however, prevailed. It was voiced by Annixter: "You're stuck. You can roar till you're black in the face, but you can't buck against the Railroad. There's nothing to be done." "You can shoot the ruffian, you can shoot S. Behrman," clamoured one of the group. "Yes, sir; by the Lord, you can shoot him."

"Poor fool," commented Annixter, turning away.

Nothing to be done. No, there was nothing to be done—not one thing. Dyke, at last alone and driving his team out of the town, turned the business confusedly over in his mind from end to end. Advice, suggestion, even offers of financial aid had been showered upon him from all directions. Friends were not wanting who heatedly presented to his consideration all manner of ingenious plans, wonderful devices. They were worthless. The tentacle held fast. He was stuck.

By degrees, as his wagon carried him farther out into the country, and open empty fields, his anger lapsed, and the numbness of bewilderment returned. He could not look one hour ahead into the future; could formulate no plans even for the next day. He did not know what to do. He was stuck.

With the limpness and inertia of a sack of sand, the reins slipping loosely in his dangling fingers, his eyes fixed, staring between the horses' heads, he allowed himself to be carried aimlessly along. He resigned himself. What did he care? What was the use of going on? He was stuck.

The team he was driving had once belonged to the Los Muertos stables and unguided as the horses were, they took the county road towards Derrick's ranch house. Dyke, all abroad, was unaware of the fact till, drawn by the smell of water, the horses halted by the trough in front of Caraher's saloon.

The ex-engineer dismounted, looking about him, realising where he was. So much the worse; it did not matter. Now that he had come so far it was as short to go home by this route as to return on his tracks. Slowly he unchecked the horses and stood at their heads, watching them drink.

"I don't see," he muttered, "just what I am going to do."

Caraher appeared at the door of his place, his red face, red beard, and flaming cravat standing sharply out from the shadow of the doorway. He called a welcome to Dyke.

"Hello, Captain."

Dyke looked up, nodding his head listlessly.

"Hello, Caraher," he answered.

"Well," continued the saloonkeeper, coming forward a step, "what's the news in town?"

Dyke told him. Caraher's red face suddenly took on a darker colour. The red glint in his eyes shot from under his eyebrows. Furious, he vented a rolling explosion of oaths.

"And now it's your turn," he vociferated. "They ain't after only the big wheat-growers, the rich men. By God, they'll even pick the poor man's pocket. Oh, they'll get their bellies full some day. It can't last forever. They'll wake up the wrong kind of man some morning, the man that's got guts in him, that will hit back when he's kicked and that will talk to 'em with a torch in one hand and a stick of dynamite in the other." He raised his clenched fists in the air. "So help me, God," he cried, "when I think it all over I go crazy, I see red. Oh, if the people only knew their strength. Oh, if I could wake 'em up. There's not only Shelgrim, but there's others. All the magnates, all the butchers, all the blood-suckers, by the thousands. Their day will come, by God, it will."

By now, the ex-engineer and the bar-keeper had retired to the saloon back of the grocery to talk over the details of this new outrage. Dyke, still a little dazed, sat down by one of the tables, preoccupied, saying but little, and Caraher as a matter of course set the whiskey bottle at his elbow.

It happened that at this same moment, Presley, returning to Los Muertos from Bonneville, his pockets full of mail, stopped in at the grocery to buy some black lead for his bicycle. In the saloon, on the other side of the narrow partition, he overheard the conversation between Dyke and Caraher. The door was open. He caught every word distinctly.

"Tell us all about it, Dyke," urged Caraher.

For the fiftieth time Dyke told the story. Already it had crystallised into a certain form. He used the same phrases with each repetition, the same sentences, the same words. In his mind it became set. Thus he would tell it to any one who would listen from now on, week after week, year after year, all the rest of his life—"And I based my calculations on a two-cent rate. So soon as they saw I was to make money they doubled the tariff—all the traffic would bear—and I mortgaged to S. Behrman—ruined me with a turn of the hand—stuck, cinched, and not one thing to be done."

As he talked, he drank glass after glass of whiskey, and the honest rage, the open, above-board fury of his mind coagulated, thickened, and sunk to a dull, evil hatred, a wicked, oblique malevolence. Caraher, sure now of winning a disciple, replenished his glass.

"Do you blame us now," he cried, "us others, the Reds? Ah, yes, it's all very well for your middle class to preach moderation. I could do it, too. You could do it, too, if your belly was fed, if your property was safe, if your wife had not been murdered if your children were not starving. Easy enough then to preach law-abiding methods, legal redress, and all such rot. But how about US?" he vociferated. "Ah, yes, I'm a loud-mouthed rum-seller, ain't I? I'm a wild-eyed striker, ain't I? I'm a blood-thirsty anarchist, ain't I? Wait till you've seen your wife brought home to you with the face you used to kiss smashed in by a horse's hoof—killed by the Trust, as it happened to me. Then talk about moderation! And you, Dyke, black-listed engineer, discharged employee, ruined agriculturist, wait till you see your little tad and your mother turned out of doors when S. Behrman forecloses. Wait till you see 'em getting thin and white, and till you hear your little girl ask you why you all don't eat a little more and that she wants her dinner and you can't give it to her. Wait till you see—at the same time that your family is dying for lack of bread—a hundred thousand acres of wheat—millions of bushels of food—grabbed and gobbled by the Railroad Trust, and then talk of moderation. That talk is just what the Trust wants to hear. It ain't frightened of that. There's one thing only it does listen to, one thing it is frightened of—the people with dynamite in their hands,—six inches of plugged gaspipe. THAT talks."

Dyke did not reply. He filled another pony of whiskey and drank it in two gulps. His frown had lowered to a scowl, his face was a dark red, his head had sunk, bull-like, between his massive shoulders; without winking he gazed long and with troubled eyes at his knotted, muscular hands, lying open on the table before him, idle, their occupation gone.

Presley forgot his black lead. He listened to Caraher. Through the open door he caught a glimpse of Dyke's back, broad, muscled, bowed down, the great shoulders stooping.

The whole drama of the doubled freight rate leaped salient and distinct in the eye of his mind. And this was but one instance, an isolated case. Because he was near at hand he happened to see it. How many others were there, the length and breadth of the State? Constantly this sort of thing must occur—little industries choked out in their very beginnings, the air full of the death rattles of little enterprises, expiring unobserved in far-off counties, up in canyons and arroyos of the foothills, forgotten by every one but the monster who was daunted by the magnitude of no business, however great, who overlooked no opportunity of plunder, however petty, who with one tentacle grabbed a hundred thousand acres of wheat, and with another pilfered a pocketful of growing hops.

He went away without a word, his head bent, his hands clutched tightly on the cork grips of the handle bars of his bicycle. His lips were white. In his heart a blind demon of revolt raged tumultuous, shrieking blasphemies.

At Los Muertos, Presley overtook Annixter. As he guided his wheel up the driveway to Derrick's ranch house, he saw the master of Quien Sabe and Harran in conversation on the steps of the porch. Magnus stood in the doorway, talking to his wife.

Occupied with the press of business and involved in the final conference with the League's lawyers on the eve of the latter's departure for Washington, Annixter had missed the train that was to take him back to Guadalajara and Quien Sabe. Accordingly, he had accepted the Governor's invitation to return with him on his buck-board to Los Muertos, and before leaving Bonneville had telephoned to his ranch to have young Vacca bring the buckskin, by way of the Lower Road, to meet him at Los Muertos. He found her waiting there for him, but before going on, delayed a few moments to tell Harran of Dyke's affair.

"I wonder what he will do now?" observed Harran when his first outburst of indignation had subsided.

"Nothing," declared Annixter. "He's stuck."

"That eats up every cent of Dyke's earnings," Harran went on. "He has been ten years saving them. Oh, I told him to make sure of the Railroad when he first spoke to me about growing hops."

"I've just seen him," said Presley, as he joined the others. "He was at Caraher's. I only saw his back. He was drinking at a table and his back was towards me. But the man looked broken—absolutely crushed. It is terrible, terrible."

"He was at Caraher's, was he?" demanded Annixter.

"Yes."

"Drinking, hey?"

"I think so. Yes, I saw a bottle."

"Drinking at Caraher's," exclaimed Annixter, rancorously; "I can see HIS finish."

There was a silence. It seemed as if nothing more was to be said. They paused, looking thoughtfully on the ground.

In silence, grim, bitter, infinitely sad, the three men as if at that moment actually standing in the bar-room of Caraher's roadside saloon, contemplated the slow sinking, the inevitable collapse and submerging of one of their companions, the wreck of a career, the ruin of an individual; an honest man, strong, fearless, upright, struck down by a colossal power, perverted by an evil influence, go reeling to his ruin.

"I see his finish," repeated Annixter. "Exit Dyke, and score another tally for S. Behrman, Shelgrim and Co."

He moved away impatiently, loosening the tie-rope with which the buckskin was fastened. He swung himself up.

"God for us all," he declared as he rode away, "and the devil take the hindmost. Good-bye, I'm going home. I still have one a little longer."

He galloped away along the Lower Road, in the direction of Quien Sabe, emerging from the grove of cypress and eucalyptus about the ranch house, and coming out upon the bare brown plain of the wheat land, stretching away from him in apparent barrenness on either hand.

It was late in the day, already his shadow was long upon the padded dust of the road in front of him. On ahead, a long ways off, and a little to the north, the venerable campanile of the Mission San Juan was glinting radiant in the last rays of the sun, while behind him, towards the north and west, the gilded dome of the courthouse at Bonneville stood silhouetted in purplish black against the flaming west. Annixter spurred the buck-skin forward. He feared he might be late to his supper. He wondered if it would be brought to him by Hilma.

Hilma! The name struck across in his brain with a pleasant, glowing tremour. All through that day of activity, of strenuous business, the minute and cautious planning of the final campaign in the great war of the League and the Trust, the idea of her and the recollection of her had been the undercurrent of his thoughts. At last he was alone. He could put all other things behind him and occupy himself solely with her.

In that glory of the day's end, in that chaos of sunshine, he saw her again. Unimaginative, crude, direct, his fancy, nevertheless, placed her before him, steeped in sunshine, saturated with glorious light, brilliant, radiant, alluring. He saw the sweet simplicity of her carriage, the statuesque evenness of the contours of her figure, the single, deep swell of her bosom, the solid masses of her hair. He remembered the small contradictory suggestions of feminine daintiness he had so often remarked about her, her slim, narrow feet, the little steel buckles of her low shoes, the knot of black ribbon she had begun to wear of late on the back of her head, and he heard her voice, low-pitched, velvety, a sweet, murmuring huskiness that seemed to come more from her chest than from her throat.

The buckskin's hoofs clattered upon the gravelly flats of Broderson's Creek underneath the Long Trestle. Annixter's mind went back to the scene of the previous evening, when he had come upon her at this place. He set his teeth with anger and disappointment. Why had she not been able to understand? What was the matter with these women, always set upon this marrying notion? Was it not enough that he wanted her more than any other girl he knew and that she wanted him? She had said as much. Did she think she was going to be mistress of Quien Sabe? Ah, that was it. She was after his property, was for marrying him because of his money. His unconquerable suspicion of the woman, his innate distrust of the feminine element would not be done away with. What fathomless duplicity was hers, that she could appear so innocent. It was almost unbelievable; in fact, was it believable?

For the first time doubt assailed him. Suppose Hilma was indeed all that she appeared to be. Suppose it was not with her a question of his property, after all; it was a poor time to think of marrying him for his property when all Quien Sabe hung in the issue of the next few months. Suppose she had been sincere. But he caught himself up. Was he to be fooled by a feemale girl at this late date? He, Buck Annixter, crafty, hard-headed, a man of affairs? Not much. Whatever transpired he would remain the master.

He reached Quien Sabe in this frame of mind. But at this hour, Annixter, for all his resolutions, could no longer control his thoughts. As he stripped the saddle from the buckskin and led her to the watering trough by the stable corral, his heart was beating thick at the very notion of being near Hilma again. It was growing dark, but covertly he glanced here and there out of the corners of his eyes to see if she was anywhere about. Annixter—how, he could not tell—had become possessed of the idea that Hilma would not inform her parents of what had passed between them the previous evening under the Long Trestle. He had no idea that matters were at an end between himself and the young woman. He must apologise, he saw that clearly enough, must eat crow, as he told himself. Well, he would eat crow. He was not afraid of her any longer, now that she had made her confession to him. He would see her as soon as possible and get this business straightened out, and begin again from a new starting point. What he wanted with Hilma, Annixter did not define clearly in his mind. At one time he had known perfectly well what he wanted. Now, the goal of his desires had become vague. He could not say exactly what it was. He preferred that things should go forward without much idea of consequences; if consequences came, they would do so naturally enough, and of themselves; all that he positively knew was that Hilma occupied his thoughts morning, noon, and night; that he was happy when he was with her, and miserable when away from her.

The Chinese cook served his supper in silence. Annixter ate and drank and lighted a cigar, and after his meal sat on the porch of his house, smoking and enjoying the twilight. The evening was beautiful, warm, the sky one powder of stars. From the direction of the stables he heard one of the Portuguese hands picking a guitar.

But he wanted to see Hilma. The idea of going to bed without at least a glimpse of her became distasteful to him. Annixter got up and descending from the porch began to walk aimlessly about between the ranch buildings, with eye and ear alert. Possibly he might meet her somewheres.

The Trees' little house, toward which inevitably Annixter directed his steps, was dark. Had they all gone to bed so soon? He made a wide circuit about it, listening, but heard no sound. The door of the dairy-house stood ajar. He pushed it open, and stepped into the odorous darkness of its interior. The pans and deep cans of polished metal glowed faintly from the corners and from the walls. The smell of new cheese was pungent in his nostrils. Everything was quiet. There was nobody there. He went out again, closing the door, and stood for a moment in the space between the dairy-house and the new barn, uncertain as to what he should do next.

As he waited there, his foreman came out of the men's bunk house, on the other side of the kitchens, and crossed over toward the barn. "Hello, Billy," muttered Annixter as he passed.

"Oh, good evening, Mr. Annixter," said the other, pausing in front of him. "I didn't know you were back. By the way," he added, speaking as though the matter was already known to Annixter, "I see old man Tree and his family have left us. Are they going to be gone long? Have they left for good?"

"What's that?" Annixter exclaimed. "When did they go? Did all of them go, all three?"

"Why, I thought you knew. Sure, they all left on the afternoon train for San Francisco. Cleared out in a hurry—took all their trunks. Yes, all three went—the young lady, too. They gave me notice early this morning. They ain't ought to have done that. I don't know who I'm to get to run the dairy on such short notice. Do you know any one, Mr. Annixter?"

"Well, why in hell did you let them go?" vociferated Annixter. "Why didn't you keep them here till I got back? Why didn't you find out if they were going for good? I can't be everywhere. What do I feed you for if it ain't to look after things I can't attend to?"

He turned on his heel and strode away straight before him, not caring where he was going. He tramped out from the group of ranch buildings; holding on over the open reach of his ranch, his teeth set, his heels digging furiously into the ground. The minutes passed. He walked on swiftly, muttering to himself from time to time.

"Gone, by the Lord. Gone, by the Lord. By the Lord Harry, she's cleared out."

As yet his head was empty of all thought. He could not steady his wits to consider this new turn of affairs. He did not even try.

"Gone, by the Lord," he exclaimed. "By the Lord, she's cleared out."

He found the irrigating ditch, and the beaten path made by the ditch tenders that bordered it, and followed it some five minutes; then struck off at right angles over the rugged surface of the ranch land, to where a great white stone jutted from the ground. There he sat down, and leaning forward, rested his elbows on his knees, and looked out vaguely into the night, his thoughts swiftly readjusting themselves.

He was alone. The silence of the night, the infinite repose of the flat, bare earth—two immensities—widened around and above him like illimitable seas. A grey half-light, mysterious, grave, flooded downward from the stars.

Annixter was in torment. Now, there could be no longer any doubt—now it was Hilma or nothing. Once out of his reach, once lost to him, and the recollection of her assailed him with unconquerable vehemence. Much as she had occupied his mind, he had never realised till now how vast had been the place she had filled in his life. He had told her as much, but even then he did not believe it.

Suddenly, a bitter rage against himself overwhelmed him as he thought of the hurt he had given her the previous evening. He should have managed differently. How, he did not know, but the sense of the outrage he had put upon her abruptly recoiled against him with cruel force. Now, he was sorry for it, infinitely sorry, passionately sorry. He had hurt her. He had brought the tears to her eyes. He had so flagrantly insulted her that she could no longer bear to breathe the same air with him. She had told her parents all. She had left Quien Sabe—had left him for good, at the very moment when he believed he had won her. Brute, beast that he was, he had driven her away.

An hour went by; then two, then four, then six. Annixter still sat in his place, groping and battling in a confusion of spirit, the like of which he had never felt before. He did not know what was the matter with him. He could not find his way out of the dark and out of the turmoil that wheeled around him. He had had no experience with women. There was no precedent to guide him. How was he to get out of this? What was the clew that would set everything straight again?

That he would give Hilma up, never once entered his head. Have her he would. She had given herself to him. Everything should have been easy after that, and instead, here he was alone in the night, wrestling with himself, in deeper trouble than ever, and Hilma farther than ever away from him.

It was true, he might have Hilma, even now, if he was willing to marry her. But marriage, to his mind, had been always a vague, most remote possibility, almost as vague and as remote as his death,—a thing that happened to some men, but that would surely never occur to him, or, if it did, it would be after long years had passed, when he was older, more settled, more mature—an event that belonged to the period of his middle life, distant as yet.

He had never faced the question of his marriage. He had kept it at an immense distance from him. It had never been a part of his order of things. He was not a marrying man.

But Hilma was an ever-present reality, as near to him as his right hand. Marriage was a formless, far distant abstraction. Hilma a tangible, imminent fact. Before he could think of the two as one; before he could consider the idea of marriage, side by side with the idea of Hilma, measureless distances had to be traversed, things as disassociated in his mind as fire and water, had to be fused together; and between the two he was torn as if upon a rack.

Slowly, by imperceptible degrees, the imagination, unused, unwilling machine, began to work. The brain's activity lapsed proportionately. He began to think less, and feel more. In that rugged composition, confused, dark, harsh, a furrow had been driven deep, a little seed planted, a little seed at first weak, forgotten, lost in the lower dark places of his character.

But as the intellect moved slower, its functions growing numb, the idea of self dwindled. Annixter no longer considered himself; no longer considered the notion of marriage from the point of view of his own comfort, his own wishes, his own advantage. He realised that in his newfound desire to make her happy, he was sincere. There was something in that idea, after all. To make some one happy—how about that now? It was worth thinking of.

Far away, low down in the east, a dim belt, a grey light began to whiten over the horizon. The tower of the Mission stood black against it. The dawn was coming. The baffling obscurity of the night was passing. Hidden things were coming into view.

Annixter, his eyes half-closed, his chin upon his fist, allowed his imagination full play. How would it be if he should take Hilma into his life, this beautiful young girl, pure as he now knew her to be; innocent, noble with the inborn nobility of dawning womanhood? An overwhelming sense of his own unworthiness suddenly bore down upon him with crushing force, as he thought of this. He had gone about the whole affair wrongly. He had been mistaken from the very first. She was infinitely above him. He did not want—he should not desire to be the master. It was she, his servant, poor, simple, lowly even, who should condescend to him.

Abruptly there was presented to his mind's eye a picture of the years to come, if he now should follow his best, his highest, his most unselfish impulse. He saw Hilma, his own, for better or for worse, for richer or for poorer, all barriers down between them, he giving himself to her as freely, as nobly, as she had given herself to him. By a supreme effort, not of the will, but of the emotion, he fought his way across that vast gulf that for a time had gaped between Hilma and the idea of his marriage. Instantly, like the swift blending of beautiful colours, like the harmony of beautiful chords of music, the two ideas melted into one, and in that moment into his harsh, unlovely world a new idea was born. Annixter stood suddenly upright, a mighty tenderness, a gentleness of spirit, such as he had never conceived of, in his heart strained, swelled, and in a moment seemed to burst. Out of the dark furrows of his soul, up from the deep rugged recesses of his being, something rose, expanding. He opened his arms wide. An immense happiness overpowered him. Actual tears came to his eyes. Without knowing why, he was not ashamed of it. This poor, crude fellow, harsh, hard, narrow, with his unlovely nature, his fierce truculency, his selfishness, his obstinacy, abruptly knew that all the sweetness of life, all the great vivifying eternal force of humanity had burst into life within him.

The little seed, long since planted, gathering strength quietly, had at last germinated.

Then as the realisation of this hardened into certainty, in the growing light of the new day that had just dawned for him, Annixter uttered a cry. Now at length, he knew the meaning of it all.

"Why—I—I, I LOVE her," he cried. Never until then had it occurred to him. Never until then, in all his thoughts of Hilma, had that great word passed his lips.

It was a Memnonian cry, the greeting of the hard, harsh image of man, rough-hewn, flinty, granitic, uttering a note of joy, acclaiming the new risen sun.

By now it was almost day. The east glowed opalescent. All about him Annixter saw the land inundated with light. But there was a change. Overnight something had occurred. In his perturbation the change seemed to him, at first, elusive, almost fanciful, unreal. But now as the light spread, he looked again at the gigantic scroll of ranch lands unrolled before him from edge to edge of the horizon. The change was not fanciful. The change was real. The earth was no longer bare. The land was no longer barren,—no longer empty, no longer dull brown. All at once Annixter shouted aloud.

There it was, the Wheat, the Wheat! The little seed long planted, germinating in the deep, dark furrows of the soil, straining, swelling, suddenly in one night had burst upward to the light. The wheat had come up. It was there before him, around him, everywhere, illimitable, immeasurable. The winter brownness of the ground was overlaid with a little shimmer of green. The promise of the sowing was being fulfilled. The earth, the loyal mother, who never failed, who never disappointed, was keeping her faith again. Once more the strength of nations was renewed. Once more the force of the world was revivified. Once more the Titan, benignant, calm, stirred and woke, and the morning abruptly blazed into glory upon the spectacle of a man whose heart leaped exuberant with the love of a woman, and an exulting earth gleaming transcendent with the radiant magnificence of an inviolable pledge.

CHAPTER III

Presley's room in the ranch house of Los Muertos was in the second story of the building. It was a corner room; one of its windows facing the south, the other the east. Its appointments were of the simplest. In one angle was the small white painted iron bed, covered with a white counterpane. The walls were hung with a white paper figured with knots of pale green leaves, very gay and bright. There was a straw matting on the floor. White muslin half-curtains hung in the windows, upon the sills of which certain plants bearing pink waxen flowers of which Presley did not know the name, grew in oblong green boxes. The walls were unadorned, save by two pictures, one a reproduction of the "Reading from Homer," the other a charcoal drawing of the Mission of San Juan de Guadalajara, which Presley had made himself. By the east window stood the plainest of deal tables, innocent of any cloth or covering, such as might have been used in a kitchen. It was Presley's work table, and was invariably littered with papers, half-finished manuscripts, drafts of poems, notebooks, pens, half-smoked cigarettes, and the like. Near at hand, upon a shelf, were his books. There were but two chairs in the room—the straight backed wooden chair, that stood in front of the table, angular, upright, and in which it was impossible to take one's ease, and the long comfortable wicker steamer chair, stretching its length in front of the south window. Presley was immensely fond of this room. It amused and interested him to maintain its air of rigorous simplicity and freshness. He abhorred cluttered bric-a-brac and meaningless objets d'art. Once in so often he submitted his room to a vigorous inspection; setting it to rights, removing everything but the essentials, the few ornaments which, in a way, were part of his life.

His writing had by this time undergone a complete change. The notes for his great Song of the West, the epic poem he once had hoped to write he had flung aside, together with all the abortive attempts at its beginning. Also he had torn up a great quantity of "fugitive" verses, preserving only a certain half-finished poem, that he called "The Toilers." This poem was a comment upon the social fabric, and had been inspired by the sight of a painting he had seen in Cedarquist's art gallery. He had written all but the last verse.

On the day that he had overheard the conversation between Dyke and Caraher, in the latter's saloon, which had acquainted him with the monstrous injustice of the increased tariff, Presley had returned to Los Muertos, white and trembling, roused to a pitch of exaltation, the like of which he had never known in all his life. His wrath was little short of even Caraher's. He too "saw red"; a mighty spirit of revolt heaved tumultuous within him. It did not seem possible that this outrage could go on much longer. The oppression was incredible; the plain story of it set down in truthful statement of fact would not be believed by the outside world.

He went up to his little room and paced the floor with clenched fists and burning face, till at last, the repression of his contending thoughts all but suffocated him, and he flung himself before his table and began to write. For a time, his pen seemed to travel of itself; words came to him without searching, shaping themselves into phrases,—the phrases building themselves up to great, forcible sentences, full of eloquence, of fire, of passion. As his prose grew more exalted, it passed easily into the domain of poetry. Soon the cadence of his paragraphs settled to an ordered beat and rhythm, and in the end Presley had thrust aside his journal and was once more writing verse.

He picked up his incomplete poem of "The Toilers," read it hastily a couple of times to catch its swing, then the Idea of the last verse—the Idea for which he so long had sought in vain—abruptly springing to his brain, wrote it off without so much as replenishing his pen with ink. He added still another verse, bringing the poem to a definite close, resuming its entire conception, and ending with a single majestic thought, simple, noble, dignified, absolutely convincing.

Presley laid down his pen and leaned back in his chair, with the certainty that for one moment he had touched untrod heights. His hands were cold, his head on fire, his heart leaping tumultuous in his breast.

Now at last, he had achieved. He saw why he had never grasped the inspiration for his vast, vague, IMPERSONAL Song of the West. At the time when he sought for it, his convictions had not been aroused; he had not then cared for the People. His sympathies had not been touched. Small wonder that he had missed it. Now he was of the People; he had been stirred to his lowest depths. His earnestness was almost a frenzy. He BELIEVED, and so to him all things were possible at once.

Then the artist in him reasserted itself. He became more interested in his poem, as such, than in the cause that had inspired it. He went over it again, retouching it carefully, changing a word here and there, and improving its rhythm. For the moment, he forgot the People, forgot his rage, his agitation of the previous hour, he remembered only that he had written a great poem.

Then doubt intruded. After all, was it so great? Did not its sublimity overpass a little the bounds of the ridiculous? Had he seen true? Had he failed again? He re-read the poem carefully; and it seemed all at once to lose force.

By now, Presley could not tell whether what he had written was true poetry or doggerel. He distrusted profoundly his own judgment. He must have the opinion of some one else, some one competent to judge. He could not wait; to-morrow would not do. He must know to a certainty before he could rest that night.

He made a careful copy of what he had written, and putting on his hat and laced boots, went down stairs and out upon the lawn, crossing over to the stables. He found Phelps there, washing down the buckboard.

"Do you know where Vanamee is to-day?" he asked the latter. Phelps put his chin in the air.

"Ask me something easy," he responded. "He might be at Guadalajara, or he might be up at Osterman's, or he might be a hundred miles away from either place. I know where he ought to be, Mr. Presley, but that ain't saying where the crazy gesabe is. He OUGHT to be range-riding over east of Four, at the head waters of Mission Creek."

"I'll try for him there, at all events," answered Presley. "If you see Harran when he comes in, tell him I may not be back in time for supper."

Presley found the pony in the corral, cinched the saddle upon him, and went off over the Lower Road, going eastward at a brisk canter.

At Hooven's he called a "How do you do" to Minna, whom he saw lying in a slat hammock under the mammoth live oak, her foot in bandages; and then galloped on over the bridge across the irrigating ditch, wondering vaguely what would become of such a pretty girl as Minna, and if in the end she would marry the Portuguese foreman in charge of the ditching-gang. He told himself that he hoped she would, and that speedily. There was no lack of comment as to Minna Hooven about the ranches. Certainly she was a good girl, but she was seen at all hours here and there about Bonneville and Guadalajara, skylarking with the Portuguese farm hands of Quien Sabe and Los Muertos. She was very pretty; the men made fools of themselves over her. Presley hoped they would not end by making a fool of her.

Just beyond the irrigating ditch, Presley left the Lower Road, and following a trail that branched off southeasterly from this point, held on across the Fourth Division of the ranch, keeping the Mission Creek on his left. A few miles farther on, he went through a gate in a barbed wire fence, and at once engaged himself in a system of little arroyos and low rolling hills, that steadily lifted and increased in size as he proceeded. This higher ground was the advance guard of the Sierra foothills, and served as the stock range for Los Muertos. The hills were huge rolling hummocks of bare ground, covered only by wild oats. At long intervals, were isolated live oaks. In the canyons and arroyos, the chaparral and manzanita grew in dark olive-green thickets. The ground was honey-combed with gopher-holes, and the gophers themselves were everywhere. Occasionally a jack rabbit bounded across the open, from one growth of chaparral to another, taking long leaps, his ears erect. High overhead, a hawk or two swung at anchor, and once, with a startling rush of wings, a covey of quail flushed from the brush at the side of the trail.

On the hillsides, in thinly scattered groups were the cattle, grazing deliberately, working slowly toward the water-holes for their evening drink, the horses keeping to themselves, the colts nuzzling at their mothers' bellies, whisking their tails, stamping their unshod feet. But once in a remoter field, solitary, magnificent, enormous, the short hair curling tight upon his forehead, his small red eyes twinkling, his vast neck heavy with muscles, Presley came upon the monarch, the king, the great Durham bull, maintaining his lonely state, unapproachable, austere.

Presley found the one-time shepherd by a water-hole, in a far distant corner of the range. He had made his simple camp for the night. His blue-grey army blanket lay spread under a live oak, his horse grazed near at hand. He himself sat on his heels before a little fire of dead manzanita roots, cooking his coffee and bacon. Never had Presley conceived so keen an impression of loneliness as his crouching figure presented. The bald, bare landscape widened about him to infinity. Vanamee was a spot in it all, a tiny dot, a single atom of human organisation, floating endlessly on the ocean of an illimitable nature.

The two friends ate together, and Vanamee, having snared a brace of quails, dressed and then roasted them on a sharpened stick. After eating, they drank great refreshing draughts from the water-hole. Then, at length, Presley having lit his cigarette, and Vanamee his pipe, the former said:

"Vanamee, I have been writing again."

Vanamee turned his lean ascetic face toward him, his black eyes fixed attentively.

"I know," he said, "your journal."

"No, this is a poem. You remember, I told you about it once. 'The Toilers,' I called it."

"Oh, verse! Well, I am glad you have gone back to it. It is your natural vehicle."

"You remember the poem?" asked Presley. "It was unfinished."

"Yes, I remember it. There was better promise in it than anything you ever wrote. Now, I suppose, you have finished it."

Without reply, Presley brought it from out the breast pocket of his shooting coat. The moment seemed propitious. The stillness of the vast, bare hills was profound. The sun was setting in a cloudless brazier of red light; a golden dust pervaded all the landscape. Presley read his poem aloud. When he had finished, his friend looked at him.

"What have you been doing lately?" he demanded. Presley, wondering, told of his various comings and goings.

"I don't mean that," returned the other. "Something has happened to you, something has aroused you. I am right, am I not? Yes, I thought so. In this poem of yours, you have not been trying to make a sounding piece of literature. You wrote it under tremendous stress. Its very imperfections show that. It is better than a mere rhyme. It is an Utterance—a Message. It is Truth. You have come back to the primal heart of things, and you have seen clearly. Yes, it is a great poem."

"Thank you," exclaimed Presley fervidly. "I had begun to mistrust myself."

"Now," observed Vanamee, "I presume you will rush it into print. To have formulated a great thought, simply to have accomplished, is not enough."

"I think I am sincere," objected Presley. "If it is good it will do good to others. You said yourself it was a Message. If it has any value, I do not think it would be right to keep it back from even a very small and most indifferent public."

"Don't publish it in the magazines at all events," Vanamee answered. "Your inspiration has come FROM the People. Then let it go straight TO the

People—not the literary readers of the monthly periodicals, the rich, who would only be indirectly interested. If you must publish it, let it be in the daily press. Don't interrupt. I know what you will say. It will be that the daily press is common, is vulgar, is undignified; and I tell you that such a poem as this of yours, called as it is, 'The Toilers,' must be read BY the Toilers. It MUST BE common; it must be vulgarised. You must not stand upon your dignity with the People, if you are to reach them."

"That is true, I suppose," Presley admitted, "but I can't get rid of the idea that it would be throwing my poem away. The great magazine gives me such—a—background; gives me such weight."

"Gives YOU such weight, gives you such background. Is it YOURSELF you think of? You helper of the helpless. Is that your sincerity? You must sink yourself; must forget yourself and your own desire of fame, of admitted success. It is your POEM, your MESSAGE, that must prevail,—not YOU, who wrote it. You preach a doctrine of abnegation, of self-obliteration, and you sign your name to your words as high on the tablets as you can reach, so that all the world may see, not the poem, but the poet. Presley, there are many like you. The social reformer writes a book on the iniquity of the possession of land, and out of the proceeds, buys a corner lot. The economist who laments the hardships of the poor, allows himself to grow rich upon the sale of his book."

But Presley would hear no further.

"No," he cried, "I know I am sincere, and to prove it to you, I will publish my poem, as you say, in the daily press, and I will accept no money for it."

They talked on for about an hour, while the evening wore away. Presley very soon noticed that Vanamee was again preoccupied. More than ever of late, his silence, his brooding had increased. By and by he rose abruptly, turning his head to the north, in the direction of the Mission church of San Juan. "I think," he said to Presley, "that I must be going."

"Going? Where to at this time of night?"

"Off there." Vanamee made an uncertain gesture toward the north. "Good-bye," and without another word he disappeared in the grey of the twilight. Presley was left alone wondering. He found his horse, and, tightening the girths, mounted and rode home under the sheen of the stars, thoughtful, his head bowed. Before he went to bed that night he sent "The Toilers" to the Sunday Editor of a daily newspaper in San Francisco.

Upon leaving Presley, Vanamee, his thumbs hooked into his empty cartridge belt, strode swiftly down from the hills of the Los Muertos stock-range and on through the silent town of Guadalajara. His lean, swarthy face, with its hollow cheeks, fine, black, pointed beard, and sad eyes, was set to the northward. As was his custom, he was bareheaded, and the rapidity of his stride made a breeze in his long, black hair. He knew where he was going. He knew what he must live through that night.

Again, the deathless grief that never slept leaped out of the shadows, and fastened upon his shoulders. It was scourging him back to that scene of a vanished happiness, a dead romance, a perished idyl,—the Mission garden in the shade of the venerable pear trees.

But, besides this, other influences tugged at his heart. There was a mystery in the garden. In that spot the night was not always empty, the darkness not always silent. Something far off stirred and listened to his cry, at times drawing nearer to him. At first this presence had been a matter for terror; but of late, as he felt it gradually drawing nearer, the terror had at long intervals given place to a feeling of an almost ineffable sweetness. But distrusting his own senses, unwilling to submit himself to such torturing, uncertain happiness, averse to the terrible confusion of spirit that followed upon a night spent in the garden, Vanamee had tried to keep away from the place. However, when the sorrow of his life reassailed him, and the thoughts and recollections of Angele brought the ache into his heart, and the tears to his eyes, the temptation to return to the garden invariably gripped him close. There were times when he could not resist. Of themselves, his footsteps turned in that direction. It was almost as if he himself had been called.

Guadalajara was silent, dark. Not even in Solotari's was there a light. The town was asleep. Only the inevitable guitar hummed from an unseen 'dobe. Vanamee pushed on. The smell of the fields and open country, and a distant scent of flowers that he knew well, came to his nostrils, as he emerged from the town by way of the road that led on towards the Mission through Quien Sabe. On either side of him lay the brown earth, silently nurturing the implanted seed. Two days before it had rained copiously, and the soil, still moist, disengaged a pungent aroma of fecundity.

Vanamee, following the road, passed through the collection of buildings of Annixter's home ranch. Everything slept. At intervals, the aer-motor on the artesian well creaked audibly, as it turned in a languid breeze from the northeast. A cat, hunting field-mice, crept from the shadow of the gigantic barn and paused uncertainly in the open, the tip of her tail twitching. From within the barn itself came the sound of the friction of a heavy body and a stir of hoofs, as one of the dozing cows lay down with a long breath.

Vanamee left the ranch house behind him and proceeded on his way. Beyond him, to the right of the road, he could make out the higher ground in the Mission enclosure, and the watching tower of the Mission itself. The minutes passed. He went steadily forward. Then abruptly he paused, his head in the air, eye and ear alert. To that strange sixth sense of his, responsive as the leaves of the sensitive plant, had suddenly come the impression of a human being near at hand. He had neither seen nor heard, but for all that he stopped an instant in his tracks; then, the sensation confirmed, went on again with slow steps, advancing warily.

At last, his swiftly roving eyes lighted upon an object, just darker than the grey-brown of the night-ridden land. It was at some distance from the roadside. Vanamee approached it cautiously, leaving the road, treading carefully upon the moist clods of earth underfoot. Twenty paces distant, he halted.

Annixter was there, seated upon a round, white rock, his back towards him. He was leaning forward, his elbows on his knees, his chin in his hands. He did not move. Silent, motionless, he gazed out upon the flat, sombre land.

It was the night wherein the master of Quien Sabe wrought out his salvation, struggling with Self from dusk to dawn. At the moment when Vanamee came upon him, the turmoil within him had only begun. The heart of the man had not yet wakened. The night was young, the dawn far distant, and all around him the fields of upturned clods lay bare and brown, empty of all life, unbroken by a single green shoot.

For a moment, the life-circles of these two men, of so widely differing characters, touched each other, there in the silence of the night under the stars. Then silently Vanamee withdrew, going on his way, wondering at the trouble that, like himself, drove this hardheaded man of affairs, untroubled by dreams, out into the night to brood over an empty land.

Then speedily he forgot all else. The material world drew off from him. Reality dwindled to a point and vanished like the vanishing of a star at moonrise. Earthly things dissolved and disappeared, as a strange, unnamed essence flowed in upon him. A new atmosphere for him pervaded his surroundings. He entered the world of the Vision, of the Legend, of the

Miracle, where all things were possible. He stood at the gate of the Mission garden.

Above him rose the ancient tower of the Mission church. Through the arches at its summit, where swung the Spanish queen's bells, he saw the slow-burning stars. The silent bats, with flickering wings, threw their dancing shadows on the pallid surface of the venerable facade.

Not the faintest chirring of a cricket broke the silence. The bees were asleep. In the grasses, in the trees, deep in the calix of punka flower and magnolia bloom, the gnats, the caterpillars, the beetles, all the microscopic, multitudinous life of the daytime drowsed and dozed. Not even the minute scuffling of a lizard over the warm, worn pavement of the colonnade disturbed the infinite repose, the profound stillness. Only within the garden, the intermittent trickling of the fountain made itself heard, flowing steadily, marking off the lapse of seconds, the progress of hours, the cycle of years, the inevitable march of centuries. At one time, the doorway before which Vanamee now stood had been hermetically closed. But he, himself, had long since changed that. He stood before it for a moment, steeping himself in the mystery and romance of the place, then raising he latch, pushed open the gate, entered, and closed it softly behind him. He was in the cloister garden.

The stars were out, strewn thick and close in the deep blue of the sky, the milky way glowing like a silver veil. Ursa Major wheeled gigantic in the north. The great nebula in Orion was a whorl of shimmering star dust. Venus flamed a lambent disk of pale saffron, low over the horizon. From edge to edge of the world marched the constellations, like the progress of emperors, and from the innumerable glory of their courses a mysterious sheen of diaphanous light disengaged itself, expanding over all the earth, serene, infinite, majestic.

The little garden revealed itself but dimly beneath the brooding light, only half emerging from the shadow. The polished surfaces of the leaves of the pear trees winked faintly back the reflected light as the trees just stirred in the uncertain breeze. A blurred shield of silver marked the ripples of the fountain. Under the flood of dull blue lustre, the gravelled walks lay vague amid the grasses, like webs of white satin on the bed of a lake. Against the eastern wall the headstones of the graves, an indistinct procession of grey cowls ranged themselves.

Vanamee crossed the garden, pausing to kiss the turf upon Angele's grave. Then he approached the line of pear trees, and laid himself down in their shadow, his chin propped upon his hands, his eyes wandering over the expanse of the little valley that stretched away from the foot of the hill upon which the Mission was built.

Once again he summoned the Vision. Once again he conjured up the Illusion. Once again, tortured with doubt, racked with a deathless grief, he craved an Answer of the night. Once again, mystic that he was, he sent his mind out from him across the enchanted sea of the Supernatural. Hope, of what he did not know, roused up within him. Surely, on such a night as this, the hallucination must define itself. Surely, the Manifestation must be vouchsafed.

His eyes closed, his will girding itself to a supreme effort, his senses exalted to a state of pleasing numbness, he called upon Angele to come to him, his voiceless cry penetrating far out into that sea of faint, ephemeral light that floated tideless over the little valley beneath him. Then motionless, prone upon the ground, he waited.

Months had passed since that first night when, at length, an Answer had come to Vanamee. At first, startled out of all composure, troubled and stirred to his lowest depths, because of the very thing for which he sought, he resolved never again to put his strange powers to the test. But for all that, he had come a second night to the garden, and a third, and a fourth. At last, his visits were habitual. Night after night he was there, surrendering himself to the influences of the place, gradually convinced that something did actually answer when he called. His faith increased as the winter grew into spring. As the spring advanced and the nights became shorter, it crystallised into certainty. Would he have her again, his love, long dead? Would she come to him once more out of the grave, out of the night? He could not tell; he could only hope. All that he knew was that his cry found an answer, that his outstretched hands, groping in the darkness, met the touch of other fingers. Patiently he waited. The nights became warmer as the spring drew on. The stars shone clearer. The nights seemed brighter. For nearly a month after the occasion of his first answer nothing new occurred. Some nights it failed him entirely; upon others it was faint, illusive.

Then, at last, the most subtle, the barest of perceptible changes began. His groping mind far-off there, wandering like a lost bird over the valley, touched upon some thing again, touched and held it and this time drew it a single step closer to him. His heart beating, the blood surging in his temples, he watched with the eyes of his imagination, this gradual approach. What was coming to him? Who was coming to him? Shrouded in the obscurity of the night, whose was the face now turned towards his? Whose the footsteps that with such infinite slowness drew nearer to where he waited? He did not dare to say.

His mind went back many years to that time before the tragedy of Angele's death, before the mystery of the Other. He waited then as he waited now. But then he had not waited in vain. Then, as now, he had seemed to feel her approach, seemed to feel her drawing nearer and nearer to their rendezvous. Now, what would happen? He did not know. He waited. He waited, hoping all things. He waited, believing all things. He waited, enduring all things. He trusted in the Vision.

Meanwhile, as spring advanced, the flowers in the Seed ranch began to come to life. Over the five hundred acres whereon the flowers were planted, the widening growth of vines and bushes spread like the waves of a green sea. Then, timidly, colours of the faintest tints began to appear. Under the moonlight, Vanamee saw them expanding, delicate pink, faint blue, tenderest variations of lavender and yellow, white shimmering with reflections of gold, all subdued and pallid in the moonlight.

By degrees, the night became impregnated with the perfume of the flowers. Illusive at first, evanescent as filaments of gossamer; then as the buds opened, emphasising itself, breathing deeper, stronger. An exquisite mingling of many odours passed continually over the Mission, from the garden of the Seed ranch, meeting and blending with the aroma of its magnolia buds and punka blossoms.

As the colours of the flowers of the Seed ranch deepened, and as their odours penetrated deeper and more distinctly, as the starlight of each succeeding night grew brighter and the air became warmer, the illusion defined itself. By imperceptible degrees, as Vanamee waited under the shadows of the pear trees, the Answer grew nearer and nearer. He saw nothing but the distant glimmer of the flowers. He heard nothing but the drip of the fountain. Nothing moved about him but the invisible, slow-passing breaths of perfume; yet he felt the approach of the Vision.

It came first to about the middle of the Seed ranch itself, some half a mile away, where the violets grew; shrinking, timid flowers, hiding close to the ground. Then it passed forward beyond the violets, and drew nearer and stood amid the mignonette, hardier blooms that dared look heavenward from out the leaves. A few nights later it left the mignonette behind, and advanced into the beds of white iris that pushed more boldly forth from the earth, their waxen petals claiming the attention. It advanced then a long step into the proud, challenging beauty of the carnations and roses; and at last, after many nights, Vanamee felt that it paused, as if trembling at its hardihood, full in the superb glory of the royal lilies themselves, that grew on the extreme border of the Seed ranch nearest to him. After this, there was a certain long wait. Then, upon a dark midnight, it advanced again. Vanamee could scarcely repress a cry. Now, the illusion emerged from the flowers. It stood, not distant, but unseen, almost at the base of the hill upon whose crest he waited, in a depression of the ground where the shadows lay thickest. It was nearly within earshot.

The nights passed. The spring grew warmer. In the daytime intermittent rains freshened all the earth. The flowers of the Seed ranch grew rapidly. Bud after bud burst forth, while those already opened expanded to full maturity. The colour of the Seed ranch deepened.

One night, after hours of waiting, Vanamee felt upon his cheek the touch of a prolonged puff of warm wind, breathing across the little valley from out the east. It reached the Mission garden and stirred the branches of the pear trees. It seemed veritably to be compounded of the very essence of the flowers. Never had the aroma been so sweet, so pervasive. It passed and faded, leaving in its wake an absolute silence. Then, at length, the silence of the night, that silence to which Vanamee had so long appealed, was broken by a tiny sound. Alert, half-risen from the ground, he listened; for now, at length, he heard something. The sound repeated itself. It came from near at hand, from the thick shadow at the foot of the hill. What it was, he could not tell, but it did not belong to a single one of the infinite similar noises of the place with which he was so familiar. It was neither the rustle of a leaf, the snap of a parted twig, the drone of an insect, the dropping of a magnolia blossom. It was a vibration merely, faint, elusive, impossible of definition; a minute notch in the fine, keen edge of stillness.

Again the nights passed. The summer stars became brighter. The warmth increased. The flowers of the Seed ranch grew still more. The five hundred acres of the ranch were carpeted with them.

At length, upon a certain midnight, a new light began to spread in the sky. The thin scimitar of the moon rose, veiled and dim behind the earth-mists. The light increased. Distant objects, until now hidden, came into view, and as the radiance brightened, Vanamee, looking down upon the little valley, saw a spectacle of incomparable beauty. All the buds of the Seed ranch had opened. The faint tints of the flowers had deepened, had asserted themselves. They challenged the eye. Pink became a royal red. Blue rose into purple. Yellow flamed into orange. Orange glowed golden and brilliant. The earth disappeared under great bands and fields of resplendent colour. Then, at length, the moon abruptly soared zenithward from out the veiling mist, passing from one filmy haze to another. For a moment there was a gleam of a golden light, and Vanamee, his eyes searching the shade at the foot of the hill, felt his heart suddenly leap, and then hang poised, refusing to beat. In that instant of passing light, something had caught his eye. Something that moved, down there, half in and half out of the shadow, at the hill's foot. It had come and gone in an instant. The haze once more screened the moonlight. The shade again engulfed the vision. What was it he had seen? He did not know. So brief had been that movement, the drowsy brain had not been quick enough to interpret the cipher message of the eye. Now it was gone. But something had been there. He had seen it. Was it the lifting of a strand of hair, the wave of a white hand, the flutter of a garment's edge? He could not tell, but it did not belong to any of those sights which he had seen so often in that place. It was neither the glancing of a moth's wing, the nodding of a wind-touched blossom, nor the noiseless flitting of a bat. It was a gleam merely, faint, elusive, impossible of definition, an intangible agitation, in the vast, dim blur of the darkness.

And that was all. Until now no single real thing had occurred, nothing that Vanamee could reduce to terms of actuality, nothing he could put into words. The manifestation, when not recognisable to that strange sixth sense of his, appealed only to the most refined, the most delicate perception of eye and ear. It was all ephemeral, filmy, dreamy, the mystic forming of the Vision—the invisible developing a concrete nucleus, the starlight coagulating, the radiance of the flowers thickening to something actual; perfume, the most delicious fragrance, becoming a tangible presence.

But into that garden the serpent intruded. Though cradled in the slow rhythm of the dream, lulled by this beauty of a summer's night, heavy with the scent of flowers, the silence broken only by a rippling fountain, the darkness illuminated by a world of radiant blossoms, Vanamee could not forget the tragedy of the Other; that terror of many years ago,—that prowler of the night, that strange, fearful figure with the unseen face, swooping in there from out the darkness, gone in an instant, yet leaving behind the trail and trace of death and of pollution.

Never had Vanamee seen this more clearly than when leaving Presley on the stock range of Los Muertos, he had come across to the Mission garden by way of the Quien Sabe ranch.

It was the same night in which Annixter out-watched the stars, coming, at last, to himself.

As the hours passed, the two men, far apart, ignoring each other, waited for the Manifestation, — Annixter on the ranch, Vanamee in the garden.

Prone upon his face, under the pear trees, his forehead buried in the hollow of his arm, Vanamee lay motionless. For the last time, raising his head, he sent his voiceless cry out into the night across the multi-coloured levels of the little valley, calling upon the miracle, summoning the darkness to give Angele back to him, resigning himself to the hallucination. He bowed his head upon his arm again and waited. The minutes passed. The fountain dripped steadily. Over the hills a haze of saffron light foretold the rising of the full moon. Nothing stirred. The silence was profound.

Then, abruptly, Vanamee's right hand shut tight upon his wrist. There — there it was. It began again, his invocation was answered. Far off there, the ripple formed again upon the still, black pool of the night. No sound, no sight; vibration merely, appreciable by some sublimated faculty of the mind as yet unnamed. Rigid, his nerves taut, motionless, prone on the ground, he waited.

It advanced with infinite slowness. Now it passed through the beds of violets, now through the mignonette. A moment later, and he knew it stood among the white iris. Then it left those behind. It was in the splendour of the red roses and carnations. It passed like a moving star into the superb abundance, the imperial opulence of the royal lilies. It was advancing slowly, but there was no pause. He held his breath, not daring to raise his head. It passed beyond the limits of the Seed ranch, and entered the shade at the foot of the hill below him. Would it come farther than this? Here it had always stopped hitherto, stopped for a moment, and then, in spite of his efforts, had slipped from his grasp and faded back into the night. But now he wondered if he had been willing to put forth his utmost strength, after all. Had there not always been an element of dread in the thought of beholding the mystery face to face? Had he not even allowed the Vision to dissolve, the Answer to recede into the obscurity whence it came?

But never a night had been so beautiful as this. It was the full period of the spring. The air was a veritable caress. The infinite repose of the little garden, sleeping under the night, was delicious beyond expression. It was a tiny corner of the world, shut off, discreet, distilling romance, a garden of dreams, of enchantments.

Below, in the little valley, the resplendent colourations of the million flowers, roses, lilies, hyacinths, carnations, violets, glowed like incandescence in the golden light of the rising moon. The air was thick with the perfume, heavy with it, clogged with it. The sweetness filled the very mouth. The throat choked with it. Overhead wheeled the illimitable procession of the constellations. Underfoot, the earth was asleep. The very flowers were dreaming. A cathedral hush overlay all the land, and a sense of benediction brooded low, — a divine kindliness manifesting itself in beauty, in peace, in absolute repose.

It was a time for visions. It was the hour when dreams come true, and lying deep in the grasses beneath the pear trees, Vanamee, dizzied with mysticism, reaching up and out toward the supernatural, felt, as it were, his mind begin to rise upward from out his body. He passed into a state of being the like of which he had not known before. He felt that his imagination was reshaping itself, preparing to receive an impression never experienced until now. His body felt light to him, then it dwindled, vanished. He saw with new eyes, heard with new ears, felt with a new heart.

"Come to me," he murmured.

Then slowly he felt the advance of the Vision. It was approaching. Every instant it drew gradually nearer. At last, he was to see. It had left the shadow at the base of the hill; it was on the hill itself. Slowly, steadily, it ascended the slope; just below him there, he heard a faint stirring. The grasses rustled under the touch of a foot. The leaves of the bushes murmured, as a hand brushed against them; a slender twig creaked. The sounds of approach were more distinct. They came nearer. They reached the top of the hill. They were within whispering distance.

Vanamee, trembling, kept his head buried in his arm. The sounds, at length, paused definitely. The Vision could come no nearer. He raised his head and looked. The moon had risen. Its great shield of gold stood over the eastern horizon. Within six feet of Vanamee, clear and distinct, against the disk of the moon, stood the figure of a young girl. She was dressed in a gown of scarlet silk, with flowing sleeves, such as Japanese wear, embroidered with flowers and figures of birds worked in gold threads. On either side of her face, making three-cornered her round, white forehead, hung the soft masses of her hair of gold. Her hands hung limply at her sides. But from between her parted lips — lips of almost an Egyptian fulness — her breath came slow and regular, and her eyes, heavy lidded, slanting upwards toward the temples, perplexing, oriental, were closed. She was asleep.

From out this life of flowers, this world of colour, this atmosphere oppressive with perfume, this darkness clogged and cloyed, and thickened with sweet odours, she came to him. She came to him from out of the flowers, the smell of the roses in her hair of gold, the aroma and the imperial red of the carnations in her lips, the whiteness of the lilies, the perfume of the lilies, and the lilies' slender, balancing grace in her neck. Her hands disengaged the scent of the heliotrope. The folds of her scarlet gown gave off the enervating smell of poppies. Her feet were redolent of hyacinth. She stood before him, a Vision realised—a dream come true. She emerged from out the invisible. He beheld her, a figure of gold and pale vermilion, redolent of perfume, poised motionless in the faint saffron sheen of the new-risen moon. She, a creation of sleep, was herself asleep. She, a dream, was herself dreaming.

Called forth from out the darkness, from the grip of the earth, the embrace of the grave, from out the memory of corruption, she rose into light and life, divinely pure. Across that white forehead was no smudge, no trace of an earthly pollution—no mark of a terrestrial dishonour. He saw in her the same beauty of untainted innocence he had known in his youth. Years had made no difference with her. She was still young. It was the old purity that returned, the deathless beauty, the ever-renascent life, the eternal consecrated and immortal youth. For a few seconds, she stood there before him, and he, upon the ground at her feet, looked up at her, spellbound. Then, slowly she withdrew. Still asleep, her eyelids closed, she turned from him, descending the slope. She was gone.

Vanamee started up, coming, as it were, to himself, looking wildly about him. Sarria was there.

"I saw her," said the priest. "It was Angele, the little girl, your Angele's daughter. She is like her mother."

But Vanamee scarcely heard. He walked as if in a trance, pushing by Sarria, going forth from the garden. Angele or Angele's daughter, it was all one with him. It was She. Death was overcome. The grave vanquished. Life, ever-renewed, alone existed. Time was naught; change was naught; all things were immortal but evil; all things eternal but grief.

Suddenly, the dawn came; the east burned roseate toward the zenith. Vanamee walked on, he knew not where. The dawn grew brighter. At length, he paused upon the crest of a hill overlooking the ranchos, and cast his eye below him to the southward. Then, suddenly flinging up his arms, he uttered a great cry.

There it was. The Wheat! The Wheat! In the night it had come up. It was there, everywhere, from margin to margin of the horizon. The earth, long empty, teemed with green life. Once more the pendulum of the seasons swung in its mighty arc, from death back to life. Life out of death, eternity rising from out dissolution. There was the lesson. Angele was not the symbol, but the PROOF of immortality. The seed dying, rotting and corrupting in the earth; rising again in life unconquerable, and in immaculate purity,— Angele dying as she gave birth to her little daughter, life springing from her death,—the pure, unconquerable, coming forth from the defiled. Why had he not had the knowledge of God? Thou fool, that which thou sowest is not quickened except it die. So the seed had died. So died Angele. And that which thou sowest, thou sowest not that body that shall be, but bare grain. It may chance of wheat, or of some other grain. The wheat called forth from out the darkness, from out the grip of the earth, of the grave, from out corruption, rose triumphant into light and life. So Angele, so life, so also the resurrection of the dead. It is sown in corruption. It is raised in incorruption. It is sown in dishonour. It is raised in glory. It is sown in weakness. It is raised in power. Death was swallowed up in Victory.

The sun rose. The night was over. The glory of the terrestrial was one, and the glory of the celestial was another. Then, as the glory of sun banished the lesser glory of moon and stars, Vanamee, from his mountain top, beholding the eternal green life of the growing Wheat, bursting its bonds, and in his heart exulting in his triumph over the grave, flung out his arms with a mighty shout:

"Oh, Death, where is thy sting? Oh, Grave, where is thy victory?"

CHAPTER IV

Presley's Socialistic poem, "The Toilers," had an enormous success. The editor of the Sunday supplement of the San Francisco paper to which it was sent, printed it in Gothic type, with a scare-head title so decorative as to be almost illegible, and furthermore caused the poem to be illustrated by one of the paper's staff artists in a most impressive fashion. The whole affair occupied an entire page. Thus advertised, the poem attracted attention. It was promptly copied in New York, Boston, and Chicago papers. It was discussed, attacked, defended, eulogised, ridiculed. It was praised with the most fulsome adulation; assailed with the most violent condemnation. Editorials were written upon it. Special articles, in literary pamphlets, dissected its rhetoric and prosody. The phrases were quoted,—were used as texts for revolutionary sermons, reactionary speeches. It was parodied; it was distorted so as to read as an advertisement for patented cereals and infants' foods. Finally, the editor of an enterprising monthly magazine reprinted the poem, supplementing it by a photograph and biography of Presley himself.

Presley was stunned, bewildered. He began to wonder at himself. Was he actually the "greatest American poet since Bryant"? He had had no thought of fame while composing "The Toilers." He had only been moved to his heart's foundations,—thoroughly in earnest, seeing clearly,— and had addressed himself to the poem's composition in a happy moment when words came easily to him, and the elaboration of fine sentences was not difficult. Was it thus fame was achieved? For a while he was tempted to cross the continent and go to New York and there come unto his own, enjoying the triumph that awaited him. But soon he denied himself this cheap reward. Now he was too much in earnest. He wanted to help his People, the community in which he lived—the little world of the San Joaquin, at grapples with the Railroad. The struggle had found its poet. He told himself that his place was here. Only the words of the manager of a lecture bureau troubled him for a moment. To range the entire nation, telling all his countrymen of the drama that was working itself out on this fringe of the continent, this ignored and distant Pacific Coast, rousing their interest and stirring them up to action—appealed to him. It might do great good. To devote himself to "the Cause," accepting no penny of remuneration; to give his life to loosing the grip of the iron-hearted monster of steel and steam would be beyond question heroic. Other States than California had their grievances. All over the country the family of cyclops was growing. He would declare himself the champion of the People in their opposition to the Trust. He would be an apostle, a prophet, a martyr of Freedom.

But Presley was essentially a dreamer, not a man of affairs. He hesitated to act at this precise psychological moment, striking while the iron was yet hot, and while he hesitated, other affairs near at hand began to absorb his attention.

One night, about an hour after he had gone to bed, he was awakened by the sound of voices on the porch of the ranch house, and, descending, found Mrs. Dyke there with Sidney. The ex-engineer's mother was talking to Magnus and Harran, and crying as she talked. It seemed that Dyke was missing. He had gone into town early that afternoon with the wagon and team, and was to have been home for supper. By now it was ten o'clock and there was no news of him. Mrs. Dyke told how she first had gone to Quien Sabe, intending to telephone from there to Bonneville, but Annixter was in San Francisco, and in his absence the house was locked up, and the over-seer, who had a duplicate key, was himself in Bonneville. She had telegraphed three times from Guadalajara to Bonneville for news of her son, but without result. Then, at last, tortured with anxiety, she had gone to Hooven's, taking Sidney with her, and had prevailed upon "Bismarck" to hitch up and drive her across Los Muertos to the Governor's, to beg him to telephone into Bonneville, to know what had become of Dyke.

While Harran rang up Central in town, Mrs. Dyke told Presley and Magnus of the lamentable change in Dyke.

"They have broken my son's spirit, Mr. Derrick," she said. "If you were only there to see. Hour after hour, he sits on the porch with his hands lying open in his lap, looking at them without a word. He won't look me in the face any more, and he don't sleep. Night after night, he has walked the floor until morning. And he will go on that way for days together, very silent, without a word, and sitting still in his chair, and then, all of a sudden, he will break out—oh, Mr. Derrick, it is terrible—into an awful rage, cursing, swearing, grinding his teeth, his hands clenched over his head, stamping so that the house shakes, and saying that if S. Behrman don't give him back his money, he will kill him with his two hands. But that isn't the worst, Mr. Derrick. He goes to Mr. Caraher's saloon now, and stays there for hours, and listens to Mr. Caraher. There is something on my son's mind; I know there is—something that he and Mr. Caraher have talked over together, and I can't find out what it is. Mr. Caraher is a bad man, and my son has fallen under his influence." The tears filled her eyes. Bravely, she turned to hide them, turning away to take Sidney in her arms, putting her head upon the little girl's shoulder.

"I—I haven't broken down before, Mr. Derrick," she said, "but after we have been so happy in our little house, just us three—and the future seemed so bright—oh, God will punish the gentlemen who own the railroad for being so hard and cruel."

Harran came out on the porch, from the telephone, and she interrupted herself, fixing her eyes eagerly upon him.

"I think it is all right, Mrs. Dyke," he said, reassuringly. "We know where he is, I believe. You and the little tad stay here, and Hooven and I will go after him."

About two hours later, Harran brought Dyke back to Los Muertos in Hooven's wagon. He had found him at Caraher's saloon, very drunk.

There was nothing maudlin about Dyke's drunkenness. In him the alcohol merely roused the spirit of evil, vengeful, reckless.

As the wagon passed out from under the eucalyptus trees about the ranch house, taking Mrs. Dyke, Sidney, and the one-time engineer back to the hop ranch, Presley leaning from his window heard the latter remark:

"Caraher is right. There is only one thing they listen to, and that's dynamite."

The following day Presley drove Magnus over to Guadalajara to take the train for San Francisco. But after he had said good-bye to the Governor, he was moved to go on to the hop ranch to see the condition of affairs in that quarter. He returned to Los Muertos overwhelmed with sadness and trembling with anger. The hop ranch that he had last seen in the full tide of prosperity was almost a ruin. Work had evidently been abandoned long since. Weeds were already choking the vines. Everywhere the poles sagged and drooped. Many had even fallen, dragging the vines with them, spreading them over the ground in an inextricable tangle of dead leaves, decaying tendrils, and snarled string. The fence was broken; the unfinished storehouse, which never was to see completion, was a lamentable spectacle of gaping doors and windows—a melancholy skeleton. Last of all, Presley had caught a glimpse of Dyke himself, seated in his rocking chair on the porch, his beard and hair unkempt, motionless, looking with vague eyes upon his hands that lay palm upwards and idle in his lap.

Magnus on his way to San Francisco was joined at Bonneville by Osterman. Upon seating himself in front of the master of Los Muertos in the smoking-car of the train, this latter, pushing back his hat and smoothing his bald head, observed:

"Governor, you look all frazeled out. Anything wrong these days?"

The other answered in the negative, but, for all that, Osterman was right. The Governor had aged suddenly. His former erectness was gone, the broad shoulders stooped a little, the strong lines of his thin-lipped mouth were relaxed, and his hand, as it clasped over the yellowed ivory knob of his cane, had an unwonted tremulousness not hitherto noticeable. But the change in Magnus was more than physical. At last, in the full tide of power, President of the League, known and talked of in every county of the State, leader in a great struggle, consulted, deferred to as the "Prominent Man," at length attaining that position, so long and vainly sought for, he yet found no pleasure in his triumph, and little but bitterness in life. His success had come by devious methods, had been reached by obscure means.

He was a briber. He could never forget that. To further his ends, disinterested, public-spirited, even philanthropic as those were, he had connived with knavery, he, the politician of the old school, of such rigorous integrity, who had abandoned a "career" rather than compromise with honesty. At this eleventh hour, involved and entrapped in the fine-spun web of a new order of things, bewildered by Osterman's dexterity, by his volubility and glibness, goaded and harassed beyond the point of reason by the aggression of the Trust he fought, he had at last failed. He had fallen he had given a bribe. He had thought that, after all, this would make but little difference with him. The affair was known only to Osterman, Broderson, and Annixter; they would not judge him, being themselves involved. He could still preserve a bold front; could still hold his head high. As time went on the affair would lose its point.

But this was not so. Some subtle element of his character had forsaken him. He felt it. He knew it. Some certain stiffness that had given him all his rigidity, that had lent force to his authority, weight to his dominance, temper to his fine, inflexible hardness, was diminishing day by day. In the decisions which he, as President of the League, was called upon to make so often, he now hesitated. He could no longer be arrogant, masterful, acting upon his own judgment, independent of opinion. He began to consult his lieutenants, asking their advice, distrusting his own opinions. He made mistakes, blunders, and when those were brought to his notice, took refuge in bluster. He knew it to be bluster—knew that sooner or later his subordinates would recognise it as such. How long could he maintain his position? So only he could keep his grip upon the lever of control till the battle was over, all would be well. If not, he would fall, and, once fallen, he knew that now, briber that he was, he would never rise again.

He was on his way at this moment to the city to consult with Lyman as to a certain issue of the contest between the Railroad and the ranchers, which, of late, had been brought to his notice.

When appeal had been taken to the Supreme Court by the League's Executive Committee, certain test cases had been chosen, which should represent all the lands in question. Neither Magnus nor Annixter had so appealed, believing, of course, that their cases were covered by the test cases on trial at Washington. Magnus had here blundered again, and the League's agents in San Francisco had written to warn him that the Railroad might be able to take advantage of a technicality, and by pretending that neither Quien Sabe nor Los Muertos were included in the appeal, attempt to put its dummy buyers in possession of the two ranches before the Supreme Court handed down its decision. The ninety days allowed for taking this appeal were nearly at an end and after then the Railroad could act. Osterman and Magnus at once decided to go up to the city, there joining Annixter (who had been absent from Quien Sabe for the last ten days), and talk the matter over with Lyman. Lyman, because of his position as Commissioner, might be cognisant of the Railroad's plans, and, at the same time, could give sound legal advice as to what was to be done should the new rumour prove true.

"Say," remarked Osterman, as the train pulled out of the Bonneville station, and the two men settled themselves for the long journey, "say Governor, what's all up with Buck Annixter these days? He's got a bean about something, sure."

"I had not noticed," answered Magnus. "Mr. Annixter has been away some time lately. I cannot imagine what should keep him so long in San Francisco."

"That's it," said Osterman, winking. "Have three guesses. Guess right and you get a cigar. I guess g-i-r-l spells Hilma Tree. And a little while ago she quit Quien Sabe and hiked out to 'Frisco. So did Buck. Do I draw the cigar? It's up to you." "I have noticed her," observed Magnus. "A fine figure of a woman. She would make some man a good wife."

"Hoh! Wife! Buck Annixter marry! Not much. He's gone a-girling at last, old Buck! It's as funny as twins. Have to josh him about it when I see him, sure."

But when Osterman and Magnus at last fell in with Annixter in the vestibule of the Lick House, on Montgomery Street, nothing could be got out of him. He was in an execrable humour. When Magnus had broached the subject of business, he had declared that all business could go to pot, and when Osterman, his tongue in his cheek, had permitted himself a most distant allusion to a feemale girl, Annixter had cursed him for a "busy-face" so vociferously and tersely, that even Osterman was cowed.

"Well," insinuated Osterman, "what are you dallying 'round 'Frisco so much for?"

"Cat fur, to make kitten-breeches," retorted Annixter with oracular vagueness.

Two weeks before this time, Annixter had come up to the city and had gone at once to a certain hotel on Bush Street, behind the First National Bank, that he knew was kept by a family connection of the Trees. In his conjecture that Hilma and her parents would stop here, he was right. Their names were on the register. Ignoring custom, Annixter marched straight up to their rooms, and before he was well aware of it, was "eating crow" before old man Tree.

Hilma and her mother were out at the time. Later on, Mrs. Tree returned alone, leaving Hilma to spend the day with one of her cousins who lived far out on Stanyan Street in a little house facing the park.

Between Annixter and Hilma's parents, a reconciliation had been effected, Annixter convincing them both of his sincerity in wishing to make Hilma his wife. Hilma, however, refused to see him. As soon as she knew he had followed her to San Francisco she had been unwilling to return to the hotel and had arranged with her cousin to spend an indefinite time at her house.

She was wretchedly unhappy during all this time; would not set foot out of doors, and cried herself to sleep night after night. She detested the city. Already she was miserably homesick for the ranch. She remembered the days she had spent in the little dairy-house, happy in her work, making butter and cheese; skimming the great pans of milk, scouring the copper vessels and vats, plunging her arms, elbow deep, into the white curds; coming and going in that atmosphere of freshness, cleanliness, and sunlight, gay, singing, supremely happy just because the sun shone. She remembered her long walks toward the Mission late in the afternoons, her excursions for cresses underneath the Long Trestle, the crowing of the cocks, the distant whistle of the passing trains, the faint sounding of the Angelus. She recalled with infinite longing the solitary expanse of the ranches, the level reaches between the horizons, full of light and silence; the heat at noon, the cloudless iridescence of the sunrise and sunset. She had been so happy in that life! Now, all those days were passed. This crude, raw city, with its crowding houses all of wood and tin, its blotting fogs, its uproarious trade winds, disturbed and saddened her. There was no outlook for the future.

At length, one day, about a week after Annixter's arrival in the city, she was prevailed upon to go for a walk in the park. She went alone, putting on for the first time the little hat of black straw with its puff of white silk her mother had bought for her, a pink shirtwaist, her belt of imitation alligator skin, her new skirt of brown cloth, and her low shoes, set off with their little steel buckles.

She found a tiny summer house, built in Japanese fashion, around a diminutive pond, and sat there for a while, her hands folded in her lap, amused with watching the goldfish, wishing—she knew not what.

Without any warning, Annixter sat down beside her. She was too frightened to move. She looked at him with wide eyes that began to fill with tears.

"Oh," she said, at last, "oh—I didn't know."

"Well," exclaimed Annixter, "here you are at last. I've been watching that blamed house till I was afraid the policeman would move me on. By the Lord," he suddenly cried, "you're pale. You—you, Hilma, do you feel well?"

"Yes—I am well," she faltered.

"No, you're not," he declared. "I know better. You are coming back to Quien Sabe with me. This place don't agree with you. Hilma, what's all the matter? Why haven't you let me see you all this time? Do you know—how things are with me? Your mother told you, didn't she? Do you know how sorry I am? Do you know that I see now that I made the mistake of my life there, that time, under the Long Trestle? I found it out the night after you went away. I sat all night on a stone out on the ranch somewhere and I don't know exactly what happened, but I've been a different man since then. I see things all different now. Why, I've only begun to live since then. I know what love means now, and instead of being ashamed of it, I'm proud of it. If I never was to see you again I would be glad I'd lived through that night, just the same. I just woke up that night. I'd been absolutely and completely selfish up to the moment I realised I really loved you, and now, whether you'll let me marry you or not, I mean to live—I don't know, in a different way. I've GOT to live different. I—well—oh, I can't make you understand, but just loving you has changed my life all around. It's made it easier to do the straight, clean thing. I want to do it, it's fun doing it. Remember, once I said I was proud of being a hard man, a driver, of being glad that people hated me and were afraid of me? Well, since I've loved you I'm ashamed of it all. I don't want to be hard any more, and nobody is going to hate me if I can help it. I'm happy and I want other people so. I love you," he suddenly exclaimed; "I love you, and if you will forgive me, and if you will come down to such a beast as I am, I want to be to you the best a man can be to a woman, Hilma. Do you understand, little girl? I want to be your husband."

Hilma looked at the goldfishes through her tears.

"Have you got anything to say to me, Hilma?" he asked, after a while.

"I don't know what you want me to say," she murmured.

"Yes, you do," he insisted. "I've followed you 'way up here to hear it. I've waited around in these beastly, draughty picnic grounds for over a week to hear it. You know what I want to hear, Hilma."

"Well—I forgive you," she hazarded.

"That will do for a starter," he answered. "But that's not IT."

"Then, I don't know what."

"Shall I say it for you?"

She hesitated a long minute, then:

"You mightn't say it right," she replied.

"Trust me for that. Shall I say it for you, Hilma?"

"I don't know what you'll say."

"I'll say what you are thinking of. Shall I say it?"

There was a very long pause. A goldfish rose to the surface of the little pond, with a sharp, rippling sound. The fog drifted overhead. There was nobody about.

"No," said Hilma, at length. "I—I—I can say it for myself. I—" All at once she turned to him and put her arms around his neck. "Oh, DO you love me?" she cried. "Is it really true? Do you mean every word of it? And you are sorry and you WILL be good to me if I will be your wife? You will be my dear, dear husband?"

The tears sprang to Annixter's eyes. He took her in his arms and held her there for a moment. Never in his life had he felt so unworthy, so undeserving of this clean, pure girl who forgave him and trusted his spoken word and believed him to be the good man he could only wish to be. She was so far above him, so exalted, so noble that he should have bowed his forehead to her feet, and instead, she took him in her arms, believing him to be good, to be her equal. He could think of no words to say. The tears overflowed his eyes and ran down upon his cheeks. She drew away from him and held him a second at arm's length, looking at him, and he saw that she, too, had been crying.

"I think," he said, "we are a couple of softies."

"No, no," she insisted. "I want to cry and want you to cry, too. Oh, dear, I haven't a handkerchief."

"Here, take mine."

They wiped each other's eyes like two children and for a long time sat in the deserted little Japanese pleasure house, their arms about each other, talking, talking, talking.

On the following Saturday they were married in an uptown Presbyterian church, and spent the week of their honeymoon at a small, family hotel on Sutter Street. As a matter of course, they saw the sights of the city together. They made the inevitable bridal trip to the Cliff House and spent an afternoon in the grewsome and made-to-order beauties of Sutro's Gardens; they went through Chinatown, the Palace Hotel, the park museum — where Hilma resolutely refused to believe in the Egyptian mummy — and they drove out in a hired hack to the Presidio and the Golden Gate.

On the sixth day of their excursions, Hilma abruptly declared they had had enough of "playing out," and must be serious and get to work.

This work was nothing less than the buying of the furniture and appointments for the rejuvenated ranch house at Quien Sabe, where they were to live. Annixter had telegraphed to his overseer to have the building repainted, replastered, and reshingled and to empty the rooms of everything but the telephone and safe. He also sent instructions to have the dimensions of each room noted down and the result forwarded to him. It was the arrival of these memoranda that had roused Hilma to action.

Then ensued a most delicious week. Armed with formidable lists, written by Annixter on hotel envelopes, they two descended upon the department stores of the city, the carpet stores, the furniture stores. Right and left they bought and bargained, sending each consignment as soon as purchased to Quien Sabe. Nearly an entire car load of carpets, curtains, kitchen furniture, pictures, fixtures, lamps, straw matting, chairs, and the like were sent down to the ranch, Annixter making a point that their new home should be entirely equipped by San Francisco dealers.

The furnishings of the bedroom and sitting-room were left to the very last. For the former, Hilma bought a "set" of pure white enamel, three chairs, a washstand and bureau, a marvellous bargain of thirty dollars, discovered by wonderful accident at a "Friday Sale." The bed was a piece by itself, bought elsewhere, but none the less a wonder. It was of brass, very brave and gay, and actually boasted a canopy! They bought it complete, just as it stood in the window of the department store and Hilma was in an ecstasy over its crisp, clean, muslin curtains, spread, and shams. Never was there such a bed, the luxury of a princess, such a bed as she had dreamed about her whole life.

Next the appointments of the sitting-room occupied her—since Annixter, himself, bewildered by this astonishing display, unable to offer a single suggestion himself, merely approved of all she bought. In the sitting-room was to be a beautiful blue and white paper, cool straw matting, set off with white wool rugs, a stand of flowers in the window, a globe of goldfish, rocking chairs, a sewing machine, and a great, round centre table of yellow oak whereon should stand a lamp covered with a deep shade of crinkly red tissue paper. On the walls were to hang several pictures—lovely affairs, photographs from life, all properly tinted—of choir boys in robes, with beautiful eyes; pensive young girls in pink gowns, with flowing yellow hair, drooping over golden harps; a coloured reproduction of "Rouget de Lisle, Singing the Marseillaise," and two "pieces" of wood carving, representing a quail and a wild duck, hung by one leg in the midst of game bags and powder horns,—quite masterpieces, both.

At last everything had been bought, all arrangements made, Hilma's trunks packed with her new dresses, and the tickets to Bonneville bought.

"We'll go by the Overland, by Jingo," declared Annixter across the table to his wife, at their last meal in the hotel where they had been stopping; "no way trains or locals for us, hey?"

"But we reach Bonneville at SUCH an hour," protested Hilma. "Five in the morning!"

"Never mind," he declared, "we'll go home in PULLMAN'S, Hilma. I'm not going to have any of those slobs in Bonneville say I didn't know how to do the thing in style, and we'll have Vacca meet us with the team. No, sir, it is Pullman's or nothing. When it comes to buying furniture, I don't shine, perhaps, but I know what's due my wife."

He was obdurate, and late one afternoon the couple boarded the Transcontinental (the crack Overland Flyer of the Pacific and Southwestern) at the Oakland mole. Only Hilma's parents were there to say good-bye. Annixter knew that Magnus and Osterman were in the city, but he had laid his plans to elude them. Magnus, he could trust to be dignified, but that goat Osterman, one could never tell what he would do next. He did not propose to start his journey home in a shower of rice. Annixter marched down the line of cars, his hands encumbered with wicker telescope baskets, satchels, and valises, his tickets in his mouth, his hat on wrong side foremost, Hilma and her parents hurrying on behind him, trying to keep up. Annixter was in a turmoil of nerves lest something should go wrong; catching a train was always for him a little crisis. He rushed ahead so furiously that when he had found his Pullman he had lost his party. He set down his valises to mark the place and charged back along the platform, waving his arms.

"Come on," he cried, when, at length, he espied the others. "We've no more time."

He shouldered and urged them forward to where he had set his valises, only to find one of them gone. Instantly he raised an outcry. Aha, a fine way to treat passengers! There was P. and S. W. management for you. He would, by the Lord, he would—but the porter appeared in the vestibule of the car to placate him. He had already taken his valises inside.

Annixter would not permit Hilma's parents to board the car, declaring that the train might pull out any moment. So he and his wife, following the porter down the narrow passage by the stateroom, took their places and, raising the window, leaned out to say good-bye to Mr. and Mrs. Tree. These latter would not return to Quien Sabe. Old man Tree had found a business chance awaiting him in the matter of supplying his relative's hotel with dairy products. But Bonneville was not too far from San Francisco; the separation was by no means final.

The porters began taking up the steps that stood by the vestibule of each sleeping-car.

"Well, have a good time, daughter," observed her father; "and come up to see us whenever you can."

From beyond the enclosure of the depot's reverberating roof came the measured clang of a bell.

"I guess we're off," cried Annixter. "Good-bye, Mrs. Tree."

"Remember your promise, Hilma," her mother hastened to exclaim, "to write every Sunday afternoon."

There came a prolonged creaking and groan of straining wood and iron work, all along the length of the train. They all began to cry their good-byes at once. The train stirred, moved forward, and gathering slow headway, rolled slowly out into the sunlight. Hilma leaned out of the window and as long as she could keep her mother in sight waved her handkerchief. Then at length she sat back in her seat and looked at her husband.

"Well," she said.

"Well," echoed Annixter, "happy?" for the tears rose in her eyes.

She nodded energetically, smiling at him bravely.

"You look a little pale," he declared, frowning uneasily; "feel well?"

"Pretty well."

Promptly he was seized with uneasiness. "But not ALL well, hey? Is that it?"

It was true that Hilma had felt a faint tremour of seasickness on the ferry-boat coming from the city to the Oakland mole. No doubt a little nausea yet remained with her. But Annixter refused to accept this explanation. He was distressed beyond expression.

"Now you're going to be sick," he cried anxiously.

"No, no," she protested, "not a bit."

"But you said you didn't feel very well. Where is it you feel sick?"

"I don't know. I'm not sick. Oh, dear me, why will you bother?"

"Headache?"

"Not the least."

"You feel tired, then. That's it. No wonder, the way rushed you 'round to-day."

"Dear, I'm NOT tired, and I'm NOT sick, and I'm all RIGHT."

"No, no; I can tell. I think we'd best have the berth made up and you lie down."

"That would be perfectly ridiculous."

"Well, where is it you feel sick? Show me; put your hand on the place. Want to eat something?"

With elaborate minuteness, he cross-questioned her, refusing to let the subject drop, protesting that she had dark circles under her eyes; that she had grown thinner.

"Wonder if there's a doctor on board," he murmured, looking uncertainly about the car. "Let me see your tongue. I know—a little whiskey is what you want, that and some pru— —"

"No, no, NO," she exclaimed. "I'm as well as I ever was in all my life. Look at me. Now, tell me, do l look likee a sick lady?"

He scrutinised her face distressfully.

"Now, don't I look the picture of health?" she challenged.

"In a way you do," he began, "and then again— —"

Hilma beat a tattoo with her heels upon the floor, shutting her fists, the thumbs tucked inside. She closed her eyes, shaking her head energetically.

"I won't listen, I won't listen, I won't listen," she cried.

"But, just the same— —"

"Gibble—gibble—gibble," she mocked. "I won't Listen, I won't listen." She put a hand over his mouth. "Look, here's the dining-car waiter, and the first call for supper, and your wife is hungry."

They went forward and had supper in the diner, while the long train, now out upon the main line, settled itself to its pace, the prolonged, even gallop that it would hold for the better part of the week, spinning out the miles as a cotton spinner spins thread.

It was already dark when Antioch was left behind. Abruptly the sunset appeared to wheel in the sky and readjusted itself to the right of the track behind Mount Diablo, here visible almost to its base. The train had turned southward. Neroly was passed, then Brentwood, then Byron. In the gathering dusk, mountains began to build themselves up on either hand, far off, blocking the horizon. The train shot forward, roaring. Between the mountains the land lay level, cut up into farms, ranches. These continually grew larger; growing wheat began to appear, billowing in the wind of the train's passage. The mountains grew higher, the land richer, and by the time the moon rose, the train was well into the northernmost limits of the valley of the San Joaquin.

Annixter had engaged an entire section, and after he and his wife went to bed had the porter close the upper berth. Hilma sat up in bed to say her prayers, both hands over her face, and then kissing Annixter good-night, went to sleep with the directness of a little child, holding his hand in both her own.

Annixter, who never could sleep on the train, dozed and tossed and fretted for hours, consulting his watch and time-table whenever there was a stop; twice he rose to get a drink of ice water, and between whiles was forever sitting up in the narrow berth, stretching himself and yawning, murmuring with uncertain relevance:

"Oh, Lord! Oh-h-h LORD!"

There were some dozen other passengers in the car—a lady with three children, a group of school-teachers, a couple of drummers, a stout gentleman with whiskers, and a well-dressed young man in a plaid travelling cap, whom Annixter had observed before supper time reading Daudet's "Tartarin" in the French.

But by nine o'clock, all these people were in their berths. Occasionally, above the rhythmic rumble of the wheels, Annixter could hear one of the lady's children fidgeting and complaining. The stout gentleman snored monotonously in two notes, one a rasping bass, the other a prolonged treble. At intervals, a brakeman or the passenger conductor pushed down the aisle, between the curtains, his red and white lamp over his arm. Looking out into the car Annixter saw in an end section where the berths had not been made up, the porter, in his white duck coat, dozing, his mouth wide open, his head on his shoulder.

The hours passed. Midnight came and went. Annixter, checking off the stations, noted their passage of Modesto, Merced, and Madeira. Then, after another broken nap, he lost count. He wondered where they were. Had they reached Fresno yet? Raising the window curtain, he made a shade with both hands on either side of his face and looked out. The night was thick, dark, clouded over. A fine rain was falling, leaving horizontal streaks on the glass of the outside window. Only the faintest grey blur indicated the sky. Everything else was impenetrable blackness.

"I think sure we must have passed Fresno," he muttered. He looked at his watch. It was about half-past three. "If we have passed Fresno," he said to himself, "I'd better wake the little girl pretty soon. She'll need about an hour to dress. Better find out for sure."

He drew on his trousers and shoes, got into his coat, and stepped out into the aisle. In the seat that had been occupied by the porter, the Pullman conductor, his cash box and car-schedules before him, was checking up his berths, a blue pencil behind his ear.

"What's the next stop, Captain?" inquired Annixter, coming up. "Have we reached Fresno yet?"

"Just passed it," the other responded, looking at Annixter over his spectacles.

"What's the next stop?"

"Goshen. We will be there in about forty-five minutes."

"Fair black night, isn't it?"

"Black as a pocket. Let's see, you're the party in upper and lower 9."

Annixter caught at the back of the nearest seat, just in time to prevent a fall, and the conductor's cash box was shunted off the surface of the plush seat and came clanking to the floor. The Pintsch lights overhead vibrated with blinding rapidity in the long, sliding jar that ran through the train from end to end, and the momentum of its speed suddenly decreasing, all but pitched the conductor from his seat. A hideous ear-splitting rasp made itself heard from the clamped-down Westinghouse gear underneath, and Annixter knew that the wheels had ceased to revolve and that the train was sliding forward upon the motionless flanges.

"Hello, hello," he exclaimed, "what's all up now?"

"Emergency brakes," declared the conductor, catching up his cash box and thrusting his papers and tickets into it. "Nothing much; probably a cow on the track."

He disappeared, carrying his lantern with him.

But the other passengers, all but the stout gentleman, were awake; heads were thrust from out the curtains, and Annixter, hurrying back to Hilma, was assailed by all manner of questions.

"What was that?"

"Anything wrong?"

"What's up, anyways?"

Hilma was just waking as Annixter pushed the curtain aside.

"Oh, I was so frightened. What's the matter, dear?" she exclaimed.

"I don't know," he answered. "Only the emergency brakes. Just a cow on the track, I guess. Don't get scared. It isn't anything."

But with a final shriek of the Westinghouse appliance, the train came to a definite halt.

At once the silence was absolute. The ears, still numb with the long-continued roar of wheels and clashing iron, at first refused to register correctly the smaller noises of the surroundings. Voices came from the other end of the car, strange and unfamiliar, as though heard at a great distance across the water. The stillness of the night outside was so profound that the rain, dripping from the car roof upon the road-bed underneath, was as distinct as the ticking of a clock.

"Well, we've sure stopped," observed one of the drummers.

"What is it?" asked Hilma again. "Are you sure there's nothing wrong?"

"Sure," said Annixter. Outside, underneath their window, they heard the sound of hurried footsteps crushing into the clinkers by the side of the ties. They passed on, and Annixter heard some one in the distance shout:

"Yes, on the other side."

Then the door at the end of their car opened and a brakeman with a red beard ran down the aisle and out upon the platform in front. The forward door closed. Everything was quiet again. In the stillness the fat gentleman's snores made themselves heard once more.

The minutes passed; nothing stirred. There was no sound but the dripping rain. The line of cars lay immobilised and inert under the night. One of the drummers, having stepped outside on the platform for a look around, returned, saying:

"There sure isn't any station anywheres about and no siding. Bet you they have had an accident of some kind."

"Ask the porter."

"I did. He don't know."

"Maybe they stopped to take on wood or water, or something."

"Well, they wouldn't use the emergency brakes for that, would they? Why, this train stopped almost in her own length. Pretty near slung me out the berth. Those were the emergency brakes. I heard some one say so."

From far out towards the front of the train, near the locomotive, came the sharp, incisive report of a revolver; then two more almost simultaneously; then, after a long interval, a fourth.

"Say, that's SHOOTING. By God, boys, they're shooting. Say, this is a hold-up."

Instantly a white-hot excitement flared from end to end of the car. Incredibly sinister, heard thus in the night, and in the rain, mysterious, fearful, those four pistol shots started confusion from out the sense of security like a frightened rabbit hunted from her burrow. Wide-eyed, the passengers of the car looked into each other's faces. It had come to them at last, this, they had so often read about. Now they were to see the real thing, now they were to face actuality, face this danger of the night, leaping in from out the blackness of the roadside, masked, armed, ready to kill. They were facing it now. They were held up.

Hilma said nothing, only catching Annixter's hand, looking squarely into his eyes.

"Steady, little girl," he said. "They can't hurt you. I won't leave you. By the Lord," he suddenly exclaimed, his excitement getting the better of him for a moment. "By the Lord, it's a hold-up."

The school-teachers were in the aisle of the car, in night gown, wrapper, and dressing sack, huddled together like sheep, holding on to each other, looking to the men, silently appealing for protection. Two of them were weeping, white to the lips.

"Oh, oh, oh, it's terrible. Oh, if they only won't hurt me."

But the lady with the children looked out from her berth, smiled reassuringly, and said:

"I'm not a bit frightened. They won't do anything to us if we keep quiet. I've my watch and jewelry all ready for them in my little black bag, see?"

She exhibited it to the passengers. Her children were all awake. They were quiet, looking about them with eager faces, interested and amused at this surprise. In his berth, the fat gentleman with whiskers snored profoundly.

"Say, I'm going out there," suddenly declared one of the drummers, flourishing a pocket revolver.

His friend caught his arm.

"Don't make a fool of yourself, Max," he said.

"They won't come near us," observed the well-dressed young man; "they are after the Wells-Fargo box and the registered mail. You won't do any good out there."

But the other loudly protested. No; he was going out. He didn't propose to be buncoed without a fight. He wasn't any coward.

"Well, you don't go, that's all," said his friend, angrily. "There's women and children in this car. You ain't going to draw the fire here."

"Well, that's to be thought of," said the other, allowing himself to be pacified, but still holding his pistol.

"Don't let him open that window," cried Annixter sharply from his place by Hilma's side, for the drummer had made as if to open the sash in one of the sections that had not been made up.

"Sure, that's right," said the others. "Don't open any windows. Keep your head in. You'll get us all shot if you aren't careful."

However, the drummer had got the window up and had leaned before the others could interfere and draw him away.

"Say, by jove," he shouted, as he turned back to the car, "our engine's gone. We're standing on a curve and you can see the end of the train. She's gone, I tell you. Well, look for yourself."

In spite of their precautions, one after another, his friends looked out. Sure enough, the train was without a locomotive.

"They've done it so we can't get away," vociferated the drummer with the pistol. "Now, by jiminy-Christmas, they'll come through the cars and stand us up. They'll be in here in a minute. LORD! WHAT WAS THAT?"

From far away up the track, apparently some half-mile ahead of the train, came the sound of a heavy explosion. The windows of the car vibrated with it.

"Shooting again."

"That isn't shooting," exclaimed Annixter. "They've pulled the express and mail car on ahead with the engine and now they are dynamiting her open."

"That must be it. Yes, sure, that's just what they are doing."

The forward door of the car opened and closed and the school-teachers shrieked and cowered. The drummer with the revolver faced about, his eyes bulging. However, it was only the train conductor, hatless, his lantern in his hand. He was soaked with rain. He appeared in the aisle.

"Is there a doctor in this car?" he asked.

Promptly the passengers surrounded him, voluble with questions. But he was in a bad temper.

"I don't know anything more than you," he shouted angrily. "It was a hold-up. I guess you know that, don't you? Well, what more do you want to know? I ain't got time to fool around. They cut off our express car and have cracked it open, and they shot one of our train crew, that's all, and I want a doctor."

"Did they shoot him—kill him, do you mean?"

"Is he hurt bad?"   ―

"Did the men get away?"

"Oh, shut up, will you all?" exclaimed the conductor.

"What do I know? Is there a DOCTOR in this car, that's what I want to know?"

The well-dressed young man stepped forward.

"I'm a doctor," he said. "Well, come along then," returned the conductor, in a surly voice, "and the passengers in this car," he added, turning back at the door and nodding his head menacingly, "will go back to bed and STAY there. It's all over and there's nothing to see."

He went out, followed by the young doctor.

Then ensued an interminable period of silence. The entire train seemed deserted. Helpless, bereft of its engine, a huge, decapitated monster it lay, half-way around a curve, rained upon, abandoned.

There was more fear in this last condition of affairs, more terror in the idea of this prolonged line of sleepers, with their nickelled fittings, their plate glass, their upholstery, vestibules, and the like, loaded down with people, lost and forgotten in the night and the rain, than there had been when the actual danger threatened.

What was to become of them now? Who was there to help them? Their engine was gone; they were helpless. What next was to happen?

Nobody came near the car. Even the porter had disappeared. The wait seemed endless, and the persistent snoring of the whiskered gentleman rasped the nerves like the scrape of a file.

"Well, how long are we going to stick here now?" began one of the drummers. "Wonder if they hurt the engine with their dynamite?"

"Oh, I know they will come through the car and rob us," wailed the school-teachers.

The lady with the little children went back to bed, and Annixter, assured that the trouble was over, did likewise. But nobody slept. From berth to berth came the sound of suppressed voices talking it all over, formulating conjectures. Certain points seemed to be settled upon, no one knew how, as indisputable. The highwaymen had been four in number and had stopped the train by pulling the bell cord. A brakeman had attempted to interfere and had been shot. The robbers had been on the train all the way from San Francisco. The drummer named Max remembered to have seen four "suspicious-looking characters" in the smoking-car at Lathrop, and had intended to speak to the conductor about them. This drummer had been in a hold-up before, and told the story of it over and over again.

At last, after what seemed to have been an hour's delay, and when the dawn had already begun to show in the east, the locomotive backed on to the train again with a reverberating jar that ran from car to car. At the jolting, the school-teachers screamed in chorus, and the whiskered gentleman stopped snoring and thrust his head from his curtains, blinking at the Pintsch lights. It appeared that he was an Englishman.

"I say," he asked of the drummer named Max, "I say, my friend, what place is this?"

The others roared with derision.

"We were HELD UP, sir, that's what we were. We were held up and you slept through it all. You missed the show of your life."

The gentleman fixed the group with a prolonged gaze. He said never a word, but little by little he was convinced that the drummers told the truth. All at once he grew wrathful, his face purpling. He withdrew his head angrily, buttoning his curtains together in a fury. The cause of his rage was inexplicable, but they could hear him resettling himself upon his pillows with exasperated movements of his head and shoulders. In a few moments the deep bass and shrill treble of his snoring once more sounded through the car.

At last the train got under way again, with useless warning blasts of the engine's whistle. In a few moments it was tearing away through the dawn at a wonderful speed, rocking around curves, roaring across culverts, making up time.

And all the rest of that strange night the passengers, sitting up in their unmade beds, in the swaying car, lighted by a strange mingling of pallid dawn and trembling Pintsch lights, rushing at break-neck speed through the misty rain, were oppressed by a vision of figures of terror, far behind them in the night they had left, masked, armed, galloping toward the mountains pistol in hand, the booty bound to the saddle bow, galloping, galloping on, sending a thrill of fear through all the country side.

The young doctor returned. He sat down in the smoking-room, lighting a cigarette, and Annixter and the drummers pressed around him to know the story of the whole affair.

"The man is dead," he declared, "the brakeman. He was shot through the lungs twice. They think the fellow got away with about five thousand in gold coin."

"The fellow? Wasn't there four of them?"

"No; only one. And say, let me tell you, he had his nerve with him. It seems he was on the roof of the express car all the time, and going as fast as we were, he jumped from the roof of the car down on to the coal on the engine's tender, and crawled over that and held up the men in the cab with his gun, took their guns from 'em and made 'em stop the train. Even ordered 'em to use the emergency gear, seems he knew all about it. Then he went back and uncoupled the express car himself.

"While he was doing this, a brakeman—you remember that brakeman that came through here once or twice—had a red mustache."

"THAT chap?" "Sure. Well, as soon as the train stopped, this brakeman guessed something was wrong and ran up, saw the fellow cutting off the express car and took a couple of shots at him, and the fireman says the fellow didn't even take his hand off the coupling-pin; just turned around as cool as how-do-you-do and NAILED the brakeman right there. They weren't five feet apart when they began shooting. The brakeman had come on him unexpected, had no idea he was so close."

"And the express messenger, all this time?"

"Well, he did his best. Jumped out with his repeating shot-gun, but the fellow had him covered before he could turn round. Held him up and took his gun away from him. Say, you know I call that nerve, just the same. One man standing up a whole train-load, like that. Then, as soon as he'd cut the express car off, he made the engineer run her up the track about half a mile to a road crossing, WHERE HE HAD A HORSE TIED. What do you think of that? Didn't he have it all figured out close? And when he got there, he dynamited the safe and got the Wells-Fargo box. He took five thousand in gold coin; the messenger says it was railroad money that the company were sending down to Bakersfield to pay off with. It was in a bag. He never touched the registered mail, nor a whole wad of greenbacks that were in the safe, but just took the coin, got on his horse, and lit out. The engineer says he went to the east'ard."

"He got away, did he?"

"Yes, but they think they'll get him. He wore a kind of mask, but the brakeman recognised him positively. We got his ante-mortem statement. The brakeman said the fellow had a grudge against the road. He was a discharged employee, and lives near Bonneville."

"Dyke, by the Lord!" exclaimed Annixter.

"That's the name," said the young doctor.

When the train arrived at Bonneville, forty minutes behind time, it landed Annixter and Hilma in the midst of the very thing they most wished to avoid—an enormous crowd. The news that the Overland had been held up thirty miles south of Fresno, a brakeman killed and the safe looted, and that Dyke alone was responsible for the night's work, had been wired on ahead from Fowler, the train conductor throwing the despatch to the station agent from the flying train.

Before the train had come to a standstill under the arched roof of the Bonneville depot, it was all but taken by assault. Annixter, with Hilma on his arm, had almost to fight his way out of the car. The depot was black with people. S. Behrman was there, Delaney, Cyrus Ruggles, the town marshal, the mayor. Genslinger, his hat on the back of his head, ranged the train from cab to rear-lights, note-book in hand, interviewing, questioning, collecting facts for his extra. As Annixter descended finally to the platform, the editor, alert as a black-and-tan terrier, his thin, osseous hands quivering with eagerness, his brown, dry face working with excitement, caught his elbow.

"Can I have your version of the affair, Mr. Annixter?"

Annixter turned on him abruptly.

"Yes!" he exclaimed fiercely. "You and your gang drove Dyke from his job because he wouldn't work for starvation wages. Then you raised freight rates on him and robbed him of all he had. You ruined him and drove him to fill himself up with Caraher's whiskey. He's only taken back what you plundered him of, and now you're going to hound him over the State, hunt him down like a wild animal, and bring him to the gallows at San Quentin. That's my version of the affair, Mister Genslinger, but it's worth your subsidy from the P. and S. W. to print it."

There was a murmur of approval from the crowd that stood around, and Genslinger, with an angry shrug of one shoulder, took himself away.

At length, Annixter brought Hilma through the crowd to where young Vacca was waiting with the team. However, they could not at once start for the ranch, Annixter wishing to ask some questions at the freight office about a final consignment of chairs. It was nearly eleven o'clock before they could start home. But to gain the Upper Road to Quien Sabe, it was necessary to traverse all of Main Street, running through the heart of Bonneville.

The entire town seemed to be upon the sidewalks. By now the rain was over and the sun shining. The story of the hold-up—the work of a man whom every one knew and liked—was in every mouth. How had Dyke come to do it? Who would have believed it of him? Think-of his poor mother and the little tad. Well, after all, he was not so much to blame; the railroad people had brought it on themselves. But he had shot a man to death. Ah, that was a serious business. Good-natured, big, broad-shouldered, jovial Dyke, the man they knew, with whom they had shaken hands only yesterday, yes, and drank with him. He had shot a man, killed him, had stood there in the dark and in the rain while they were asleep in their beds, and had killed a man. Now where was he? Instinctively eyes were turned eastward, over the tops of the houses, or down vistas of side streets to where the foothills of the mountains rose dim and vast over the edge of the valley. He was in amongst them; somewhere, in all that pile of blue crests and purple canyons he was hidden away. Now for weeks of searching, false alarms, clews, trailings, watchings, all the thrill and heart-bursting excitement of a man-hunt. Would he get away? Hardly a man on the sidewalks of the town that day who did not hope for it.

As Annixter's team trotted through the central portion of the town, young Vacca pointed to a denser and larger crowd around the rear entrance of the City Hall. Fully twenty saddle horses were tied to the iron rail underneath the scant, half-grown trees near by, and as Annixter and Hilma drove by, the crowd parted and a dozen men with revolvers on their hips pushed their way to the curbstone, and, mounting their horses, rode away at a gallop.

"It's the posse," said young Vacca.

Outside the town limits the ground was level. There was nothing to obstruct the view, and to the north, in the direction of Osterman's ranch, Vacca made out another party of horsemen, galloping eastward, and beyond these still another.

"There're the other posses," he announced. "That further one is Archie Moore's. He's the sheriff. He came down from Visalia on a special engine this morning."

When the team turned into the driveway to the ranch house, Hilma uttered a little cry, clasping her hands joyfully. The house was one glitter of new white paint, the driveway had been freshly gravelled, the flower-beds replenished. Mrs. Vacca and her daughter, who had been busy putting on the finishing touches, came to the door to welcome them.

"What's this case here?" asked Annixter, when, after helping his wife from the carry-all, his eye fell upon a wooden box of some three by five feet that stood on the porch and bore the red Wells-Fargo label.

"It came here last night, addressed to you, sir," exclaimed Mrs. Vacca. "We were sure it wasn't any of your furniture, so we didn't open it."

"Oh, maybe it's a wedding present," exclaimed Hilma, her eyes sparkling.

"Well, maybe it is," returned her husband. "Here, m' son, help me in with this."

Annixter and young Vacca bore the case into the sitting-room of the house, and Annixter, hammer in hand, attacked it vigorously. Vacca discreetly withdrew on signal from his mother, closing the door after him. Annixter and his wife were left alone.

"Oh, hurry, hurry," cried Hilma, dancing around him.

"I want to see what it is. Who do you suppose could have sent it to us? And so heavy, too. What do you think it can be?"

Annixter put the claw of the hammer underneath the edge of the board top and wrenched with all his might. The boards had been clamped together by a transverse bar and the whole top of the box came away in one piece. A layer of excelsior was disclosed, and on it a letter addressed by typewriter to Annixter. It bore the trade-mark of a business firm of Los Angeles. Annixter glanced at this and promptly caught it up before Hilma could see, with an exclamation of intelligence.

"Oh, I know what this is," he observed, carelessly trying to restrain her busy hands. "It isn't anything. Just some machinery. Let it go." But already she had pulled away the excelsior. Underneath, in temporary racks, were two dozen Winchester repeating rifles.

"Why—what—what—" murmured Hilma blankly.

"Well, I told you not to mind," said Annixter. "It isn't anything. Let's look through the rooms."

"But you said you knew what it was," she protested, bewildered. "You wanted to make believe it was machinery. Are you keeping anything from me? Tell me what it all means. Oh, why are you getting—these?"

She caught his arm, looking with intense eagerness into his face. She half understood already. Annixter saw that.

"Well," he said, lamely, "YOU know—it may not come to anything at all, but you know—well, this League of ours—suppose the Railroad tries to jump Quien Sabe or Los Muertos or any of the other ranches—we made up our minds—the Leaguers have—that we wouldn't let it. That's all."

"And I thought," cried Hilma, drawing back fearfully from the case of rifles, "and I thought it was a wedding present."

And that was their home-coming, the end of their bridal trip. Through the terror of the night, echoing with pistol shots, through that scene of robbery and murder, into this atmosphere of alarms, a man-hunt organising, armed horsemen silhouetted against the horizons, cases of rifles where wedding presents should have been, Annixter brought his young wife to be mistress of a home he might at any moment be called upon to defend with his life.

The days passed. Soon a week had gone by. Magnus Derrick and Osterman returned from the city without any definite idea as to the Corporation's plans. Lyman had been reticent. He knew nothing as to the progress of the land cases in Washington. There was no news. The Executive Committee of the League held a perfunctory meeting at Los Muertos at which nothing but routine business was transacted. A scheme put forward by Osterman for a conference with the railroad managers fell through because of the refusal of the company to treat with the ranchers upon any other basis than that of the new grading. It was impossible to learn whether or not the company considered Los Muertos, Quien Sabe, and the ranches around Bonneville covered by the test cases then on appeal.

Meanwhile there was no decrease in the excitement that Dyke's hold-up had set loose over all the county. Day after day it was the one topic of conversation, at street corners, at cross-roads, over dinner tables, in office, bank, and store. S. Behrman placarded the town with a notice of $500.00 reward for the ex-engineer's capture, dead or alive, and the express company supplemented this by another offer of an equal amount. The country was thick with parties of horsemen, armed with rifles and revolvers, recruited from Visalia, Goshen, and the few railroad sympathisers around Bonneville and Guadlajara. One after another of these returned, empty-handed, covered with dust and mud, their horses exhausted, to be met and passed by fresh posses starting out to continue the pursuit. The sheriff of Santa Clara County sent down his bloodhounds from San Jose—small, harmless-looking dogs, with a terrific bay—to help in the chase. Reporters from the San Francisco papers appeared, interviewing every one, sometimes even accompanying the searching bands. Horse hoofs clattered over the roads at night; bells were rung, the "Mercury" issued extra after extra; the bloodhounds bayed, gun butts clashed on the asphalt pavements of Bonneville; accidental discharges of revolvers brought the whole town into the street; farm hands called to each other across the fences of ranch-divisions—in a word, the country-side was in an uproar.

And all to no effect. The hoof-marks of Dyke's horse had been traced in the mud of the road to within a quarter of a mile of the foot-hills and there irretrievably lost. Three days after the hold-up, a sheep-herder was found who had seen the highwayman on a ridge in the higher mountains, to the northeast of Taurusa. And that was absolutely all. Rumours were thick, promising clews were discovered, new trails taken up, but nothing transpired to bring the pursuers and pursued any closer together. Then, after ten days of strain, public interest began to flag. It was believed that Dyke had succeeded in getting away. If this was true, he had gone to the southward, after gaining the mountains, and it would be his intention to work out of the range somewhere near the southern part of the San Joaquin, near Bakersfield. Thus, the sheriffs, marshals, and deputies decided. They had hunted too many criminals in these mountains before not to know the usual courses taken. In time, Dyke MUST come out of the mountains to get water and provisions. But this time passed, and from not one of the watched points came any word of his appearance. At last the posses began to disband. Little by little the pursuit was given up.

Only S. Behrman persisted. He had made up his mind to bring Dyke in. He succeeded in arousing the same degree of determination in Delaney—by now, a trusted aide of the Railroad—and of his own cousin, a real estate broker, named Christian, who knew the mountains and had once been marshal of Visalia in the old stock-raising days. These two went into the Sierras, accompanied by two hired deputies, and carrying with them a month's provisions and two of the bloodhounds loaned by the Santa Clara sheriff.

On a certain Sunday, a few days after the departure of Christian and Delaney, Annixter, who had been reading "David Copperfield" in his hammock on the porch of the ranch house, put down the book and went to find Hilma, who was helping Louisa Vacca set the table for dinner. He found her in the dining-room, her hands full of the gold-bordered china plates, only used on special occasions and which Louisa was forbidden to touch.

His wife was more than ordinarily pretty that day. She wore a dress of flowered organdie over pink sateen with pink ribbons about her waist and neck, and on her slim feet the low shoes she always affected, with their smart, bright buckles. Her thick, brown, sweet-smelling hair was heaped high upon her head and set off with a bow of black velvet, and underneath the shadow of its coils, her wide-open eyes, rimmed with the thin, black line of her lashes, shone continually, reflecting the sunlight. Marriage had only accentuated the beautiful maturity of Hilma's figure—now no longer precocious—defining the single, deep swell from her throat to her waist, the strong, fine amplitude of her hips, the sweet feminine undulation of her neck and shoulders. Her cheeks were pink with health, and her large round arms carried the piled-up dishes with never a tremour. Annixter, observant enough where his wife was concerned noted how the reflection of the white china set a glow of pale light underneath her chin.

"Hilma," he said, "I've been wondering lately about things. We're so blamed happy ourselves it won't do for us to forget about other people who are down, will it? Might change our luck. And I'm just likely to forget that way, too. It's my nature."

His wife looked up at him joyfully. Here was the new Annixter, certainly.

"In all this hullabaloo about Dyke," he went on "there's some one nobody ain't thought about at all. That's MRS. Dyke—and the little tad. I wouldn't be surprised if they were in a hole over there. What do you say we drive over to the hop ranch after dinner and see if she wants anything?"

Hilma put down the plates and came around the table and kissed him without a word.

As soon as their dinner was over, Annixter had the carry-all hitched up, and, dispensing with young Vacca, drove over to the hop ranch with Hilma.

Hilma could not keep back the tears as they passed through the lamentable desolation of the withered, brown vines, symbols of perished hopes and abandoned effort, and Annixter swore between his teeth.

Though the wheels of the carry-all grated loudly on the roadway in front of the house, nobody came to the door nor looked from the windows. The place seemed tenantless, infinitely lonely, infinitely sad. Annixter tied the team, and with Hilma approached the wide-open door, scuffling and tramping on the porch to attract attention. Nobody stirred. A Sunday stillness pervaded the place. Outside, the withered hop-leaves rustled like dry paper in the breeze. The quiet was ominous. They peered into the front room from the doorway, Hilma holding her husband's hand. Mrs. Dyke was there. She sat at the table in the middle of the room, her head, with its white hair, down upon her arm. A clutter of unwashed dishes were strewed over the red and white tablecloth. The unkempt room, once a marvel of neatness, had not been cleaned for days. Newspapers, Genslinger's extras and copies of San Francisco and Los Angeles dailies were scattered all over the room. On the table itself were crumpled yellow telegrams, a dozen of them, a score of them, blowing about in the draught from the door. And in the midst of all this disarray, surrounded by the published accounts of her son's crime, the telegraphed answers to her pitiful appeals for tidings fluttering about her head, the highwayman's mother, worn out, abandoned and forgotten, slept through the stillness of the Sunday afternoon.

Neither Hilma nor Annixter ever forgot their interview with Mrs. Dyke that day. Suddenly waking, she had caught sight of Annixter, and at once exclaimed eagerly:

"Is there any news?"

For a long time afterwards nothing could be got from her. She was numb to all other issues than the one question of Dyke's capture. She did not answer their questions nor reply to their offers of assistance. Hilma and Annixter conferred together without lowering their voices, at her very elbow, while she looked vacantly at the floor, drawing one hand over the other in a persistent, maniacal gesture. From time to time she would start suddenly from her chair, her eyes wide, and as if all at once realising Annixter's presence, would cry out:

"Is there any news?"

"Where is Sidney, Mrs. Dyke?" asked Hilma for the fourth time. "Is she well? Is she taken care of?"

"Here's the last telegram," said Mrs. Dyke, in a loud, monotonous voice. "See, it says there is no news. He didn't do it," she moaned, rocking herself back and forth, drawing one hand over the other, "he didn't do it, he didn't do it, he didn't do it. I don't know where he is."

When at last she came to herself, it was with a flood of tears. Hilma put her arms around the poor, old woman, as she bowed herself again upon the table, sobbing and weeping.

"Oh, my son, my son," she cried, "my own boy, my only son! If I could have died for you to have prevented this. I remember him when he was little. Such a splendid little fellow, so brave, so loving, with never an unkind thought, never a mean action. So it was all his life. We were never apart. It was always 'dear little son,' and 'dear mammy' between us—never once was he unkind, and he loved me and was the gentlest son to me. And he was a GOOD man. He is now, he is now. They don't understand him. They are not even sure that he did this. He never meant it. They don't know my son. Why, he wouldn't have hurt a kitten. Everybody loved him. He was driven to it. They hounded him down, they wouldn't let him alone. He was not right in his mind. They hounded him to it," she cried fiercely, "they hounded him to it. They drove him and goaded him till he couldn't stand it any longer, and now they mean to kill him for turning on them. They are hunting him with dogs; night after night I have stood on the porch and heard the dogs baying far off. They are tracking my boy with dogs like a wild animal. May God never forgive them." She rose to her feet, terrible, her white hair unbound. "May God punish them as they deserve, may they never prosper—on my knees I shall pray for it every night—may their money be a curse to them, may their sons, their first-born, only sons, be taken from them in their youth."

But Hilma interrupted, begging her to be silent, to be quiet. The tears came again then and the choking sobs. Hilma took her in her arms.

"Oh, my little boy, my little boy," she cried. "My only son, all that I had, to have come to this! He was not right in his mind or he would have known it would break my heart. Oh, my son, my son, if I could have died for you."

Sidney came in, clinging to her dress, weeping, imploring her not to cry, protesting that they never could catch her papa, that he would come back soon. Hilma took them both, the little child and the broken-down old woman, in the great embrace of her strong arms, and they all three sobbed together.

Annixter stood on the porch outside, his back turned, looking straight before him into the wilderness of dead vines, his teeth shut hard, his lower lip thrust out.

"I hope S. Behrman is satisfied with all this," he muttered. "I hope he is satisfied now, damn his soul!"

All at once an idea occurred to him. He turned about and reentered the room.

"Mrs Dyke," he began, "I want you and Sidney to come over and live at Quien Sabe. I know—you can't make me believe that the reporters and officers and officious busy-faces that pretend to offer help just so as they can satisfy their curiosity aren't nagging you to death. I want you to let me take care of you and the little tad till all this trouble of yours is over with. There's plenty of place for you. You can have the house my wife's people used to live in. You've got to look these things in the face. What are you going to do to get along? You must be very short of money. S. Behrman will foreclose on you and take the whole place in a little while, now. I want you to let me help you, let Hilma and me be good friends to you. It would be a privilege."

Mrs. Dyke tried bravely to assume her pride, insisting that she could manage, but her spirit was broken. The whole affair ended unexpectedly, with Annixter and Hilma bringing Dyke's mother and little girl back to Quien Sabe in the carry-all.

Mrs. Dyke would not take with her a stick of furniture nor a single ornament. It would only serve to remind her of a vanished happiness. She packed a few clothes of her own and Sidney's in a little trunk, Hilma helping her, and Annixter stowed the trunk under the carry-all's back seat. Mrs. Dyke turned the key in the door of the house and Annixter helped her to her seat beside his wife. They drove through the sear, brown hop vines. At the angle of the road Mrs. Dyke turned around and looked back at the ruin of the hop ranch, the roof of the house just showing above the trees. She never saw it again.

As soon as Annixter and Hilma were alone, after their return to Quien Sabe—Mrs. Dyke and Sidney having been installed in the Trees' old house—Hilma threw her arms around her husband's neck.

"Fine," she exclaimed, "oh, it was fine of you, dear to think of them and to be so good to them. My husband is such a GOOD man. So unselfish. You wouldn't have thought of being kind to Mrs. Dyke and Sidney a little while ago. You wouldn't have thought of them at all. But you did now, and it's just because you love me true, isn't it? Isn't it? And because it's made you a better man. I'm so proud and glad to think it's so. It is so, isn't it? Just because you love me true."

"You bet it is, Hilma," he told her.

As Hilma and Annixter were sitting down to the supper which they found waiting for them, Louisa Vacca came to the door of the dining-room to say that Harran Derrick had telephoned over from Los Muertos for Annixter, and had left word for him to ring up Los Muertos as soon as he came in.

"He said it was important," added Louisa Vacca.

"Maybe they have news from Washington," suggested Hilma.

Annixter would not wait to have supper, but telephoned to Los Muertos at once. Magnus answered the call. There was a special meeting of the Executive Committee of the League summoned for the next day, he told Annixter. It was for the purpose of considering the new grain tariff prepared by the Railroad Commissioners. Lyman had written that the schedule of this tariff had just been issued, that he had not been able to construct it precisely according to the wheat-growers' wishes, and that he, himself, would come down to Los Muertos and explain its apparent discrepancies. Magnus said Lyman would be present at the session.

Annixter, curious for details, forbore, nevertheless, to question. The connection from Los Muertos to Quien Sabe was made through Bonneville, and in those troublesome times no one could be trusted. It could not be known who would overhear conversations carried on over the lines. He assured Magnus that he would be on hand. The time for the Committee meeting had been set for seven o'clock in the evening, in order to accommodate Lyman, who wrote that he would be down on the evening train, but would be compelled, by pressure of business, to return to the city early the next morning.

At the time appointed, the men composing the Committee gathered about the table in the dining-room of the Los Muertos ranch house. It was almost a reproduction of the scene of the famous evening when Osterman had proposed the plan of the Ranchers' Railroad Commission. Magnus Derrick sat at the head of the table, in his buttoned frock coat. Whiskey bottles and siphons of soda-water were within easy reach. Presley, who by now was considered the confidential friend of every member of the Committee, lounged as before on the sofa, smoking cigarettes, the cat Nathalie on his knee. Besides Magnus and Annixter, Osterman was present, and old Broderson and Harran; Garnet from the Ruby Rancho and Gethings of the San Pablo, who were also members of the Executive Committee, were on hand, preoccupied, bearded men, smoking black cigars, and, last of all, Dabney, the silent old man, of whom little was known but his name, and who had been made a member of the Committee, nobody could tell why.

"My son Lyman should be here, gentlemen, within at least ten minutes. I have sent my team to meet him at Bonneville," explained Magnus, as he called the meeting to order. "The Secretary will call the roll."

Osterman called the roll, and, to fill in the time, read over the minutes of the previous meeting. The treasurer was making his report as to the funds at the disposal of the League when Lyman arrived.

Magnus and Harran went forward to meet him, and the Committee rather awkwardly rose and remained standing while the three exchanged greetings, the members, some of whom had never seen their commissioner, eyeing him out of the corners of their eyes.

Lyman was dressed with his usual correctness. His cravat was of the latest fashion, his clothes of careful design and unimpeachable fit. His shoes, of patent leather, reflected the lamplight, and he carried a drab overcoat over his arm. Before being introduced to the Committee, he excused himself a moment and ran to see his mother, who waited for him in the adjoining sitting-room. But in a few moments he returned, asking pardon for the delay.

He was all affability; his protruding eyes, that gave such an unusual, foreign appearance to his very dark face, radiated geniality. He was evidently anxious to please, to produce a good impression upon the grave, clumsy farmers before whom he stood. But at the same time, Presley, watching him from his place on the sofa, could imagine that he was rather nervous. He was too nimble in his cordiality, and the little gestures he made in bringing his cuffs into view and in touching the ends of his tight, black mustache with the ball of his thumb were repeated with unnecessary frequency.

"Mr. Broderson, my son, Lyman, my eldest son. Mr. Annixter, my son, Lyman."

The Governor introduced him to the ranchers, proud of Lyman's good looks, his correct dress, his ease of manner. Lyman shook hands all around, keeping up a flow of small talk, finding a new phrase for each member, complimenting Osterman, whom he already knew, upon his talent for organisation, recalling a mutual acquaintance to the mind of old Broderson. At length, however, he sat down at the end of the table, opposite his brother. There was a silence.

Magnus rose to recapitulate the reasons for the extra session of the Committee, stating again that the Board of Railway Commissioners which they — the ranchers — had succeeded in seating had at length issued the new schedule of reduced rates, and that Mr. Derrick had been obliging enough to offer to come down to Los Muertos in person to acquaint the wheat-growers of the San Joaquin with the new rates for the carriage of their grain.

But Lyman very politely protested, addressing his father punctiliously as "Mr. Chairman," and the other ranchers as "Gentlemen of the Executive Committee of the League." He had no wish, he said, to disarrange the regular proceedings of the Committee. Would it not be preferable to defer the reading of his report till "new business" was called for? In the meanwhile, let the Committee proceed with its usual work. He understood the necessarily delicate nature of this work, and would be pleased to withdraw till the proper time arrived for him to speak.

"Good deal of backing and filling about the reading of a column of figures," muttered Annixter to the man at his elbow.

Lyman "awaited the Committee's decision." He sat down, touching the ends of his mustache.

"Oh, play ball," growled Annixter.

Gethings rose to say that as the meeting had been called solely for the purpose of hearing and considering the new grain tariff, he was of the opinion that routine business could be dispensed with and the schedule read at once. It was so ordered.

Lyman rose and made a long speech. Voluble as Osterman himself, he, nevertheless, had at his command a vast number of ready-made phrases, the staples of a political speaker, the stock in trade of the commercial lawyer, which rolled off his tongue with the most persuasive fluency. By degrees, in the course of his speech, he began to insinuate the idea that the wheat-growers had never expected to settle their difficulties with the Railroad by the work of a single commission; that they had counted upon a long, continued campaign of many years, railway commission succeeding railway commission, before the desired low rates should be secured; that the present Board of Commissioners was only the beginning and that too great results were not expected from them. All this he contrived to mention casually, in the talk, as if it were a foregone conclusion, a matter understood by all.

As the speech continued, the eyes of the ranchers around the table were fixed with growing attention upon this well-dressed, city-bred young man, who spoke so fluently and who told them of their own intentions. A feeling of perplexity began to spread, and the first taint of distrust invaded their minds.

"But the good work has been most auspiciously inaugurated," continued Lyman. "Reforms so sweeping as the one contemplated cannot be accomplished in a single night. Great things grow slowly, benefits to be permanent must accrue gradually. Yet, in spite of all this, your commissioners have done much. Already the phalanx of the enemy is pierced, already his armour is dinted. Pledged as were your commissioners to an average ten per cent. reduction in rates for the carriage of grain by the Pacific and Southwestern Railroad, we have rigidly adhered to the demands of our constituency, we have obeyed the People. The main problem has not yet been completely solved; that is for later, when we shall have gathered sufficient strength to attack the enemy in his very stronghold; BUT AN AVERAGE TEN PER CENT. CUT HAS BEEN MADE ALL OVER THE STATE. We have made a great advance, have taken a great step forward, and if the work is carried ahead, upon the lines laid down by the present commissioners and their constituents, there is every reason to believe that within a very few years equitable and stable rates for the shipment of grain from the San Joaquin Valley to Stockton, Port Costa, and tidewater will be permanently imposed."

"Well, hold on," exclaimed Annixter, out of order and ignoring the Governor's reproof, "hasn't your commission reduced grain rates in the San Joaquin?"

"We have reduced grain rates by ten per cent. all over the State," rejoined Lyman. "Here are copies of the new schedule."

He drew them from his valise and passed them around the table.

"You see," he observed, "the rate between Mayfield and Oakland, for instance, has been reduced by twenty-five cents a ton."

"Yes—but—but—" said old Broderson, "it is rather unusual, isn't it, for wheat in that district to be sent to Oakland?" "Why, look here," exclaimed Annixter, looking up from the schedule, "where is there any reduction in rates in the San Joaquin—from Bonneville and Guadalajara, for instance? I don't see as you've made any reduction at all. Is this right? Did you give me the right schedule?"

"Of course, ALL the points in the State could not be covered at once," returned Lyman. "We never expected, you know, that we could cut rates in the San Joaquin the very first move; that is for later. But you will see we made very material reductions on shipments from the upper Sacramento Valley; also the rate from Ione to Marysville has been reduced eighty cents a ton."

"Why, rot," cried Annixter, "no one ever ships wheat that way."

"The Salinas rate," continued Lyman, "has been lowered seventy-five cents; the St. Helena rate fifty cents, and please notice the very drastic cut from Red Bluff, north, along the Oregon route, to the Oregon State Line."

"Where not a carload of wheat is shipped in a year," commented Gethings of the San Pablo.

"Oh, you will find yourself mistaken there, Mr. Gethings," returned Lyman courteously. "And for the matter of that, a low rate would stimulate wheat-production in that district."

The order of the meeting was broken up, neglected; Magnus did not even pretend to preside. In the growing excitement over the inexplicable schedule, routine was not thought of. Every one spoke at will.

"Why, Lyman," demanded Magnus, looking across the table to his son, "is this schedule correct? You have not cut rates in the San Joaquin at all. We—these gentlemen here and myself, we are no better off than we were before we secured your election as commissioner."

"We were pledged to make an average ten per cent. cut, sir——" "It IS an average ten per cent. cut," cried Osterman. "Oh, yes, that's plain. It's an average ten per cent. cut all right, but you've made it by cutting grain rates between points where practically no grain is shipped. We, the wheat-growers in the San Joaquin, where all the wheat is grown, are right where we were before. The Railroad won't lose a nickel. By Jingo, boys," he glanced around the table, "I'd like to know what this means."

"The Railroad, if you come to that," returned Lyman, "has already lodged a protest against the new rate."

Annixter uttered a derisive shout.

"A protest! That's good, that is. When the P. and S. W. objects to rates it don't 'protest,' m' son. The first you hear from Mr. Shelgrim is an injunction from the courts preventing the order for new rates from taking effect. By the Lord," he cried angrily, leaping to his feet, "I would like to know what all this means, too. Why didn't you reduce our grain rates? What did we elect you for?"

"Yes, what did we elect you for?" demanded Osterman and Gethings, also getting to their feet.

"Order, order, gentlemen," cried Magnus, remembering the duties of his office and rapping his knuckles on the table. "This meeting has been allowed to degenerate too far already."

"You elected us," declared Lyman doggedly, "to make an average ten per cent. cut on grain rates. We have done it. Only because you don't benefit at once, you object. It makes a difference whose ox is gored, it seems."

"Lyman!"

It was Magnus who spoke. He had drawn himself to his full six feet. His eyes were flashing direct into his son's. His voice rang with severity.

"Lyman, what does this mean?"

The other spread out his hands.

"As you see, sir. We have done our best. I warned you not to expect too much. I told you that this question of transportation was difficult. You would not wish to put rates so low that the action would amount to confiscation of property."

"Why did you not lower rates in the valley of the San Joaquin?"

"That was not a PROMINENT issue in the affair," responded Lyman, carefully emphasising his words. "I understand, of course, it was to be approached IN TIME. The main point was AN AVERAGE TEN PER CENT. REDUCTION. Rates WILL be lowered in the San Joaquin. The ranchers around Bonneville will be able to ship to Port Costa at equitable rates, but so radical a measure as that cannot be put through in a turn of the hand. We must study— —"

"You KNEW the San Joaquin rate was an issue," shouted Annixter, shaking his finger across the table. "What do we men who backed you care about rates up in Del Norte and Siskiyou Counties? Not a whoop in hell. It was the San Joaquin rate we were fighting for, and we elected you to reduce that. You didn't do it and you don't intend to, and, by the Lord Harry, I want to know why."

"You'll know, sir—" began Lyman.

"Well, I'll tell you why," vociferated Osterman. "I'll tell you why. It's because we have been sold out. It's because the P. and S. W. have had their spoon in this boiling. It's because our commissioners have betrayed us. It's because we're a set of damn fool farmers and have been cinched again."

Lyman paled under his dark skin at the direct attack. He evidently had not expected this so soon. For the fraction of one instant he lost his poise. He strove to speak, but caught his breath, stammering.

"What have you to say, then?" cried Harran, who, until now, had not spoken.

"I have this to say," answered Lyman, making head as best he might, "that this is no proper spirit in which to discuss business. The Commission has fulfilled its obligations. It has adjusted rates to the best of its ability. We have been at work for two months on the preparation of this schedule——"

"That's a lie," shouted Annixter, his face scarlet; "that's a lie. That schedule was drawn in the offices of the Pacific and Southwestern and you know it. It's a scheme of rates made for the Railroad and by the Railroad and you were bought over to put your name to it."

There was a concerted outburst at the words. All the men in the room were on their feet, gesticulating and vociferating.

"Gentlemen, gentlemen," cried Magnus, "are we schoolboys, are we ruffians of the street?"

"We're a set of fool farmers and we've been betrayed," cried Osterman.

"Well, what have you to say? What have you to say?" persisted Harran, leaning across the table toward his brother. "For God's sake, Lyman, you've got SOME explanation."

"You've misunderstood," protested Lyman, white and trembling. "You've misunderstood. You've expected too much. Next year,—next year,—soon now, the Commission will take up the—the Commission will consider the San Joaquin rate. We've done our best, that is all."

"Have you, sir?" demanded Magnus.

The Governor's head was in a whirl; a sensation, almost of faintness, had seized upon him. Was it possible? Was it possible?

"Have you done your best?" For a second he compelled Lyman's eye. The glances of father and son met, and, in spite of his best efforts, Lyman's eyes wavered. He began to protest once more, explaining the matter over again from the beginning. But Magnus did not listen. In that brief lapse of time he was convinced that the terrible thing had happened, that the unbelievable had come to pass. It was in the air. Between father and son, in some subtle fashion, the truth that was a lie stood suddenly revealed. But even then Magnus would not receive it. Lyman do this! His son, his eldest son, descend to this! Once more and for the last time he turned to him and in his voice there was that ring that compelled silence.

"Lyman," he said, "I adjure you—I—I demand of you as you are my son and an honourable man, explain yourself. What is there behind all this? It is no longer as Chairman of the Committee I speak to you, you a member of the Railroad Commission. It is your father who speaks, and I address you as my son. Do you understand the gravity of this crisis; do you realise the responsibility of your position; do you not see the importance of this moment? Explain yourself."

"There is nothing to explain."

"You have not reduced rates in the San Joaquin? You have not reduced rates between Bonneville and tidewater?"

"I repeat, sir, what I said before. An average ten per cent. cut——"

"Lyman, answer me, yes or no. Have you reduced the Bonneville rate?"

"It could not be done so soon. Give us time. We——"

"Yes or no! By God, sir, do you dare equivocate with me? Yes or no; have you reduced the Bonneville rate?"

"No."

"And answer ME," shouted Harran, leaning far across the table, "answer ME. Were you paid by the Railroad to leave the San Joaquin rate untouched?"

Lyman, whiter than ever, turned furious upon his brother.

"Don't you dare put that question to me again."

"No, I won't," cried Harran, "because I'll TELL you to your villain's face that you WERE paid to do it."

On the instant the clamour burst forth afresh. Still on their feet, the ranchers had, little by little, worked around the table, Magnus alone keeping his place. The others were in a group before Lyman, crowding him, as it were, to the wall, shouting into his face with menacing gestures. The truth that was a lie, the certainty of a trust betrayed, a pledge ruthlessly broken, was plain to every one of them.

"By the Lord! men have been shot for less than this," cried Osterman. "You've sold us out, you, and if you ever bring that dago face of yours on a level with mine again, I'll slap it."

"Keep your hands off," exclaimed Lyman quickly, the aggressiveness of the cornered rat flaming up within him. "No violence. Don't you go too far."

"How much were you paid? How much were you paid?" vociferated Harran.

"Yes, yes, what was your price?" cried the others. They were beside themselves with anger; their words came harsh from between their set teeth; their gestures were made with their fists clenched.

"You know the Commission acted in good faith," retorted Lyman. "You know that all was fair and above board."

"Liar," shouted Annixter; "liar, bribe-eater. You were bought and paid for," and with the words his arm seemed almost of itself to leap out from his shoulder. Lyman received the blow squarely in the face and the force of it sent him staggering backwards toward the wall. He tripped over his valise and fell half way, his back supported against the closed door of the room. Magnus sprang forward. His son had been struck, and the instincts of a father rose up in instant protest; rose for a moment, then forever died away in his heart. He checked the words that flashed to his mind. He lowered his upraised arm. No, he had but one son. The poor, staggering creature with the fine clothes, white face, and blood-streaked lips was no longer his. A blow could not dishonour him more than he had dishonoured himself.

But Gethings, the older man, intervened, pulling Annixter back, crying:

"Stop, this won't do. Not before his father."

"I am no father to this man, gentlemen," exclaimed Magnus. "From now on, I have but one son. You, sir," he turned to Lyman, "you, sir, leave my house."

Lyman, his handkerchief to his lips, his smart cravat in disarray, caught up his hat and coat. He was shaking with fury, his protruding eyes were blood-shot. He swung open the door.

"Ruffians," he shouted from the threshold, "ruffians, bullies. Do your own dirty business yourselves after this. I'm done with you. How is it, all of a sudden you talk about honour? How is it that all at once you're so clean and straight? You weren't so particular at Sacramento just before the nominations. How was the Board elected? I'm a bribe-eater, am I? Is it any worse than GIVING a bribe? Ask Magnus Derrick what he thinks about that. Ask him how much he paid the Democratic bosses at Sacramento to swing the convention."

He went out, slamming the door.

Presley followed. The whole affair made him sick at heart, filled him with infinite disgust, infinite weariness. He wished to get away from it all. He left the dining-room and the excited, clamouring men behind him and stepped out on the porch of the ranch house, closing the door behind him. Lyman was nowhere in sight. Presley was alone. It was late, and after the lamp-heated air of the dining-room, the coolness of the night was delicious, and its vast silence, after the noise and fury of the committee meeting, descended from the stars like a benediction. Presley stepped to the edge of the porch, looking off to southward.

And there before him, mile after mile, illimitable, covering the earth from horizon to horizon, lay the Wheat. The growth, now many days old, was already high from the ground. There it lay, a vast, silent ocean, shimmering a pallid green under the moon and under the stars; a mighty force, the strength of nations, the life of the world. There in the night, under the dome of the sky, it was growing steadily. To Presley's mind, the scene in the room he had just left dwindled to paltry insignificance before this sight. Ah, yes, the Wheat—it was over this that the Railroad, the ranchers, the traitor false to his trust, all the members of an obscure conspiracy, were wrangling. As if human agency could affect this colossal power! What were these heated, tiny squabbles, this feverish, small bustle of mankind, this minute swarming of the human insect, to the great, majestic, silent ocean of the Wheat itself! Indifferent, gigantic, resistless, it moved in its appointed grooves. Men, Liliputians, gnats in the sunshine, buzzed impudently in their tiny battles, were born, lived through their little day, died, and were forgotten; while the Wheat, wrapped in Nirvanic calm, grew steadily under the night, alone with the stars and with God.

CHAPTER V

Jack-rabbits were a pest that year and Presley occasionally found amusement in hunting them with Harran's half-dozen greyhounds, following the chase on horseback. One day, between two and three months after Lyman s visit to Los Muertos, as he was returning toward the ranch house from a distant and lonely quarter of Los Muertos, he came unexpectedly upon a strange sight.

Some twenty men, Annixter's and Osterman's tenants, and small ranchers from east of Guadalajara—all members of the League—were going through the manual of arms under Harran Derrick's supervision. They were all equipped with new Winchester rifles. Harran carried one of these himself and with it he illustrated the various commands he gave. As soon as one of the men under his supervision became more than usually proficient, he was told off to instruct a file of the more backward. After the manual of arms, Harran gave the command to take distance as skirmishers, and when the line had opened out so that some half-dozen feet intervened between each man, an advance was made across the field, the men stooping low and snapping the hammers of their rifles at an imaginary enemy.

The League had its agents in San Francisco, who watched the movements of the Railroad as closely as was possible, and some time before this, Annixter had received word that the Marshal and his deputies were coming down to Bonneville to put the dummy buyers of his ranch in possession. The report proved to be but the first of many false alarms, but it had stimulated the League to unusual activity, and some three or four hundred men were furnished with arms and from time to time were drilled in secret.

Among themselves, the ranchers said that if the Railroad managers did not believe they were terribly in earnest in the stand they had taken, they were making a fatal mistake.

Harran reasserted this statement to Presley on the way home to the ranch house that same day. Harran had caught up with him by the time he reached the Lower Road, and the two jogged homeward through the miles of standing wheat.

"They may jump the ranch, Pres," he said, "if they try hard enough, but they will never do it while I am alive. By the way," he added, "you know we served notices yesterday upon S. Behrman and Cy. Ruggles to quit the country. Of course, they won't do it, but they won't be able to say they didn't have warning."

About an hour later, the two reached the ranch house, but as Harran rode up the driveway, he uttered an exclamation.

"Hello," he said, "something is up. That's Genslinger's buckboard."

In fact, the editor's team was tied underneath the shade of a giant eucalyptus tree near by. Harran, uneasy under this unexpected visit of the enemy's friend, dismounted without stabling his horse, and went at once to the dining-room, where visitors were invariably received. But the dining-room was empty, and his mother told him that Magnus and the editor were in the "office." Magnus had said they were not to be disturbed.

Earlier in the afternoon, the editor had driven up to the porch and had asked Mrs. Derrick, whom he found reading a book of poems on the porch, if he could see Magnus. At the time, the Governor had gone with Phelps to inspect the condition of the young wheat on Hooven's holding, but within half an hour he returned, and Genslinger had asked him for a "few moments' talk in private."

The two went into the "office," Magnus locking the door behind him. "Very complete you are here, Governor," observed the editor in his alert, jerky manner, his black, bead-like eyes twinkling around the room from behind his glasses. "Telephone, safe, ticker, account-books—well, that's progress, isn't it? Only way to manage a big ranch these days. But the day of the big ranch is over. As the land appreciates in value, the temptation to sell off small holdings will be too strong. And then the small holding can be cultivated to better advantage. I shall have an editorial on that some day."

"The cost of maintaining a number of small holdings," said Magnus, indifferently, "is, of course, greater than if they were all under one management."

"That may be, that may be," rejoined the other.

There was a long pause. Genslinger leaned back in his chair and rubbed a knee. Magnus, standing erect in front of the safe, waited for him to speak.

"This is an unfortunate business, Governor," began the editor, "this misunderstanding between the ranchers and the Railroad. I wish it could be adjusted. HERE are two industries that MUST be in harmony with one another, or we all go to pot."

"I should prefer not to be interviewed on the subject, Mr. Genslinger," said Magnus.

"Oh, no, oh, no. Lord love you, Governor, I don't want to interview you. We all know how you stand."

Again there was a long silence. Magnus wondered what this little man, usually so garrulous, could want of him. At length, Genslinger began again. He did not look at Magnus, except at long intervals.

"About the present Railroad Commission," he remarked. "That was an interesting campaign you conducted in Sacramento and San Francisco."

Magnus held his peace, his hands shut tight. Did Genslinger know of Lyman's disgrace? Was it for this he had come? Would the story of it be the leading article in to-morrow's Mercury?

"An interesting campaign," repeated Genslinger, slowly; "a very interesting campaign. I watched it with every degree of interest. I saw its every phase, Mr. Derrick."

"The campaign was not without its interest," admitted Magnus.

"Yes," said Genslinger, still more deliberately, "and some phases of it were—more interesting than others, as, for instance, let us say the way in which you—personally—secured the votes of certain chairmen of delegations—NEED I particularise further? Yes, those men—the way you got their votes. Now, THAT I should say, Mr. Derrick, was the most interesting move in the whole game—to you. Hm, curious," he murmured, musingly. "Let's see. You deposited two one-thousand dollar bills and four five-hundred dollar bills in a box—three hundred and eight was the number—in a box in the Safety Deposit Vaults in San Francisco, and then— let's see, you gave a key to this box to each of the gentlemen in question, and after the election the box was empty. Now, I call that interesting—curious, because it's a new, safe, and highly ingenious method of bribery. How did you happen to think of it, Governor?"

"Do you know what you are doing, sir?" Magnus burst forth. "Do you know what you are insinuating, here, in my own house?"

"Why, Governor," returned the editor, blandly, "I'm not INSINUATING anything. I'm talking about what I KNOW."

"It's a lie."

Genslinger rubbed his chin reflectively.

"Well," he answered, "you can have a chance to prove it before the Grand Jury, if you want to."

"My character is known all over the State," blustered Magnus. "My politics are pure politics. My——"

"No one needs a better reputation for pure politics than the man who sets out to be a briber," interrupted Genslinger, "and I might as well tell you, Governor, that you can't shout me down. I can put my hand on the two chairmen you bought before it's dark to-day. I've had their depositions in my safe for the last six weeks. We could make the arrests to-morrow, if we wanted. Governor, you sure did a risky thing when you went into that Sacramento fight, an awful risky thing. Some men can afford to have bribery charges preferred against them, and it don't hurt one little bit, but YOU— Lord, it would BUST you, Governor, bust you dead. I know all about the whole shananigan business from A to Z, and if you don't believe it—here," he drew a long strip of paper from his pocket, "here's a galley proof of the story."

Magnus took it in his hands. There, under his eyes, scare-headed, double-leaded, the more important clauses printed in bold type, was the detailed account of the "deal" Magnus had made with the two delegates. It was pitiless, remorseless, bald. Every statement was substantiated, every statistic verified with Genslinger's meticulous love for exactness. Besides all that, it had the ring of truth. It was exposure, ruin, absolute annihilation.

"That's about correct, isn't it?" commented Genslinger, as Derrick finished reading. Magnus did not reply. "I think it is correct enough," the editor continued. "But I thought it would only be fair to you to let you see it before it was published."

The one thought uppermost in Derrick's mind, his one impulse of the moment was, at whatever cost, to preserve his dignity, not to allow this man to exult in the sight of one quiver of weakness, one trace of defeat, one suggestion of humiliation. By an effort that put all his iron rigidity to the test, he forced himself to look straight into Genslinger's eyes.

"I congratulate you," he observed, handing back the proof, "upon your journalistic enterprise. Your paper will sell to-morrow." "Oh, I don't know as I want to publish this story," remarked the editor, indifferently, putting away the galley. "I'm just like that. The fun for me is running a good story to earth, but once I've got it, I lose interest. And, then, I wouldn't like to see you—holding the position you do, President of the League and a leading man of the county—I wouldn't like to see a story like this smash you over. It's worth more to you to keep it out of print than for me to put it in. I've got nothing much to gain but a few extra editions, but you—Lord, you would lose everything. Your committee was in the deal right enough. But your League, all the San Joaquin Valley, everybody in the State believes the commissioners were fairly elected."

"Your story," suddenly exclaimed Magnus, struck with an idea, "will be thoroughly discredited just so soon as the new grain tariff is published. I have means of knowing that the San Joaquin rate—the issue upon which the board was elected—is not to be touched. Is it likely the ranchers would secure the election of a board that plays them false?"

"Oh, we know all about that," answered Genslinger, smiling. "You thought you were electing Lyman easily. You thought you had got the Railroad to walk right into your trap. You didn't understand how you could pull off your deal so easily. Why, Governor, LYMAN WAS PLEDGED TO THE RAILROAD TWO YEARS AGO. He was THE ONE PARTICULAR man the corporation wanted for commissioner. And your people elected him—saved the Railroad all the trouble of campaigning for him. And you can't make any counter charge of bribery there. No, sir, the corporation don't use such amateurish methods as that. Confidentially and between us two, all that the Railroad has done for Lyman, in order to attach him to their interests, is to promise to back him politically in the next campaign for Governor. It's too bad," he continued, dropping his voice, and changing his position. "It really is too bad to see good men trying to bunt a stone wall over with their bare heads. You couldn't have won at any stage of the game. I wish I could have talked to you and your friends before you went into that Sacramento fight. I could have told you then how little chance you had. When will you people realise that you can't buck against the Railroad? Why, Magnus, it's like me going out in a paper boat and shooting peas at a battleship."

"Is that all you wished to see me about, Mr. Genslinger?" remarked Magnus, bestirring himself. "I am rather occupied to-day." "Well," returned the other, "you know what the publication of this article would mean for you." He paused again, took off his glasses, breathed on them, polished the lenses with his handkerchief and readjusted them on his nose. "I've been thinking, Governor," he began again, with renewed alertness, and quite irrelevantly, "of enlarging the scope of the 'Mercury.' You see, I'm midway between the two big centres of the State, San Francisco and Los Angeles, and I want to extend the 'Mercury's' sphere of influence as far up and down the valley as I can. I want to illustrate the paper. You see, if I had a photo-engraving plant of my own, I could do a good deal of outside jobbing as well, and the investment would pay ten per cent. But it takes money to make money. I wouldn't want to put in any dinky, one-horse affair. I want a good plant. I've been figuring out the business. Besides the plant, there would be the expense of a high grade paper. Can't print half-tones on anything but coated paper, and that COSTS. Well, what with this and with that and running expenses till the thing began to pay, it would cost me about ten thousand dollars, and I was wondering if, perhaps, you couldn't see your way clear to accommodating me."

"Ten thousand?"

"Yes. Say five thousand down, and the balance within sixty days."

Magnus, for the moment blind to what Genslinger had in mind, turned on him in astonishment.

"Why, man, what security could you give me for such an amount?"

"Well, to tell the truth," answered the editor, "I hadn't thought much about securities. In fact, I believed you would see how greatly it was to your advantage to talk business with me. You see, I'm not going to print this article about you, Governor, and I'm not going to let it get out so as any one else can print it, and it seems to me that one good turn deserves another. You understand?"

Magnus understood. An overwhelming desire suddenly took possession of him to grip this blackmailer by the throat, to strangle him where he stood; or, if not, at least to turn upon him with that old-time terrible anger, before which whole conventions had once cowered. But in the same moment the Governor realised this was not to be. Only its righteousness had made his wrath terrible; only the justice of his anger had made him feared. Now the foundation was gone from under his feet; he had knocked it away himself. Three times feeble was he whose quarrel was unjust. Before this country editor, this paid speaker of the Railroad, he stood, convicted. The man had him at his mercy. The detected briber could not resent an insult. Genslinger rose, smoothing his hat.

"Well," he said, "of course, you want time to think it over, and you can't raise money like that on short notice. I'll wait till Friday noon of this week. We begin to set Saturday's paper at about four, Friday afternoon, and the forms are locked about two in the morning. I hope," he added, turning back at the door of the room, "that you won't find anything disagreeable in your Saturday morning 'Mercury,' Mr. Derrick."

He went out, closing the door behind him, and in a moment, Magnus heard the wheels of his buckboard grating on the driveway.

The following morning brought a letter to Magnus from Gethings, of the San Pueblo ranch, which was situated very close to Visalia. The letter was to the effect that all around Visalia, upon the ranches affected by the regrade of the Railroad, men were arming and drilling, and that the strength of the League in that quarter was undoubted. "But to refer," continued the letter, "to a most painful recollection. You will, no doubt, remember that, at the close of our last committee meeting, specific charges were made as to fraud in the nomination and election of one of our commissioners, emanating, most unfortunately, from the commissioner himself. These charges, my dear Mr. Derrick, were directed at yourself. How the secrets of the committee have been noised about, I cannot understand. You may be, of course, assured of my own unquestioning confidence and loyalty. However, I regret exceedingly to state not only that the rumour of the charges referred to above is spreading in this district, but that also they are made use of by the enemies of the League. It is to be deplored that some of the Leaguers themselves—you know, we number in our ranks many small farmers, ignorant Portuguese and foreigners—have listened to these stories and have permitted a feeling of uneasiness to develop among them. Even though it were admitted that fraudulent means had been employed in the elections, which, of course, I personally do not admit, I do not think it would make very much difference in the confidence which the vast majority of the Leaguers repose in their chiefs. Yet we have so insisted upon the probity of our position as opposed to Railroad chicanery, that I believe it advisable to quell this distant suspicion at once; to publish a denial of these rumoured charges would only be to give them too much importance. However, can you not write me a letter, stating exactly how the campaign was conducted, and the commission nominated and elected? I could show this to some of the more disaffected, and it would serve to allay all suspicion on the instant. I think it would be well to write as though the initiative came, not from me, but from yourself, ignoring this present letter. I offer this only as a suggestion, and will confidently endorse any decision you may arrive at."

The letter closed with renewed protestations of confidence.

Magnus was alone when he read this. He put it carefully away in the filing cabinet in his office, and wiped the sweat from his forehead and face. He stood for one moment, his hands rigid at his sides, his fists clinched.

"This is piling up," he muttered, looking blankly at the opposite wall. "My God, this is piling up. What am I to do?"

Ah, the bitterness of unavailing regret, the anguish of compromise with conscience, the remorse of a bad deed done in a moment of excitement. Ah, the humiliation of detection, the degradation of being caught, caught like a schoolboy pilfering his fellows' desks, and, worse than all, worse than all, the consciousness of lost self-respect, the knowledge of a prestige vanishing, a dignity impaired, knowledge that the grip which held a multitude in check was trembling, that control was wavering, that command was being weakened. Then the little tricks to deceive the crowd, the little subterfuges, the little pretences that kept up appearances, the lies, the bluster, the pose, the strut, the gasconade, where once was iron authority; the turning of the head so as not to see that which could not be prevented; the suspicion of suspicion, the haunting fear of the Man on the Street, the uneasiness of the direct glance, the questioning as to motives—why had this been said, what was meant by that word, that gesture, that glance?

Wednesday passed, and Thursday. Magnus kept to himself, seeing no visitors, avoiding even his family. How to break through the mesh of the net, how to regain the old position, how to prevent discovery? If there were only some way, some vast, superhuman effort by which he could rise in his old strength once more, crushing Lyman with one hand, Genslinger with the other, and for one more moment, the last, to stand supreme again, indomitable, the leader; then go to his death, triumphant at the end, his memory untarnished, his fame undimmed. But the plague-spot was in himself, knitted forever into the fabric of his being. Though Genslinger should be silenced, though Lyman should be crushed, though even the League should overcome the Railroad, though he should be the acknowledged leader of a resplendent victory, yet the plague-spot would remain. There was no success for him now. However conspicuous the outward achievement, he, he himself, Magnus Derrick, had failed, miserably and irredeemably.

Petty, material complications intruded, sordid considerations. Even if Genslinger was to be paid, where was the money to come from? His legal battles with the Railroad, extending now over a period of many years, had cost him dear; his plan of sowing all of Los Muertos to wheat, discharging the tenants, had proved expensive, the campaign resulting in Lyman's election had drawn heavily upon his account. All along he had been relying upon a "bonanza crop" to reimburse him. It was not believable that the Railroad would "jump" Los Muertos, but if this should happen, he would be left without resources. Ten thousand dollars! Could he raise the amount? Possibly. But to pay it out to a blackmailer! To be held up thus in road-agent fashion, without a single means of redress! Would it not cripple him financially? Genslinger could do his worst. He, Magnus, would brave it out. Was not his character above suspicion?

Was it? This letter of Gethings's. Already the murmur of uneasiness made itself heard. Was this not the thin edge of the wedge? How the publication of Genslinger's story would drive it home! How the spark of suspicion would flare into the blaze of open accusation! There would be investigations. Investigation! There was terror in the word. He could not stand investigation. Magnus groaned aloud, covering his head with his clasped hands. Briber, corrupter of government, ballot-box stuffer, descending to the level of back-room politicians, of bar-room heelers, he, Magnus Derrick, statesman of the old school, Roman in his iron integrity, abandoning a career rather than enter the "new politics," had, in one moment of weakness, hazarding all, even honour, on a single stake, taking great chances to achieve great results, swept away the work of a lifetime.

Gambler that he was, he had at last chanced his highest stake, his personal honour, in the greatest game of his life, and had lost.

It was Presley's morbidly keen observation that first noticed the evidence of a new trouble in the Governor's face and manner. Presley was sure that Lyman's defection had not so upset him. The morning after the committee meeting, Magnus had called Harran and Annie Derrick into the office, and, after telling his wife of Lyman's betrayal, had forbidden either of them to mention his name again. His attitude towards his prodigal son was that of stern, unrelenting resentment. But now, Presley could not fail to detect traces of a more deep-seated travail. Something was in the wind, the times were troublous. What next was about to happen? What fresh calamity impended?

One morning, toward the very end of the week, Presley woke early in his small, white-painted iron bed. He hastened to get up and dress. There was much to be done that day. Until late the night before, he had been at work on a collection of some of his verses, gathered from the magazines in which they had first appeared. Presley had received a liberal offer for the publication of these verses in book form. "The Toilers" was to be included in this book, and, indeed, was to give it its name—"The Toilers and Other Poems." Thus it was that, until the previous midnight, he had been preparing the collection for publication, revising, annotating, arranging. The book was to be sent off that morning.

But also Presley had received a typewritten note from Annixter, inviting him to Quien Sabe that same day. Annixter explained that it was Hilma's birthday, and that he had planned a picnic on the high ground of his ranch, at the headwaters of Broderson Creek. They were to go in the carry-all, Hilma, Presley, Mrs. Dyke, Sidney, and himself, and were to make a day of it. They would leave Quien Sabe at ten in the morning. Presley had at once resolved to go. He was immensely fond of Annixter—more so than ever since his marriage with Hilma and the astonishing transformation of his character. Hilma, as well, was delightful as Mrs. Annixter; and Mrs. Dyke and the little tad had always been his friends. He would have a good time.

But nobody was to go into Bonneville that morning with the mail, and if he wished to send his manuscript, he would have to take it in himself. He had resolved to do this, getting an early start, and going on horseback to Quien Sabe, by way of Bonneville.

It was barely six o'clock when Presley sat down to his coffee and eggs in the dining-room of Los Muertos. The day promised to be hot, and for the first time, Presley had put on a new khaki riding suit, very English-looking, though in place of the regulation top-boots, he wore his laced knee-boots, with a great spur on the left heel. Harran joined him at breakfast, in his working clothes of blue canvas. He was bound for the irrigating ditch to see how the work was getting on there.

"How is the wheat looking?" asked Presley.

"Bully," answered the other, stirring his coffee. "The Governor has had his usual luck. Practically, every acre of the ranch was sown to wheat, and everywhere the stand is good. I was over on Two, day before yesterday, and if nothing happens, I believe it will go thirty sacks to the acre there. Cutter reports that there are spots on Four where we will get forty-two or three. Hooven, too, brought up some wonderful fine ears for me to look at. The grains were just beginning to show. Some of the ears carried twenty grains. That means nearly forty bushels of wheat to every acre. I call it a bonanza year."

"Have you got any mail?" said Presley, rising. "I'm going into town."

Harran shook his head, and took himself away, and Presley went down to the stable-corral to get his pony.

As he rode out of the stable-yard and passed by the ranch house, on the driveway, he was surprised to see Magnus on the lowest step of the porch.

"Good morning, Governor," called Presley. "Aren't you up pretty early?"

"Good morning, Pres, my boy." The Governor came forward and, putting his hand on the pony's withers, walked along by his side.

"Going to town, Pres?" he asked.

"Yes, sir. Can I do anything for you, Governor?"

Magnus drew a sealed envelope from his pocket.

"I wish you would drop in at the office of the Mercury for me," he said, "and see Mr. Genslinger personally, and give him this envelope. It is a package of papers, but they involve a considerable sum of money, and you must be careful of them. A few years ago, when our enmity was not so strong, Mr. Genslinger and I had some business dealings with each other. I thought it as well just now, considering that we are so openly opposed, to terminate the whole affair, and break off relations. We came to a settlement a few days ago. These are the final papers. They must be given to him in person, Presley. You understand."

Presley cantered on, turning into the county road and holding northward by the mammoth watering tank and Broderson's popular windbreak. As he passed Caraher's, he saw the saloon-keeper in the doorway of his place, and waved him a salutation which the other returned.

By degrees, Presley had come to consider Caraher in a more favourable light. He found, to his immense astonishment, that Caraher knew something of Mill and Bakounin, not, however, from their books, but from extracts and quotations from their writings, reprinted in the anarchistic journals to which he subscribed. More than once, the two had held long conversations, and from Caraher's own lips, Presley heard the terrible story of the death of his wife, who had been accidentally killed by Pinkertons during a "demonstration" of strikers. It invested the saloon-keeper, in Presley's imagination, with all the dignity of the tragedy. He could not blame Caraher for being a "red." He even wondered how it was the saloon-keeper had not put his theories into practice, and adjusted his ancient wrong with his "six inches of plugged gas-pipe." Presley began to conceive of the man as a "character."

"You wait, Mr. Presley," the saloon-keeper had once said, when Presley had protested against his radical ideas. "You don't know the Railroad yet. Watch it and its doings long enough, and you'll come over to my way of thinking, too."

It was about half-past seven when Presley reached Bonneville. The business part of the town was as yet hardly astir; he despatched his manuscript, and then hurried to the office of the "Mercury." Genslinger, as he feared, had not yet put in appearance, but the janitor of the building gave Presley the address of the editor's residence, and it was there he found him in the act of sitting down to breakfast. Presley was hardly courteous to the little man, and abruptly refused his offer of a drink. He delivered Magnus's envelope to him and departed.

It had occurred to him that it would not do to present himself at Quien Sabe on Hilma's birthday, empty-handed, and, on leaving Genslinger's house, he turned his pony's head toward the business part of the town again pulling up in front of the jeweller's, just as the clerk was taking down the shutters.

At the jeweller's, he purchased a little brooch for Hilma and at the cigar stand in the lobby of the Yosemite House, a box of superfine cigars, which, when it was too late, he realised that the master of Quien Sabe would never smoke, holding, as he did, with defiant inconsistency, to miserable weeds, black, bitter, and flagrantly doctored, which he bought, three for a nickel, at Guadalajara.

Presley arrived at Quien Sabe nearly half an hour behind the appointed time; but, as he had expected, the party were in no way ready to start. The carry-all, its horses covered with white fly-nets, stood under a tree near the house, young Vacca dozing on the seat. Hilma and Sidney, the latter exuberant with a gayety that all but brought the tears to Presley's eyes, were making sandwiches on the back porch. Mrs. Dyke was nowhere to be seen, and Annixter was shaving himself in his bedroom.

This latter put a half-lathered face out of the window as Presley cantered through the gate, and waved his razor with a beckoning motion.

"Come on in, Pres," he cried. "Nobody's ready yet. You're hours ahead of time."

Presley came into the bedroom, his huge spur clinking on the straw matting. Annixter was without coat, vest or collar, his blue silk suspenders hung in loops over either hip, his hair was disordered, the crown lock stiffer than ever.

"Glad to see you, old boy," he announced, as Presley came in. "No, don't shake hands, I'm all lather. Here, find a chair, will you? I won't be long."

"I thought you said ten o'clock," observed Presley, sitting down on the edge of the bed.

"Well, I did, but— —"

"But, then again, in a way, you didn't, hey?" his friend interrupted.

Annixter grunted good-humouredly, and turned to strop his razor. Presley looked with suspicious disfavour at his suspenders.

"Why is it," he observed, "that as soon as a man is about to get married, he buys himself pale blue suspenders, silk ones? Think of it. You, Buck Annixter, with sky-blue, silk suspenders. It ought to be a strap and a nail."

"Old fool," observed Annixter, whose repartee was the heaving of brick bats. "Say," he continued, holding the razor from his face, and jerking his head over his shoulder, while he looked at Presley's reflection in his mirror; "say, look around. Isn't this a nifty little room? We refitted the whole house, you know. Notice she's all painted?"

"I have been looking around," answered Presley, sweeping the room with a series of glances. He forebore criticism. Annixter was so boyishly proud of the effect that it would have been unkind to have undeceived him. Presley looked at the marvellous, department-store bed of brass, with its brave, gay canopy; the mill-made wash-stand, with its pitcher and bowl of blinding red and green china, the straw-framed lithographs of symbolic female figures against the multi-coloured, new wall-paper; the inadequate spindle chairs of white and gold; the sphere of tissue paper hanging from the gas fixture, and the plumes of pampas grass tacked to the wall at artistic angles, and overhanging two astonishing oil paintings, in dazzling golden frames.

"Say, how about those paintings, Prēs?" inquired Annixter a little uneasily. "I don't know whether they're good or not. They were painted by a three-fingered Chinaman in Monterey, and I got the lot for thirty dollars, frames thrown in. Why, I think the frames alone are worth thirty dollars."

"Well, so do I," declared Presley. He hastened to change the subject.

"Buck," he said, "I hear you've brought Mrs. Dyke and Sidney to live with you. You know, I think that's rather white of you."

"Oh, rot, Pres," muttered Annixter, turning abruptly to his shaving.

"And you can't fool me, either, old man," Presley continued. "You're giving this picnic as much for Mrs. Dyke and the little tad as you are for your wife, just to cheer them up a bit."

"Oh, pshaw, you make me sick."

"Well, that's the right thing to do, Buck, and I'm as glad for your sake as I am for theirs. There was a time when you would have let them all go to grass, and never so much as thought of them. I don't want to seem to be officious, but you've changed for the better, old man, and I guess I know why. She—" Presley caught his friend's eye, and added gravely, "She's a good woman, Buck."

Annixter turned around abruptly, his face flushing under its lather.

"Pres," he exclaimed, "she's made a man of me. I was a machine before, and if another man, or woman, or child got in my way, I rode 'em down, and I never DREAMED of anybody else but myself. But as soon as I woke up to the fact that I really loved her, why, it was glory hallelujah all in a minute, and, in a way, I kind of loved everybody then, and wanted to be everybody's friend. And I began to see that a fellow can't live FOR himself any more than he can live BY himself. He's got to think of others. If he's got brains, he's got to think for the poor ducks that haven't 'em, and not give 'em a boot in the backsides because they happen to be stupid; and if he's got money, he's got to help those that are busted, and if he's got a house, he's got to think of those that ain't got anywhere to go. I've got a whole lot of ideas since I began to love Hilma, and just as soon as I can, I'm going to get in and HELP people, and I'm going to keep to that idea the rest of my natural life. That ain't much of a religion, but it's the best I've got, and Henry Ward Beecher couldn't do any more than that. And it's all come about because of Hilma, and because we cared for each other."

Presley jumped up, and caught Annixter about the shoulders with one arm, gripping his hand hard. This absurd figure, with dangling silk suspenders, lathered chin, and tearful eyes, seemed to be suddenly invested with true nobility. Beside this blundering struggle to do right, to help his fellows, Presley's own vague schemes, glittering systems of reconstruction, collapsed to ruin, and he himself, with all his refinement, with all his poetry, culture, and education, stood, a bungler at the world's workbench.

"You're all RIGHT, old man," he exclaimed, unable to think of anything adequate. "You're all right. That's the way to talk, and here, by the way, I brought you a box of cigars."

Annixter stared as Presley laid the box on the edge of the washstand.

"Old fool," he remarked, "what in hell did you do that for?"

"Oh, just for fun."

"I suppose they're rotten stinkodoras, or you wouldn't give 'em away."

"This cringing gratitude—" Presley began.

"Shut up," shouted Annixter, and the incident was closed.

Annixter resumed his shaving, and Presley lit a cigarette.

"Any news from Washington?" he queried.

"Nothing that's any good," grunted Annixter. "Hello," he added, raising his head, "there's somebody in a hurry for sure."

The noise of a horse galloping so fast that the hoof-beats sounded in one uninterrupted rattle, abruptly made itself heard. The noise was coming from the direction of the road that led from the Mission to Quien Sabe. With incredible swiftness, the hoof-beats drew nearer. There was that in their sound which brought Presley to his feet. Annixter threw open the window.

"Runaway," exclaimed Presley.

Annixter, with thoughts of the Railroad, and the "Jumping" of the ranch, flung his hand to his hip pocket.

"What is it, Vacca?" he cried.

Young Vacca, turning in his seat in the carryall, was looking up the road. All at once, he jumped from his place, and dashed towards the window. "Dyke," he shouted. "Dyke, it's Dyke."

While the words were yet in his mouth, the sound of the hoof-beats rose to a roar, and a great, bell-toned voice shouted:

"Annixter, Annixter, Annixter!"

It was Dyke's voice, and the next instant he shot into view in the open square in front of the house.

"Oh, my God!" cried Presley.

The ex-engineer threw the horse on its haunches, springing from the saddle; and, as he did so, the beast collapsed, shuddering, to the ground. Annixter sprang from the window, and ran forward, Presley following.

There was Dyke, hatless, his pistol in his hand, a gaunt terrible figure the beard immeasurably long, the cheeks fallen in, the eyes sunken. His clothes ripped and torn by weeks of flight and hiding in the chaparral, were ragged beyond words, the boots were shreds of leather, bloody to the ankle with furious spurring.

"Annixter," he shouted, and again, rolling his sunken eyes, "Annixter, Annixter!"

"Here, here," cried Annixter.

The other turned, levelling his pistol.

"Give me a horse, give me a horse, quick, do you hear? Give me a horse, or I'll shoot."

"Steady, steady. That won't do. You know me, Dyke. We're friends here."

The other lowered his weapon.

"I know, I know," he panted. "I'd forgotten. I'm unstrung, Mr. Annixter, and I'm running for my life. They're not ten minutes behind me."

"Come on, come on," shouted Annixter, dashing stablewards, his suspenders flying.

"Here's a horse."

"Mine?" exclaimed Presley. "He wouldn't carry you a mile."

Annixter was already far ahead, trumpeting orders.

"The buckskin," he yelled. "Get her out, Billy. Where's the stable-man? Get out that buckskin. Get out that saddle."

Then followed minutes of furious haste, Presley, Annixter, Billy the stable-man, and Dyke himself, darting hither and thither about the yellow mare, buckling, strapping, cinching, their lips pale, their fingers trembling with excitement.

"Want anything to eat?" Annixter's head was under the saddle flap as he tore at the cinch. "Want anything to eat? Want any money? Want a gun?"

"Water," returned Dyke. "They've watched every spring. I'm killed with thirst."

"There's the hydrant. Quick now."

"I got as far as the Kern River, but they turned me back," he said between breaths as he drank.

"Don't stop to talk."

"My mother, and the little tad — —"

"I'm taking care of them. They're stopping with me."

Here?

"You won't see 'em; by the Lord, you won't. You'll get away. Where's that back cinch strap, BILLY? God damn it, are you going to let him be shot before he can get away? Now, Dyke, up you go. She'll kill herself running before they can catch you."

"God bless you, Annixter. Where's the little tad? Is she well, Annixter, and the mother? Tell them——"

"Yes, yes, yes. All clear, Pres? Let her have her own gait, Dyke. You're on the best horse in the county now. Let go her head, Billy. Now, Dyke,— shake hands? You bet I will. That's all right. Yes, God bless you. Let her go. You're OFF."

Answering the goad of the spur, and already quivering with the excitement of the men who surrounded her, the buckskin cleared the stable-corral in two leaps; then, gathering her legs under her, her head low, her neck stretched out, swung into the road from out the driveway disappearing in a blur of dust.

With the agility of a monkey, young Vacca swung himself into the framework of the artesian well, clambering aloft to its very top. He swept the country with a glance.

"Well?" demanded Annixter from the ground. The others cocked their heads to listen.

"I see him; I see him!" shouted Vacca. "He's going like the devil. He's headed for Guadalajara."

"Look back, up the road, toward the Mission. Anything there?"

The answer came down in a shout of apprehension.

"There's a party of men. Three or four—on horse-back. There's dogs with 'em. They're coming this way. Oh, I can hear the dogs. And, say, oh, say, there's another party coming down the Lower Road, going towards Guadalajara, too. They got guns. I can see the shine of the barrels. And, oh, Lord, say, there's three more men on horses coming down on the jump from the hills on the Los Muertos stock range. They're making towards Guadalajara. And I can hear the courthouse bell in Bonneville ringing. Say, the whole county is up."

As young Vacca slid down to the ground, two small black-and-tan hounds, with flapping ears and lolling tongues, loped into view on the road in front of the house. They were grey with dust, their noses were to the ground. At the gate where Dyke had turned into the ranch house grounds, they halted in confusion a moment. One started to follow the highwayman's trail towards the stable corral, but the other, quartering over the road with lightning swiftness, suddenly picked up the new scent leading on towards Guadalajara. He tossed his head in the air, and Presley abruptly shut his hands over his ears.

Ah, that terrible cry! deep-toned, reverberating like the bourdon of a great bell. It was the trackers exulting on the trail of the pursued, the prolonged, raucous howl, eager, ominous, vibrating with the alarm of the tocsin, sullen with the heavy muffling note of death. But close upon the bay of the hounds, came the gallop of horses. Five men, their eyes upon the hounds, their rifles across their pommels, their horses reeking and black with sweat, swept by in a storm of dust, glinting hoofs, and streaming manes.

"That was Delaney's gang," exclaimed Annixter. "I saw him."

"The other was that chap Christian," said Vacca, "S. Behrman's cousin. He had two deputies with him; and the chap in the white slouch hat was the sheriff from Visalia."

"By the Lord, they aren't far behind," declared Annixter.

As the men turned towards the house again they saw Hilma and Mrs. Dyke in the doorway of the little house where the latter lived. They were looking out, bewildered, ignorant of what had happened. But on the porch of the Ranch house itself, alone, forgotten in the excitement, Sidney—the little tad—stood, with pale face and serious, wide-open eyes. She had seen everything, and had understood. She said nothing. Her head inclined towards the roadway, she listened to the faint and distant baying of the dogs.

Dyke thundered across the railway tracks by the depot at Guadalajara not five minutes ahead of his pursuers. Luck seemed to have deserted him. The station, usually so quiet, was now occupied by the crew of a freight train that lay on the down track; while on the up line, near at hand and headed in the same direction, was a detached locomotive, whose engineer and fireman recognized him, he was sure, as the buckskin leaped across the rails.

He had had no time to formulate a plan since that morning, when, tortured with thirst, he had ventured near the spring at the headwaters of Broderson Creek, on Quien Sabe, and had all but fallen into the hands of the posse that had been watching for that very move. It was useless now to regret that he had tried to foil pursuit by turning back on his tracks to regain the mountains east of Bonneville. Now Delaney was almost on him.

To distance that posse, was the only thing to be thought of now. It was no longer a question of hiding till pursuit should flag; they had driven him out from the shelter of the mountains, down into this populous countryside, where an enemy might be met with at every turn of the road. Now it was life or death. He would either escape or be killed. He knew very well that he would never allow himself to be taken alive. But he had no mind to be killed—to turn and fight—till escape was blocked. His one thought was to leave pursuit behind.

Weeks of flight had sharpened Dyke's every sense. As he turned into the Upper Road beyond Guadalajara, he saw the three men galloping down from Derrick's stock range, making for the road ahead of him. They would cut him off there. He swung the buckskin about. He must take the Lower Road across Los Muertos from Guadalajara, and he must reach it before Delaney's dogs and posse. Back he galloped, the buckskin measuring her length with every leap. Once more the station came in sight. Rising in his stirrups, he looked across the fields in the direction of the Lower Road. There was a cloud of dust there. From a wagon? No, horses on the run, and their riders were armed! He could catch the flash of gun barrels. They were all closing in on him, converging on Guadalajara by every available road. The Upper Road west of Guadalajara led straight to Bonneville. That way was impossible. Was he in a trap? Had the time for fighting come at last?

But as Dyke neared the depot at Guadalajara, his eye fell upon the detached locomotive that lay quietly steaming on the up line, and with a thrill of exultation, he remembered that he was an engineer born and bred. Delaney's dogs were already to be heard, and the roll of hoofs on the Lower Road was dinning in his ears, as he leaped from the buckskin before the depot. The train crew scattered like frightened sheep before him, but Dyke ignored them. His pistol was in his hand as, once more on foot, he sprang toward the lone engine.

"Out of the cab," he shouted. "Both of you. Quick, or I'll kill you both."

The two men tumbled from the iron apron of the tender as Dyke swung himself up, dropping his pistol on the floor of the cab and reaching with the old instinct for the familiar levers. The great compound hissed and trembled as the steam was released, and the huge drivers stirred, turning slowly on the tracks. But there was a shout. Delaney's posse, dogs and men, swung into view at the turn of the road, their figures leaning over as they took the curve at full speed. Dyke threw everything wide open and caught up his revolver. From behind came the challenge of a Winchester. The party on the Lower Road were even closer than Delaney. They had seen his manoeuvre, and the first shot of the fight shivered the cab windows above the engineer's head.

But spinning futilely at first, the drivers of the engine at last caught the rails. The engine moved, advanced, travelled past the depot and the freight train, and gathering speed, rolled out on the track beyond. Smoke, black and boiling, shot skyward from the stack; not a joint that did not shudder with the mighty strain of the steam; but the great iron brute—one of Baldwin's newest and best—came to call, obedient and docile as soon as ever the great pulsing heart of it felt a master hand upon its levers. It gathered its speed, bracing its steel muscles, its thews of iron, and roared out upon the open track, filling the air with the rasp of its tempest-breath, blotting the sunshine with the belch of its hot, thick smoke. Already it was lessening in the distance, when Delaney, Christian, and the sheriff of Visalia dashed up to the station.

The posse had seen everything.

"Stuck. Curse the luck!" vociferated the cow-Puncher.

But the sheriff was already out of the saddle and into the telegraph office.

"There's a derailing switch between here and Pixley, isn't there?" he cried.

"Yes."

"Wire ahead to open it. We'll derail him there. Come on;" he turned to Delaney and the others. They sprang into the cab of the locomotive that was attached to the freight train.

"Name of the State of California," shouted the sheriff to the bewildered engineer. "Cut off from your train."

The sheriff was a man to be obeyed without hesitating. Time was not allowed the crew of the freight train for debating as to the right or the wrong of requisitioning the engine, and before anyone thought of the safety or danger of the affair, the freight engine was already flying out upon the down line, hot in pursuit of Dyke, now far ahead upon the up track.

"I remember perfectly well there's a derailing switch between here and Pixley," shouted the sheriff above the roar of the locomotive. "They use it in case they have to derail runaway engines. It runs right off into the country. We'll pile him up there. Ready with your guns, boys."

"If we should meet another train coming up on this track——" protested the frightened engineer.

"Then we'd jump or be smashed. Hi! look! There he is." As the freight engine rounded a curve, Dyke's engine came into view, shooting on some quarter of a mile ahead of them, wreathed in whirling smoke.

"The switch ain't much further on," clamoured the engineer. "You can see Pixley now."

Dyke, his hand on the grip of the valve that controlled the steam, his head out of the cab window, thundered on. He was back in his old place again; once more he was the engineer; once more he felt the engine quiver under him; the familiar noises were in his ears; the familiar buffeting of the wind surged, roaring at his face; the familiar odours of hot steam and smoke reeked in his nostrils, and on either side of him, parallel panoramas, the two halves of the landscape sliced, as it were, in two by the clashing wheels of his engine, streamed by in green and brown blurs.

He found himself settling to the old position on the cab seat, leaning on his elbow from the window, one hand on the controller. All at once, the instinct of the pursuit that of late had become so strong within him, prompted him to shoot a glance behind. He saw the other engine on the down line, plunging after him, rocking from side to side with the fury of its gallop. Not yet had he shaken the trackers from his heels; not yet was he out of the reach of danger. He set his teeth and, throwing open the fire-door, stoked vigorously for a few moments. The indicator of the steam gauge rose; his speed increased; a glance at the telegraph poles told him he was doing his fifty miles an hour. The freight engine behind him was never built for that pace. Barring the terrible risk of accident, his chances were good.

But suddenly—the engineer dominating the highway-man—he shut off his steam and threw back his brake to the extreme notch. Directly ahead of him rose a semaphore, placed at a point where evidently a derailing switch branched from the line. The semaphore's arm was dropped over the track, setting the danger signal that showed the switch was open.

In an instant, Dyke saw the trick. They had meant to smash him here; had been clever enough, quick-witted enough to open the switch, but had forgotten the automatic semaphore that worked simultaneously with the movement of the rails. To go forward was certain destruction. Dyke reversed. There was nothing for it but to go back. With a wrench and a spasm of all its metal fibres, the great compound braced itself, sliding with rigid wheels along the rails. Then, as Dyke applied the reverse, it drew back from the greater danger, returning towards the less. Inevitably now the two engines, one on the up, the other on the down line, must meet and pass each other.

Dyke released the levers, reaching for his revolver. The engineer once more became the highwayman, in peril of his life. Now, beyond all doubt, the time for fighting was at hand.

The party in the heavy freight engine, that lumbered after in pursuit, their eyes fixed on the smudge of smoke on ahead that marked the path of the fugitive, suddenly raised a shout.

"He's stopped. He's broke down. Watch, now, and see if he jumps off."

"Broke NOTHING. HE'S COMING BACK. Ready, now, he's got to pass us."

The engineer applied the brakes, but the heavy freight locomotive, far less mobile than Dyke's flyer, was slow to obey. The smudge on the rails ahead grew swiftly larger.

"He's coming. He's coming—look out, there's a shot. He's shooting already."

A bright, white sliver of wood leaped into the air from the sooty window sill of the cab.

"Fire on him! Fire on him!"

While the engines were yet two hundred yards apart, the duel began, shot answering shot, the sharp staccato reports punctuating the thunder of wheels and the clamour of steam.

Then the ground trembled and rocked; a roar as of heavy ordnance developed with the abruptness of an explosion. The two engines passed each other, the men firing the while, emptying their revolvers, shattering wood, shivering glass, the bullets clanging against the metal work as they struck and struck and struck. The men leaned from the cabs towards each other, frantic with excitement, shouting curses, the engines rocking, the steam roaring; confusion whirling in the scene like the whirl of a witch's dance, the white clouds of steam, the black eddies from the smokestack, the blue wreaths from the hot mouths of revolvers, swirling together in a blinding maze of vapour, spinning around them, dazing them, dizzying them, while the head rang with hideous clamour and the body twitched and trembled with the leap and jar of the tumult of machinery.

Roaring, clamouring, reeking with the smell of powder and hot oil, spitting death, resistless, huge, furious, an abrupt vision of chaos, faces, rage-distorted, peering through smoke, hands gripping outward from sudden darkness, prehensile, malevolent; terrible as thunder, swift as lightning, the two engines met and passed.

"He's hit," cried Delaney. "I know I hit him. He can't go far now. After him again. He won't dare go through Bonneville."

It was true. Dyke had stood between cab and tender throughout all the duel, exposed, reckless, thinking only of attack and not of defence, and a bullet from one of the pistols had grazed his hip. How serious was the wound he did not know, but he had no thought of giving up. He tore back through the depot at Guadalajara in a storm of bullets, and, clinging to the broken window ledge of his cab, was carried towards Bonneville, on over the Long Trestle and Broderson Creek and through the open country between the two ranches of Los Muertos and Quien Sabe.

But to go on to Bonneville meant certain death. Before, as well as behind him, the roads were now blocked. Once more he thought of the mountains. He resolved to abandon the engine and make another final attempt to get into the shelter of the hills in the northernmost corner of Quien Sabe. He set his teeth. He would not give in. There was one more fight left in him yet. Now to try the final hope.

He slowed the engine down, and, reloading his revolver, jumped from the platform to the road. He looked about him, listening. All around him widened an ocean of wheat. There was no one in sight.

The released engine, alone, unattended, drew slowly away from him, jolting ponderously over the rail joints. As he watched it go, a certain indefinite sense of abandonment, even in that moment, came over Dyke. His last friend, that also had been his first, was leaving him. He remembered that day, long ago, when he had opened the throttle of his first machine. To-day, it was leaving him alone, his last friend turning against him. Slowly it was going back towards Bonneville, to the shops of the Railroad, the camp of the enemy, that enemy that had ruined him and wrecked him. For the last time in his life, he had been the engineer. Now, once more, he became the highwayman, the outlaw against whom all hands were raised, the fugitive skulking in the mountains, listening for the cry of dogs.

But he would not give in. They had not broken him yet. Never, while he could fight, would he allow S. Behrman the triumph of his capture.

He found his wound was not bad. He plunged into the wheat on Quien Sabe, making northward for a division house that rose with its surrounding trees out of the wheat like an island. He reached it, the blood squelching in his shoes. But the sight of two men, Portuguese farm-hands, staring at him from an angle of the barn, abruptly roused him to action. He sprang forward with peremptory commands, demanding a horse.

At Guadalajara, Delaney and the sheriff descended from the freight engine.

"Horses now," declared the sheriff. "He won't go into Bonneville, that's certain. He'll leave the engine between here and there, and strike off into the country. We'll follow after him now in the saddle. Soon as he leaves his engine, HE'S on foot. We've as good as got him now."

Their horses, including even the buckskin mare that Dyke had ridden, were still at the station. The party swung themselves up, Delaney exclaiming, "Here's MY mount," as he bestrode the buckskin.

At Guadalajara, the two bloodhounds were picked up again. Urging the jaded horses to a gallop, the party set off along the Upper Road, keeping a sharp lookout to right and left for traces of Dyke's abandonment of the engine.

Three miles beyond the Long Trestle, they found S. Behrman holding his saddle horse by the bridle, and looking attentively at a trail that had been broken through the standing wheat on Quien Sabe. The party drew rein.

"The engine passed me on the tracks further up, and empty," said S. Behrman. "Boys, I think he left her here."

But before anyone could answer, the bloodhounds gave tongue again, as they picked up the scent.

"That's him," cried S. Behrman. "Get on, boys."

They dashed forward, following the hounds. S. Behrman laboriously climbed to his saddle, panting, perspiring, mopping the roll of fat over his coat collar, and turned in after them, trotting along far in the rear, his great stomach and tremulous jowl shaking with the horse's gait.

"What a day," he murmured. "What a day."

Dyke's trail was fresh, and was followed as easily as if made on new-fallen snow. In a short time, the posse swept into the open space around the division house. The two Portuguese were still there, wide-eyed, terribly excited.

Yes, yes, Dyke had been there not half an hour since, had held them up, taken a horse and galloped to the northeast, towards the foothills at the headwaters of Broderson Creek.

On again, at full gallop, through the young wheat, trampling it under the flying hoofs; the hounds hot on the scent, baying continually; the men, on fresh mounts, secured at the division house, bending forward in their saddles, spurring relentlessly. S. Behrman jolted along far in the rear.

And even then, harried through an open country, where there was no place to hide, it was a matter of amazement how long a chase the highwayman led them. Fences were passed; fences whose barbed wire had been slashed apart by the fugitive's knife. The ground rose under foot; the hills were at hand; still the pursuit held on. The sun, long past the meridian, began to turn earthward. Would night come on before they were up with him?

"Look! Look! There he is! Quick, there he goes!"

High on the bare slope of the nearest hill, all the posse, looking in the direction of Delaney's gesture, saw the figure of a horseman emerge from an arroyo, filled with chaparral, and struggle at a labouring gallop straight up the slope. Suddenly, every member of the party shouted aloud. The horse had fallen, pitching the rider from the saddle. The man rose to his feet, caught at the bridle, missed it and the horse dashed on alone. The man, pausing for a second looked around, saw the chase drawing nearer, then, turning back, disappeared in the chaparral. Delaney raised a great whoop.

"We've got you now." Into the slopes and valleys of the hills dashed the band of horsemen, the trail now so fresh that it could be easily discerned by all. On and on it led them, a furious, wild scramble straight up the slopes. The minutes went by. The dry bed of a rivulet was passed; then another fence; then a tangle of manzanita; a meadow of wild oats, full of agitated cattle; then an arroyo, thick with chaparral and scrub oaks, and then, without warning, the pistol shots ripped out and ran from rider to rider with the rapidity of a gatling discharge, and one of the deputies bent forward in the saddle, both hands to his face, the blood jetting from between his fingers.

Dyke was there, at bay at last, his back against a bank of rock, the roots of a fallen tree serving him as a rampart, his revolver smoking in his hand.

"You're under arrest, Dyke," cried the sheriff. "It's not the least use to fight. The whole country is up."

Dyke fired again, the shot splintering the foreleg of the horse the sheriff rode.

The posse, four men all told—the wounded deputy having crawled out of the fight after Dyke's first shot—fell back after the preliminary fusillade, dismounted, and took shelter behind rocks and trees. On that rugged ground, fighting from the saddle was impracticable. Dyke, in the meanwhile, held his fire, for he knew that, once his pistol was empty, he would never be allowed time to reload.

"Dyke," called the sheriff again, "for the last time, I summon you to surrender."

Dyke did not reply. The sheriff, Delaney, and the man named Christian conferred together in a low voice. Then Delaney and Christian left the others, making a wide detour up the sides of the arroyo, to gain a position to the left and somewhat to the rear of Dyke.

But it was at this moment that S. Behrman arrived. It could not be said whether it was courage or carelessness that brought the Railroad's agent within reach of Dyke's revolver. Possibly he was really a brave man; possibly occupied with keeping an uncertain seat upon the back of his labouring, scrambling horse, he had not noticed that he was so close upon that scene of battle. He certainly did not observe the posse lying upon the ground behind sheltering rocks and trees, and before anyone could call a warning, he had ridden out into the open, within thirty paces of Dyke's intrenchment.

Dyke saw. There was the arch-enemy; the man of all men whom he most hated; the man who had ruined him, who had exasperated him and driven him to crime, and who had instigated tireless pursuit through all those past terrible weeks. Suddenly, inviting death, he leaped up and forward; he had forgotten all else, all other considerations, at the sight of this man. He would die, gladly, so only that S. Behrman died before him.

"I've got YOU, anyway," he shouted, as he ran forward.

The muzzle of the weapon was not ten feet from S. Behrman's huge stomach as Dyke drew the trigger. Had the cartridge exploded, death, certain and swift, would have followed, but at this, of all moments, the revolver missed fire.

S. Behrman, with an unexpected agility, leaped from the saddle, and, keeping his horse between him and Dyke, ran, dodging and ducking, from tree to tree. His first shot a failure, Dyke fired again and again at his enemy, emptying his revolver, reckless of consequences. His every shot went wild, and before he could draw his knife, the whole posse was upon him.

Without concerted plans, obeying no signal but the promptings of the impulse that snatched, unerring, at opportunity—the men, Delaney and Christian from one side, the sheriff and the deputy from the other, rushed in. They did not fire. It was Dyke alive they wanted. One of them had a riata snatched from a saddle-pommel, and with this they tried to bind him.

The fight was four to one—four men with law on their side, to one wounded freebooter, half-starved, exhausted by days and nights of pursuit, worn down with loss of sleep, thirst, privation, and the grinding, nerve-racking consciousness of an ever-present peril.

They swarmed upon him from all sides, gripping at his legs, at his arms, his throat, his head, striking, clutching, kicking, falling to the ground, rolling over and over, now under, now above, now staggering forward, now toppling back. Still Dyke fought. Through that scrambling, struggling group, through that maze of twisting bodies, twining arms, straining legs, S. Behrman saw him from moment to moment, his face flaming, his eyes bloodshot, his hair matted with sweat. Now he was down, pinned under, two men across his legs, and now half-way up again, struggling to one knee. Then upright again, with half his enemies hanging on his back. His colossal strength seemed doubled; when his arms were held, he fought bull-like with his head. A score of times, it seemed as if they were about to secure him finally and irrevocably, and then he would free an arm, a leg, a shoulder, and the group that, for the fraction of an instant, had settled, locked and rigid, on its prey, would break up again as he flung a man from him, reeling and bloody, and he himself twisting, squirming, dodging, his great fists working like pistons, backed away, dragging and carrying the others with him.

More than once, he loosened almost every grip, and for an instant stood nearly free, panting, rolling his eyes, his clothes torn from his body, bleeding, dripping with sweat, a terrible figure, nearly free. The sheriff, under his breath, uttered an exclamation:

"By God, he'll get away yet."

S. Behrman watched the fight complacently.

"That all may show obstinacy," he commented, "but it don't show common sense."

Yet, however Dyke might throw off the clutches and fettering embraces that encircled him, however he might disintegrate and scatter the band of foes that heaped themselves upon him, however he might gain one instant of comparative liberty, some one of his assailants always hung, doggedly, blindly to an arm, a leg, or a foot, and the others, drawing a second's breath, closed in again, implacable, unconquerable, ferocious, like hounds upon a wolf.

At length, two of the men managed to bring Dyke's wrists close enough together to allow the sheriff to snap the handcuffs on. Even then, Dyke, clasping his hands, and using the handcuffs themselves as a weapon, knocked down Delaney by the crushing impact of the steel bracelets upon the cow-puncher's forehead. But he could no longer protect himself from attacks from behind, and the riata was finally passed around his body, pinioning his arms to his sides. After this it was useless to resist.

The wounded deputy sat with his back to a rock, holding his broken jaw in both hands. The sheriff's horse, with its splintered foreleg, would have to be shot. Delaney's head was cut from temple to cheekbone. The right wrist of the sheriff was all but dislocated. The other deputy was so exhausted he had to be helped to his horse. But Dyke was taken.

He himself had suddenly lapsed into semi-unconsciousness, unable to walk. They sat him on the buckskin, S. Behrman supporting him, the sheriff, on foot, leading the horse by the bridle. The little procession formed, and descended from the hills, turning in the direction of Bonneville. A special train, one car and an engine, would be made up there, and the highwayman would sleep in the Visalia jail that night.

Delaney and S. Behrman found themselves in the rear of the cavalcade as it moved off. The cow-puncher turned to his chief:

"Well, captain," he said, still panting, as he bound up his forehead; "well—we GOT him."

CHAPTER VI

Osterman cut his wheat that summer before any of the other ranchers, and as soon as his harvest was over organized a jack-rabbit drive. Like Annixter's barn-dance, it was to be an event in which all the country-side should take part. The drive was to begin on the most western division of the Osterman ranch, whence it would proceed towards the southeast, crossing into the northern part of Quien Sabe—on which Annixter had sown no wheat—and ending in the hills at the headwaters of Broderson Creek, where a barbecue was to be held.

Early on the morning of the day of the drive, as Harran and Presley were saddling their horses before the stables on Los Muertos, the foreman, Phelps, remarked:

"I was into town last night, and I hear that Christian has been after Ruggles early and late to have him put him in possession here on Los Muertos, and Delaney is doing the same for Quien Sabe."

It was this man Christian, the real estate broker, and cousin of S. Behrman, one of the main actors in the drama of Dyke's capture, who had come forward as a purchaser of Los Muertos when the Railroad had regraded its holdings on the ranches around Bonneville.

"He claims, of course," Phelps went on, "that when he bought Los Muertos of the Railroad he was guaranteed possession, and he wants the place in time for the harvest."

"That's almost as thin," muttered Harran as he thrust the bit into his horse's mouth, "as Delaney buying Annixter's Home ranch. That slice of Quien Sabe, according to the Railroad's grading, is worth about ten thousand dollars; yes, even fifteen, and I don't believe Delaney is worth the price of a good horse. Why, those people don't even try to preserve appearances. Where would Christian find the money to buy Los Muertos? There's no one man in all Bonneville rich enough to do it. Damned rascals! as if we didn't see that Christian and Delaney are S. Behrman's right and left hands. Well, he'll get 'em cut off," he cried with sudden fierceness, "if he comes too near the machine."

"How is it, Harran," asked Presley as the two young men rode out of the stable yard, "how is it the Railroad gang can do anything before the Supreme Court hands down a decision?"

"Well, you know how they talk," growled Harran. "They have claimed that the cases taken up to the Supreme Court were not test cases as WE claim they ARE, and that because neither Annixter nor the Governor appealed, they've lost their cases by default. It's the rottenest kind of sharp practice, but it won't do any good. The League is too strong. They won't dare move on us yet awhile. Why, Pres, the moment they'd try to jump any of these ranches around here, they would have six hundred rifles cracking at them as quick as how-do-you-do. Why, it would take a regiment of U. S. soldiers to put any one of us off our land. No, sir; they know the League means business this time."

As Presley and Harran trotted on along the county road they continually passed or overtook other horsemen, or buggies, carry-alls, buck-boards or even farm wagons, going in the same direction. These were full of the farming people from all the country round about Bonneville, on their way to the rabbit drive—the same people seen at the barn-dance—in their Sunday finest, the girls in muslin frocks and garden hats, the men with linen dusters over their black clothes; the older women in prints and dotted calicoes. Many of these latter had already taken off their bonnets—the day was very hot—and pinning them in newspapers, stowed them under the seats. They tucked their handkerchiefs into the collars of their dresses, or knotted them about their fat necks, to keep out the dust. From the axle trees of the vehicles swung carefully covered buckets of galvanised iron, in which the lunch was packed. The younger children, the boys with great frilled collars, the girls with ill-fitting shoes cramping their feet, leaned from the sides of buggy and carry-all, eating bananas and "macaroons," staring about with ox-like stolidity. Tied to the axles, the dogs followed the horses' hoofs with lolling tongues coated with dust.

The California summer lay blanket-wise and smothering over all the land. The hills, bone-dry, were browned and parched. The grasses and wild-oats, sear and yellow, snapped like glass filaments under foot. The roads, the bordering fences, even the lower leaves and branches of the trees, were thick and grey with dust. All colour had been burned from the landscape, except in the irrigated patches, that in the waste of brown and dull yellow glowed like oases.

The wheat, now close to its maturity, had turned from pale yellow to golden yellow, and from that to brown. Like a gigantic carpet, it spread itself over all the land. There was nothing else to be seen but the limitless sea of wheat as far as the eye could reach, dry, rustling, crisp and harsh in the rare breaths of hot wind out of the southeast. As Harran and Presley went along the county road, the number of vehicles and riders increased. They overtook and passed Hooven and his family in the former's farm wagon, a saddled horse tied to the back board. The little Dutchman, wearing the old frock coat of Magnus Derrick, and a new broad-brimmed straw hat, sat on the front seat with Mrs. Hooven. The little girl Hilda, and the older daughter Minna, were behind them on a board laid across the sides of the wagon. Presley and Harran stopped to shake hands. "Say," cried Hooven, exhibiting an old, but extremely well kept, rifle, "say, bei Gott, me, I tek some schatz at dose rebbit, you bedt. Ven he hef shtop to run und sit oop soh, bei der hind laigs on, I oop mit der guhn und—bing! I cetch um."

"The marshals won't allow you to shoot, Bismarck," observed Presley, looking at Minna.

Hooven doubled up with merriment.

"Ho! dot's hell of some fine joak. Me, I'M ONE OAF DOSE MAIRSCHELL MINE-SELLUF," he roared with delight, beating his knee. To his notion, the joke was irresistible. All day long, he could be heard repeating it. "Und Mist'r Praicelie, he say, 'Dose mairschell woand led you schoot, Bismarck,' und ME, ach Gott, ME, aindt I mine-selluf one oaf dose mairschell?"

As the two friends rode on, Presley had in his mind the image of Minna Hooven, very pretty in a clean gown of pink gingham, a cheap straw sailor hat from a Bonneville store on her blue black hair. He remembered her very pale face, very red lips and eyes of greenish blue,—a pretty girl certainly, always trailing a group of men behind her. Her love affairs were the talk of all Los Muertos.

"I hope that Hooven girl won't go to the bad," Presley said to Harran.

"Oh, she's all right," the other answered. "There's nothing vicious about Minna, and I guess she'll marry that foreman on the ditch gang, right enough."

"Well, as a matter of course, she's a good girl," Presley hastened to reply, "only she's too pretty for a poor girl, and too sure of her prettiness besides. That's the kind," he continued, "who would find it pretty easy to go wrong if they lived in a city."

Around Caraher's was a veritable throng. Saddle horses and buggies by the score were clustered underneath the shed or hitched to the railings in front of the watering trough. Three of Broderson's Portuguese tenants and a couple of workmen from the railroad shops in Bonneville were on the porch, already very drunk.

Continually, young men, singly or in groups, came from the doorway, wiping their lips with sidelong gestures of the hand. The whole place exhaled the febrile bustle of the saloon on a holiday morning.

The procession of teams streamed on through Bonneville, reenforced at every street corner. Along the Upper Road from Quien Sabe and Guadalajara came fresh auxiliaries, Spanish-Mexicans from the town itself,—swarthy young men on capering horses, dark-eyed girls and matrons, in red and black and yellow, more Portuguese in brand-new overalls, smoking long thin cigars. Even Father Sarria appeared.

"Look," said Presley, "there goes Annixter and Hilma. He's got his buckskin back." The master of Quien Sabe, in top laced boots and campaign hat, a cigar in his teeth, followed along beside the carry-all. Hilma and Mrs. Derrick were on the back seat, young Vacca driving. Harran and Presley bowed, taking off their hats.

"Hello, hello, Pres," cried Annixter, over the heads of the intervening crowd, standing up in his stirrups and waving a hand, "Great day! What a mob, hey? Say when this thing is over and everybody starts to walk into the barbecue, come and have lunch with us. I'll look for you, you and Harran. Hello, Harran, where's the Governor?"

"He didn't come to-day," Harran shouted back, as the crowd carried him further away from Annixter. "Left him and old Broderson at Los Muertos."

The throng emerged into the open country again, spreading out upon the Osterman ranch. From all directions could be seen horses and buggies driving across the stubble, converging upon the rendezvous. Osterman's Ranch house was left to the eastward; the army of the guests hurrying forward—for it began to be late—to where around a flag pole, flying a red flag, a vast crowd of buggies and horses was already forming. The marshals began to appear. Hooven, descending from the farm wagon, pinned his white badge to his hat brim and mounted his horse. Osterman, in marvellous riding clothes of English pattern, galloped up and down upon his best thoroughbred, cracking jokes with everybody, chaffing, joshing, his great mouth distended in a perpetual grin of amiability.

"Stop here, stop here," he vociferated, dashing along in front of Presley and Harran, waving his crop. The procession came to a halt, the horses' heads pointing eastward. The line began to be formed. The marshals perspiring, shouting, fretting, galloping about, urging this one forward, ordering this one back, ranged the thousands of conveyances and cavaliers in a long line, shaped like a wide open crescent. Its wings, under the command of lieutenants, were slightly advanced. Far out before its centre Osterman took his place, delighted beyond expression at his conspicuousness, posing for the gallery, making his horse dance.

"Wail, aindt dey gowun to gommence den bretty soohn," exclaimed Mrs. Hooven, who had taken her husband's place on the forward seat of the wagon.

"I never was so warm," murmured Minna, fanning herself with her hat. All seemed in readiness. For miles over the flat expanse of stubble, curved the interminable lines of horses and vehicles. At a guess, nearly five thousand people were present. The drive was one of the largest ever held. But no start was made; immobilized, the vast crescent stuck motionless under the blazing sun. Here and there could be heard voices uplifted in jocular remonstrance.

"Oh, I say, get a move on, somebody."

"ALL aboard."

"Say, I'll take root here pretty soon."

Some took malicious pleasure in starting false alarms.

"Ah, HERE we go."

"Off, at last."

"We're off."

Invariably these jokes fooled some one in the line. An old man, or some old woman, nervous, hard of hearing, always gathered up the reins and started off, only to be hustled and ordered back into the line by the nearest marshal. This manoeuvre never failed to produce its effect of hilarity upon those near at hand. Everybody laughed at the blunderer, the joker jeering audibly.

"Hey, come back here."

"Oh, he's easy."

"Don't be in a hurry, Grandpa."

"Say, you want to drive all the rabbits yourself."

Later on, a certain group of these fellows started a huge "josh."

"Say, that's what we're waiting for, the 'do-funny.'"

"The do-funny?"

"Sure, you can't drive rabbits without the 'do-funny.'"

"What's the do-funny?"   .

"Oh, say, she don't know what the do-funny is. We can't start without it, sure. Pete went back to get it."

"Oh, you're joking me, there's no such thing."

"Well, aren't we WAITING for it?"

"Oh, look, look," cried some women in a covered rig. "See, they are starting already 'way over there."

In fact, it did appear as if the far extremity of the line was in motion. Dust rose in the air above it.

"They ARE starting. Why don't we start?"

"No, they've stopped. False alarm."

"They've not, either. Why don't we move?"

But as one or two began to move off, the nearest marshal shouted wrathfully:

"Get back there, get back there."

"Well, they've started over there."

"Get back, I tell you."

"Where's the 'do-funny?'"

"Say, we're going to miss it all. They've all started over there."

A lieutenant came galloping along in front of the line, shouting:

"Here, what's the matter here? Why don't you start?"

There was a great shout. Everybody simultaneously uttered a prolonged "Oh-h."

"We're off."

"Here we go for sure this time."

"Remember to keep the alignment," roared the lieutenant. "Don't go too fast."

And the marshals, rushing here and there on their sweating horses to points where the line bulged forward, shouted, waving their arms: "Not too fast, not too fast....Keep back here....Here, keep closer together here. Do you want to let all the rabbits run back between you?"

A great confused sound rose into the air,—the creaking of axles, the jolt of iron tires over the dry clods, the click of brittle stubble under the horses' hoofs, the barking of dogs, the shouts of conversation and laughter.

The entire line, horses, buggies, wagons, gigs, dogs, men and boys on foot, and armed with clubs, moved slowly across the fields, sending up a cloud of white dust, that hung above the scene like smoke. A brisk gaiety was in the air. Everyone was in the best of humor, calling from team to team, laughing, skylarking, joshing. Garnett, of the Ruby Rancho, and Gethings, of the San Pablo, both on horseback, found themselves side by side. Ignoring the drive and the spirit of the occasion, they kept up a prolonged and serious conversation on an expected rise in the price of wheat. Dabney, also on horseback, followed them, listening attentively to every word, but hazarding no remark.

Mrs. Derrick and Hilma sat in the back seat of the carry-all, behind young Vacca. Mrs. Derrick, a little disturbed by such a great concourse of people, frightened at the idea of the killing of so many rabbits, drew back in her place, her young-girl eyes troubled and filled with a vague distress. Hilma, very much excited, leaned from the carry-all, anxious to see everything, watching for rabbits, asking innumerable questions of Annixter, who rode at her side.

The change that had been progressing in Hilma, ever since the night of the famous barn-dance, now seemed to be approaching its climax; first the girl, then the woman, last of all the Mother. Conscious dignity, a new element in her character, developed. The shrinking, the timidity of the girl just awakening to the consciousness of sex, passed away from her. The confusion, the troublous complexity of the woman, a mystery even to herself, disappeared. Motherhood dawned, the old simplicity of her maiden days came back to her. It was no longer a simplicity of ignorance, but of supreme knowledge, the simplicity of the perfect, the simplicity of greatness. She looked the world fearlessly in the eyes. At last, the confusion of her ideas, like frightened birds, re-settling, adjusted itself, and she emerged from the trouble calm, serene, entering into her divine right, like a queen into the rule of a realm of perpetual peace.

And with this, with the knowledge that the crown hung poised above her head, there came upon Hilma a gentleness infinitely beautiful, infinitely pathetic; a sweetness that touched all who came near her with the softness of a caress. She moved surrounded by an invisible atmosphere of Love. Love was in her wide-opened brown eyes, Love—the dim reflection of that descending crown poised over her head—radiated in a faint lustre from her dark, thick hair. Around her beautiful neck, sloping to her shoulders with full, graceful curves, Love lay encircled like a necklace—Love that was beyond words, sweet, breathed from her parted lips. From her white, large arms downward to her pink finger-tips—Love, an invisible electric fluid, disengaged itself, subtle, alluring. In the velvety huskiness of her voice, Love vibrated like a note of unknown music.

Annixter, her uncouth, rugged husband, living in this influence of a wife, who was also a mother, at all hours touched to the quick by this sense of nobility, of gentleness and of love, the instincts of a father already clutching and tugging at his heart, was trembling on the verge of a mighty transformation. The hardness and inhumanity of the man was fast breaking up. One night, returning late to the Ranch house, after a compulsory visit to the city, he had come upon Hilma asleep. He had never forgotten that night. A realization of his boundless happiness in this love he gave and received, the thought that Hilma TRUSTED him, a knowledge of his own unworthiness, a vast and humble thankfulness that his God had chosen him of all men for this great joy, had brought him to his knees for the first time in all his troubled, restless life of combat and aggression. He prayed, he knew not what,—vague words, wordless thoughts, resolving fiercely to do right, to make some return for God's gift thus placed within his hands.

Where once Annixter had thought only of himself, he now thought only of Hilma. The time when this thought of another should broaden and widen into thought of OTHERS, was yet to come; but already it had expanded to include the unborn child—already, as in the case of Mrs. Dyke, it had broadened to enfold another child and another mother bound to him by no ties other than those of humanity and pity. In time, starting from this point it would reach out more and more till it should take in all men and all women, and the intolerant selfish man, while retaining all of his native strength, should become tolerant and generous, kind and forgiving.

For the moment, however, the two natures struggled within him. A fight was to be fought, one more, the last, the fiercest, the attack of the enemy who menaced his very home and hearth, was to be resisted. Then, peace attained, arrested development would once more proceed.

Hilma looked from the carry-all, scanning the open plain in front of the advancing line of the drive.

"Where are the rabbits?" she asked of Annixter. "I don't see any at all."

"They are way ahead of us yet," he said. "Here, take the glasses."

He passed her his field glasses, and she adjusted them.

"Oh, yes," she cried, "I see. I can see five or six, but oh, so far off."

"The beggars run 'way ahead, at first."

"I should say so. See them run,—little specks. Every now and then they sit up, their ears straight up, in the air."

"Here, look, Hilma, there goes one close by."

From out of the ground apparently, some twenty yards distant, a great jack sprang into view, bounding away with tremendous leaps, his black-tipped ears erect. He disappeared, his grey body losing itself against the grey of the ground.

"Oh, a big fellow."

"Hi, yonder's another."

"Yes, yes, oh, look at him run." From off the surface of the ground, at first apparently empty of all life, and seemingly unable to afford hiding place for so much as a field-mouse, jack-rabbits started up at every moment as the line went forward. At first, they appeared singly and at long intervals; then in twos and threes, as the drive continued to advance. They leaped across the plain, and stopped in the distance, sitting up with straight ears, then ran on again, were joined by others; sank down flush to the soil—their ears flattened; started up again, ran to the side, turned back once more, darted away with incredible swiftness, and were lost to view only to be replaced by a score of others.

Gradually, the number of jacks to be seen over the expanse of stubble in front of the line of teams increased. Their antics were infinite. No two acted precisely alike. Some lay stubbornly close in a little depression between two clods, till the horses' hoofs were all but upon them, then sprang out from their hiding-place at the last second. Others ran forward but a few yards at a time, refusing to take flight, scenting a greater danger before them than behind. Still others, forced up at the last moment, doubled with lightning alacrity in their tracks, turning back to scuttle between the teams, taking desperate chances. As often as this occurred, it was the signal for a great uproar.

"Don't let him get through; don t let him get through."

"Look out for him, there he goes."

Horns were blown, bells rung, tin pans clamorously beaten. Either the jack escaped, or confused by the noise, darted back again, fleeing away as if his life depended on the issue of the instant. Once even, a bewildered rabbit jumped fair into Mrs. Derrick's lap as she sat in the carry-all, and was out again like a flash.

"Poor frightened thing," she exclaimed; and for a long time afterward, she retained upon her knees the sensation of the four little paws quivering with excitement, and the feel of the trembling furry body, with its wildly beating heart, pressed against her own.

By noon the number of rabbits discernible by Annixter's field glasses on ahead was far into the thousands. What seemed to be ground resolved itself, when seen through the glasses, into a maze of small, moving bodies, leaping, ducking, doubling, running back and forth—a wilderness of agitated ears, white tails and twinkling legs. The outside wings of the curved line of vehicles began to draw in a little; Osterman's ranch was left behind, the drive continued on over Quien Sabe.

As the day advanced, the rabbits, singularly enough, became less wild. When flushed, they no longer ran so far nor so fast, limping off instead a few feet at a time, and crouching down, their ears close upon their backs. Thus it was, that by degrees the teams began to close up on the main herd. At every instant the numbers increased. It was no longer thousands, it was tens of thousands. The earth was alive with rabbits.

Denser and denser grew the throng. In all directions nothing was to be seen but the loose mass of the moving jacks. The horns of the crescent of teams began to contract. Far off the corral came into sight. The disintegrated mass of rabbits commenced, as it were, to solidify, to coagulate. At first, each jack was some three feet distant from his nearest neighbor, but this space diminished to two feet, then to one, then to but a few inches. The rabbits began leaping over one another.

Then the strange scene defined itself. It was no longer a herd covering the earth. It was a sea, whipped into confusion, tossing incessantly, leaping, falling, agitated by unseen forces. At times the unexpected tameness of the rabbits all at once vanished. Throughout certain portions of the herd eddies of terror abruptly burst forth. A panic spread; then there would ensue a blind, wild rushing together of thousands of crowded bodies, and a furious scrambling over backs, till the scuffing thud of innumerable feet over the earth rose to a reverberating murmur as of distant thunder, here and there pierced by the strange, wild cry of the rabbit in distress.

The line of vehicles was halted. To go forward now meant to trample the rabbits under foot. The drive came to a standstill while the herd entered the corral. This took time, for the rabbits were by now too crowded to run. However, like an opened sluice-gate, the extending flanks of the entrance of the corral slowly engulfed the herd. The mass, packed tight as ever, by degrees diminished, precisely as a pool of water when a dam is opened. The last stragglers went in with a rush, and the gate was dropped.

"Come, just have a lock in here," called Annixter.

Hilma, descending from the carry-all and joined by Presley and Harran, approached and looked over the high board fence.

"Oh, did you ever see anything like that?" she exclaimed.

The corral, a really large enclosure, had proved all too small for the number of rabbits collected by the drive. Inside it was a living, moving, leaping, breathing, twisting mass. The rabbits were packed two, three, and four feet deep. They were in constant movement; those beneath struggling to the top, those on top sinking and disappearing below their fellows. All wildness, all fear of man, seemed to have entirely disappeared. Men and boys reaching over the sides of the corral, picked up a jack in each hand, holding them by the ears, while two reporters from San Francisco papers took photographs of the scene. The noise made by the tens of thousands of moving bodies was as the noise of wind in a forest, while from the hot and sweating mass there rose a strange odor, penetrating, ammoniacal, savouring of wild life.

On signal, the killing began. Dogs that had been brought there for that purpose when let into the corral refused, as had been half expected, to do the work. They snuffed curiously at the pile, then backed off, disturbed, perplexed. But the men and boys—Portuguese for the most part—were more eager. Annixter drew Hilma away, and, indeed, most of the people set about the barbecue at once.

In the corral, however, the killing went forward. Armed with a club in each hand, the young fellows from Guadalajara and Bonneville, and the farm boys from the ranches, leaped over the rails of the corral. They walked unsteadily upon the myriad of crowding bodies underfoot, or, as space was cleared, sank almost waist deep into the mass that leaped and squirmed about them. Blindly, furiously, they struck and struck. The Anglo-Saxon spectators round about drew back in disgust, but the hot, degenerated blood of Portuguese, Mexican, and mixed Spaniard boiled up in excitement at this wholesale slaughter.

But only a few of the participants of the drive cared to look on. All the guests betook themselves some quarter of a mile farther on into the hills.

The picnic and barbecue were to be held around the spring where Broderson Creek took its rise. Already two entire beeves were roasting there; teams were hitched, saddles removed, and men, women, and children, a great throng, spread out under the shade of the live oaks. A vast confused clamour rose in the air, a babel of talk, a clatter of tin plates, of knives and forks. Bottles were uncorked, napkins and oil-cloths spread over the ground. The men lit pipes and cigars, the women seized the occasion to nurse their babies.

Osterman, ubiquitous as ever, resplendent in his boots and English riding breeches, moved about between the groups, keeping up an endless flow of talk, cracking jokes, winking, nudging, gesturing, putting his tongue in his cheek, never at a loss for a reply, playing the goat.

"That josher, Osterman, always at his monkey-shines, but a good fellow for all that; brainy too. Nothing stuck up about him either, like Magnus Derrick."

"Everything all right, Buck?" inquired Osterman, coming up to where Annixter, Hilma and Mrs. Derrick were sitting down to their lunch.

"Yes, yes, everything right. But we've no cork-screw."

"No screw-cork—no scare-crow? Here you are," and he drew from his pocket a silver-plated jack-knife with a cork-screw attachment. Harran and Presley came up, bearing between them a great smoking, roasted portion of beef just off the fire. Hilma hastened to put forward a huge china platter.

Osterman had a joke to crack with the two boys, a joke that was rather broad, but as he turned about, the words almost on his lips, his glance fell upon Hilma herself, whom he had not seen for more than two months.

She had handed Presley the platter, and was now sitting with her back against the tree, between two boles of the roots. The position was a little elevated and the supporting roots on either side of her were like the arms of a great chair—a chair of state. She sat thus, as on a throne, raised above the rest, the radiance of the unseen crown of motherhood glowing from her forehead, the beauty of the perfect woman surrounding her like a glory.

And the josh died away on Osterman's lips, and unconsciously and swiftly he bared his head. Something was passing there in the air about him that he did not understand, something, however, that imposed reverence and profound respect. For the first time in his life, embarrassment seized upon him, upon this joker, this wearer of clothes, this teller of funny stories, with his large, red ears, bald head and comic actor's face. He stammered confusedly and took himself away, for the moment abstracted, serious, lost in thought.

By now everyone was eating. It was the feeding of the People, elemental, gross, a great appeasing of appetite, an enormous quenching of thirst. Quarters of beef, roasts, ribs, shoulders, haunches were consumed, loaves of bread by the thousands disappeared, whole barrels of wine went down the dry and dusty throats of the multitude. Conversation lagged while the People ate, while hunger was appeased. Everybody had their fill. One ate for the sake of eating, resolved that there should be nothing left, considering it a matter of pride to exhibit a clean plate.

After dinner, preparations were made for games. On a flat plateau at the top of one of the hills the contestants were to strive. There was to be a footrace of young girls under seventeen, a fat men's race, the younger fellows were to put the shot, to compete in the running broad jump, and the standing high jump, in the hop, skip, and step and in wrestling.

Presley was delighted with it all. It was Homeric, this feasting, this vast consuming of meat and bread and wine, followed now by games of strength. An epic simplicity and directness, an honest Anglo-Saxon mirth and innocence, commended it. Crude it was; coarse it was, but no taint of viciousness was here. These people were good people, kindly, benignant even, always readier to give than to receive, always more willing to help than to be helped. They were good stock. Of such was the backbone of the nation—sturdy Americans everyone of them. Where else in the world round were such strong, honest men, such strong, beautiful women?

Annixter, Harran, and Presley climbed to the level plateau where the games were to be held, to lay out the courses, and mark the distances. It was the very place where once Presley had loved to lounge entire afternoons, reading his books of poems, smoking and dozing. From this high point one dominated the entire valley to the south and west. The view was superb. The three men paused for a moment on the crest of the hill to consider it.

Young Vacca came running and panting up the hill after them, calling for Annixter.

"Well, well, what is it?"

"Mr. Osterman's looking for you, sir, you and Mr. Harran. Vanamee, that cow-boy over at Derrick's, has just come from the Governor with a message. I guess it's important."

"Hello, what's up now?" muttered Annixter, as they turned back.

They found Osterman saddling his horse in furious haste. Near-by him was Vanamee holding by the bridle an animal that was one lather of sweat. A few of the picnickers were turning their heads curiously in that direction. Evidently something of moment was in the wind.

"What's all up?" demanded Annixter, as he and Harran, followed by Presley, drew near.

"There's hell to pay," exclaimed Osterman under his breath. "Read that. Vanamee just brought it."

He handed Annixter a sheet of note paper, and turned again to the cinching of his saddle.

"We've got to be quick," he cried. "They've stolen a march on us."

Annixter read the note, Harran and Presley looking over his shoulder.

"Ah, it's them, is it," exclaimed Annixter.

Harran set his teeth. "Now for it," he exclaimed. "They've been to your place already, Mr. Annixter," said Vanamee. "I passed by it on my way up. They have put Delaney in possession, and have set all your furniture out in the road."

Annixter turned about, his lips white. Already Presley and Harran had run to their horses.

"Vacca," cried Annixter, "where's Vacca? Put the saddle on the buckskin, QUICK. Osterman, get as many of the League as are here together at THIS spot, understand. I'll be back in a minute. I must tell Hilma this."

Hooven ran up as Annixter disappeared. His little eyes were blazing, he was dragging his horse with him.

"Say, dose fellers come, hey? Me, I'm alretty, see I hev der guhn."

"They've jumped the ranch, little girl," said Annixter, putting one arm around Hilma. "They're in our house now. I'm off. Go to Derrick's and wait for me there."

She put her arms around his neck.

"You're going?" she demanded.

"I must. Don't be frightened. It will be all right. Go to Derrick's and—good-bye."

She said never a word. She looked once long into his eyes, then kissed him on the mouth.

Meanwhile, the news had spread. The multitude rose to its feet. Women and men, with pale faces, looked at each other speechless, or broke forth into inarticulate exclamations. A strange, unfamiliar murmur took the place of the tumultuous gaiety of the previous moments. A sense of dread, of confusion, of impending terror weighed heavily in the air. What was now to happen?

When Annixter got back to Osterman, he found a number of the Leaguers already assembled. They were all mounted. Hooven was there and Harran, and besides these, Garnett of the Ruby ranch and Gethings of the San Pablo, Phelps the foreman of Los Muertos, and, last of all, Dabney, silent as ever, speaking to no one. Presley came riding up.

"Best keep out of this, Pres," cried Annixter.

"Are we ready?" exclaimed Gethings.

"Ready, ready, we're all here."

"ALL. Is this all of us?" cried Annixter. "Where are the six hundred men who were going to rise when this happened?"

They had wavered, these other Leaguers. Now, when the actual crisis impended, they were smitten with confusion. Ah, no, they were not going to stand up and be shot at just to save Derrick's land. They were not armed. What did Annixter and Osterman take them for? No, sir; the Railroad had stolen a march on them. After all his big talk Derrick had allowed them to be taken by surprise. The only thing to do was to call a meeting of the Executive Committee. That was the only thing. As for going down there with no weapons in their hands, NO, sir. That was asking a little TOO much. "Come on, then, boys," shouted Osterman, turning his back on the others. "The Governor says to meet him at Hooven's. We'll make for the Long Trestle and strike the trail to Hooven's there."

They set off. It was a terrible ride. Twice during the scrambling descent from the hills, Presley's pony fell beneath him. Annixter, on his buckskin, and Osterman, on his thoroughbred, good horsemen both, led the others, setting a terrific pace. The hills were left behind. Broderson Creek was crossed and on the levels of Quien Sabe, straight through the standing wheat, the nine horses, flogged and spurred, stretched out to their utmost. Their passage through the wheat sounded like the rip and tear of a gigantic web of cloth. The landscape on either hand resolved itself into a long blur. Tears came to the eyes, flying pebbles, clods of earth, grains of wheat flung up in the flight, stung the face like shot. Osterman's thoroughbred took the second crossing of Broderson's Creek in a single leap. Down under the Long Trestle tore the cavalcade in a shower of mud and gravel; up again on the further bank, the horses blowing like steam engines; on into the trail to Hooven's, single file now, Presley's pony lagging, Hooven's horse bleeding at the eyes, the buckskin, game as a fighting cock, catching her second wind, far in the lead now, distancing even the English thoroughbred that Osterman rode.

At last Hooven's unpainted house, beneath the enormous live oak tree, came in sight. Across the Lower Road, breaking through fences and into the yard around the house, thundered the Leaguers. Magnus was waiting for them.

The riders dismounted, hardly less exhausted than their horses.

"Why, where's all the men?" Annixter demanded of Magnus.

"Broderson is here and Cutter," replied the Governor, "no one else. I thought YOU would bring more men with you."

"There are only nine of us."

"And the six hundred Leaguers who were going to rise when this happened!" exclaimed Garnett, bitterly.

"Rot the League," cried Annixter. "It's gone to pot—went to pieces at the first touch."

"We have been taken by surprise, gentlemen, after all," said Magnus. "Totally off our guard. But there are eleven of us. It is enough."

"Well, what's the game? Has the marshal come? How many men are with him?"

"The United States marshal from San Francisco," explained Magnus, "came down early this morning and stopped at Guadalajara. We learned it all through our friends in Bonneville about an hour ago. They telephoned me and Mr. Broderson. S. Behrman met him and provided about a dozen deputies. Delaney, Ruggles, and Christian joined them at Guadalajara. They left Guadalajara, going towards Mr. Annixter's ranch house on Quien Sabe. They are serving the writs in ejectment and putting the dummy buyers in possession. They are armed. S. Behrman is with them."

"Where are they now?"

"Cutter is watching them from the Long Trestle. They returned to Guadalajara. They are there now."

"Well," observed Gethings, "From Guadalajara they can only go to two places. Either they will take the Upper Road and go on to Osterman's next, or they will take the Lower Road to Mr. Derrick's."

"That is as I supposed," said Magnus. "That is why I wanted you to come here. From Hooven's, here, we can watch both roads simultaneously."

"Is anybody on the lookout on the Upper Road?"

"Cutter. He is on the Long Trestle."

"Say," observed Hooven, the instincts of the old-time soldier stirring him, "say, dose feller pretty demn schmart, I tink. We got to put some picket way oudt bei der Lower Roadt alzoh, und he tek dose glassus Mist'r Ennixt'r got bei um. Say, look at dose irregation ditsch. Dot ditsch he run righd across BOTH dose road, hey? Dat's some fine entrenchment, you bedt. We fighd um from dose ditsch."

In fact, the dry irrigating ditch was a natural trench, admirably suited to the purpose, crossing both roads as Hooven pointed out and barring approach from Guadalajara to all the ranches save Annixter's—which had already been seized.

Gethings departed to join Cutter on the Long Trestle, while Phelps and Harran, taking Annixter's field glasses with them, and mounting their horses, went out towards Guadalajara on the Lower Road to watch for the marshal's approach from that direction.

After the outposts had left them, the party in Hooven's cottage looked to their weapons. Long since, every member of the League had been in the habit of carrying his revolver with him. They were all armed and, in addition, Hooven had his rifle. Presley alone carried no weapon.

The main room of Hooven's house, in which the Leaguers were now assembled, was barren, poverty-stricken, but tolerably clean. An old clock ticked vociferously on a shelf. In one corner was a bed, with a patched, faded quilt. In the centre of the room, straddling over the bare floor, stood a pine table. Around this the men gathered, two or three occupying chairs, Annixter sitting sideways on the table, the rest standing.

"I believe, gentlemen," said Magnus, "that we can go through this day without bloodshed. I believe not one shot need be fired. The Railroad will not force the issue, will not bring about actual fighting. When the marshal realises that we are thoroughly in earnest, thoroughly determined, I am convinced that he will withdraw."

There were murmurs of assent.

"Look here," said Annixter, "if this thing can by any means be settled peaceably, I say let's do it, so long as we don't give in."

The others stared. Was this Annixter who spoke—the Hotspur of the League, the quarrelsome, irascible fellow who loved and sought a quarrel? Was it Annixter, who now had been the first and only one of them all to suffer, whose ranch had been seized, whose household possessions had been flung out into the road?

"When you come right down to it," he continued, "killing a man, no matter what he's done to you, is a serious business. I propose we make one more attempt to stave this thing off. Let's see if we can't get to talk with the marshal himself; at any rate, warn him of the danger of going any further. Boys, let's not fire the first shot. What do you say?"

The others agreed unanimously and promptly; and old Broderson, tugging uneasily at his long beard, added:

"No—no—no violence, no UNNECESSARY violence, that is. I should hate to have innocent blood on my hands—that is, if it IS innocent. I don't know, that S. Behrman—ah, he is a—a—surely he had innocent blood on HIS head. That Dyke affair, terrible, terrible; but then Dyke WAS in the wrong—driven to it, though; the Railroad did drive him to it. I want to be fair and just to everybody."

"There's a team coming up the road from Los Muertos," announced Presley from the door.

"Fair and just to everybody," murmured old Broderson, wagging his head, frowning perplexedly. "I don't want to—to—to harm anybody unless they harm me."

"Is the team going towards Guadalajara?" enquired Garnett, getting up and coming to the door.

"Yes, it's a Portuguese, one of the garden truck men."

"We must turn him back," declared Osterman. "He can't go through here. We don't want him to take any news on to the marshal and S. Behrman."

"I'll turn him back," said Presley.

He rode out towards the market cart, and the others, watching from the road in front of Hooven's, saw him halt it. An excited interview followed. They could hear the Portuguese expostulating volubly, but in the end he turned back.

"Martial law on Los Muertos, isn't it?" observed Osterman. "Steady all," he exclaimed as he turned about, "here comes Harran."

Harran rode up at a gallop. The others surrounded him.

"I saw them," he cried. "They are coming this way. S. Behrman and Ruggles are in a two-horse buggy. All the others are on horseback. There are eleven of them. Christian and Delaney are with them. Those two have rifles. I left Hooven watching them."

"Better call in Gethings and Cutter right away," said Annixter. "We'll need all our men."

"I'll call them in," Presley volunteered at once. "Can I have the buckskin? My pony is about done up."

He departed at a brisk gallop, but on the way met Gethings and Cutter returning. They, too, from their elevated position, had observed the marshal's party leaving Guadalajara by the Lower Road. Presley told them of the decision of the Leaguers not to fire until fired upon.

"All right," said Gethings. "But if it comes to a gun-fight, that means it's all up with at least one of us. Delaney never misses his man."

When they reached Hooven's again, they found that the Leaguers had already taken their position in the ditch. The plank bridge across it had been torn up. Magnus, two long revolvers lying on the embankment in front of him, was in the middle, Harran at his side. On either side, some five feet intervening between each man, stood the other Leaguers, their revolvers ready. Dabney, the silent old man, had taken off his coat.

"Take your places between Mr. Osterman and Mr. Broderson," said Magnus, as the three men rode up. "Presley," he added, "I forbid you to take any part in this affair."

"Yes, keep him out of it," cried Annixter from his position at the extreme end of the line. "Go back to Hooven's house, Pres, and look after the horses," he added. "This is no business of yours. And keep the road behind us clear. Don't let ANY ONE come near, not ANY ONE, understand?"

Presley withdrew, leading the buckskin and the horses that Gethings and Cutter had ridden. He fastened them under the great live oak and then came out and stood in the road in front of the house to watch what was going on.

In the ditch, shoulder deep, the Leaguers, ready, watchful, waited in silence, their eyes fixed on the white shimmer of the road leading to Guadalajara.

"Where's Hooven?" enquired Cutter.

"I don't know," Osterman replied. "He was out watching the Lower Road with Harran Derrick. Oh, Harran," he called, "isn't Hooven coming in?"

"I don't know what he is waiting for," answered Harran. "He was to have come in just after me. He thought maybe the marshal's party might make a feint in this direction, then go around by the Upper Road, after all. He wanted to watch them a little longer. But he ought to be here now."

"Think he'll take a shot at them on his own account?"

"Oh, no, he wouldn't do that."

"Maybe they took him prisoner."

"Well, that's to be thought of, too."

Suddenly there was a cry. Around the bend of the road in front of them came a cloud of dust. From it emerged a horse's head.

"Hello, hello, there's something."

"Remember, we are not to fire first."

"Perhaps that's Hooven; I can't see. Is it? There only seems to be one horse."

"Too much dust for one horse."

Annixter, who had taken his field glasses from Harran, adjusted them to his eyes.

"That's not them," he announced presently, "nor Hooven either. That's a cart." Then after another moment, he added, "The butcher's cart from Guadalajara."

The tension was relaxed. The men drew long breaths, settling back in their places.

"Do we let him go on, Governor?"

"The bridge is down. He can't go by and we must not let him go back. We shall have to detain him and question him. I wonder the marshal let him pass."

The cart approached at a lively trot.

"Anybody else in that cart, Mr. Annixter?" asked Magnus. "Look carefully. It may be a ruse. It is strange the marshal should have let him pass."

The Leaguers roused themselves again. Osterman laid his hand on his revolver.

"No," called Annixter, in another instant, "no, there's only one man in it."

The cart came up, and Cutter and Phelps, clambering from the ditch, stopped it as it arrived in front of the party.

"Hey—what—what?" exclaimed the young butcher, pulling up. "Is that bridge broke?"

But at the idea of being held, the boy protested at top voice, badly frightened, bewildered, not knowing what was to happen next.

"No, no, I got my meat to deliver. Say, you let me go. Say, I ain't got nothing to do with you."

He tugged at the reins, trying to turn the cart about. Cutter, with his jack-knife, parted the reins just back of the bit.

"You'll stay where you are, m' son, for a while. We're not going to hurt you. But you are not going back to town till we say so. Did you pass anybody on the road out of town?"

In reply to the Leaguers' questions, the young butcher at last told them he had passed a two-horse buggy and a lot of men on horseback just beyond the railroad tracks. They were headed for Los Muertos.

"That's them, all right," muttered Annixter. "They're coming by this road, sure."

The butcher's horse and cart were led to one side of the road, and the horse tied to the fence with one of the severed lines. The butcher, himself, was passed over to Presley, who locked him in Hooven's barn.

"Well, what the devil," demanded Osterman, "has become of Bismarck?"

In fact, the butcher had seen nothing of Hooven. The minutes were passing, and still he failed to appear.

"What's he up to, anyways?"

"Bet you what you like, they caught him. Just like that crazy Dutchman to get excited and go too near. You can always depend on Hooven to lose his head."

Five minutes passed, then ten. The road towards Guadalajara lay empty, baking and white under the sun.

"Well, the marshal and S. Behrman don't seem to be in any hurry, either."

"Shall I go forward and reconnoitre, Governor?" asked Harran.

But Dabney, who stood next to Annixter, touched him on the shoulder and, without speaking, pointed down the road. Annixter looked, then suddenly cried out:

"Here comes Hooven."

The German galloped into sight, around the turn of the road, his rifle laid across his saddle. He came on rapidly, pulled up, and dismounted at the ditch.

"Dey're commen," he cried, trembling with excitement. "I watch um long dime bei der side oaf der roadt in der busches. Dey shtop bei der gate oder side der relroadt trecks and talk long dime mit one n'udder. Den dey gome on. Dey're gowun sure do zum monkey-doodle pizeness. Me, I see Gritschun put der kertridges in his guhn. I tink dey gowun to gome MY blace first. Dey gowun to try put me off, tek my home, bei Gott."

"All right, get down in here and keep quiet, Hooven. Don't fire unless——"

"Here they are."

A half-dozen voices uttered the cry at once.

There could be no mistake this time. A buggy, drawn by two horses, came into view around the curve of the road. Three riders accompanied it, and behind these, seen at intervals in a cloud of dust were two—three—five—six others.

This, then, was S. Behrman with the United States marshal and his posse. The event that had been so long in preparation, the event which it had been said would never come to pass, the last trial of strength, the last fight between the Trust and the People, the direct, brutal grapple of armed men, the law defied, the Government ignored, behold, here it was close at hand.

Osterman cocked his revolver, and in the profound silence that had fallen upon the scene, the click was plainly audible from end to end of the line.

"Remember our agreement, gentlemen," cried Magnus, in a warning voice. "Mr. Osterman, I must ask you to let down the hammer of your weapon."

No one answered. In absolute quiet, standing motionless in their places, the Leaguers watched the approach of the marshal.

Five minutes passed. The riders came on steadily. They drew nearer. The grind of the buggy wheels in the grit and dust of the road, and the prolonged clatter of the horses' feet began to make itself heard. The Leaguers could distinguish the faces of their enemies.

In the buggy were S. Behrman and Cyrus Ruggles, the latter driving. A tall man in a frock coat and slouched hat—the marshal, beyond question— rode at the left of the buggy; Delaney, carrying a Winchester, at the right. Christian, the real estate broker, S. Behrman's cousin, also with a rifle, could be made out just behind the marshal. Back of these, riding well up, was a group of horsemen, indistinguishable in the dust raised by the buggy's wheels.

Steadily the distance between the Leaguers and the posse diminished.

"Don't let them get too close, Governor," whispered Harran.

When S. Behrman's buggy was about one hundred yards distant from the irrigating ditch, Magnus sprang out upon the road, leaving his revolvers behind him. He beckoned Garnett and Gethings to follow, and the three ranchers, who, with the exception of Broderson, were the oldest men present, advanced, without arms, to meet the marshal.

Magnus cried aloud:

"Halt where you are."

From their places in the ditch, Annixter, Osterman, Dabney, Harran, Hooven, Broderson, Cutter, and Phelps, their hands laid upon their revolvers, watched silently, alert, keen, ready for anything.

At the Governor's words, they saw Ruggles pull sharply on the reins. The buggy came to a standstill, the riders doing likewise. Magnus approached the marshal, still followed by Garnett and Gethings, and began to speak. His voice was audible to the men in the ditch, but his words could not be made out. They heard the marshal reply quietly enough and the two shook hands. Delaney came around from the side of the buggy, his horse standing before the team across the road. He leaned from the saddle, listening to what was being said, but made no remark. From time to time, S. Behrman and Ruggles, from their seats in the buggy, interposed a sentence or two into the conversation, but at first, so far as the Leaguers could discern, neither Magnus nor the marshal paid them any attention. They saw, however, that the latter repeatedly shook his head and once they heard him exclaim in a loud voice:

"I only know my duty, Mr. Derrick."

Then Gethings turned about, and seeing Delaney close at hand, addressed an unheard remark to him. The cow-puncher replied curtly and the words seemed to anger Gethings. He made a gesture, pointing back to the ditch, showing the intrenched Leaguers to the posse. Delaney appeared to communicate the news that the Leaguers were on hand and prepared to resist, to the other members of the party. They all looked toward the ditch and plainly saw the ranchers there, standing to their arms.

But meanwhile Ruggles had addressed himself more directly to Magnus, and between the two an angry discussion was going forward. Once even Harran heard his father exclaim:

"The statement is a lie and no one knows it better than yourself."

"Here," growled Annixter to Dabney, who stood next him in the ditch, "those fellows are getting too close. Look at them edging up. Don't Magnus see that?"

The other members of the marshal's force had come forward from their places behind the buggy and were spread out across the road. Some of them were gathered about Magnus, Garnett, and Gethings; and some were talking together, looking and pointing towards the ditch. Whether acting upon signal or not, the Leaguers in the ditch could not tell, but it was certain that one or two of the posse had moved considerably forward. Besides this, Delaney had now placed his horse between Magnus and the ditch, and two others riding up from the rear had followed his example. The posse surrounded the three ranchers, and by now, everybody was talking at once.

"Look here," Harran called to Annixter, "this won't do. I don't like the looks of this thing. They all seem to be edging up, and before we know it they may take the Governor and the other men prisoners."

"They ought to come back," declared Annixter.

"Somebody ought to tell them that those fellows are creeping up."

By now, the angry argument between the Governor and Ruggles had become more heated than ever. Their voices were raised; now and then they made furious gestures.

"They ought to come back," cried Osterman. "We couldn't shoot now if anything should happen, for fear of hitting them."

"Well, it sounds as though something were going to happen pretty soon."

They could hear Gethings and Delaney wrangling furiously; another deputy joined in.

"I'm going to call the Governor back," exclaimed Annixter, suddenly clambering out of the ditch. "No, no," cried Osterman, "keep in the ditch. They can't drive us out if we keep here."

Hooven and Harran, who had instinctively followed Annixter, hesitated at Osterman's words and the three halted irresolutely on the road before the ditch, their weapons in their hands.

"Governor," shouted Harran, "come on back. You can't do anything."

Still the wrangle continued, and one of the deputies, advancing a little from out the group, cried out:

"Keep back there! Keep back there, you!"

"Go to hell, will you?" shouted Harran on the instant. "You're on my land."

"Oh, come back here, Harran," called Osterman. "That ain't going to do any good."

"There—listen," suddenly exclaimed Harran. "The Governor is calling us. Come on; I'm going."

Osterman got out of the ditch and came forward, catching Harran by the arm and pulling him back.

"He didn't call. Don't get excited. You'll ruin everything. Get back into the ditch again."

But Cutter, Phelps, and the old man Dabney, misunderstanding what was happening, and seeing Osterman leave the ditch, had followed his example. All the Leaguers were now out of the ditch, and a little way down the road, Hooven, Osterman, Annixter, and Harran in front, Dabney, Phelps, and Cutter coming up from behind.

"Keep back, you," cried the deputy again.

In the group around S. Behrman's buggy, Gethings and Delaney were yet quarrelling, and the angry debate between Magnus, Garnett, and the marshal still continued.

Till this moment, the real estate broker, Christian, had taken no part in the argument, but had kept himself in the rear of the buggy. Now, however, he pushed forward. There was but little room for him to pass, and, as he rode by the buggy, his horse scraped his flank against the hub of the wheel. The animal recoiled sharply, and, striking against Garnett, threw him to the ground. Delaney's horse stood between the buggy and the Leaguers gathered on the road in front of the ditch; the incident, indistinctly seen by them, was misinterpreted.

Garnett had not yet risen when Hooven raised a great shout:

"HOCH, DER KAISER! HOCH, DER VATERLAND!"

With the words, he dropped to one knee, and sighting his rifle carefully, fired into the group of men around the buggy.

Instantly the revolvers and rifles seemed to go off of themselves. Both sides, deputies and Leaguers, opened fire simultaneously. At first, it was nothing but a confused roar of explosions; then the roar lapsed to an irregular, quick succession of reports, shot leaping after shot; then a moment's silence, and, last of all, regular as clock-ticks, three shots at exact intervals. Then stillness.

Delaney, shot through the stomach, slid down from his horse, and, on his hands and knees, crawled from the road into the standing wheat. Christian fell backward from the saddle toward the buggy, and hung suspended in that position, his head and shoulders on the wheel, one stiff leg still across his saddle. Hooven, in attempting to rise from his kneeling position, received a rifle ball squarely in the throat, and rolled forward upon his face. Old Broderson, crying out, "Oh, they've shot me, boys," staggered sideways, his head bent, his hands rigid at his sides, and fell into the ditch. Osterman, blood running from his mouth and nose, turned about and walked back. Presley helped him across the irrigating ditch and Osterman laid himself down, his head on his folded arms. Harran Derrick dropped where he stood, turning over on his face, and lay motionless, groaning terribly, a pool of blood forming under his stomach. The old man Dabney, silent as ever, received his death, speechless. He fell to his knees, got up again, fell once more, and died without a word. Annixter, instantly killed, fell his length to the ground, and lay without movement, just as he had fallen, one arm across his face.

CHAPTER VII

On their way to Derrick's ranch house, Hilma and Mrs. Derrick heard the sounds of distant firing.

"Stop!" cried Hilma, laying her hand upon young Vacca's arm. "Stop the horses. Listen, what was that?"

The carry-all came to a halt and from far away across the rustling wheat came the faint rattle of rifles and revolvers.

"Say," cried Vacca, rolling his eyes, "oh, say, they're fighting over there."

Mrs. Derrick put her hands over her face.

"Fighting," she cried, "oh, oh, it's terrible. Magnus is there—and Harran."

"Where do you think it is?" demanded Hilma. "That's over toward Hooven's."

"I'm going. Turn back. Drive to Hooven's, quick."

"Better not, Mrs. Annixter," protested the young man. "Mr. Annixter said we were to go to Derrick's. Better keep away from Hooven's if there's trouble there. We wouldn't get there till it's all over, anyhow."

"Yes, yes, let's go home," cried Mrs. Derrick, "I'm afraid. Oh, Hilma, I'm afraid."

"Come with me to Hooven's then."

"There, where they are fighting? Oh, I couldn't. I—I can't. It would be all over before we got there as Vacca says."

"Sure," repeated young Vacca.

"Drive to Hooven's," commanded Hilma. "If you won't, I'll walk there." She threw off the lap-robes, preparing to descend. "And you," she exclaimed, turning to Mrs. Derrick, "how CAN you—when Harran and your husband may be—may—are in danger."

Grumbling, Vacca turned the carry-all about and drove across the open fields till he reached the road to Guadalajara, just below the Mission.

"Hurry!" cried Hilma.

The horses started forward under the touch of the whip. The ranch houses of Quien Sabe came in sight.

"Do you want to stop at the house?" inquired Vacca over his shoulder.

"No, no; oh, go faster—make the horses run."

They dashed through the houses of the Home ranch.

"Oh, oh," cried Hilma suddenly, "look, look there. Look what they have done."

Vacca pulled the horses up, for the road in front of Annixter's house was blocked.

A vast, confused heap of household effects was there—chairs, sofas, pictures, fixtures, lamps. Hilma's little home had been gutted; everything had been taken from it and ruthlessly flung out upon the road, everything that she and her husband had bought during that wonderful week after their marriage. Here was the white enamelled "set" of the bedroom furniture, the three chairs, wash-stand and bureau,—the bureau drawers falling out, spilling their contents into the dust; there were the white wool rugs of the sitting-room, the flower stand, with its pots all broken, its flowers wilting; the cracked goldfish globe, the fishes already dead; the rocking chair, the sewing machine, the great round table of yellow oak, the lamp with its deep shade of crinkly red tissue paper, the pretty tinted photographs that had hung on the wall—the choir boys with beautiful eyes, the pensive young girls in pink gowns—the pieces of wood carving that represented quails and ducks, and, last of all, its curtains of crisp, clean muslin, cruelly torn and crushed—the bed, the wonderful canopied bed so brave and gay, of which Hilma had been so proud, thrust out there into the common road, torn from its place, from the discreet intimacy of her bridal chamber, violated, profaned, flung out into the dust and garish sunshine for all men to stare at, a mockery and a shame.

To Hilma it was as though something of herself, of her person, had been thus exposed and degraded; all that she held sacred pilloried, gibbeted, and exhibited to the world's derision. Tears of anguish sprang to her eyes, a red flame of outraged modesty overspread her face.

"Oh," she cried, a sob catching her throat, "oh, how could they do it?" But other fears intruded; other greater terrors impended.

"Go on," she cried to Vacca, "go on quickly."

But Vacca would go no further. He had seen what had escaped Hilma's attention, two men, deputies, no doubt, on the porch of the ranch house. They held possession there, and the evidence of the presence of the enemy in this raid upon Quien Sabe had daunted him.

"No, SIR," he declared, getting out of the carry-all, "I ain't going to take you anywhere where you're liable to get hurt. Besides, the road's blocked by all this stuff. You can't get the team by."

Hilma sprang from the carry-all.

"Come," she said to Mrs. Derrick.

The older woman, trembling, hesitating, faint with dread, obeyed, and Hilma, picking her way through and around the wreck of her home, set off by the trail towards the Long Trestle and Hooven's.

When she arrived, she found the road in front of the German's house, and, indeed, all the surrounding yard, crowded with people. An overturned buggy lay on the side of the road in the distance, its horses in a tangle of harness, held by two or three men. She saw Caraher's buckboard under the live oak and near it a second buggy which she recognised as belonging to a doctor in Guadalajara.

"Oh, what has happened; oh, what has happened?" moaned Mrs. Derrick.

"Come," repeated Hilma. The young girl took her by the hand and together they pushed their way through the crowd of men and women and entered the yard.

The throng gave way before the two women, parting to right and left without a word.

"Presley," cried Mrs. Derrick, as she caught sight of him in the doorway of the house, "oh, Presley, what has happened? Is Harran safe? Is Magnus safe? Where are they?"

"Don't go in, Mrs. Derrick," said Presley, coming forward, "don't go in."

"Where is my husband?" demanded Hilma.

Presley turned away and steadied himself against the jamb of the door.

Hilma, leaving Mrs. Derrick, entered the house. The front room was full of men. She was dimly conscious of Cyrus Ruggles and S. Behrman, both deadly pale, talking earnestly and in whispers to Cutter and Phelps. There was a strange, acrid odour of an unfamiliar drug in the air. On the table before her was a satchel, surgical instruments, rolls of bandages, and a blue, oblong paper box full of cotton. But above the hushed noises of voices and footsteps, one terrible sound made itself heard—the prolonged, rasping sound of breathing, half choked, laboured, agonised.

"Where is my husband?" she cried. She pushed the men aside. She saw Magnus, bareheaded, three or four men lying on the floor, one half naked, his body swathed in white bandages; the doctor in shirt sleeves, on one knee beside a figure of a man stretched out beside him.

Garnett turned a white face to her.

"Where is my husband?"

The other did not reply, but stepped aside and Hilma saw the dead body of her husband lying upon the bed. She did not cry out. She said no word. She went to the bed, and sitting upon it, took Annixter's head in her lap, holding it gently between her hands. Thereafter she did not move, but sat holding her dead husband's head in her lap, looking vaguely about from face to face of those in the room, while, without a sob, without a cry, the great tears filled her wide-opened eyes and rolled slowly down upon her cheeks.

On hearing that his wife was outside, Magnus came quickly forward. She threw herself into his arms.

"Tell me, tell me," she cried, "is Harran—is——"

"We don't know yet," he answered. "Oh, Annie——"

Then suddenly the Governor checked himself. He, the indomitable, could not break down now.

"The doctor is with him," he said; "we are doing all we can. Try and be brave, Annie. There is always hope. This is a terrible day's work. God forgive us all."

She pressed forward, but he held her back.

"No, don't see him now. Go into the next room. Garnett, take care of her."

But she would not be denied. She pushed by Magnus, and, breaking through the group that surrounded her son, sank on her knees beside him, moaning, in compassion and terror.

Harran lay straight and rigid upon the floor, his head propped by a pillow, his coat that had been taken off spread over his chest. One leg of his trousers was soaked through and through with blood. His eyes were half-closed, and with the regularity of a machine, the eyeballs twitched and twitched. His face was so white that it made his yellow hair look brown, while from his opened mouth, there issued that loud and terrible sound of guttering, rasping, laboured breathing that gagged and choked and gurgled with every inhalation.

"Oh, Harrie, Harrie," called Mrs. Derrick, catching at one of his hands.

The doctor shook his head.

"He is unconscious, Mrs. Derrick."

"Where was he—where is—the—the——"

"Through the lungs."

"Will he get well? Tell me the truth."

"I don't know. Mrs. Derrick."

She had all but fainted, and the old rancher, Garnett, half-carrying, half-leading her, took her to the one adjoining room—Minna Hooven's bedchamber. Dazed, numb with fear, she sat down on the edge of the bed, rocking herself back and forth, murmuring:

"Harrie, Harrie, oh, my son, my little boy."

In the outside room, Presley came and went, doing what he could to be of service, sick with horror, trembling from head to foot.

The surviving members of both Leaguers and deputies—the warring factions of the Railroad and the People—mingled together now with no thought of hostility. Presley helped the doctor to cover Christian's body. S. Behrman and Ruggles held bowls of water while Osterman was attended to. The horror of that dreadful business had driven all other considerations from the mind. The sworn foes of the last hour had no thought of anything but to care for those whom, in their fury, they had shot down. The marshal, abandoning for that day the attempt to serve the writs, departed for San Francisco.

The bodies had been brought in from the road where they fell. Annixter's corpse had been laid upon the bed; those of Dabney and Hooven, whose wounds had all been in the face and head, were covered with a tablecloth. Upon the floor, places were made for the others. Cutter and Ruggles rode into Guadalajara to bring out the doctor there, and to telephone to Bonneville for others.

Osterman had not at any time since the shooting, lost consciousness. He lay upon the floor of Hooven's house, bare to the waist, bandages of adhesive tape reeved about his abdomen and shoulder. His eyes were half-closed. Presley, who looked after him, pending the arrival of a hack from Bonneville that was to take him home, knew that he was in agony.

But this poser, this silly fellow, this cracker of jokes, whom no one had ever taken very seriously, at the last redeemed himself. When at length, the doctor had arrived, he had, for the first time, opened his eyes.

"I can wait," he said. "Take Harran first." And when at length, his turn had come, and while the sweat rolled from his forehead as the doctor began probing for the bullet, he had reached out his free arm and taken Presley's hand in his, gripping it harder and harder, as the probe entered the wound. His breath came short through his nostrils; his face, the face of a comic actor, with its high cheek bones, bald forehead, and salient ears, grew paler and paler, his great slit of a mouth shut tight, but he uttered no groan.

When the worst anguish was over and he could find breath to speak, his first words had been:

"Were any of the others badly hurt?"

As Presley stood by the door of the house after bringing in a pail of water for the doctor, he was aware of a party of men who had struck off from the road on the other side of the irrigating ditch and were advancing cautiously into the field of wheat. He wondered what it meant and Cutter, coming up at that moment, Presley asked him if he knew.

"It's Delaney," said Cutter. "It seems that when he was shot he crawled off into the wheat. They are looking for him there."

Presley had forgotten all about the buster and had only a vague recollection of seeing him slide from his horse at the beginning of the fight. Anxious to know what had become of him, he hurried up and joined the party of searchers.

"We better look out," said one of the young men, "how we go fooling around in here. If he's alive yet he's just as liable as not to think we're after him and take a shot at us."

"I guess there ain't much fight left in him," another answered. "Look at the wheat here."

"Lord! He's bled like a stuck pig."

"Here's his hat," abruptly exclaimed the leader of the party. "He can't be far off. Let's call him."

They called repeatedly without getting any answer, then proceeded cautiously. All at once the men in advance stopped so suddenly that those following carromed against them. There was an outburst of exclamation.

"Here he is!"

"Good Lord! Sure, that's him."

"Poor fellow, poor fellow."

The cow-puncher lay on his back, deep in the wheat, his knees drawn up, his eyes wide open, his lips brown. Rigidly gripped in one hand was his empty revolver.

The men, farm hands from the neighbouring ranches, young fellows from Guadalajara, drew back in instinctive repulsion. One at length ventured near, peering down into the face.

"Is he dead?" inquired those in the rear.

"I don't know."

"Well, put your hand on his heart." "No! I—I don't want to."

"What you afraid of?"

"Well, I just don't want to touch him, that's all. It's bad luck. YOU feel his heart."

"You can't always tell by that."

"How can you tell, then? Pshaw, you fellows make me sick. Here, let me get there. I'll do it."

There was a long pause, as the other bent down and laid his hand on the cow-puncher's breast.

"Well?"

"I can't tell. Sometimes I think I feel it beat and sometimes I don't. I never saw a dead man before."

"Well, you can't tell by the heart."

"What's the good of talking so blame much. Dead or not, let's carry him back to the house."

Two or three ran back to the road for planks from the broken bridge. When they returned with these a litter was improvised, and throwing their coats over the body, the party carried it back to the road. The doctor was summoned and declared the cow-puncher to have been dead over half an hour.

"What did I tell you?" exclaimed one of the group.

"Well, I never said he wasn't dead," protested the other. "I only said you couldn't always tell by whether his heart beat or not."

But all at once there was a commotion. The wagon containing Mrs. Hooven, Minna, and little Hilda drove up.

"Eh, den, my men," cried Mrs. Hooven, wildly interrogating the faces of the crowd. "Whadt has happun? Sey, den, dose vellers, hev dey hurdt my men, eh, whadt?"

She sprang from the wagon, followed by Minna with Hilda in her arms. The crowd bore back as they advanced, staring at them in silence.

"Eh, whadt has happun, whadt has happun?" wailed Mrs. Hooven, as she hurried on, her two hands out before her, the fingers spread wide. "Eh, Hooven, eh, my men, are you alle righdt?"

She burst into the house. Hooven's body had been removed to an adjoining room, the bedroom of the house, and to this room Mrs. Hooven—Minna still at her heels—proceeded, guided by an instinct born of the occasion. Those in the outside room, saying no word, made way for them. They entered, closing the door behind them, and through all the rest of that terrible day, no sound nor sight of them was had by those who crowded into and about that house of death. Of all the main actors of the tragedy of the fight in the ditch, they remained the least noted, obtruded themselves the least upon the world's observation. They were, for the moment, forgotten.

But by now Hooven's house was the centre of an enormous crowd. A vast concourse of people from Bonneville, from Guadalajara, from the ranches, swelled by the thousands who had that morning participated in the rabbit drive, surged about the place; men and women, young boys, young girls, farm hands, villagers, townspeople, ranchers, railroad employees, Mexicans, Spaniards, Portuguese. Presley, returning from the search for Delaney's body, had to fight his way to the house again.

And from all this multitude there rose an indefinable murmur. As yet, there was no menace in it, no anger. It was confusion merely, bewilderment, the first long-drawn "oh!" that greets the news of some great tragedy. The people had taken no thought as yet. Curiosity was their dominant impulse. Every one wanted to see what had been done; failing that, to hear of it, and failing that, to be near the scene of the affair. The crowd of people packed the road in front of the house for nearly a quarter of a mile in either direction. They balanced themselves upon the lower strands of the barbed wire fence in their effort to see over each others' shoulders; they stood on the seats of their carts, buggies, and farm wagons, a few even upon the saddles of their riding horses. They crowded, pushed, struggled, surged forward and back without knowing why, converging incessantly upon Hooven's house.

When, at length, Presley got to the gate, he found a carry-all drawn up before it. Between the gate and the door of the house a lane had been formed, and as he paused there a moment, a group of Leaguers, among whom were Garnett and Gethings, came slowly from the door carrying old Broderson in their arms. The doctor, bareheaded and in his shirt sleeves, squinting in the sunlight, attended them, repeating at every step:

"Slow, slow, take it easy, gentlemen."

Old Broderson was unconscious. His face was not pale, no bandages could be seen. With infinite precautions, the men bore him to the carry-all and deposited him on the back seat; the rain flaps were let down on one side to shut off the gaze of the multitude.

But at this point a moment of confusion ensued. Presley, because of half a dozen people who stood in his way, could not see what was going on. There were exclamations, hurried movements. The doctor uttered a sharp command and a man ran back to the house returning on the instant with the doctor's satchel. By this time, Presley was close to the wheels of the carry-all and could see the doctor inside the vehicle bending over old Broderson.

"Here it is, here it is," exclaimed the man who had been sent to the house.

"I won't need it," answered the doctor, "he's dying now."

At the words a great hush widened throughout the throng near at hand. Some men took off their hats.

"Stand back," protested the doctor quietly, "stand back, good people, please."

The crowd bore back a little. In the silence, a woman began to sob. The seconds passed, then a minute. The horses of the carry-all shifted their feet and whisked their tails, driving off the flies. At length, the doctor got down from the carry-all, letting down the rain-flaps on that side as well.

"Will somebody go home with the body?" he asked. Gethings stepped forward and took his place by the driver. The carry-all drove away.

Presley reentered the house. During his absence it had been cleared of all but one or two of the Leaguers, who had taken part in the fight. Hilma still sat on the bed with Annixter's head in her lap. S. Behrman, Ruggles, and all the railroad party had gone. Osterman had been taken away in a hack and the tablecloth over Dabney's body replaced with a sheet. But still unabated, agonised, raucous, came the sounds of Harran's breathing. Everything possible had already been done. For the moment it was out of the question to attempt to move him. His mother and father were at his side, Magnus, with a face of stone, his look fixed on those persistently twitching eyes, Annie Derrick crouching at her son's side, one of his hands in hers, fanning his face continually with the crumpled sheet of an old newspaper.

Presley on tip-toes joined the group, looking on attentively. One of the surgeons who had been called from Bonneville stood close by, watching Harran's face, his arms folded.

"How is he?" Presley whispered.

"He won't live," the other responded.

By degrees the choke and gurgle of the breathing became more irregular and the lids closed over the twitching eyes. All at once the breath ceased. Magnus shot an inquiring glance at the surgeon.

"He is dead, Mr. Derrick," the surgeon replied.

Annie Derrick, with a cry that rang through all the house, stretched herself over the body of her son, her head upon his breast, and the Governor's great shoulders bowed never to rise again.

"God help me and forgive me," he groaned.

Presley rushed from the house, beside himself with grief, with horror, with pity, and with mad, insensate rage. On the porch outside Caraher met him.

"Is he—is he—" began the saloon-keeper.

"Yes, he's dead," cried Presley. "They're all dead, murdered, shot down, dead, dead, all of them. Whose turn is next?"

"That's the way they killed my wife, Presley."

"Caraher," cried Presley, "give me your hand. I've been wrong all the time. The League is wrong. All the world is wrong. You are the only one of us all who is right. I'm with you from now on. BY GOD, I TOO, I'M A RED!"

In course of time, a farm wagon from Bonneville arrived at Hooven's. The bodies of Annixter and Harran were placed in it, and it drove down the Lower Road towards the Los Muertos ranch houses.

The bodies of Delaney and Christian had already been carried to Guadalajara and thence taken by train to Bonneville.

Hilma followed the farm wagon in the Derricks' carry-all, with Magnus and his wife. During all that ride none of them spoke a word. It had been arranged that, since Quien Sabe was in the hands of the Railroad, Hilma should come to Los Muertos. To that place also Annixter's body was carried.

Later on in the day, when it was almost evening, the undertaker's black wagon passed the Derricks' Home ranch on its way from Hooven's and turned into the county road towards Bonneville. The initial excitement of the affair of the irrigating ditch had died down; the crowd long since had dispersed. By the time the wagon passed Caraher's saloon, the sun had set. Night was coming on.

And the black wagon went on through the darkness, unattended, ignored, solitary, carrying the dead body of Dabney, the silent old man of whom nothing was known but his name, who made no friends, whom nobody knew or spoke to, who had come from no one knew whence and who went no one knew whither.

Towards midnight of that same day, Mrs. Dyke was awakened by the sounds of groaning in the room next to hers. Magnus Derrick was not so occupied by Harran's death that he could not think of others who were in distress, and when he had heard that Mrs. Dyke and Sidney, like Hilma, had been turned out of Quien Sabe, he had thrown open Los Muertos to them.

"Though," he warned them, "it is precarious hospitality at the best."

Until late, Mrs. Dyke had sat up with Hilma, comforting her as best she could, rocking her to and fro in her arms, crying with her, trying to quiet her, for once having given way to her grief, Hilma wept with a terrible anguish and a violence that racked her from head to foot, and at last, worn out, a little child again, had sobbed herself to sleep in the older woman's arms, and as a little child, Mrs. Dyke had put her to bed and had retired herself.

Aroused a few hours later by the sounds of a distress that was physical, as well as mental, Mrs. Dyke hurried into Hilma's room, carrying the lamp with her. Mrs. Dyke needed no enlightenment. She woke Presley and besought him to telephone to Bonneville at once, summoning a doctor. That night Hilma in great pain suffered a miscarriage.

Presley did not close his eyes once during the night; he did not even remove his clothes. Long after the doctor had departed and that house of tragedy had quieted down, he still remained in his place by the open window of his little room, looking off across the leagues of growing wheat, watching the slow kindling of the dawn. Horror weighed intolerably upon him. Monstrous things, huge, terrible, whose names he knew only too well, whirled at a gallop through his imagination, or rose spectral and grisly before the eyes of his mind. Harran dead, Annixter dead, Broderson dead, Osterman, perhaps, even at that moment dying. Why, these men had made up his world. Annixter had been his best friend, Harran, his almost daily companion; Broderson and Osterman were familiar to him as brothers. They were all his associates, his good friends, the group was his environment, belonging to his daily life. And he, standing there in the dust of the road by the irrigating ditch, had seen them shot. He found himself suddenly at his table, the candle burning at his elbow, his journal before him, writing swiftly, the desire for expression, the craving for outlet to the thoughts that clamoured tumultuous at his brain, never more insistent, more imperious. Thus he wrote:

"Dabney dead, Hooven dead, Harran dead, Annixter dead, Broderson dead, Osterman dying, S. Behrman alive, successful; the Railroad in possession of Quien Sabe. I saw them shot. Not twelve hours since I stood there at the irrigating ditch. Ah, that terrible moment of horror and confusion! powder smoke—flashing pistol barrels—blood stains—rearing horses—men staggering to their death—Christian in a horrible posture, one rigid leg high in the air across his saddle—Broderson falling sideways into the ditch—Osterman laying himself down, his head on his arms, as if tired, tired out. These things, I have seen them. The picture of this day's work is from henceforth part of my mind, part of ME. They have done it, S. Behrman and the owners of the railroad have done it, while all the world looked on, while the people of these United States looked on. Oh, come now and try your theories upon us, us of the ranchos, us, who have suffered, us, who KNOW. Oh, talk to US now of the 'rights of Capital,' talk to US of the Trust, talk to US of the 'equilibrium between the classes.' Try your ingenious ideas upon us. WE KNOW. I cannot tell whether or not your theories are excellent. I do not know if your ideas are plausible. I do not know how practical is your scheme of society. I do not know if the Railroad has a right to our lands, but I DO know that Harran is dead, that Annixter is dead, that Broderson is dead, that Hooven is dead, that Osterman is dying, and that S. Behrman is alive, successful, triumphant; that he has ridden into possession of a principality over the dead bodies of five men shot down by his hired associates.

"I can see the outcome. The Railroad will prevail. The Trust will overpower us. Here in this corner of a great nation, here, on the edge of the continent, here, in this valley of the West, far from the great centres, isolated, remote, lost, the great iron hand crushes life from us, crushes liberty and the pursuit of happiness from us, and our little struggles, our moment's convulsion of death agony causes not one jar in the vast, clashing machinery of the nation's life; a fleck of grit in the wheels, perhaps, a grain of sand in the cogs—the momentary creak of the axle is the mother's wail of bereavement, the wife's cry of anguish—and the great wheel turns, spinning smooth again, even again, and the tiny impediment of a second, scarce noticed, is forgotten. Make the people believe that the faint tremour in their great engine is a menace to its function? What a folly to think of it. Tell them of the danger and they will laugh at you. Tell them, five years from now, the story of the fight between the League of the San Joaquin and the Railroad and it will not be believed. What! a pitched battle between Farmer and Railroad, a battle that cost the lives of seven men? Impossible, it could not have happened. Your story is fiction—is exaggerated.

"Yet it is Lexington—God help us, God enlighten us, God rouse us from our lethargy—it is Lexington; farmers with guns in their hands fighting for Liberty. Is our State of California the only one that has its ancient and hereditary foe? Are there no other Trusts between the oceans than this of the Pacific and Southwestern Railroad? Ask yourselves, you of the Middle West, ask yourselves, you of the North, ask yourselves, you of the East, ask yourselves, you of the South—ask yourselves, every citizen of every State from Maine to Mexico, from the Dakotas to the Carolinas, have you not the monster in your boundaries? If it is not a Trust of transportation, it is only another head of the same Hydra. Is not our death struggle typical? Is it not one of many, is it not symbolical of the great and terrible conflict that is going on everywhere in these United States? Ah, you people, blind, bound, tricked, betrayed, can you not see it? Can you not see how the monsters have plundered your treasures and holding them in the grip of their iron claws, dole them out to you only at the price of your blood, at the price of the lives of your wives and your little children? You give your babies to Moloch for the loaf of bread you have kneaded yourselves. You offer your starved wives to Juggernaut for the iron nail you have yourselves compounded."

He spent the night over his journal, writing down such thoughts as these or walking the floor from wall to wall, or, seized at times with unreasoning horror and blind rage, flinging himself face downward upon his bed, vowing with inarticulate cries that neither S. Behrman nor Shelgrim should ever live to consummate their triumph.

Morning came and with it the daily papers and news. Presley did not even glance at the "Mercury." Bonneville published two other daily journals that professed to voice the will and reflect the temper of the people and these he read eagerly.

Osterman was yet alive and there were chances of his recovery. The League—some three hundred of its members had gathered at Bonneville over night and were patrolling the streets and, still resolved to keep the peace, were even guarding the railroad shops and buildings. Furthermore, the Leaguers had issued manifestoes, urging all citizens to preserve law and order, yet summoning an indignation meeting to be convened that afternoon at the City Opera House.

It appeared from the newspapers that those who obstructed the marshal in the discharge of his duty could be proceeded against by the District Attorney on information or by bringing the matter before the Grand Jury. But the Grand Jury was not at that time in session, and it was known that there were no funds in the marshal's office to pay expenses for the summoning of jurors or the serving of processes. S. Behrman and Ruggles in interviews stated that the Railroad withdrew entirely from the fight; the matter now, according to them, was between the Leaguers and the United States Government; they washed their hands of the whole business. The ranchers could settle with Washington. But it seemed that Congress had recently forbade the use of troops for civil purposes; the whole matter of the League-Railroad contest was evidently for the moment to be left in status quo.

But to Presley's mind the most important piece of news that morning was the report of the action of the Railroad upon hearing of the battle.

Instantly Bonneville had been isolated. Not a single local train was running, not one of the through trains made any halt at the station. The mails were not moved. Further than this, by some arrangement difficult to understand, the telegraph operators at Bonneville and Guadalajara, acting under orders, refused to receive any telegrams except those emanating from railway officials. The story of the fight, the story creating the first impression, was to be told to San Francisco and the outside world by S. Behrman, Ruggles, and the local P. and S. W. agents.

An hour before breakfast, the undertakers arrived and took charge of the bodies of Harran and Annixter. Presley saw neither Hilma, Magnus, nor Mrs. Derrick. The doctor came to look after Hilma. He breakfasted with Mrs. Dyke and Presley, and from him Presley learned that Hilma would recover both from the shock of her husband's death and from her miscarriage of the previous night.

"She ought to have her mother with her," said the physician. "She does nothing but call for her or beg to be allowed to go to her. I have tried to get a wire through to Mrs. Tree, but the company will not take it, and even if I could get word to her, how could she get down here? There are no trains."

But Presley found that it was impossible for him to stay at Los Muertos that day. Gloom and the shadow of tragedy brooded heavy over the place. A great silence pervaded everything, a silence broken only by the subdued coming and going of the undertaker and his assistants. When Presley, having resolved to go into Bonneville, came out through the doorway of the house, he found the undertaker tying a long strip of crape to the bell-handle.

Presley saddled his pony and rode into town. By this time, after long hours of continued reflection upon one subject, a sombre brooding malevolence, a deep-seated desire of revenge, had grown big within his mind. The first numbness had passed off; familiarity with what had been done had blunted the edge of horror, and now the impulse of retaliation prevailed. At first, the sullen anger of defeat, the sense of outrage, had only smouldered, but the more he brooded, the fiercer flamed his rage. Sudden paroxysms of wrath gripped him by the throat; abrupt outbursts of fury injected his eyes with blood. He ground his teeth, his mouth filled with curses, his hands clenched till they grew white and bloodless. Was the Railroad to triumph then in the end? After all those months of preparation, after all those grandiloquent resolutions, after all the arrogant presumption of the League! The League! what a farce; what had it amounted to when the crisis came? Was the Trust to crush them all so easily? Was S. Behrman to swallow Los Muertos? S. Behrman! Presley saw him plainly, huge, rotund, white; saw his jowl tremulous and obese, the roll of fat over his collar sprinkled with sparse hairs, the great stomach with its brown linen vest and heavy watch chain of hollow links, clinking against the buttons of imitation pearl. And this man was to crush Magnus Derrick—had already stamped the life from such men as Harran and Annixter. This man, in the name of the Trust, was to grab Los Muertos as he had grabbed Quien Sabe, and after Los Muertos, Broderson's ranch, then Osterman's, then others, and still others, the whole valley, the whole State.

Presley beat his forehead with his clenched fist as he rode on.

"No," he cried, "no, kill him, kill him, kill him with my hands."

The idea of it put him beside himself. Oh, to sink his fingers deep into the white, fat throat of the man, to clutch like iron into the great puffed jowl of him, to wrench out the life, to batter it out, strangle it out, to pay him back for the long years of extortion and oppression, to square accounts for bribed jurors, bought judges, corrupted legislatures, to have justice for the trick of the Ranchers' Railroad Commission, the charlatanism of the "ten per cent. cut," the ruin of Dyke, the seizure of Quien Sabe, the murder of Harran, the assassination of Annixter!

It was in such mood that he reached Caraher's. The saloon-keeper had just opened his place and was standing in his doorway, smoking his pipe. Presley dismounted and went in and the two had a long talk.

When, three hours later, Presley came out of the saloon and rode on towards Bonneville, his face was very pale, his lips shut tight, resolute, determined. His manner was that of a man whose mind is made up. The hour for the mass meeting at the Opera House had been set for one o'clock, but long before noon the street in front of the building and, in fact, all the streets in its vicinity, were packed from side to side with a shifting, struggling, surging, and excited multitude. There were few women in the throng, but hardly a single male inhabitant of either Bonneville or Guadalajara was absent. Men had even come from Visalia and Pixley. It was no longer the crowd of curiosity seekers that had thronged around Hooven's place by the irrigating ditch; the People were no longer confused, bewildered. A full realisation of just what had been done the day before was clear now in the minds of all. Business was suspended; nearly all the stores were closed. Since early morning the members of the League had put in an appearance and rode from point to point, their rifles across their saddle pommels. Then, by ten o'clock, the streets had begun to fill up, the groups on the corners grew and merged into one another; pedestrians, unable to find room on the sidewalks, took to the streets. Hourly the crowd increased till shoulders touched and elbows, till free circulation became impeded, then congested, then impossible. The crowd, a solid mass, was wedged tight from store front to store front. And from all this throng, this single unit, this living, breathing organism—the People—there rose a droning, terrible note. It was not yet the wild, fierce clamour of riot and insurrection, shrill, high pitched; but it was a beginning, the growl of the awakened brute, feeling the iron in its flank, heaving up its head with bared teeth, the throat vibrating to the long, indrawn snarl of wrath.

Thus the forenoon passed, while the people, their bulk growing hourly vaster, kept to the streets, moving slowly backward and forward, oscillating in the grooves of the thoroughfares, the steady, low-pitched growl rising continually into the hot, still air.

Then, at length, about twelve o'clock, the movement of the throng assumed definite direction. It set towards the Opera House. Presley, who had left his pony at the City livery stable, found himself caught in the current and carried slowly forward in its direction. His arms were pinioned to his sides by the press, the crush against his body was all but rib-cracking, he could hardly draw his breath. All around him rose and fell wave after wave of faces, hundreds upon hundreds, thousands upon thousands, red, lowering, sullen. All were set in one direction and slowly, slowly they advanced, crowding closer, till they almost touched one another. For reasons that were inexplicable, great, tumultuous heavings, like ground-swells of an incoming tide, surged over and through the multitude. At times, Presley, lifted from his feet, was swept back, back, back, with the crowd, till the entrance of the Opera House was half a block away; then, the returning billow beat back again and swung him along, gasping, staggering, clutching, till he was landed once more in the vortex of frantic action in front of the foyer. Here the waves were shorter, quicker, the crushing pressure on all sides of his body left him without strength to utter the cry that rose to his lips; then, suddenly the whole mass of struggling, stamping, fighting, writhing men about him seemed, as it were, to rise, to lift, multitudinous, swelling, gigantic. A mighty rush dashed Presley forward in its leap. There was a moment's whirl of confused sights, congested faces, opened mouths, bloodshot eyes, clutching hands; a moment's outburst of furious sound, shouts, cheers, oaths; a moment's jam wherein Presley veritably believed his ribs must snap like pipestems and he was carried, dazed, breathless, helpless, an atom on the crest of a storm-driven wave, up the steps of the Opera House, on into the vestibule, through the doors, and at last into the auditorium of the house itself.

There was a mad rush for places; men disdaining the aisle, stepped from one orchestra chair to another, striding over the backs of seats, leaving the print of dusty feet upon the red plush cushions. In a twinkling the house was filled from stage to topmost gallery. The aisles were packed solid, even on the edge of the stage itself men were sitting, a black fringe on either side of the footlights.

The curtain was up, disclosing a half-set scene,—the flats, leaning at perilous angles,—that represented some sort of terrace, the pavement, alternate squares of black and white marble, while red, white, and yellow flowers were represented as growing from urns and vases. A long, double row of chairs stretched across the scene from wing to wing, flanking a table covered with a red cloth, on which was set a pitcher of water and a speaker's gavel.

Promptly these chairs were filled up with members of the League, the audience cheering as certain well-known figures made their appearance—Garnett of the Ruby ranch, Gethings of the San Pablo, Keast of the ranch of the same name, Chattern of the Bonanza, elderly men, bearded, slow of speech, deliberate.

Garnett opened the meeting; his speech was plain, straightforward, matter-of-fact. He simply told what had happened. He announced that certain resolutions were to be drawn up. He introduced the next speaker.

This one pleaded for moderation. He was conservative. All along he had opposed the idea of armed resistance except as the very last resort. He "deplored" the terrible affair of yesterday. He begged the people to wait in patience, to attempt no more violence. He informed them that armed guards of the League were, at that moment, patrolling Los Muertos, Broderson's, and Osterman's. It was well known that the United States marshal confessed himself powerless to serve the writs. There would be no more bloodshed.

"We have had," he continued, "bloodshed enough, and I want to say right here that I am not so sure but what yesterday's terrible affair might have been avoided. A gentleman whom we all esteem, who from the first has been our recognised leader, is, at this moment, mourning the loss of a young son, killed before his eyes. God knows that I sympathise, as do we all, in the affliction of our President. I am sorry for him. My heart goes out to him in this hour of distress, but, at the same time, the position of the League must be defined. We owe it to ourselves, we owe it to the people of this county. The League armed for the very purpose of preserving the peace, not of breaking it. We believed that with six hundred armed and drilled men at our disposal, ready to muster at a moment's call, we could so overawe any attempt to expel us from our lands that such an attempt would not be made until the cases pending before the Supreme Court had been decided. If when the enemy appeared in our midst yesterday they had been met by six hundred rifles, it is not conceivable that the issue would have been forced. No fight would have ensued, and to-day we would not have to mourn the deaths of four of our fellow-citizens. A mistake has been made and we of the League must not be held responsible."

The speaker sat down amidst loud applause from the Leaguers and less pronounced demonstrations on the part of the audience.

A second Leaguer took his place, a tall, clumsy man, half-rancher, half-politician.

"I want to second what my colleague has just said," he began. "This matter of resisting the marshal when he tried to put the Railroad dummies in possession on the ranches around here, was all talked over in the committee meetings of the League long ago. It never was our intention to fire a single shot. No such absolute authority as was assumed yesterday was delegated to anybody. Our esteemed President is all right, but we all know that he is a man who loves authority and who likes to go his own gait without accounting to anybody. We—the rest of us Leaguers—never were informed as to what was going on. We supposed, of course, that watch was being kept on the Railroad so as we wouldn't be taken by surprise as we were yesterday. And it seems no watch was kept at all, or if there was, it was mighty ineffective. Our idea was to forestall any movement on the part of the Railroad and then when we knew the marshal was coming down, to call a meeting of our Executive Committee and decide as to what should be done. We ought to have had time to call out the whole League. Instead of that, what happens? While we're all off chasing rabbits, the Railroad is allowed to steal a march on us and when it is too late, a handful of Leaguers is got together and a fight is precipitated and our men killed. I'M sorry for our President, too. No one is more so, but I want to put myself on record as believing he did a hasty and inconsiderate thing. If he had managed right, he could have had six hundred men to oppose the Railroad and there would not have been any gun fight or any killing. He DIDN'T manage right and there WAS a killing and I don't see as how the League ought to be held responsible. The idea of the League, the whole reason why it was organised, was to protect ALL the ranches of this valley from the Railroad, and it looks to me as if the lives of our fellow-citizens had been sacrificed, not in defending ALL of our ranches, but just in defence of one of them—Los Muertos—the one that Mr. Derrick owns."

The speaker had no more than regained his seat when a man was seen pushing his way from the back of the stage towards Garnett. He handed the rancher a note, at the same time whispering in his ear. Garnett read the note, then came forward to the edge of the stage, holding up his hand. When the audience had fallen silent he said:

"I have just received sad news. Our friend and fellow-citizen, Mr. Osterman, died this morning between eleven and twelve o'clock."

Instantly there was a roar. Every man in the building rose to his feet, shouting, gesticulating. The roar increased, the Opera House trembled to it, the gas jets in the lighted chandeliers vibrated to it. It was a raucous howl of execration, a bellow of rage, inarticulate, deafening.

A tornado of confusion swept whirling from wall to wall and the madness of the moment seized irresistibly upon Presley. He forgot himself; he no longer was master of his emotions or his impulses. All at once he found himself upon the stage, facing the audience, flaming with excitement, his imagination on fire, his arms uplifted in fierce, wild gestures, words leaping to his mind in a torrent that could not be withheld.

"One more dead," he cried, "one more. Harran dead, Annixter dead, Broderson dead, Dabney dead, Osterman dead, Hooven dead; shot down, killed, killed in the defence of their homes, killed in the defence of their rights, killed for the sake of liberty. How long must it go on? How long must we suffer? Where is the end; what is the end? How long must the iron-hearted monster feed on our life's blood? How long must this terror of steam and steel ride upon our necks? Will you never be satisfied, will you never relent, you, our masters, you, our lords, you, our kings, you, our task-masters, you, our Pharoahs. Will you never listen to that command 'LET MY PEOPLE GO'? Oh, that cry ringing down the ages. Hear it, hear it. It is the voice of the Lord God speaking in his prophets. Hear it, hear it—'Let My people go!' Rameses heard it in his pylons at Thebes, Caesar heard it on the Palatine, the Bourbon Louis heard it at Versailles, Charles Stuart heard it at Whitehall, the white Czar heard it in the Kremlin,—'LET MY PEOPLE GO.'

It is the cry of the nations, the great voice of the centuries; everywhere it is raised. The voice of God is the voice of the People. The people cry out 'Let us, the People, God's people, go.' You, our masters, you, our kings, you, our tyrants, don't you hear us? Don't you hear God speaking in us? Will you never let us go? How long at length will you abuse our patience? How long will you drive us? How long will you harass us? Will nothing daunt you? Does nothing check you? Do you not know that to ignore our cry too long is to wake the Red Terror? Rameses refused to listen to it and perished miserably. Caesar refused to listen and was stabbed in the Senate House. The Bourbon Louis refused to listen and died on the guillotine; Charles Stuart refused to listen and died on the block; the white Czar refused to listen and was blown up in his own capital. Will you let it come to that? Will you drive us to it? We who boast of our land of freedom, we who live in the country of liberty? Go on as you have begun and it WILL come to that. Turn a deaf ear to that cry of 'Let My people go' too long and another cry will be raised, that you cannot choose but hear, a cry that you cannot shut out. It will be the cry of the man on the street, the 'a la Bastille' that wakes the Red Terror and unleashes Revolution. Harassed, plundered, exasperated, desperate, the people will turn at last as they have turned so many, many times before. You, our lords, you, our task-masters, you, our kings; you have caught your Samson, you have made his strength your own. You have shorn his head; you have put out his eyes; you have set him to turn your millstones, to grind the grist for your mills; you have made him a shame and a mock. Take care, oh, as you love your lives, take care, lest some day calling upon the Lord his God he reach not out his arms for the pillars of your temples."

The audience, at first bewildered, confused by this unexpected invective, suddenly took fire at his last words. There was a roar of applause; then, more significant than mere vociferation, Presley's listeners, as he began to speak again, grew suddenly silent. His next sentences were uttered in the midst of a profound stillness.

"They own us, these task-masters of ours; they own our homes, they own our legislatures. We cannot escape from them. There is no redress. We are told we can defeat them by the ballot-box. They own the ballot-box. We are told that we must look to the courts for redress; they own the courts. We know them for what they are,—ruffians in politics, ruffians in finance, ruffians in law, ruffians in trade, bribers, swindlers, and tricksters. No outrage too great to daunt them, no petty larceny too small to shame them; despoiling a government treasury of a million dollars, yet picking the pockets of a farm hand of the price of a loaf of bread.

"They swindle a nation of a hundred million and call it Financiering; they levy a blackmail and call it Commerce; they corrupt a legislature and call it Politics; they bribe a judge and call it Law; they hire blacklegs to carry out their plans and call it Organisation; they prostitute the honour of a State and call it Competition.

"And this is America. We fought Lexington to free ourselves; we fought Gettysburg to free others. Yet the yoke remains; we have only shifted it to the other shoulder. We talk of liberty—oh, the farce of it, oh, the folly of it! We tell ourselves and teach our children that we have achieved liberty, that we no longer need fight for it. Why, the fight is just beginning and so long as our conception of liberty remains as it is to-day, it will continue.

"For we conceive of Liberty in the statues we raise to her as a beautiful woman, crowned, victorious, in bright armour and white robes, a light in her uplifted hand—a serene, calm, conquering goddess. Oh, the farce of it, oh, the folly of it! Liberty is NOT a crowned goddess, beautiful, in spotless garments, victorious, supreme. Liberty is the Man In the Street, a terrible figure, rushing through powder smoke, fouled with the mud and ordure of the gutter, bloody, rampant, brutal, yelling curses, in one hand a smoking rifle, in the other, a blazing torch.

"Freedom is NOT given free to any who ask; Liberty is not born of the gods. She is a child of the People, born in the very height and heat of battle, born from death, stained with blood, grimed with powder. And she grows to be not a goddess, but a Fury, a fearful figure, slaying friend and foe alike, raging, insatiable, merciless, the Red Terror."

Presley ceased speaking. Weak, shaking, scarcely knowing what he was about, he descended from the stage. A prolonged explosion of applause followed, the Opera House roaring to the roof, men cheering, stamping, waving their hats. But it was not intelligent applause. Instinctively as he made his way out, Presley knew that, after all, he had not once held the hearts of his audience. He had talked as he would have written; for all his scorn of literature, he had been literary. The men who listened to him, ranchers, country people, store-keepers, attentive though they were, were not once sympathetic. Vaguely they had felt that here was something which other men—more educated—would possibly consider eloquent. They applauded vociferously but perfunctorily, in order to appear to understand.

Presley, for all his love of the people, saw clearly for one moment that he was an outsider to their minds. He had not helped them nor their cause in the least; he never would.

Disappointed, bewildered, ashamed, he made his way slowly from the Opera House and stood on the steps outside, thoughtful, his head bent.

He had failed, thus he told himself. In that moment of crisis, that at the time he believed had been an inspiration, he had failed. The people would not consider him, would not believe that he could do them service. Then suddenly he seemed to remember. The resolute set of his lips returned once more. Pushing his way through the crowded streets, he went on towards the stable where he had left his pony.

Meanwhile, in the Opera House, a great commotion had occurred. Magnus Derrick had appeared.

Only a sense of enormous responsibility, of gravest duty could have prevailed upon Magnus to have left his house and the dead body of his son that day. But he was the President of the League, and never since its organisation had a meeting of such importance as this one been held. He had been in command at the irrigating ditch the day before. It was he who had gathered the handful of Leaguers together. It was he who must bear the responsibility of the fight.

When he had entered the Opera House, making his way down the central aisle towards the stage, a loud disturbance had broken out, partly applause, partly a meaningless uproar. Many had pressed forward to shake his hand, but others were not found wanting who, formerly his staunch supporters, now scenting opposition in the air, held back, hesitating, afraid to compromise themselves by adhering to the fortunes of a man whose actions might be discredited by the very organisation of which he was the head.

Declining to take the chair of presiding officer which Garnett offered him, the Governor withdrew to an angle of the stage, where he was joined by Keast.

This one, still unalterably devoted to Magnus, acquainted him briefly with the tenor of the speeches that had been made.

"I am ashamed of them, Governor," he protested indignantly, "to lose their nerve now! To fail you now! it makes my blood boil. If you had succeeded yesterday, if all had gone well, do you think we would have heard of any talk of 'assumption of authority,' or 'acting without advice and consent'? As if there was any time to call a meeting of the Executive Committee. If you hadn't acted as you did, the whole county would have been grabbed by the Railroad. Get up, Governor, and bring 'em all up standing. Just tear 'em all to pieces, show 'em that you are the head, the boss. That's what they need. That killing yesterday has shaken the nerve clean out of them."

For the instant the Governor was taken all aback. What, his lieutenants were failing him? What, he was to be questioned, interpolated upon yesterday's "irrepressible conflict"? Had disaffection appeared in the ranks of the League—at this, of all moments? He put from him his terrible grief. The cause was in danger. At the instant he was the President of the League only, the chief, the master. A royal anger surged within him, a wide, towering scorn of opposition. He would crush this disaffection in its incipiency, would vindicate himself and strengthen the cause at one and the same time. He stepped forward and stood in the speaker's place, turning partly toward the audience, partly toward the assembled Leaguers.

"Gentlemen of the League," he began, "citizens of Bonneville"

But at once the silence in which the Governor had begun to speak was broken by a shout. It was as though his words had furnished a signal. In a certain quarter of the gallery, directly opposite, a man arose, and in a voice partly of derision, partly of defiance, cried out:

"How about the bribery of those two delegates at Sacramento? Tell us about that. That's what we want to hear about."

A great confusion broke out. The first cry was repeated not only by the original speaker, but by a whole group of which he was but a part. Others in the audience, however, seeing in the disturbance only the clamour of a few Railroad supporters, attempted to howl them down, hissing vigorously and exclaiming:

"Put 'em out, put 'em out."

"Order, order," called Garnett, pounding with his gavel. The whole Opera House was in an uproar.

But the interruption of the Governor's speech was evidently not unpremeditated. It began to look like a deliberate and planned attack. Persistently, doggedly, the group in the gallery vociferated: "Tell us how you bribed the delegates at Sacramento. Before you throw mud at the Railroad, let's see if you are clean yourself."

"Put 'em out, put 'em out."

"Briber, briber—Magnus Derrick, unconvicted briber! Put him out."

Keast, beside himself with anger, pushed down the aisle underneath where the recalcitrant group had its place and, shaking his fist, called up at them:

"You were paid to break up this meeting. If you have anything to say; you will be afforded the opportunity, but if you do not let the gentleman proceed, the police will be called upon to put you out."

But at this, the man who had raised the first shout leaned over the balcony rail, and, his face flaming with wrath, shouted:

"YAH! talk to me of your police. Look out we don't call on them first to arrest your President for bribery. You and your howl about law and justice and corruption! Here"—he turned to the audience—"read about him, read the story of how the Sacramento convention was bought by Magnus Derrick, President of the San Joaquin League. Here's the facts printed and proved."

With the words, he stooped down and from under his seat dragged forth a great package of extra editions of the "Bonneville Mercury," not an hour off the presses. Other equally large bundles of the paper appeared in the hands of the surrounding group. The strings were cut and in handfuls and armfuls the papers were flung out over the heads of the audience underneath. The air was full of the flutter of the newly printed sheets. They swarmed over the rim of the gallery like clouds of monstrous, winged insects, settled upon the heads and into the hands of the audience, were passed swiftly from man to man, and within five minutes of the first outbreak every one in the Opera House had read Genslinger's detailed and substantiated account of Magnus Derrick's "deal" with the political bosses of the Sacramento convention.

Genslinger, after pocketing the Governor's hush money, had "sold him out."⌐

Keast, one quiver of indignation, made his way back upon the stage. The Leaguers were in wild confusion. Half the assembly of them were on their feet, bewildered, shouting vaguely. From proscenium wall to foyer, the Opera House was a tumult of noise. The gleam of the thousands of the "Mercury" extras was like the flash of white caps on a troubled sea.

Keast faced the audience.

"Liars," he shouted, striving with all the power of his voice to dominate the clamour, "liars and slanderers. Your paper is the paid organ of the corporation. You have not one shadow of proof to back you up. Do you choose this, of all times, to heap your calumny upon the head of an honourable gentleman, already prostrated by your murder of his son? Proofs—we demand your proofs!"

"We've got the very assemblymen themselves," came back the answering shout. "Let Derrick speak. Where is he hiding? If this is a lie, let him deny it. Let HIM DISPROVE the charge." "Derrick, Derrick," thundered the Opera House.

Keast wheeled about. Where was Magnus? He was not in sight upon the stage. He had disappeared. Crowding through the throng of Leaguers, Keast got from off the stage into the wings. Here the crowd was no less dense. Nearly every one had a copy of the "Mercury." It was being read aloud to groups here and there, and once Keast overheard the words, "Say, I wonder if this is true, after all?"

"Well, and even if it was," cried Keast, turning upon the speaker, "we should be the last ones to kick. In any case, it was done for our benefit. It elected the Ranchers' Commission."

"A lot of benefit we got out of the Ranchers' Commission," retorted the other.

"And then," protested a third speaker, "that ain't the way to do—if he DID do it—bribing legislatures. Why, we were bucking against corrupt politics. We couldn't afford to be corrupt."

Keast turned away with a gesture of impatience. He pushed his way farther on. At last, opening a small door in a hallway back of the stage, he came upon Magnus.

The room was tiny. It was a dressing-room. Only two nights before it had been used by the leading actress of a comic opera troupe which had played for three nights at Bonneville. A tattered sofa and limping toilet table occupied a third of the space. The air was heavy with the smell of stale grease paint, ointments, and sachet. Faded photographs of young women in tights and gauzes ornamented the mirror and the walls. Underneath the sofa was an old pair of corsets. The spangled skirt of a pink dress, turned inside out, hung against the wall.

And in the midst of such environment, surrounded by an excited group of men who gesticulated and shouted in his very face, pale, alert, agitated, his thin lips pressed tightly together, stood Magnus Derrick.

"Here," cried Keast, as he entered, closing the door behind him, "where's the Governor? Here, Magnus, I've been looking for you. The crowd has gone wild out there. You've got to talk 'em down. Come out there and give those blacklegs the lie. They are saying you are hiding."

But before Magnus could reply, Garnett turned to Keast.

"Well, that's what we want him to do, and he won't do it."

"Yes, yes," cried the half-dozen men who crowded around Magnus, "yes, that's what we want him to do."

Keast turned to Magnus.

"Why, what's all this, Governor?" he exclaimed. "You've got to answer that. Hey? why don't you give 'em the lie?"

"I—I," Magnus loosened the collar about his throat "it is a lie. I will not stoop—I would not—would be—it would be beneath my—my—it would be beneath me."

Keast stared in amazement. Was this the Great Man the Leader, indomitable, of Roman integrity, of Roman valour, before whose voice whole conventions had quailed? Was it possible he was AFRAID to face those hired villifiers?

"Well, how about this?" demanded Garnett suddenly. "It is a lie, isn't it? That Commission was elected honestly, wasn't it?"

"How dare you, sir!" Magnus burst out. "How dare you question me—call me to account! Please understand, sir, that I tolerate——"

"Oh, quit it!" cried a voice from the group. "You can't scare us, Derrick. That sort of talk was well enough once, but it don't go any more. We want a yes or no answer."

It was gone—that old-time power of mastery, that faculty of command. The ground crumbled beneath his feet. Long since it had been, by his own hand, undermined. Authority was gone. Why keep up this miserable sham any longer? Could they not read the lie in his face, in his voice? What a folly to maintain the wretched pretence! He had failed. He was ruined. Harran was gone. His ranch would soon go; his money was gone. Lyman was worse than dead. His own honour had been prostituted. Gone, gone, everything he held dear, gone, lost, and swept away in that fierce struggle. And suddenly and all in a moment the last remaining shells of the fabric of his being, the sham that had stood already wonderfully long, cracked and collapsed.

"Was the Commission honestly elected?" insisted Garnett. "Were the delegates—did you bribe the delegates?"

"We were obliged to shut our eyes to means," faltered Magnus. "There was no other way to—" Then suddenly and with the last dregs of his resolution, he concluded with: "Yes, I gave them two thousand dollars each."

"Oh, hell! Oh, my God!" exclaimed Keast, sitting swiftly down upon the ragged sofa.

There was a long silence. A sense of poignant embarrassment descended upon those present. No one knew what to say or where to look. Garnett, with a laboured attempt at nonchalance, murmured:

"I see. Well, that's what I was trying to get at. Yes, I see."

"Well," said Gethings at length, bestirring himself, "I guess I'LL go home."

There was a movement. The group broke up, the men making for the door. One by one they went out. The last to go was Keast. He came up to Magnus and shook the Governor's limp hand.

"Good-bye, Governor," he said. "I'll see you again pretty soon. Don't let this discourage you. They'll come around all right after a while. So long."

He went out, shutting the door.

And seated in the one chair of the room, Magnus Derrick remained a long time, looking at his face in the cracked mirror that for so many years had reflected the painted faces of soubrettes, in this atmosphere of stale perfume and mouldy rice powder.

It had come—his fall, his ruin. After so many years of integrity and honest battle, his life had ended here—in an actress's dressing-room, deserted by his friends, his son murdered, his dishonesty known, an old man, broken, discarded, discredited, and abandoned. Before nightfall of that day, Bonneville was further excited by an astonishing bit of news. S. Behrman lived in a detached house at some distance from the town, surrounded by a grove of live oak and eucalyptus trees. At a little after half-past six, as he was sitting down to his supper, a bomb was thrown through the window of his dining-room, exploding near the doorway leading into the hall. The room was wrecked and nearly every window of the house shattered. By a miracle, S. Behrman, himself, remained untouched.

CHAPTER VIII

On a certain afternoon in the early part of July, about a month after the fight at the irrigating ditch and the mass meeting at Bonneville, Cedarquist, at the moment opening his mail in his office in San Francisco, was genuinely surprised to receive a visit from Presley.

"Well, upon my word, Pres," exclaimed the manufacturer, as the young man came in through the door that the office boy held open for him, "upon my word, have you been sick? Sit down, my boy. Have a glass of sherry. I always keep a bottle here."

Presley accepted the wine and sank into the depths of a great leather chair near by.

"Sick?" he answered. "Yes, I have been sick. I'm sick now. I'm gone to pieces, sir."

His manner was the extreme of listlessness—the listlessness of great fatigue. "Well, well," observed the other. "I'm right sorry to hear that. What's the trouble, Pres?"

"Oh, nerves mostly, I suppose, and my head, and insomnia, and weakness, a general collapse all along the line, the doctor tells me. 'Over-cerebration,' he says; 'over-excitement.' I fancy I rather narrowly missed brain fever."

"Well, I can easily suppose it," answered Cedarquist gravely, "after all you have been through."

Presley closed his eyes—they were sunken in circles of dark brown flesh—and pressed a thin hand to the back of his head.

"It is a nightmare," he murmured. "A frightful nightmare, and it's not over yet. You have heard of it all only through the newspaper reports. But down there, at Bonneville, at Los Muertos—oh, you can have no idea of it, of the misery caused by the defeat of the ranchers and by this decision of the Supreme Court that dispossesses them all. We had gone on hoping to the last that we would win there. We had thought that in the Supreme Court of the United States, at least, we could find justice. And the news of its decision was the worst, last blow of all. For Magnus it was the last—positively the very last."

"Poor, poor Derrick," murmured Cedarquist. "Tell me about him, Pres. How does he take it? What is he going to do?"

"It beggars him, sir. He sunk a great deal more than any of us believed in his ranch, when he resolved to turn off most of the tenants and farm the ranch himself. Then the fight he made against the Railroad in the Courts and the political campaign he went into, to get Lyman on the Railroad Commission, took more of it. The money that Genslinger blackmailed him of, it seems, was about all he had left. He had been gambling—you know the Governor—on another bonanza crop this year to recoup him. Well, the bonanza came right enough—just in time for S. Behrman and the Railroad to grab it. Magnus is ruined."

"What a tragedy! what a tragedy!" murmured the other. "Lyman turning rascal, Harran killed, and now this; and all within so short a time—all at the SAME time, you might almost say."

"If it had only killed him," continued Presley; "but that is the worst of it."

"How the worst?"

"I'm afraid, honestly, I'm afraid it is going to turn his wits, sir. It's broken him; oh, you should see him, you should see him. A shambling, stooping, trembling old man, in his dotage already. He sits all day in the dining-room, turning over papers, sorting them, tying them up, opening them again, forgetting them—all fumbling and mumbling and confused. And at table sometimes he forgets to eat. And, listen, you know, from the house we can hear the trains whistling for the Long Trestle. As often as that happens the Governor seems to be—oh, I don't know, frightened. He will sink his head between his shoulders, as though he were dodging something, and he won't fetch a long breath again till the train is out of hearing. He seems to have conceived an abject, unreasoned terror of the Railroad."

"But he will have to leave Los Muertos now, of course?"

"Yes, they will all have to leave. They have a fortnight more. The few tenants that were still on Los Muertos are leaving. That is one thing that brings me to the city. The family of one of the men who was killed—Hooven was his name—have come to the city to find work. I think they are liable to be in great distress, unless they have been wonderfully lucky, and I am trying to find them in order to look after them."

"You need looking after yourself, Pres."

"Oh, once away from Bonneville and the sight of the ruin there, I'm better. But I intend to go away. And that makes me think, I came to ask you if you could help me. If you would let me take passage on one of your wheat ships. The Doctor says an ocean voyage would set me up."

"Why, certainly, Pres," declared Cedarquist. "But I'm sorry you'll have to go. We expected to have you down in the country with us this winter."

Presley shook his head. "No," he answered. "I must go. Even if I had all my health, I could not bring myself to stay in California just now. If you can introduce me to one of your captains—"

"With pleasure. When do you want to go? You may have to wait a few weeks. Our first ship won't clear till the end of the month."

"That would do very well. Thank you, sir."

But Cedarquist was still interested in the land troubles of the Bonneville farmers, and took the first occasion to ask:

"So, the Railroad are in possession on most of the ranches?" "On all of them," returned Presley. "The League went all to pieces, so soon as Magnus was forced to resign. The old story—they got quarrelling among themselves. Somebody started a compromise party, and upon that issue a new president was elected. Then there were defections. The Railroad offered to lease the lands in question to the ranchers—the ranchers who owned them," he exclaimed bitterly, "and because the terms were nominal—almost nothing—plenty of the men took the chance of saving themselves. And, of course, once signing the lease, they acknowledged the Railroad's title. But the road would not lease to Magnus. S. Behrman takes over Los Muertos in a few weeks now."

"No doubt, the road made over their title in the property to him," observed Cedarquist, "as a reward of his services."

"No doubt," murmured Presley wearily. He rose to go.

"By the way," said Cedarquist, "what have you on hand for, let us say, Friday evening? Won't you dine with us then? The girls are going to the country Monday of next week, and you probably won't see them again for some time if you take that ocean voyage of yours."

"I'm afraid I shall be very poor company, sir," hazarded Presley. "There's no 'go,' no life in me at all these days. I am like a clock with a broken spring."

"Not broken, Pres, my boy;" urged the other, "only run down. Try and see if we can't wind you up a bit. Say that we can expect you. We dine at seven."

"Thank you, sir. Till Friday at seven, then."

Regaining the street, Presley sent his valise to his club (where he had engaged a room) by a messenger boy, and boarded a Castro Street car. Before leaving Bonneville, he had ascertained, by strenuous enquiry, Mrs. Hooven's address in the city, and thitherward he now directed his steps.

When Presley had told Cedarquist that he was ill, that he was jaded, worn out, he had only told half the truth. Exhausted he was, nerveless, weak, but this apathy was still invaded from time to time with fierce incursions of a spirit of unrest and revolt, reactions, momentary returns of the blind, undirected energy that at one time had prompted him to a vast desire to acquit himself of some terrible deed of readjustment, just what, he could not say, some terrifying martyrdom, some awe-inspiring immolation, consummate, incisive, conclusive. He fancied himself to be fired with the purblind, mistaken heroism of the anarchist, hurling his victim to destruction with full knowledge that the catastrophe shall sweep him also into the vortex it creates.

But his constitutional irresoluteness obstructed his path continually; brain-sick, weak of will, emotional, timid even, he temporised, procrastinated, brooded; came to decisions in the dark hours of the night, only to abandon them in the morning.

Once only he had ACTED. And at this moment, as he was carried through the windy, squalid streets, he trembled at the remembrance of it. The horror of "what might have been" incompatible with the vengeance whose minister he fancied he was, oppressed him. The scene perpetually reconstructed itself in his imagination. He saw himself under the shade of the encompassing trees and shrubbery, creeping on his belly toward the house, in the suburbs of Bonneville, watching his chances, seizing opportunities, spying upon the lighted windows where the raised curtains afforded a view of the interior. Then had come the appearance in the glare of the gas of the figure of the man for whom he waited. He saw himself rise and run forward. He remembered the feel and weight in his hand of Caraher's bomb—the six inches of plugged gas pipe. His uraised arm shot forward. There was a shiver of smashed window-panes, then—a void—a red whirl of confusion, the air rent, the ground rocking, himself flung headlong, flung off the spinning circumference of things out into a place of terror and vacancy and darkness. And then after a long time the return of reason, the consciousness that his feet were set upon the road to Los Muertos, and that he was fleeing terror-stricken, gasping, all but insane with hysteria. Then the never-to-be-forgotten night that ensued, when he descended into the pit, horrified at what he supposed he had done, at one moment ridden with remorse, at another raging against his own feebleness, his lack of courage, his wretched, vacillating spirit. But morning had come, and with it the knowledge that he had failed, and the baser assurance that he was not even remotely suspected. His own escape had been no less miraculous than that of his enemy, and he had fallen on his knees in inarticulate prayer, weeping, pouring out his thanks to God for the deliverance from the gulf to the very brink of which his feet had been drawn.

After this, however, there had come to Presley a deep-rooted suspicion that he was—of all human beings, the most wretched—a failure. Everything to which he had set his mind failed—his great epic, his efforts to help the people who surrounded him, even his attempted destruction of the enemy, all these had come to nothing. Girding his shattered strength together, he resolved upon one last attempt to live up to the best that was in him, and to that end had set himself to lift out of the despair into which they had been thrust, the bereaved family of the German, Hooven.

After all was over, and Hooven, together with the seven others who had fallen at the irrigating ditch, was buried in the Bonneville cemetery, Mrs. Hooven, asking no one's aid or advice, and taking with her Minna and little Hilda, had gone to San Francisco—had gone to find work, abandoning Los Muertos and her home forever. Presley only learned of the departure of the family after fifteen days had elapsed.

At once, however, the suspicion forced itself upon him that Mrs. Hooven—and Minna, too for the matter of that—country-bred, ignorant of city ways, might easily come to grief in the hard, huge struggle of city life. This suspicion had swiftly hardened to a conviction, acting at last upon which Presley had followed them to San Francisco, bent upon finding and assisting them.

The house to which Presley was led by the address in his memorandum book was a cheap but fairly decent hotel near the power house of the Castro Street cable. He inquired for Mrs. Hooven.

The landlady recollected the Hoovens perfectly.

"German woman, with a little girl-baby, and an older daughter, sure. The older daughter was main pretty. Sure I remember them, but they ain't here no more. They left a week ago. I had to ask them for their room. As it was, they owed a week's room-rent. Mister, I can't afford — —"

"Well, do you know where they went? Did you hear what address they had their trunk expressed to?"

"Ah, yes, their trunk," vociferated the woman, clapping her hands to her hips, her face purpling. "Their trunk, ah, sure. I got their trunk, and what are you going to do about it? I'm holding it till I get my money. What have you got to say about it? Let's hear it."

Presley turned away with a gesture of discouragement, his heart sinking. On the street corner he stood for a long time, frowning in trouble and perplexity. His suspicions had been only too well founded. So long ago as a week, the Hoovens had exhausted all their little store of money. For seven days now they had been without resources, unless, indeed, work had been found; "and what," he asked himself, "what work in God's name could they find to do here in the city?"

Seven days! He quailed at the thought of it. Seven days without money, knowing not a soul in all that swarming city. Ignorant of city life as both Minna and her mother were, would they even realise that there were institutions built and generously endowed for just such as they? He knew them to have their share of pride, the dogged sullen pride of the peasant; even if they knew of charitable organisations, would they, could they bring themselves to apply there? A poignant anxiety thrust itself sharply into Presley's heart. Where were they now? Where had they slept last night? Where breakfasted this morning? Had there even been any breakfast this morning? Had there even been any bed last night? Lost, and forgotten in the plexus of the city's life, what had befallen them? Towards what fate was the ebb tide of the streets drifting them?

Was this to be still another theme wrought out by iron hands upon the old, the world-old, world-wide keynote? How far were the consequences of that dreadful day's work at the irrigating ditch to reach? To what length was the tentacle of the monster to extend?

Presley returned toward the central, the business quarter of the city, alternately formulating and dismissing from his mind plan after plan for the finding and aiding of Mrs. Hooven and her daughters. He reached Montgomery Street, and turned toward his club, his imagination once more reviewing all the causes and circumstances of the great battle of which for the last eighteen months he had been witness.

All at once he paused, his eye caught by a sign affixed to the wall just inside the street entrance of a huge office building, and smitten with an idea, stood for an instant motionless, upon the sidewalk, his eyes wide, his fists shut tight.

The building contained the General Office of the Pacific and Southwestern Railroad. Large though it was, it nevertheless, was not pretentious, and during his visits to the city, Presley must have passed it, unheeding, many times.

But for all that it was the stronghold of the enemy—the centre of all that vast ramifying system of arteries that drained the life-blood of the State; the nucleus of the web in which so many lives, so many fortunes, so many destinies had been enmeshed. From this place—so he told himself—had emanated that policy of extortion, oppression and injustice that little by little had shouldered the ranchers from their rights, till, their backs to the wall, exasperated and despairing they had turned and fought and died. From here had come the orders to S. Behrman, to Cyrus Ruggles and to Genslinger, the orders that had brought Dyke to a prison, that had killed Annixter, that had ruined Magnus, that had corrupted Lyman. Here was the keep of the castle, and here, behind one of those many windows, in one of those many offices, his hand upon the levers of his mighty engine, sat the master, Shelgrim himself.

Instantly, upon the realisation of this fact an ungovernable desire seized upon Presley, an inordinate curiosity. Why not see, face to face, the man whose power was so vast, whose will was so resistless, whose potency for evil so limitless, the man who for so long and so hopelessly they had all been fighting. By reputation he knew him to be approachable; why should he not then approach him? Presley took his resolution in both hands. If he failed to act upon this impulse, he knew he would never act at all. His heart beating, his breath coming short, he entered the building, and in a few moments found himself seated in an ante-room, his eyes fixed with hypnotic intensity upon the frosted pane of an adjoining door, whereon in gold letters was inscribed the word, "PRESIDENT."

In the end, Presley had been surprised to find that Shelgrim was still in. It was already very late, after six o'clock, and the other offices in the building were in the act of closing. Many of them were already deserted. At every instant, through the open door of the ante-room, he caught a glimpse of clerks, office boys, book-keepers, and other employees hurrying towards the stairs and elevators, quitting business for the day. Shelgrim, it seemed, still remained at his desk, knowing no fatigue, requiring no leisure.

"What time does Mr. Shelgrim usually go home?" inquired Presley of the young man who sat ruling forms at the table in the ante-room.

"Anywhere between half-past six and seven," the other answered, adding, "Very often he comes back in the evening."

And the man was seventy years old. Presley could not repress a murmur of astonishment. Not only mentally, then, was the President of the P. and S. W. a giant. Seventy years of age and still at his post, holding there with the energy, with a concentration of purpose that would have wrecked the health and impaired the mind of many men in the prime of their manhood.

But the next instant Presley set his teeth.

"It is an ogre's vitality," he said to himself. "Just so is the man-eating tiger strong. The man should have energy who has sucked the life-blood from an entire People."

A little electric bell on the wall near at hand trilled a warning. The young man who was ruling forms laid down his pen, and opening the door of the President's office, thrust in his head, then after a word exchanged with the unseen occupant of the room, he swung the door wide, saying to Presley:

"Mr. Shelgrim will see you, sir."

Presley entered a large, well lighted, but singularly barren office. A well-worn carpet was on the floor, two steel engravings hung against the wall, an extra chair or two stood near a large, plain, littered table. That was absolutely all, unless he excepted the corner wash-stand, on which was set a pitcher of ice water, covered with a clean, stiff napkin. A man, evidently some sort of manager's assistant, stood at the end of the table, leaning on the back of one of the chairs. Shelgrim himself sat at the table.

He was large, almost to massiveness. An iron-grey beard and a mustache that completely hid the mouth covered the lower part of his face. His eyes were a pale blue, and a little watery; here and there upon his face were moth spots. But the enormous breadth of the shoulders was what, at first, most vividly forced itself upon Presley's notice. Never had he seen a broader man; the neck, however, seemed in a manner to have settled into the shoulders, and furthermore they were humped and rounded, as if to bear great responsibilities, and great abuse.

At the moment he was wearing a silk skull-cap, pushed to one side and a little awry, a frock coat of broadcloth, with long sleeves, and a waistcoat from the lower buttons of which the cloth was worn and, upon the edges, rubbed away, showing the metal underneath. At the top this waistcoat was unbuttoned and in the shirt front disclosed were two pearl studs.

Presley, uninvited, unnoticed apparently, sat down. The assistant manager was in the act of making a report. His voice was not lowered, and Presley heard every word that was spoken.

The report proved interesting. It concerned a book-keeper in the office of the auditor of disbursements. It seems he was at most times thoroughly reliable, hard-working, industrious, ambitious. But at long intervals the vice of drunkenness seized upon the man and for three days rode him like a hag. Not only during the period of this intemperance, but for the few days immediately following, the man was useless, his work untrustworthy. He was a family man and earnestly strove to rid himself of his habit; he was, when sober, valuable. In consideration of these facts, he had been pardoned again and again.

"You remember, Mr. Shelgrim," observed the manager, "that you have more than once interfered in his behalf, when we were disposed to let him go. I don't think we can do anything with him, sir. He promises to reform continually, but it is the same old story. This last time we saw nothing of him for four days. Honestly, Mr. Shelgrim, I think we ought to let Tentell out. We can't afford to keep him. He is really losing us too much money. Here's the order ready now, if you care to let it go."

There was a pause. Presley all attention, listened breathlessly. The assistant manager laid before his President the typewritten order in question. The silence lengthened; in the hall outside, the wrought-iron door of the elevator cage slid to with a clash. Shelgrim did not look at the order. He turned his swivel chair about and faced the windows behind him, looking out with unseeing eyes. At last he spoke:

"Tentell has a family, wife and three children. How much do we pay him?"

"One hundred and thirty."

"Let's double that, or say two hundred and fifty. Let's see how that will do."

"Why—of course—if you say so, but really, Mr. Shelgrim"

"Well, we'll try that, anyhow."

Presley had not time to readjust his perspective to this new point of view of the President of the P. and S. W. before the assistant manager had withdrawn. Shelgrim wrote a few memoranda on his calendar pad, and signed a couple of letters before turning his attention to Presley. At last, he looked up and fixed the young man with a direct, grave glance. He did not smile. It was some time before he spoke. At last, he said:

"Well, sir."

Presley advanced and took a chair nearer at hand. Shelgrim turned and from his desk picked up and consulted Presley's card. Presley observed that he read without the use of glasses.

"You," he said, again facing about, "you are the young man who wrote the poem called 'The Toilers.'"

"Yes, sir."

"It seems to have made a great deal of talk. I've read it, and I've seen the picture in Cedarquist's house, the picture you took the idea from."

Presley, his senses never more alive, observed that, curiously enough, Shelgrim did not move his body. His arms moved, and his head, but the great bulk of the man remained immobile in its place, and as the interview proceeded and this peculiarity emphasised itself, Presley began to conceive the odd idea that Shelgrim had, as it were, placed his body in the chair to rest, while his head and brain and hands went on working independently. A saucer of shelled filberts stood near his elbow, and from time to time he picked up one of these in a great thumb and forefinger and put it between his teeth.

"I've seen the picture called 'The Toilers,'" continued Shelgrim, "and of the two, I like the picture better than the poem."

"The picture is by a master," Presley hastened to interpose.

"And for that reason," said Shelgrim, "it leaves nothing more to be said. You might just as well have kept quiet. There's only one best way to say anything. And what has made the picture of 'The Toilers' great is that the artist said in it the BEST that could be said on the subject."

"I had never looked at it in just that light," observed Presley. He was confused, all at sea, embarrassed. What he had expected to find in Shelgrim, he could not have exactly said. But he had been prepared to come upon an ogre, a brute, a terrible man of blood and iron, and instead had discovered a sentimentalist and an art critic. No standards of measurement in his mental equipment would apply to the actual man, and it began to dawn upon him that possibly it was not because these standards were different in kind, but that they were lamentably deficient in size. He began to see that here was the man not only great, but large; many-sided, of vast sympathies, who understood with equal intelligence, the human nature in an habitual drunkard, the ethics of a masterpiece of painting, and the financiering and operation of ten thousand miles of railroad.

"I had never looked at it in just that light," repeated Presley. "There is a great deal in what you say."

"If I am to listen," continued Shelgrim, "to that kind of talk, I prefer to listen to it first hand. I would rather listen to what the great French painter has to say, than to what YOU have to say about what he has already said."

His speech, loud and emphatic at first, when the idea of what he had to say was fresh in his mind, lapsed and lowered itself at the end of his sentences as though he had already abandoned and lost interest in that thought, so that the concluding words were indistinct, beneath the grey beard and mustache. Also at times there was the faintest suggestion of a lisp.

"I wrote that poem," hazarded Presley, "at a time when I was terribly upset. I live," he concluded, "or did live on the Los Muertos ranch in Tulare County—Magnus Derrick's ranch."

"The Railroad's ranch LEASED to Mr. Derrick," observed Shelgrim.

Presley spread out his hands with a helpless, resigned gesture.

"And," continued the President of the P. and S. W. with grave intensity, looking at Presley keenly, "I suppose you believe I am a grand old rascal."

"I believe," answered Presley, "I am persuaded——" He hesitated, searching for his words.

"Believe this, young man," exclaimed Shelgrim, laying a thick powerful forefinger on the table to emphasise his words, "try to believe this—to begin with—THAT RAILROADS BUILD THEMSELVES. Where there is a demand sooner or later there will be a supply. Mr. Derrick, does he grow his wheat? The Wheat grows itself. What does he count for? Does he supply the force? What do I count for? Do I build the Railroad? You are dealing with forces, young man, when you speak of Wheat and the Railroads, not with men. There is the Wheat, the supply. It must be carried to feed the People. There is the demand. The Wheat is one force, the Railroad, another, and there is the law that governs them—supply and demand. Men have only little to do in the whole business. Complications may arise, conditions that bear hard on the individual—crush him maybe—BUT THE WHEAT WILL BE CARRIED TO FEED THE PEOPLE as inevitably as it will grow. If you want to fasten the blame of the affair at Los Muertos on any one person, you will make a mistake. Blame conditions, not men."

"But—but," faltered Presley, "you are the head, you control the road."

"You are a very young man. Control the road! Can I stop it? I can go into bankruptcy if you like. But otherwise if I run my road, as a business proposition, I can do nothing. I can not control it. It is a force born out of certain conditions, and I—no man—can stop it or control it. Can your Mr. Derrick stop the Wheat growing? He can burn his crop, or he can give it away, or sell it for a cent a bushel—just as I could go into bankruptcy—but otherwise his Wheat must grow. Can any one stop the Wheat? Well, then no more can I stop the Road."

Presley regained the street stupefied, his brain in a whirl. This new idea, this new conception dumfounded him. Somehow, he could not deny it. It rang with the clear reverberation of truth. Was no one, then, to blame for the horror at the irrigating ditch? Forces, conditions, laws of supply and demand—were these then the enemies, after all? Not enemies; there was no malevolence in Nature. Colossal indifference only, a vast trend toward appointed goals. Nature was, then, a gigantic engine, a vast cyclopean power, huge, terrible, a leviathan with a heart of steel, knowing no compunction, no forgiveness, no tolerance; crushing out the human atom standing in its way, with nirvanic calm, the agony of destruction sending never a jar, never the faintest tremour through all that prodigious mechanism of wheels and cogs. He went to his club and ate his supper alone, in gloomy agitation. He was sombre, brooding, lost in a dark maze of gloomy reflections. However, just as he was rising from the table an incident occurred that for the moment roused him and sharply diverted his mind.

His table had been placed near a window and as he was sipping his after-dinner coffee, he happened to glance across the street. His eye was at once caught by the sight of a familiar figure. Was it Minna Hooven? The figure turned the street corner and was lost to sight; but it had been strangely like. On the moment, Presley had risen from the table and, clapping on his hat, had hurried into the streets, where the lamps were already beginning to shine.

But search though he would, Presley could not again come upon the young woman, in whom he fancied he had seen the daughter of the unfortunate German. At last, he gave up the hunt, and returning to his club— at this hour almost deserted—smoked a few cigarettes, vainly attempted to read from a volume of essays in the library, and at last, nervous, distraught, exhausted, retired to his bed.

But none the less, Presley had not been mistaken. The girl whom he had tried to follow had been indeed Minna Hooven.

When Minna, a week before this time, had returned to the lodging house on Castro Street, after a day's unsuccessful effort to find employment, and was told that her mother and Hilda had gone, she was struck speechless with surprise and dismay. She had never before been in any town larger than Bonneville, and now knew not which way to turn nor how to account for the disappearance of her mother and little Hilda. That the landlady was on the point of turning them out, she understood, but it had been agreed that the family should be allowed to stay yet one more day, in the hope that Minna would find work. Of this she reminded the land-lady. But this latter at once launched upon her such a torrent of vituperation, that the girl was frightened to speechless submission.

"Oh, oh," she faltered, "I know. I am sorry. I know we owe you money, but where did my mother go? I only want to find her."

"Oh, I ain't going to be bothered," shrilled the other. "How do I know?"

The truth of the matter was that Mrs. Hooven, afraid to stay in the vicinity of the house, after her eviction, and threatened with arrest by the landlady if she persisted in hanging around, had left with the woman a note scrawled on an old blotter, to be given to Minna when she returned. This the landlady had lost. To cover her confusion, she affected a vast indignation, and a turbulent, irascible demeanour.

"I ain't going to be bothered with such cattle as you," she vociferated in Minna's face. "I don't know where your folks is. Me, I only have dealings with honest people. I ain't got a word to say so long as the rent is paid. But when I'm soldiered out of a week's lodging, then I'm done. You get right along now. I don't know you. I ain't going to have my place get a bad name by having any South of Market Street chippies hanging around. You get along, or I'll call an officer."

Minna sought the street, her head in a whirl. It was about five o'clock. In her pocket was thirty-five cents, all she had in the world. What now?

All at once, the Terror of the City, that blind, unreasoned fear that only the outcast knows, swooped upon her, and clutched her vulture-wise, by the throat.

Her first few days' experience in the matter of finding employment, had taught her just what she might expect from this new world upon which she had been thrown. What was to become of her? What was she to do, where was she to go? Unanswerable, grim questions, and now she no longer had herself to fear for. Her mother and the baby, little Hilda, both of them equally unable to look after themselves, what was to become of them, where were they gone? Lost, lost, all of them, herself as well. But she rallied herself, as she walked along. The idea of her starving, of her mother and Hilda starving, was out of all reason. Of course, it would not come to that, of course not. It was not thus that starvation came. Something would happen, of course, it would—in time. But meanwhile, meanwhile, how to get through this approaching night, and the next few days. That was the thing to think of just now.

The suddenness of it all was what most unnerved her. During all the nineteen years of her life, she had never known what it meant to shift for herself. Her father had always sufficed for the family; he had taken care of her, then, all of a sudden, her father had been killed, her mother snatched from her. Then all of a sudden there was no help anywhere. Then all of a sudden a terrible voice demanded of her, "Now just what can you do to keep yourself alive?" Life faced her; she looked the huge stone image squarely in the lustreless eyes.

It was nearly twilight. Minna, for the sake of avoiding observation— for it seemed to her that now a thousand prying glances followed her— assumed a matter-of-fact demeanour, and began to walk briskly toward the business quarter of the town.

She was dressed neatly enough, in a blue cloth skirt with a blue plush belt, fairly decent shoes, once her mother's, a pink shirt waist, and jacket and a straw sailor. She was, in an unusual fashion, pretty. Even her troubles had not dimmed the bright light of her pale, greenish-blue eyes, nor faded the astonishing redness of her lips, nor hollowed her strangely white face. Her blue-black hair was trim. She carried her well-shaped, well-rounded figure erectly. Even in her distress, she observed that men looked keenly at her, and sometimes after her as she went along. But this she noted with a dim sub-conscious faculty. The real Minna, harassed, terrified, lashed with a thousand anxieties, kept murmuring under her breath:

"What shall I do, what shall I do, oh, what shall I do, now?"

After an interminable walk, she gained Kearney Street, and held it till the well-lighted, well-kept neighbourhood of the shopping district gave place to the vice-crowded saloons and concert halls of the Barbary Coast. She turned aside in avoidance of this, only to plunge into the purlieus of Chinatown, whence only she emerged, panic-stricken and out of breath, after a half hour of never-to-be-forgotten terrors, and at a time when it had grown quite dark.

On the corner of California and Dupont streets, she stood a long moment, pondering.

"I MUST do something," she said to herself. "I must do SOMETHING." She was tired out by now, and the idea occurred to her to enter the Catholic church in whose shadow she stood, and sit down and rest. This she did. The evening service was just being concluded. But long after the priests and altar boys had departed from the chancel, Minna still sat in the dim, echoing interior, confronting her desperate situation as best she might.

Two or three hours later, the sexton woke her. The church was being closed; she must leave. Once more, chilled with the sharp night air, numb with long sitting in the same attitude, still oppressed with drowsiness, confused, frightened, Minna found herself on the pavement. She began to be hungry, and, at length, yielding to the demand that every moment grew more imperious, bought and eagerly devoured a five-cent bag of fruit. Then, once more she took up the round of walking.

At length, in an obscure street that branched from Kearney Street, near the corner of the Plaza, she came upon an illuminated sign, bearing the inscription, "Beds for the Night, 15 and 25 cents."

Fifteen cents! Could she afford it? It would leave her with only that much more, that much between herself and a state of privation of which she dared not think; and, besides, the forbidding look of the building frightened her. It was dark, gloomy, dirty, a place suggestive of obscure crimes and hidden terrors. For twenty minutes or half an hour, she hesitated, walking twice and three times around the block. At last, she made up her mind. Exhaustion such as she had never known, weighed like lead upon her shoulders and dragged at her heels. She must sleep. She could not walk the streets all night. She entered the door-way under the sign, and found her way up a filthy flight of stairs. At the top, a man in a blue checked "jumper" was filling a lamp behind a high desk. To him Minna applied.

"I should like," she faltered, "to have a room—a bed for the night. One of those for fifteen cents will be good enough, I think."

"Well, this place is only for men," said the man, looking up from the lamp.

"Oh," said Minna, "oh—I—I didn't know."

She looked at him stupidly, and he, with equal stupidity, returned the gaze. Thus, for a long moment, they held each other's eyes.

"I—I didn't know," repeated Minna.

"Yes, it's for men," repeated the other. She slowly descended the stairs, and once more came out upon the streets.

And upon those streets that, as the hours advanced, grew more and more deserted, more and more silent, more and more oppressive with the sense of the bitter hardness of life towards those who have no means of living, Minna Hooven spent the first night of her struggle to keep her head above the ebb-tide of the city's sea, into which she had been plunged.

Morning came, and with it renewed hunger. At this time, she had found her way uptown again, and towards ten o'clock was sitting upon a bench in a little park full of nurse-maids and children. A group of the maids drew their baby-buggies to Minna's bench, and sat down, continuing a conversation they had already begun. Minna listened. A friend of one of the maids had suddenly thrown up her position, leaving her "madame" in what would appear to have been deserved embarrassment.

"Oh," said Minna, breaking in, and lying with sudden unwonted fluency, "I am a nurse-girl. I am out of a place. Do you think I could get that one?"

The group turned and fixed her—so evidently a country girl—with a supercilious indifference.

"Well, you might try," said one of them. "Got good references?"

"References?" repeated Minna blankly. She did not know what this meant.

"Oh, Mrs. Field ain't the kind to stick about references," spoke up the other, "she's that soft. Why, anybody could work her."

"I'll go there," said Minna. "Have you the address?" It was told to her.

"Lorin," she murmured. "Is that out of town?"

"Well, it's across the Bay."

"Across the Bay."

"Um. You're from the country, ain't you?"

"Yes. How—how do I get there? Is it far?"

"Well, you take the ferry at the foot of Market Street, and then the train on the other side. No, it ain't very far. Just ask any one down there. They'll tell you."

It was a chance; but Minna, after walking down to the ferry slips, found that the round trip would cost her twenty cents. If the journey proved fruitless, only a dime would stand between her and the end of everything. But it was a chance; the only one that had, as yet, presented itself. She made the trip.

And upon the street-railway cars, upon the ferryboats, on the locomotives and way-coaches of the local trains, she was reminded of her father's death, and of the giant power that had reduced her to her present straits, by the letters, P. and S. W. R. R. To her mind, they occurred everywhere. She seemed to see them in every direction. She fancied herself surrounded upon every hand by the long arms of the monster.

Minute after minute, her hunger gnawed at her. She could not keep her mind from it. As she sat on the boat, she found herself curiously scanning the faces of the passengers, wondering how long since such a one had breakfasted, how long before this other should sit down to lunch.

When Minna descended from the train, at Lorin on the other side of the Bay, she found that the place was one of those suburban towns, not yet become fashionable, such as may be seen beyond the outskirts of any large American city. All along the line of the railroad thereabouts, houses, small villas—contractors' ventures—were scattered, the advantages of suburban lots and sites for homes being proclaimed in seven-foot letters upon mammoth bill-boards close to the right of way. Without much trouble, Minna found the house to which she had been directed, a pretty little cottage, set back from the street and shaded by palms, live oaks, and the inevitable eucalyptus. Her heart warmed at the sight of it. Oh, to find a little niche for herself here, a home, a refuge from those horrible city streets, from the rat of famine, with its relentless tooth. How she would work, how strenuously she would endeavour to please, how patient of rebuke she would be, how faithful, how conscientious. Nor were her pretensions altogether false; upon her, while at home, had devolved almost continually the care of the baby Hilda, her little sister. She knew the wants and needs of children.

Her heart beating, her breath failing, she rang the bell set squarely in the middle of the front door.

The lady of the house herself, an elderly lady, with pleasant, kindly face, opened the door. Minna stated her errand.

"But I have already engaged a girl," she said.

"Oh," murmured Minna, striving with all her might to maintain appearances. "Oh—I thought perhaps—" She turned away.

"I'm sorry," said the lady. Then she added, "Would you care to look after so many as three little children, and help around in light housework between whiles?"

"Yes, ma'am." "Because my sister—she lives in North Berkeley, above here—she's looking far a girl. Have you had lots of experience? Got good references?"

"Yes, ma'am."

"Well, I'll give you the address. She lives up in North Berkeley."

She turned back into the house a moment, and returned, handing Minna a card.

"That's where she lives—careful not to BLOT it, child, the ink's wet yet—you had better see her."

"Is it far? Could I walk there?"

"My, no; you better take the electric cars, about six blocks above here."

When Minna arrived in North Berkeley, she had no money left. By a cruel mistake, she had taken a car going in the wrong direction, and though her error was rectified easily enough, it had cost her her last five-cent piece. She was now to try her last hope. Promptly it crumbled away. Like the former, this place had been already filled, and Minna left the door of the house with the certainty that her chance had come to naught, and that now she entered into the last struggle with life—the death struggle—shorn of her last pitiful defence, her last safeguard, her last penny.

As she once more resumed her interminable walk, she realised she was weak, faint; and she knew that it was the weakness of complete exhaustion, and the faintness of approaching starvation. Was this the end coming on? Terror of death aroused her.

"I MUST, I MUST do something, oh, anything. I must have something to eat."

At this late hour, the idea of pawning her little jacket occurred to her, but now she was far away from the city and its pawnshops, and there was no getting back.

She walked on. An hour passed. She lost her sense of direction, became confused, knew not where she was going, turned corners and went up by-streets without knowing why, anything to keep moving, for she fancied that so soon as she stood still, the rat in the pit of her stomach gnawed more eagerly.

At last, she entered what seemed to be, if not a park, at least some sort of public enclosure. There were many trees; the place was beautiful; well-kept roads and walks led sinuously and invitingly underneath the shade. Through the trees upon the other side of a wide expanse of turf, brown and sear under the summer sun, she caught a glimpse of tall buildings and a flagstaff. The whole place had a vaguely public, educational appearance, and Minna guessed, from certain notices affixed to the trees, warning the public against the picking of flowers, that she had found her way into the grounds of the State University. She went on a little further. The path she was following led her, at length, into a grove of gigantic live oaks, whose lower branches all but swept the ground. Here the grass was green, the few flowers in bloom, the shade very thick. A more lovely spot she had seldom seen. Near at hand was a bench, built around the trunk of the largest live oak, and here, at length, weak from hunger, exhausted to the limits of her endurance, despairing, abandoned, Minna Hooven sat down to enquire of herself what next she could do.

But once seated, the demands of the animal—so she could believe—became more clamorous, more insistent. To eat, to rest, to be safely housed against another night, above all else, these were the things she craved; and the craving within her grew so mighty that she crisped her poor, starved hands into little fists, in an agony of desire, while the tears ran from her eyes, and the sobs rose thick from her breast and struggled and strangled in her aching throat.

But in a few moments Minna was aware that a woman, apparently of some thirty years of age, had twice passed along the walk in front of the bench where she sat, and now, as she took more notice of her, she remembered that she had seen her on the ferry-boat coming over from the city.

The woman was gowned in silk, tightly corseted, and wore a hat of rather ostentatious smartness. Minna became convinced that the person was watching her, but before she had a chance to act upon this conviction she was surprised out of all countenance by the stranger coming up to where she sat and speaking to her.

"Here is a coincidence," exclaimed the new-comer, as she sat down; "surely you are the young girl who sat opposite me on the boat. Strange I should come across you again. I've had you in mind ever since."

On this nearer view Minna observed that the woman's face bore rather more than a trace of enamel and that the atmosphere about was impregnated with sachet. She was not otherwise conspicuous, but there was a certain hardness about her mouth and a certain droop of fatigue in her eyelids which, combined with an indefinite self-confidence of manner, held Minna's attention.

"Do you know," continued the woman, "I believe you are in trouble. I thought so when I saw you on the boat, and I think so now. Are you? Are you in trouble? You're from the country, ain't you?"

Minna, glad to find a sympathiser, even in this chance acquaintance, admitted that she was in distress; that she had become separated from her mother, and that she was indeed from the country.

"I've been trying to find a situation," she hazarded in conclusion, "but I don't seem to succeed. I've never been in a city before, except Bonneville."

"Well, it IS a coincidence," said the other. "I know I wasn't drawn to you for nothing. I am looking for just such a young girl as you. You see, I live alone a good deal and I've been wanting to find a nice, bright, sociable girl who will be a sort of COMPANION to me. Understand? And there's something about you that I like. I took to you the moment I saw you on the boat. Now shall we talk this over?"

Towards the end of the week, one afternoon, as Presley was returning from his club, he came suddenly face to face with Minna upon a street corner.

"Ah," he cried, coming toward her joyfully. "Upon my word, I had almost given you up. I've been looking everywhere for you. I was afraid you might not be getting along, and I wanted to see if there was anything I could do. How are your mother and Hilda? Where are you stopping? Have you got a good place?"

"I don't know where mamma is," answered Minna. "We got separated, and I never have been able to find her again."

Meanwhile, Presley had been taking in with a quick eye the details of Minna's silk dress, with its garniture of lace, its edging of velvet, its silver belt-buckle. Her hair was arranged in a new way and on her head was a wide hat with a flare to one side, set off with a gilt buckle and a puff of bright blue plush. He glanced at her sharply.

"Well, but—but how are you getting on?" he demanded.

Minna laughed scornfully.

"I?" she cried. "Oh, I'VE gone to hell. It was either that or starvation."

Presley regained his room at the club, white and trembling. Worse than the worst he had feared had happened. He had not been soon enough to help. He had failed again. A superstitious fear assailed him that he was, in a manner, marked; that he was foredoomed to fail. Minna had come—had been driven to this; and he, acting too late upon his tardy resolve, had not been able to prevent it. Were the horrors, then, never to end? Was the grisly spectre of consequence to forever dance in his vision? Were the results, the far-reaching results of that battle at the irrigating ditch to cross his path forever? When would the affair be terminated, the incident closed? Where was that spot to which the tentacle of the monster could not reach?

By now, he was sick with the dread of it all. He wanted to get away, to be free from that endless misery, so that he might not see what he could no longer help. Cowardly he now knew himself to be. He thought of himself only with loathing.

Bitterly self-contemptuous that he could bring himself to a participation in such trivialities, he began to dress to keep his engagement to dine with the Cedarquists.

He arrived at the house nearly half an hour late, but before he could take off his overcoat, Mrs. Cedarquist appeared in the doorway of the drawing-room at the end of the hall. She was dressed as if to go out.

"My DEAR Presley," she exclaimed, her stout, over-dressed body bustling toward him with a great rustle of silk. "I never was so glad. You poor, dear poet, you are thin as a ghost. You need a better dinner than I can give you, and that is just what you are to have."

"Have I blundered?" Presley hastened to exclaim. "Did not Mr. Cedarquist mention Friday evening?"

"No, no, no," she cried; "it was he who blundered. YOU blundering in a social amenity! Preposterous! No; Mr. Cedarquist forgot that we were dining out ourselves to-night, and when he told me he had asked you here for the same evening, I fell upon the man, my dear, I did actually, tooth and nail. But I wouldn't hear of his wiring you. I just dropped a note to our hostess, asking if I could not bring you, and when I told her who you WERE, she received the idea with, oh, empressement. So, there it is, all settled. Cedarquist and the girls are gone on ahead, and you are to take the old lady like a dear, dear poet. I believe I hear the carriage. Allons! En voiture!"

Once settled in the cool gloom of the coupe, odorous of leather and upholstery, Mrs. Cedarquist exclaimed:

"And I've never told you who you were to dine with; oh, a personage, really. Fancy, you will be in the camp of your dearest foes. You are to dine with the Gerard people, one of the Vice-Presidents of your bete noir, the P. and S. W. Railroad."

Presley started, his fists clenching so abruptly as to all but split his white gloves. He was not conscious of what he said in reply, and Mrs. Cedarquist was so taken up with her own endless stream of talk that she did not observe his confusion.

"Their daughter Honora is going to Europe next week; her mother is to take her, and Mrs. Gerard is to have just a few people to dinner—very informal, you know—ourselves, you and, oh, I don't know, two or three others. Have you ever seen Honora? The prettiest little thing, and will she be rich? Millions, I would not dare say how many. Tiens. Nous voici."

The coupe drew up to the curb, and Presley followed Mrs. Cedarquist up the steps to the massive doors of the great house. In a confused daze, he allowed one of the footmen to relieve him of his hat and coat; in a daze he rejoined Mrs. Cedarquist in a room with a glass roof, hung with pictures, the art gallery, no doubt, and in a daze heard their names announced at the entrance of another room, the doors of which were hung with thick, blue curtains.

He entered, collecting his wits for the introductions and presentations that he foresaw impended.

The room was very large, and of excessive loftiness. Flat, rectagonal pillars of a rose-tinted, variegated marble, rose from the floor almost flush with the walls, finishing off at the top with gilded capitals of a Corinthian design, which supported the ceiling. The ceiling itself, instead of joining the walls at right angles, curved to meet them, a device that produced a sort of dome-like effect. This ceiling was a maze of golden involutions in very high relief, that adjusted themselves to form a massive framing for a great picture, nymphs and goddesses, white doves, golden chariots and the like, all wreathed about with clouds and garlands of roses. Between the pillars around the sides of the room were hangings of silk, the design—of a Louis Quinze type—of beautiful simplicity and faultless taste. The fireplace was a marvel. It reached from floor to ceiling; the lower parts, black marble, carved into crouching Atlases, with great muscles that upbore the superstructure. The design of this latter, of a kind of purple marble, shot through with white veinings, was in the same style as the design of the silk hangings. In its midst was a bronze escutcheon, bearing an undecipherable monogram and a Latin motto. Andirons of brass, nearly six feet high, flanked the hearthstone.

The windows of the room were heavily draped in sombre brocade and ecru lace, in which the initials of the family were very beautifully worked. But directly opposite the fireplace, an extra window, lighted from the adjoining conservatory, threw a wonderful, rich light into the apartment. It was a Gothic window of stained glass, very large, the centre figures being armed warriors, Parsifal and Lohengrin; the one with a banner, the other with a swan. The effect was exquisite, the window a veritable masterpiece, glowing, flaming, and burning with a hundred tints and colours—opalescent, purple, wine-red, clouded pinks, royal blues, saffrons, violets so dark as to be almost black.

Under foot, the carpet had all the softness of texture of grass; skins (one of them of an enormous polar bear) and rugs of silk velvet were spread upon the floor. A Renaissance cabinet of ebony, many feet taller than Presley's head, and inlaid with ivory and silver, occupied one corner of the room, while in its centre stood a vast table of Flemish oak, black, heavy as iron, massive. A faint odour of sandalwood pervaded the air. From the conservatory near-by, came the splashing of a fountain. A row of electric bulbs let into the frieze of the walls between the golden capitals, and burning dimly behind hemispheres of clouded glass, threw a subdued light over the whole scene.

Mrs. Gerard came forward.

"This is Mr. Presley, of course, our new poet of whom we are all so proud. I was so afraid you would be unable to come. You have given me a real pleasure in allowing me to welcome you here."

The footman appeared at her elbow.

"Dinner is served, madame," he announced.

When Mrs. Hooven had left the boarding-house on Castro Street, she had taken up a position on a neighbouring corner, to wait for Minna's reappearance. Little Hilda, at this time hardly more than six years of age, was with her, holding to her hand.

Mrs. Hooven was by no means an old woman, but hard work had aged her. She no longer had any claim to good looks. She no longer took much interest in her personal appearance. At the time of her eviction from the Castro Street boarding-house, she wore a faded black bonnet, garnished with faded artificial flowers of dirty pink. A plaid shawl was about her shoulders. But this day of misfortune had set Mrs. Hooven adrift in even worse condition than her daughter. Her purse, containing a miserable handful of dimes and nickels, was in her trunk, and her trunk was in the hands of the landlady. Minna had been allowed such reprieve as her thirty-five cents would purchase. The destitution of Mrs. Hooven and her little girl had begun from the very moment of her eviction.

While she waited for Minna, watching every street car and every approaching pedestrian, a policeman appeared, asked what she did, and, receiving no satisfactory reply, promptly moved her on.

Minna had had little assurance in facing the life struggle of the city. Mrs. Hooven had absolutely none. In her, grief, distress, the pinch of poverty, and, above all, the nameless fear of the turbulent, fierce life of the streets, had produced a numbness, an embruted, sodden, silent, speechless condition of dazed mind, and clogged, unintelligent speech. She was dumb, bewildered, stupid, animated but by a single impulse. She clung to life, and to the life of her little daughter Hilda, with the blind tenacity of purpose of a drowning cat.

Thus, when ordered to move on by the officer, she had silently obeyed, not even attempting to explain her situation. She walked away to the next street-crossing. Then, in a few moments returned, taking up her place on the corner near the boarding-house, spying upon the approaching cable cars, peeping anxiously down the length of the sidewalks.

Once more, the officer ordered her away, and once more, unprotesting, she complied. But when for the third time the policeman found her on the forbidden spot, he had lost his temper. This time when Mrs. Hooven departed, he had followed her, and when, bewildered, persistent, she had attempted to turn back, he caught her by the shoulder.

"Do you want to get arrested, hey?" he demanded. "Do you want me to lock you up? Say, do you, speak up?"

The ominous words at length reached Mrs. Hooven's comprehension. Arrested! She was to be arrested. The countrywoman's fear of the Jail nipped and bit eagerly at her unwilling heels. She hurried off, thinking to return to her post after the policeman should have gone away. But when, at length, turning back, she tried to find the boarding-house, she suddenly discovered that she was on an unfamiliar street. Unwittingly, no doubt, she had turned a corner. She could not retrace her steps. She and Hilda were lost.

"Mammy, I'm tired," Hilda complained.

Her mother picked her up.

"Mammy, where're we gowun, mammy?"

Where, indeed? Stupefied, Mrs. Hooven looked about her at the endless blocks of buildings, the endless procession of vehicles in the streets, the endless march of pedestrians on the sidewalks. Where was Minna; where was she and her baby to sleep that night? How was Hilda to be fed?

She could not stand still. There was no place to sit down; but one thing was left, walk.

Ah, that via dolorosa of the destitute, that chemin de la croix of the homeless. Ah, the mile after mile of granite pavement that MUST be, MUST be traversed. Walk they must. Move, they must; onward, forward, whither they cannot tell; why, they do not know. Walk, walk, walk with bleeding feet and smarting joints; walk with aching back and trembling knees; walk, though the senses grow giddy with fatigue, though the eyes droop with sleep, though every nerve, demanding rest, sets in motion its tiny alarm of pain. Death is at the end of that devious, winding maze of paths, crossed and re-crossed and crossed again. There is but one goal to the via dolorosa; there is no escape from the central chamber of that labyrinth. Fate guides the feet of them that are set therein. Double on their steps though they may, weave in and out of the myriad corners of the city's streets, return, go forward, back, from side to side, here, there, anywhere, dodge, twist, wind, the central chamber where Death sits is reached inexorably at the end.

Sometimes leading and sometimes carrying Hilda, Mrs. Hooven set off upon her objectless journey. Block after block she walked, street after street. She was afraid to stop, because of the policemen. As often as she so much as slackened her pace, she was sure to see one of these terrible figures in the distance, watching her, so it seemed to her, waiting for her to halt for the fraction of a second, in order that he might have an excuse to arrest her.

Hilda fretted incessantly.

"Mammy, where're we gowun? Mammy, I'm tired." Then, at last, for the first time, that plaint that stabbed the mother's heart:

"Mammy, I'm hungry."

"Be qui-ut, den," said Mrs. Hooven. "Bretty soon we'll hev der subber."

Passers-by on the sidewalk, men and women in the great six o'clock homeward march, jostled them as they went along. With dumb, dull curiousness, she looked into one after another of the limitless stream of faces, and she fancied she saw in them every emotion but pity. The faces were gay, were anxious, were sorrowful, were mirthful, were lined with thought, or were merely flat and expressionless, but not one was turned toward her in compassion. The expressions of the faces might be various, but an underlying callousness was discoverable beneath every mask. The people seemed removed from her immeasurably; they were infinitely above her. What was she to them, she and her baby, the crippled outcasts of the human herd, the unfit, not able to survive, thrust out on the heath to perish?

To beg from these people did not yet occur to her. There was no pride, however, in the matter. She would have as readily asked alms of so many sphinxes.

She went on. Without willing it, her feet carried her in a wide circle. Soon she began to recognise the houses; she had been in that street before. Somehow, this was distasteful to her; so, striking off at right angles, she walked straight before her for over a dozen blocks. By now, it was growing darker. The sun had set. The hands of a clock on the power-house of a cable line pointed to seven. No doubt, Minna had come long before this time, had found her mother gone, and had—just what had she done, just what COULD she do? Where was her daughter now? Walking the streets herself, no doubt. What was to become of Minna, pretty girl that she was, lost, houseless and friendless in the maze of these streets? Mrs. Hooven, roused from her lethargy, could not repress an exclamation of anguish. Here was misfortune indeed; here was calamity. She bestirred herself, and remembered the address of the boarding-house. She might inquire her way back thither. No doubt, by now the policeman would be gone home for the night. She looked about. She was in the district of modest residences, and a young man was coming toward her, carrying a new garden hose looped around his shoulder.

"Say, Meest'r; say, blease——"

The young man gave her a quick look and passed on, hitching the coil of hose over his shoulder. But a few paces distant, he slackened in his walk and fumbled in his vest pocket with his fingers. Then he came back to Mrs. Hooven and put a quarter into her hand.

Mrs. Hooven stared at the coin stupefied. The young man disappeared. He thought, then, that she was begging. It had come to that; she, independent all her life, whose husband had held five hundred acres of wheat land, had been taken for a beggar. A flush of shame shot to her face. She was about to throw the money after its giver. But at the moment, Hilda again exclaimed:

"Mammy, I'm hungry."

With a movement of infinite lassitude and resigned acceptance of the situation, Mrs. Hooven put the coin in her pocket. She had no right to be proud any longer. Hilda must have food.

That evening, she and her child had supper at a cheap restaurant in a poor quarter of the town, and passed the night on the benches of a little uptown park.

Unused to the ways of the town, ignorant as to the customs and possibilities of eating-houses, she spent the whole of her quarter upon supper for herself and Hilda, and had nothing left wherewith to buy a lodging.

The night was dreadful; Hilda sobbed herself to sleep on her mother's shoulder, waking thereafter from hour to hour, to protest, though wrapped in her mother's shawl, that she was cold, and to enquire why they did not go to bed. Drunken men snored and sprawled near at hand. Towards morning, a loafer, reeking of alcohol, sat down beside her, and indulged in an incoherent soliloquy, punctuated with oaths and obscenities. It was not till far along towards daylight that she fell asleep.

She awoke to find it broad day. Hilda—mercifully—slept. Her mother's limbs were stiff and lame with cold and damp; her head throbbed. She moved to another bench which stood in the rays of the sun, and for a long two hours sat there in the thin warmth, till the moisture of the night that clung to her clothes was evaporated.

A policeman came into view. She woke Hilda, and carrying her in her arms, took herself away.

"Mammy," began Hilda as soon as she was well awake; "Mammy, I'm hungry. I want mein breakfest."

"Sure, sure, soon now, leedle tochter."

She herself was hungry, but she had but little thought of that. How was Hilda to be fed? She remembered her experience of the previous day, when the young man with the hose had given her money. Was it so easy, then, to beg? Could charity be had for the asking? So it seemed; but all that was left of her sturdy independence revolted at the thought. SHE beg! SHE hold out the hand to strangers!

"Mammy, I'm hungry."

There was no other way. It must come to that in the end. Why temporise, why put off the inevitable? She sought out a frequented street where men and women were on their way to work. One after another, she let them go by, searching their faces, deterred at the very last moment by some trifling variation of expression, a firm set mouth, a serious, level eyebrow, an advancing chin. Then, twice, when she had made a choice, and brought her resolution to the point of speech, she quailed, shrinking, her ears tingling, her whole being protesting against the degradation. Every one must be looking at her. Her shame was no doubt the object of an hundred eyes.

"Mammy, I'm hungry," protested Hilda again.

She made up her mind. What, though, was she to say? In what words did beggars ask for assistance?

She tried to remember how tramps who had appeared at her back door on Los Muertos had addressed her; how and with what formula certain mendicants of Bonneville had appealed to her. Then, having settled upon a phrase, she approached a whiskered gentleman with a large stomach, walking briskly in the direction of the town.

"Say, den, please hellup a boor womun."

The gentleman passed on.

"Perhaps he doand hear me," she murmured.

Two well-dressed women advanced, chattering gayly.

"Say, say, den, please hellup a boor womun."

One of the women paused, murmuring to her companion, and from her purse extracted a yellow ticket which she gave to Mrs. Hooven with voluble explanations. But Mrs. Hooven was confused, she did not understand. What could the ticket mean? The women went on their way.

The next person to whom she applied was a young girl of about eighteen, very prettily dressed.

"Say, say, den, please hellup a boor womun."

In evident embarrassment, the young girl paused and searched in her little pocketbook. "I think I have—I think—I have just ten cents here somewhere," she murmured again and again.

In the end, she found a dime, and dropped it into Mrs. Hooven's palm.

That was the beginning. The first step once taken, the others became easy. All day long, Mrs. Hooven and Hilda followed the streets, begging, begging. Here it was a nickel, there a dime, here a nickel again. But she was not expert in the art, nor did she know where to buy food the cheapest; and the entire day's work resulted only in barely enough for two meals of bread, milk, and a wretchedly cooked stew. Tuesday night found the pair once more shelterless.

Once more, Mrs. Hooven and her baby passed the night on the park benches. But early on Wednesday morning, Mrs. Hooven found herself assailed by sharp pains and cramps in her stomach. What was the cause she could not say; but as the day went on, the pains increased, alternating with hot flushes over all her body, and a certain weakness and faintness. As the day went on, the pain and the weakness increased. When she tried to walk, she found she could do so only with the greatest difficulty. Here was fresh misfortune. To beg, she must walk. Dragging herself forward a half-block at a time, she regained the street once more. She succeeded in begging a couple of nickels, bought a bag of apples from a vender, and, returning to the park, sank exhausted upon a bench.

Here she remained all day until evening, Hilda alternately whimpering for her bread and milk, or playing languidly in the gravel walk at her feet. In the evening, she started out again. This time, it was bitter hard. Nobody seemed inclined to give. Twice she was "moved on" by policemen. Two hours' begging elicited but a single dime. With this, she bought Hilda's bread and milk, and refusing herself to eat, returned to the bench—the only home she knew—and spent the night shivering with cold, burning with fever.

From Wednesday morning till Friday evening, with the exception of the few apples she had bought, and a quarter of a loaf of hard bread that she found in a greasy newspaper—scraps of a workman's dinner—Mrs. Hooven had nothing to eat. In her weakened condition, begging became hourly more difficult, and such little money as was given her, she resolutely spent on Hilda's bread and milk in the morning and evening.

By Friday afternoon, she was very weak, indeed. Her eyes troubled her. She could no longer see distinctly, and at times there appeared to her curious figures, huge crystal goblets of the most graceful shapes, floating and swaying in the air in front of her, almost within arm's reach. Vases of elegant forms, made of shimmering glass, bowed and courtesied toward her. Glass bulbs took graceful and varying shapes before her vision, now rounding into globes, now evolving into hour-glasses, now twisting into pretzel-shaped convolutions.

"Mammy, I'm hungry," insisted Hilda, passing her hands over her face. Mrs. Hooven started and woke. It was Friday evening. Already the street lamps were being lit.

"Gome, den, leedle girl," she said, rising and taking Hilda's hand. "Gome, den, we go vind subber, hey?"

She issued from the park and took a cross street, directly away from the locality where she had begged the previous days. She had had no success there of late. She would try some other quarter of the town. After a weary walk, she came out upon Van Ness Avenue, near its junction with Market Street. She turned into the avenue, and went on toward the Bay, painfully traversing block after block, begging of all whom she met (for she no longer made any distinction among the passers-by).

"Say, say, den, blease hellup a boor womun."

"Mammy, mammy, I'm hungry."

It was Friday night, between seven and eight. The great deserted avenue was already dark. A sea fog was scudding overhead, and by degrees descending lower. The warmth was of the meagerest, and the street lamps, birds of fire in cages of glass, fluttered and danced in the prolonged gusts of the trade wind that threshed and weltered in the city streets from off the ocean.

Presley entered the dining-room of the Gerard mansion with little Miss Gerard on his arm. The other guests had preceded them—Cedarquist with Mrs. Gerard; a pale-faced, languid young man (introduced to Presley as Julian Lambert) with Presley's cousin Beatrice, one of the twin daughters of Mr. and Mrs. Cedarquist; his brother Stephen, whose hair was straight as an Indian's, but of a pallid straw color, with Beatrice's sister; Gerard himself, taciturn, bearded, rotund, loud of breath, escorted Mrs. Cedarquist. Besides these, there were one or two other couples, whose names Presley did not remember.

The dining-room was superb in its appointments. On three sides of the room, to the height of some ten feet, ran a continuous picture, an oil painting, divided into long sections by narrow panels of black oak. The painting represented the personages in the Romaunt de la Rose, and was conceived in an atmosphere of the most delicate, most ephemeral allegory. One saw young chevaliers, blue-eyed, of elemental beauty and purity; women with crowns, gold girdles, and cloudy wimples; young girls, entrancing in their loveliness, wearing snow-white kerchiefs, their golden hair unbound and flowing, dressed in white samite, bearing armfuls of flowers; the whole procession defiling against a background of forest glades, venerable oaks, half-hidden fountains, and fields of asphodel and roses.

Otherwise, the room was simple. Against the side of the wall unoccupied by the picture stood a sideboard of gigantic size, that once had adorned the banquet hall of an Italian palace of the late Renaissance. It was black with age, and against its sombre surfaces glittered an array of heavy silver dishes and heavier cut-glass bowls and goblets.

The company sat down to the first course of raw Blue Point oysters, served upon little pyramids of shaved ice, and the two butlers at once began filling the glasses of the guests with cool Haut Sauterne.

Mrs. Gerard, who was very proud of her dinners, and never able to resist the temptation of commenting upon them to her guests, leaned across to Presley and Mrs. Cedarquist, murmuring, "Mr. Presley, do you find that Sauterne too cold? I always believe it is so bourgeois to keep such a delicate wine as Sauterne on the ice, and to ice Bordeaux or Burgundy—oh, it is nothing short of a crime."

"This is from your own vineyard, is it not?" asked Julian Lambert. "I think I recognise the bouquet."

He strove to maintain an attitude of fin gourmet, unable to refrain from comment upon the courses as they succeeded one another.

Little Honora Gerard turned to Presley:

"You know," she explained, "Papa has his own vineyards in southern France. He is so particular about his wines; turns up his nose at California wines. And I am to go there next summer. Ferrieres is the name of the place where our vineyards are, the dearest village!" She was a beautiful little girl of a dainty porcelain type, her colouring low in tone. She wore no jewels, but her little, undeveloped neck and shoulders, of an exquisite immaturity, rose from the tulle bodice of her first decollete gown.

"Yes," she continued; "I'm to go to Europe for the first time. Won't it be gay? And I am to have my own bonne, and Mamma and I are to travel—so many places, Baden, Homburg, Spa, the Tyrol. Won't it be gay?"

Presley assented in meaningless words. He sipped his wine mechanically, looking about that marvellous room, with its subdued saffron lights, its glitter of glass and silver, its beautiful women in their elaborate toilets, its deft, correct servants; its array of tableware—cut glass, chased silver, and Dresden crockery. It was Wealth, in all its outward and visible forms, the signs of an opulence so great that it need never be husbanded. It was the home of a railway "Magnate," a Railroad King. For this, then, the farmers paid. It was for this that S. Behrman turned the screw, tightened the vise. It was for this that Dyke had been driven to outlawry and a jail. It was for this that Lyman Derrick had been bought, the Governor ruined and broken, Annixter shot down, Hooven killed.

The soup, puree a la Derby, was served, and at the same time, as hors d'oeuvres, ortolan patties, together with a tiny sandwich made of browned toast and thin slices of ham, sprinkled over with Parmesan cheese. The wine, so Mrs. Gerard caused it to be understood, was Xeres, of the 1815 vintage.

Mrs. Hooven crossed the avenue. It was growing late. Without knowing it, she had come to a part of the city that experienced beggars shunned. There was nobody about. Block after block of residences stretched away on either hand, lighted, full of people. But the sidewalks were deserted.

"Mammy," whimpered Hilda. "I'm tired, carry me."

Using all her strength, Mrs. Hooven picked her up and moved on aimlessly.

Then again that terrible cry, the cry of the hungry child appealing to the helpless mother:

"Mammy, I'm hungry."

"Ach, Gott, leedle girl," exclaimed Mrs. Hooven, holding her close to her shoulder, the tears starting from her eyes. "Ach, leedle tochter. Doand, doand, doand. You praik my hairt. I cen't vind any subber. We got noddings to eat, noddings, noddings."

"When do we have those bread'n milk again, Mammy?"

"To-morrow—soon—py-and-py, Hilda. I doand know what pecome oaf us now, what pecome oaf my leedle babby."

She went on, holding Hilda against her shoulder with one arm as best she might, one hand steadying herself against the fence railings along the sidewalk. At last, a solitary pedestrian came into view, a young man in a top hat and overcoat, walking rapidly. Mrs. Hooven held out a quivering hand as he passed her.

"Say, say, den, Meest'r, blease hellup a boor womun."

The other hurried on.

The fish course was grenadins of bass and small salmon, the latter stuffed, and cooked in white wine and mushroom liquor.

"I have read your poem, of course, Mr. Presley," observed Mrs. Gerard. "'The Toilers,' I mean. What a sermon you read us, you dreadful young man. I felt that I ought at once to 'sell all that I have and give to the poor.' Positively, it did stir me up. You may congratulate yourself upon making at least one convert. Just because of that poem Mrs. Cedarquist and I have started a movement to send a whole shipload of wheat to the starving people in India. Now, you horrid reactionnaire, are you satisfied?"

"I am very glad," murmured Presley.

"But I am afraid," observed Mrs. Cedarquist, "that we may be too late. They are dying so fast, those poor people. By the time our ship reaches India the famine may be all over."

"One need never be afraid of being 'too late' in the matter of helping the destitute," answered Presley. "Unfortunately, they are always a fixed quantity. 'The poor ye have always with you.'"

"How very clever that is," said Mrs. Gerard.

Mrs. Cedarquist tapped the table with her fan in mild applause.

"Brilliant, brilliant," she murmured, "epigrammatical."

"Honora," said Mrs. Gerard, turning to her daughter, at that moment in conversation with the languid Lambert, "Honora, entends-tu, ma cherie, l'esprit de notre jeune Lamartine."

Mrs. Hooven went on, stumbling from street to street, holding Hilda to her breast. Famine gnawed incessantly at her stomach; walk though she might, turn upon her tracks up and down the streets, back to the avenue again, incessantly and relentlessly the torture dug into her vitals. She was hungry, hungry, and if the want of food harassed and rended her, full-grown woman that she was, what must it be in the poor, starved stomach of her little girl? Oh, for some helping hand now, oh, for one little mouthful, one little nibble! Food, food, all her wrecked body clamoured for nourishment; anything to numb those gnawing teeth—an abandoned loaf, hard, mouldered; a half-eaten fruit, yes, even the refuse of the gutter, even the garbage of the ash heap. On she went, peering into dark corners, into the areaways, anywhere, everywhere, watching the silent prowling of cats, the intent rovings of stray dogs. But she was growing weaker; the pains and cramps in her stomach returned. Hilda's weight bore her to the pavement. More than once a great giddiness, a certain wheeling faintness all but overcame her. Hilda, however, was asleep. To wake her would only mean to revive her to the consciousness of hunger; yet how to carry her further? Mrs. Hooven began to fear that she would fall with her child in her arms. The terror of a collapse upon those cold pavements glistening with fog-damp roused her; she must make an effort to get through the night. She rallied all her strength, and pausing a moment to shift the weight of her baby to the other arm, once more set off through the night. A little while later she found on the edge of the sidewalk the peeling of a banana. It had been trodden upon and it was muddy, but joyfully she caught it up.

"Hilda," she cried, "wake oop, leedle girl. See, loog den, dere's somedings to eat. Look den, hey? Dat's goot, ain't it? Zum bunaner."

But it could not be eaten. Decayed, dirty, all but rotting, the stomach turned from the refuse, nauseated.

"No, no," cried Hilda, "that's not good. I can't eat it. Oh, Mammy, please gif me those bread'n milk."

By now the guests of Mrs. Gerard had come to the entrees—Londonderry pheasants, escallops of duck, and rissolettes a la pompadour. The wine was Chateau Latour.

All around the table conversations were going forward gayly. The good wines had broken up the slight restraint of the early part of the evening and a spirit of good humour and good fellowship prevailed. Young Lambert and Mr. Gerard were deep in reminiscences of certain mutual duck-shooting expeditions. Mrs. Gerard and Mrs. Cedarquist discussed a novel—a strange mingling of psychology, degeneracy, and analysis of erotic conditions— which had just been translated from the Italian. Stephen Lambert and Beatrice disputed over the merits of a Scotch collie just given to the young lady. The scene was gay, the electric bulbs sparkled, the wine flashing back the light. The entire table was a vague glow of white napery, delicate china, and glass as brilliant as crystal. Behind the guests the serving-men came and went, filling the glasses continually, changing the covers, serving the entrees, managing the dinner without interruption, confusion, or the slightest unnecessary noise.

But Presley could find no enjoyment in the occasion. From that picture of feasting, that scene of luxury, that atmosphere of decorous, well-bred refinement, his thoughts went back to Los Muertos and Quien Sabe and the irrigating ditch at Hooven's. He saw them fall, one by one, Harran, Annixter, Osterman, Broderson, Hooven. The clink of the wine glasses was drowned in the explosion of revolvers. The Railroad might indeed be a force only, which no man could control and for which no man was responsible, but his friends had been killed, but years of extortion and oppression had wrung money from all the San Joaquin, money that had made possible this very scene in which he found himself. Because Magnus had been beggared, Gerard had become Railroad King; because the farmers of the valley were poor, these men were rich.

The fancy grew big in his mind, distorted, caricatured, terrible. Because the farmers had been killed at the irrigation ditch, these others, Gerard and his family, fed full. They fattened on the blood of the People, on the blood of the men who had been killed at the ditch. It was a half-ludicrous, half-horrible "dog eat dog," an unspeakable cannibalism. Harran, Annixter, and Hooven were being devoured there under his eyes. These dainty women, his cousin Beatrice and little Miss Gerard, frail, delicate; all these fine ladies with their small fingers and slender necks, suddenly were transfigured in his tortured mind into harpies tearing human flesh. His head swam with the horror of it, the terror of it. Yes, the People WOULD turn some day, and turning, rend those who now preyed upon them. It would be "dog eat dog" again, with positions reversed, and he saw for one instant of time that splendid house sacked to its foundations, the tables overturned, the pictures torn, the hangings blazing, and Liberty, the red-handed Man in the Street, grimed with powder smoke, foul with the gutter, rush yelling, torch in hand, through every door.

At ten o'clock Mrs. Hooven fell.

Luckily she was leading Hilda by the hand at the time and the little girl was not hurt. In vain had Mrs. Hooven, hour after hour, walked the streets. After a while she no longer made any attempt to beg; nobody was stirring, nor did she even try to hunt for food with the stray dogs and cats. She had made up her mind to return to the park in order to sit upon the benches there, but she had mistaken the direction, and following up Sacramento Street, had come out at length, not upon the park, but upon a great vacant lot at the very top of the Clay Street hill. The ground was unfenced and rose above her to form the cap of the hill, all overgrown with bushes and a few stunted live oaks. It was in trying to cross this piece of ground that she fell. She got upon her feet again.

"Ach, Mammy, did you hurt yourself?" asked Hilda.

"No, no."

"Is that house where we get those bread'n milk?"

Hilda pointed to a single rambling building just visible in the night, that stood isolated upon the summit of the hill in a grove of trees.

"No, no, dere aindt no braid end miluk, leedle tochter."

Hilda once more began to sob.

"Ach, Mammy, please, PLEASE, I want it. I'm hungry."

The jangled nerves snapped at last under the tension, and Mrs. Hooven, suddenly shaking Hilda roughly, cried out: "Stop, stop. Doand say ut egen, you. My Gott, you kill me yet."

But quick upon this came the reaction. The mother caught her little girl to her, sinking down upon her knees, putting her arms around her, holding her close.

"No, no, gry all so mudge es you want. Say dot you are hongry. Say ut egen, say ut all de dime, ofer end ofer egen. Say ut, poor, starfing, leedle babby. Oh, mein poor, leedle tochter. My Gott, oh, I go crazy bretty soon, I guess. I cen't hellup you. I cen't ged you noddings to eat, noddings, noddings. Hilda, we gowun to die togedder. Put der arms roundt me, soh, tighd, leedle babby. We gowun to die, we gowun to vind Popper. We aindt gowun to be hongry eny more."

"Vair we go now?" demanded Hilda.

"No places. Mommer's soh tiredt. We stop heir, leedle while, end rest."

Underneath a large bush that afforded a little shelter from the wind, Mrs. Hooven lay down, taking Hilda in her arms and wrapping her shawl about her. The infinite, vast night expanded gigantic all around them. At this elevation they were far above the city. It was still. Close overhead whirled the chariots of the fog, galloping landward, smothering lights, blurring outlines. Soon all sight of the town was shut out; even the solitary house on the hilltop vanished. There was nothing left but grey, wheeling fog, and the mother and child, alone, shivering in a little strip of damp ground, an island drifting aimlessly in empty space.

Hilda's fingers touched a leaf from the bush and instinctively closed upon it and carried it to her mouth.

"Mammy," she said, "I'm eating those leaf. Is those good?"

Her mother did not reply.

"You going to sleep, Mammy?" inquired Hilda, touching her face.

Mrs. Hooven roused herself a little.

"Hey? Vat you say? Asleep? Yais, I guess I wass asleep."

Her voice trailed unintelligibly to silence again. She was not, however, asleep. Her eyes were open. A grateful numbness had begun to creep over her, a pleasing semi-insensibility. She no longer felt the pain and cramps of her stomach, even the hunger was ceasing to bite.

"These stuffed artichokes are delicious, Mrs. Gerard," murmured young Lambert, wiping his lips with a corner of his napkin. "Pardon me for mentioning it, but your dinner must be my excuse."

"And this asparagus—since Mr. Lambert has set the bad example," observed Mrs. Cedarquist, "so delicate, such an exquisite flavour. How do you manage?"

"We get all our asparagus from the southern part of the State, from one particular ranch," explained Mrs. Gerard. "We order it by wire and get it only twenty hours after cutting. My husband sees to it that it is put on a special train. It stops at this ranch just to take on our asparagus. Extravagant, isn't it, but I simply cannot eat asparagus that has been cut more than a day."

"Nor I," exclaimed Julian Lambert, who posed as an epicure. "I can tell to an hour just how long asparagus has been picked."

"Fancy eating ordinary market asparagus," said Mrs. Gerard, "that has been fingered by Heaven knows how many hands."

"Mammy, mammy, wake up," cried Hilda, trying to push open Mrs. Hooven's eyelids, at last closed. "Mammy, don't. You're just trying to frighten me."

Feebly Hilda shook her by the shoulder. At last Mrs. Hooven's lips stirred. Putting her head down, Hilda distinguished the whispered words:

"I'm sick. Go to schleep....Sick....Noddings to eat."

The dessert was a wonderful preparation of alternate layers of biscuit glaces, ice cream, and candied chestnuts.

"Delicious, is it not?" observed Julian Lambert, partly to himself, partly to Miss Cedarquist. "This Moscovite fouette—upon my word, I have never tasted its equal."

"And you should know, shouldn't you?" returned the young lady.

"Mammy, mammy, wake up," cried Hilda. "Don't sleep so. I'm frightenedt."

Repeatedly she shook her; repeatedly she tried to raise the inert eyelids with the point of her finger. But her mother no longer stirred. The gaunt, lean body, with its bony face and sunken eye-sockets, lay back, prone upon the ground, the feet upturned and showing the ragged, worn soles of the shoes, the forehead and grey hair beaded with fog, the poor, faded bonnet awry, the poor, faded dress soiled and torn. Hilda drew close to her mother, kissing her face, twining her arms around her neck. For a long time, she lay that way, alternately sobbing and sleeping. Then, after a long time, there was a stir. She woke from a doze to find a police officer and two or three other men bending over her. Some one carried a lantern. Terrified, smitten dumb, she was unable to answer the questions put to her. Then a woman, evidently a mistress of the house on the top of the hill, arrived and took Hilda in her arms and cried over her.

"I'll take the little girl," she said to the police officer.

"But the mother, can you save her? Is she too far gone?"

"I've sent for a doctor," replied the other.

Just before the ladies left the table, young Lambert raised his glass of Madeira. Turning towards the wife of the Railroad King, he said:

"My best compliments for a delightful dinner."

The doctor who had been bending over Mrs. Hooven, rose.

"It's no use," he said; "she has been dead some time—exhaustion from starvation."

CHAPTER IX

On Division Number Three of the Los Muertos ranch the wheat had already been cut, and S. Behrman on a certain morning in the first week of August drove across the open expanse of stubble toward the southwest, his eyes searching the horizon for the feather of smoke that would mark the location of the steam harvester. However, he saw nothing. The stubble extended onward apparently to the very margin of the world.

At length, S. Behrman halted his buggy and brought out his field glasses from beneath the seat. He stood up in his place and, adjusting the lenses, swept the prospect to the south and west. It was the same as though the sea of land were, in reality, the ocean, and he, lost in an open boat, were scanning the waste through his glasses, looking for the smoke of a steamer, hull down, below the horizon. "Wonder," he muttered, "if they're working on Four this morning?"

At length, he murmured an "Ah" of satisfaction. Far to the south into the white sheen of sky, immediately over the horizon, he made out a faint smudge—the harvester beyond doubt.

Thither S. Behrman turned his horse's head. It was all of an hour's drive over the uneven ground and through the crackling stubble, but at length he reached the harvester. He found, however, that it had been halted. The sack sewers, together with the header-man, were stretched on the ground in the shade of the machine, while the engineer and separator-man were pottering about a portion of the works.

"What's the matter, Billy?" demanded S. Behrman reining up.

The engineer turned about.

"The grain is heavy in here. We thought we'd better increase the speed of the cup-carrier, and pulled up to put in a smaller sprocket."

S. Behrman nodded to say that was all right, and added a question.

"How is she going?"

"Anywheres from twenty-five to thirty sacks to the acre right along here; nothing the matter with THAT I guess."

"Nothing in the world, Bill."

One of the sack sewers interposed:

"For the last half hour we've been throwing off three bags to the minute."

"That's good, that's good."

It was more than good; it was "bonanza," and all that division of the great ranch was thick with just such wonderful wheat. Never had Los Muertos been more generous, never a season more successful. S. Behrman drew a long breath of satisfaction. He knew just how great was his share in the lands which had just been absorbed by the corporation he served, just how many thousands of bushels of this marvellous crop were his property. Through all these years of confusion, bickerings, open hostility and, at last, actual warfare he had waited, nursing his patience, calm with the firm assurance of ultimate success. The end, at length, had come; he had entered into his reward and saw himself at last installed in the place he had so long, so silently coveted; saw himself chief of a principality, the Master of the Wheat.

The sprocket adjusted, the engineer called up the gang and the men took their places. The fireman stoked vigorously, the two sack sewers resumed their posts on the sacking platform, putting on the goggles that kept the chaff from their eyes. The separator-man and header-man gripped their levers.

The harvester, shooting a column of thick smoke straight upward, vibrating to the top of the stack, hissed, clanked, and lurched forward. Instantly, motion sprang to life in all its component parts; the header knives, cutting a thirty-six foot swath, gnashed like teeth; beltings slid and moved like smooth flowing streams; the separator whirred, the agitator jarred and crashed; cylinders, augers, fans, seeders and elevators, drapers and chaff-carriers clattered, rumbled, buzzed, and clanged. The steam hissed and rasped; the ground reverberated a hollow note, and the thousands upon thousands of wheat stalks sliced and slashed in the clashing shears of the header, rattled like dry rushes in a hurricane, as they fell inward, and were caught up by an endless belt, to disappear into the bowels of the vast brute that devoured them.

It was that and no less. It was the feeding of some prodigious monster, insatiable, with iron teeth, gnashing and threshing into the fields of standing wheat; devouring always, never glutted, never satiated, swallowing an entire harvest, snarling and slobbering in a welter of warm vapour, acrid smoke, and blinding, pungent clouds of chaff. It moved belly-deep in the standing grain, a hippopotamus, half-mired in river ooze, gorging rushes, snorting, sweating; a dinosaur wallowing through thick, hot grasses, floundering there, crouching, grovelling there as its vast jaws crushed and tore, and its enormous gullet swallowed, incessant, ravenous, and inordinate.

S. Behrman, very much amused, changed places with one of the sack sewers, allowing him to hold his horse while he mounted the sacking platform and took his place. The trepidation and jostling of the machine shook him till his teeth chattered in his head. His ears were shocked and assaulted by a myriad-tongued clamour, clashing steel, straining belts, jarring woodwork, while the impalpable chaff powder from the separators settled like dust in his hair, his ears, eyes, and mouth.

Directly in front of where he sat on the platform was the chute from the cleaner, and from this into the mouth of a half-full sack spouted an unending gush of grain, winnowed, cleaned, threshed, ready for the mill.

The pour from the chute of the cleaner had for S. Behrman an immense satisfaction. Without an instant's pause, a thick rivulet of wheat rolled and dashed tumultuous into the sack. In half a minute—sometimes in twenty seconds—the sack was full, was passed over to the second sewer, the mouth reeved up, and the sack dumped out upon the ground, to be picked up by the wagons and hauled to the railroad.

S. Behrman, hypnotised, sat watching that river of grain. All that shrieking, bellowing machinery, all that gigantic organism, all the months of labour, the ploughing, the planting, the prayers for rain, the years of preparation, the heartaches, the anxiety, the foresight, all the whole business of the ranch, the work of horses, of steam, of men and boys, looked to this spot—the grain chute from the harvester into the sacks. Its volume was the index of failure or success, of riches or poverty. And at this point, the labour of the rancher ended. Here, at the lip of the chute, he parted company with his grain, and from here the wheat streamed forth to feed the world. The yawning mouths of the sacks might well stand for the unnumbered mouths of the People, all agape for food; and here, into these sacks, at first so lean, so flaccid, attenuated like starved stomachs, rushed the living stream of food, insistent, interminable, filling the empty, fattening the shrivelled, making it sleek and heavy and solid.

Half an hour later, the harvester stopped again. The men on the sacking platform had used up all the sacks. But S. Behrman's foreman, a new man on

Los Muertos, put in an appearance with the report that the wagon bringing a fresh supply was approaching.

"How is the grain elevator at Port Costa getting on, sir?"

"Finished," replied S. Behrman.

The new master of Los Muertos had decided upon accumulating his grain in bulk in a great elevator at the tide-water port, where the grain ships for Liverpool and the East took on their cargoes. To this end, he had bought and greatly enlarged a building at Port Costa, that was already in use for that purpose, and to this elevator all the crop of Los Muertos was to be carried. The P. and S. W. made S. Behrman a special rate.

"By the way," said S. Behrman to his superintendent, "we're in luck. Fallon's buyer was in Bonneville yesterday. He's buying for Fallon and for Holt, too. I happened to run into him, and I've sold a ship load."

"A ship load!"

"Of Los Muertos wheat. He's acting for some Indian Famine Relief Committee—lot of women people up in the city—and wanted a whole cargo. I made a deal with him. There's about fifty thousand tons of disengaged shipping in San Francisco Bay right now, and ships are fighting for charters. I wired McKissick and got a long distance telephone from him this morning. He got me a barque, the 'Swanhilda.' She'll dock day after to-morrow, and begin loading."

"Hadn't I better take a run up," observed the superintendent, "and keep an eye on things?"

"No," answered S. Behrman, "I want you to stop down here, and see that those carpenters hustle the work in the ranch house. Derrick will be out by then. You see this deal is peculiar. I'm not selling to any middle-man—not to Fallon's buyer. He only put me on to the thing. I'm acting direct with these women people, and I've got to have some hand in shipping this stuff myself. But I made my selling figure cover the price of a charter. It's a queer, mixed-up deal, and I don't fancy it much, but there's boodle in it. I'll go to Port Costa myself."

A little later on in the day, when S. Behrman had satisfied himself that his harvesting was going forward favourably, he reentered his buggy and driving to the County Road turned southward towards the Los Muertos ranch house. He had not gone far, however, before he became aware of a familiar figure on horse-back, jogging slowly along ahead of him. He recognised Presley; he shook the reins over his horse's back and very soon ranging up by the side of the young man passed the time of day with him.

"Well, what brings you down here again, Mr. Presley?" he observed. "I thought we had seen the last of you."

"I came down to say good-bye to my friends," answered Presley shortly.

"Going away?"

"Yes—to India."

"Well, upon my word. For your health, hey?"

"Yes."

"You LOOK knocked up," asserted the other. "By the way," he added, "I suppose you've heard the news?"

Presley shrank a little. Of late the reports of disasters had followed so swiftly upon one another that he had begun to tremble and to quail at every unexpected bit of information.

"What news do you mean?" he asked.

"About Dyke. He has been convicted. The judge sentenced him for life."

For life! Riding on by the side of this man through the ranches by the County Road, Presley repeated these words to himself till the full effect of them burst at last upon him.

Jailed for life! No outlook. No hope for the future. Day after day, year after year, to tread the rounds of the same gloomy monotony. He saw the grey stone walls, the iron doors; the flagging of the "yard" bare of grass or trees—the cell, narrow, bald, cheerless; the prison garb, the prison fare, and round all the grim granite of insuperable barriers, shutting out the world, shutting in the man with outcasts, with the pariah dogs of society, thieves, murderers, men below the beasts, lost to all decency, drugged with opium, utter reprobates. To this, Dyke had been brought, Dyke, than whom no man had been more honest, more courageous, more jovial. This was the end of him, a prison; this was his final estate, a criminal.

Presley found an excuse for riding on, leaving S. Behrman behind him. He did not stop at Caraher's saloon, for the heat of his rage had long since begun to cool, and dispassionately, he saw things in their true light. For all the tragedy of his wife's death, Caraher was none the less an evil influence among the ranchers, an influence that worked only to the inciting of crime. Unwilling to venture himself, to risk his own life, the anarchist saloon-keeper had goaded Dyke and Presley both to murder; a bad man, a plague spot in the world of the ranchers, poisoning the farmers' bodies with alcohol and their minds with discontent.

At last, Presley arrived at the ranch house of Los Muertos. The place was silent; the grass on the lawn was half dead and over a foot high; the beginnings of weeds showed here and there in the driveway. He tied his horse to a ring in the trunk of one of the larger eucalyptus trees and entered the house.

Mrs. Derrick met him in the dining-room. The old look of uneasiness, almost of terror, had gone from her wide-open brown eyes. There was in them instead, the expression of one to whom a contingency, long dreaded, has arrived and passed. The stolidity of a settled grief, of an irreparable calamity, of a despair from which there was no escape was in her look, her manner, her voice. She was listless, apathetic, calm with the calmness of a woman who knows she can suffer no further.

"We are going away," she told Presley, as the two sat down at opposite ends of the dining table. "Just Magnus and myself—all there is left of us. There is very little money left; Magnus can hardly take care of himself, to say nothing of me. I must look after him now. We are going to Marysville."

"Why there?"

"You see," she explained, "it happens that my old place is vacant in the Seminary there. I am going back to teach—literature." She smiled wearily. "It is beginning all over again, isn't it? Only there is nothing to look forward to now. Magnus is an old man already, and I must take care of him."

"He will go with you, then," Presley said, "that will be some comfort to you at least."

"I don't know," she said slowly, "you have not seen Magnus lately."

"Is he—how do you mean? Isn't he any better?"

"Would you like to see him? He is in the office. You can go right in."

Presley rose. He hesitated a moment, then:

"Mrs. Annixter," he asked, "Hilma—is she still with you? I should like to see her before I go." "Go in and see Magnus," said Mrs. Derrick. "I will tell her you are here."

Presley stepped across the stone-paved hallway with the glass roof, and after knocking three times at the office door pushed it open and entered.

Magnus sat in the chair before the desk and did not look up as Presley entered. He had the appearance of a man nearer eighty than sixty. All the old-time erectness was broken and bent. It was as though the muscles that once had held the back rigid, the chin high, had softened and stretched. A certain fatness, the obesity of inertia, hung heavy around the hips and abdomen, the eye was watery and vague, the cheeks and chin unshaven and unkempt, the grey hair had lost its forward curl towards the temples and hung thin and ragged around the ears. The hawk-like nose seemed hooked to meet the chin; the lips were slack, the mouth half-opened.

Where once the Governor had been a model of neatness in his dress, the frock coat buttoned, the linen clean, he now sat in his shirt sleeves, the waistcoat open and showing the soiled shirt. His hands were stained with ink, and these, the only members of his body that yet appeared to retain their activity, were busy with a great pile of papers, — oblong, legal documents, that littered the table before him. Without a moment's cessation, these hands of the Governor's came and went among the papers, deft, nimble, dexterous.

Magnus was sorting papers. From the heap upon his left hand he selected a document, opened it, glanced over it, then tied it carefully, and laid it away upon a second pile on his right hand. When all the papers were in one pile, he reversed the process, taking from his right hand to place upon his left, then back from left to right again, then once more from right to left. He spoke no word, he sat absolutely still, even his eyes did not move, only his hands, swift, nervous, agitated, seemed alive.

"Why, how are you, Governor?" said Presley, coming forward. Magnus turned slowly about and looked at him and at the hand in which he shook his own.

"Ah," he said at length, "Presley...yes."

Then his glance fell, and he looked aimlessly about upon the floor. "I've come to say good-bye, Governor," continued Presley, "I'm going away."

"Going away...yes, why it's Presley. Good-day, Presley."

"Good-day, Governor. I'm going away. I've come to say good-bye."

"Good-bye?" Magnus bent his brows, "what are you saying good-bye for?"

"I'm going away, sir."

The Governor did not answer. Staring at the ledge of the desk, he seemed lost in thought. There was a long silence. Then, at length, Presley said:

"How are you getting on, Governor?"

Magnus looked up slowly.

"Why it's Presley," he said. "How do you do, Presley."

"Are you getting on all right, sir?"

"Yes," said Magnus after a while, "yes, all right. I am going away. I've come to say good-bye. No—" He interrupted himself with a deprecatory smile, "YOU said THAT, didn't you?"

"Well, you are going away, too, your wife tells me."

"Yes, I'm going away. I can't stay on..." he hesitated a long time, groping for the right word, "I can't stay on—on—what's the name of this place?"

"Los Muertos," put in Presley.

"No, it isn't. Yes, it is, too, that's right, Los Muertos. I don't know where my memory has gone to of late."

"Well, I hope you will be better soon, Governor."

As Presley spoke the words, S. Behrman entered the room, and the Governor sprang up with unexpected agility and stood against the wall, drawing one long breath after another, watching the railroad agent with intent eyes.

S. Behrman saluted both men affably and sat down near the desk, drawing the links of his heavy watch chain through his fat fingers.

"There wasn't anybody outside when I knocked, but I heard your voice in here, Governor, so I came right in. I wanted to ask you, Governor, if my carpenters can begin work in here day after to-morrow. I want to take down that partition there, and throw this room and the next into one. I guess that will be O. K., won't it? You'll be out of here by then, won't you?"

There was no vagueness about Magnus's speech or manner now. There was that same alertness in his demeanour that one sees in a tamed lion in the presence of its trainer.

"Yes, yes," he said quickly, "you can send your men here. I will be gone by to-morrow."

"I don't want to seem to hurry you, Governor." "No, you will not hurry me. I am ready to go now."

"Anything I can do for you, Governor?"

"Nothing."

"Yes, there is, Governor," insisted S. Behrman. "I think now that all is over we ought to be good friends. I think I can do something for you. We still want an assistant in the local freight manager's office. Now, what do you say to having a try at it? There's a salary of fifty a month goes with it. I guess you must be in need of money now, and there's always the wife to support; what do you say? Will you try the place?"

Presley could only stare at the man in speechless wonder. What was he driving at? What reason was there back of this new move, and why should it be made thus openly and in his hearing? An explanation occurred to him. Was this merely a pleasantry on the part of S. Behrman, a way of enjoying to the full his triumph; was he testing the completeness of his victory, trying to see just how far he could go, how far beneath his feet he could push his old-time enemy?

"What do you say?" he repeated. "Will you try the place?"

"You—you INSIST?" inquired the Governor.

"Oh, I'm not insisting on anything," cried S. Behrman. "I'm offering you a place, that's all. Will you take it?"

"Yes, yes, I'll take it."

"You'll come over to our side?"

"Yes, I'll come over."

"You'll have to turn 'railroad,' understand?"

"I'll turn railroad."

"Guess there may be times when you'll have to take orders from me."

"I'll take orders from you."

"You'll have to be loyal to railroad, you know. No funny business."

"I'll be loyal to the railroad."

"You would like the place then?"

"Yes."

S. Behrman turned from Magnus, who at once resumed his seat and began again to sort his papers.

"Well, Presley," said the railroad agent: "I guess I won't see you again."

"I hope not," answered the other.

"Tut, tut, Presley, you know you can't make me angry."

He put on his hat of varnished straw and wiped his fat forehead with his handkerchief. Of late, he had grown fatter than ever, and the linen vest, stamped with a multitude of interlocked horseshoes, strained tight its imitation pearl buttons across the great protuberant stomach.

Presley looked at the man a moment before replying.

But a few weeks ago he could not thus have faced the great enemy of the farmers without a gust of blind rage blowing tempestuous through all his bones. Now, however, he found to his surprise that his fury had lapsed to a profound contempt, in which there was bitterness, but no truculence. He was tired, tired to death of the whole business.

"Yes," he answered deliberately, "I am going away. You have ruined this place for me. I couldn't live here where I should have to see you, or the results of what you have done, whenever I stirred out of doors."

"Nonsense, Presley," answered the other, refusing to become angry. "That's foolishness, that kind of talk; though, of course, I understand how you feel. I guess it was you, wasn't it, who threw that bomb into my house?"

"It was."

"Well, that don't show any common sense, Presley," returned S. Behrman with perfect aplomb. "What could you have gained by killing me?"

"Not so much probably as you have gained by killing Harran and Annixter. But that's all passed now. You're safe from me." The strangeness of this talk, the oddity of the situation burst upon him and he laughed aloud. "It don't seem as though you could be brought to book, S. Behrman, by anybody, or by any means, does it? They can't get at you through the courts,—the law can't get you, Dyke's pistol missed fire for just your benefit, and you even escaped Caraher's six inches of plugged gas pipe. Just what are we going to do with you?"

"Best give it up, Pres, my boy," returned the other. "I guess there ain't anything can touch me. Well, Magnus," he said, turning once more to the Governor. "Well, I'll think over what you say, and let you know if I can get the place for you in a day or two. You see," he added, "you're getting pretty old, Magnus Derrick."

Presley flung himself from the room, unable any longer to witness the depths into which Magnus had fallen. What other scenes of degradation were enacted in that room, how much further S. Behrman carried the humiliation, he did not know. He suddenly felt that the air of the office was choking him.

He hurried up to what once had been his own room. On his way he could not but note that much of the house was in disarray, a great packing-up was in progress; trunks, half-full, stood in the hallways, crates and cases in a litter of straw encumbered the rooms. The servants came and went with armfuls of books, ornaments, articles of clothing.

Presley took from his room only a few manuscripts and note-books, and a small valise full of his personal effects; at the doorway he paused and, holding the knob of the door in his hand, looked back into the room a very long time.

He descended to the lower floor and entered the dining-room. Mrs. Derrick had disappeared. Presley stood for a long moment in front of the fireplace, looking about the room, remembering the scenes that he had witnessed there—the conference when Osterman had first suggested the fight for Railroad Commissioner and then later the attack on Lyman Derrick and the sudden revelation of that inconceivable treachery. But as he stood considering these things a door to his right opened and Hilma entered the room.

Presley came forward, holding out his hand, all unable to believe his eyes. It was a woman, grave, dignified, composed, who advanced to meet him. Hilma was dressed in black, the cut and fashion of the gown severe, almost monastic. All the little feminine and contradictory daintinesses were nowhere to be seen. Her statuesque calm evenness of contour yet remained, but it was the calmness of great sorrow, of infinite resignation. Beautiful she still remained, but she was older. The seriousness of one who has gained the knowledge of the world—knowledge of its evil—seemed to envelope her. The calm gravity of a great suffering past, but not forgotten, sat upon her. Not yet twenty-one, she exhibited the demeanour of a woman of forty.

The one-time amplitude of her figure, the fulness of hip and shoulder, the great deep swell from waist to throat were gone. She had grown thinner and, in consequence, seemed unusually, almost unnaturally tall. Her neck was slender, the outline of her full lips and round chin was a little sharp; her arms, those wonderful, beautiful arms of hers, were a little shrunken. But her eyes were as wide open as always, rimmed as ever by the thin, intensely black line of the lashes and her brown, fragrant hair was still thick, still, at times, glittered and coruscated in the sun. When she spoke, it was with the old-time velvety huskiness of voice that Annixter had learned to love so well.

"Oh, it is you," she said, giving him her hand. "You were good to want to see me before you left. I hear that you are going away."

She sat down upon the sofa.

"Yes," Presley answered, drawing a chair near to her, "yes, I felt I could not stay—down here any longer. I am going to take a long ocean voyage. My ship sails in a few days. But you, Mrs. Annixter, what are you going to do? Is there any way I can serve you?"

"No," she answered, "nothing. Papa is doing well. We are living here now."

"You are well?"

She made a little helpless gesture with both her hands, smiling very sadly.

"As you see," she answered.

As he talked, Presley was looking at her intently. Her dignity was a new element in her character and the certain slender effect of her figure, emphasised now by the long folds of the black gown she wore, carried it almost superbly. She conveyed something of the impression of a queen in exile. But she had lost none of her womanliness; rather, the contrary. Adversity had softened her, as well as deepened her. Presley saw that very clearly. Hilma had arrived now at her perfect maturity; she had known great love and she had known great grief, and the woman that had awakened in her with her affection for Annixter had been strengthened and infinitely ennobled by his death. What if things had been different? Thus, as he conversed with her, Presley found himself wondering. Her sweetness, her beautiful gentleness, and tenderness were almost like palpable presences. It was almost as if a caress had been laid softly upon his cheek, as if a gentle hand closed upon his. Here, he knew, was sympathy; here, he knew, was an infinite capacity for love.

Then suddenly all the tired heart of him went out towards her. A longing to give the best that was in him to the memory of her, to be strong and noble because of her, to reshape his purposeless, half-wasted life with her nobility and purity and gentleness for his inspiration leaped all at once within him, leaped and stood firm, hardening to a resolve stronger than any he had ever known.

For an instant he told himself that the suddenness of this new emotion must be evidence of its insincerity. He was perfectly well aware that his impulses were abrupt and of short duration. But he knew that this was not sudden. Without realising it, he had been from the first drawn to Hilma, and all through these last terrible days, since the time he had seen her at Los Muertos, just after the battle at the ditch, she had obtruded continually upon his thoughts. The sight of her to-day, more beautiful than ever, quiet, strong, reserved, had only brought matters to a culmination.

"Are you," he asked her, "are you so unhappy, Hilma, that you can look forward to no more brightness in your life?"

"Unless I could forget—forget my husband," she answered, "how can I be happy? I would rather be unhappy in remembering him than happy in forgetting him. He was my whole world, literally and truly. Nothing seemed to count before I knew him, and nothing can count for me now, after I have lost him."

"You think now," he answered, "that in being happy again you would be disloyal to him. But you will find after a while—years from now—that it need not be so. The part of you that belonged to your husband can always keep him sacred, that part of you belongs to him and he to it. But you are young; you have all your life to live yet. Your sorrow need not be a burden to you. If you consider it as you should—as you WILL some day, believe me—it will only be a great help to you. It will make you more noble, a truer woman, more generous."

"I think I see," she answered, "and I never thought about it in that light before."

"I want to help you," he answered, "as you have helped me. I want to be your friend, and above all things I do not want to see your life wasted. I am going away and it is quite possible I shall never see you again, but you will always be a help to me."

"I do not understand," she answered, "but I know you mean to be very, very kind to me. Yes, I hope when you come back—if you ever do—you will still be that. I do not know why you should want to be so kind, unless—yes, of course—you were my husband's dearest friend."

They talked a little longer, and at length Presley rose.

"I cannot bring myself to see Mrs. Derrick again," he said. "It would only serve to make her very unhappy. Will you explain that to her? I think she will understand."

"Yes," answered Hilma. "Yes, I will."

There was a pause. There seemed to be nothing more for either of them to say. Presley held out his hand.

"Good-bye," she said, as she gave him hers.

He carried it to his lips.

"Good-bye," he answered. "Good-bye and may God bless you."

He turned away abruptly and left the room. But as he was quietly making his way out of the house, hoping to get to his horse unobserved, he came suddenly upon Mrs. Dyke and Sidney on the porch of the house. He had forgotten that since the affair at the ditch, Los Muertos had been a home to the engineer's mother and daughter.

"And you, Mrs. Dyke," he asked as he took her hand, "in this break-up of everything, where do you go?"

"To the city," she answered, "to San Francisco. I have a sister there who will look after the little tad."

"But you, how about yourself, Mrs. Dyke?"

She answered him in a quiet voice, monotonous, expressionless:

"I am going to die very soon, Mr. Presley. There is no reason why I should live any longer. My son is in prison for life, everything is over for me, and I am tired, worn out."

"You mustn't talk like that, Mrs. Dyke," protested Presley, "nonsense; you will live long enough to see the little tad married." He tried to be cheerful. But he knew his words lacked the ring of conviction. Death already overshadowed the face of the engineer's mother. He felt that she spoke the truth, and as he stood there speaking to her for the last time, his arm about little Sidney's shoulder, he knew that he was seeing the beginnings of the wreck of another family and that, like Hilda Hooven, another baby girl was to be started in life, through no fault of hers, fearfully handicapped, weighed down at the threshold of existence with a load of disgrace. Hilda Hooven and Sidney Dyke, what was to be their histories? the one, sister of an outcast; the other, daughter of a convict. And he thought of that other young girl, the little Honora Gerard, the heiress of millions, petted, loved, receiving adulation from all who came near to her, whose only care was to choose from among the multitude of pleasures that the world hastened to present to her consideration.

"Good-bye," he said, holding out his hand.

"Good-bye."

"Good-bye, Sidney."

He kissed the little girl, clasped Mrs. Dyke's hand a moment with his; then, slinging his satchel about his shoulders by the long strap with which it was provided, left the house, and mounting his horse rode away from Los Muertos never to return.

Presley came out upon the County Road. At a little distance to his left he could see the group of buildings where once Broderson had lived. These were being remodelled, at length, to suit the larger demands of the New Agriculture. A strange man came out by the road gate; no doubt, the new proprietor. Presley turned away, hurrying northwards along the County Road by the mammoth watering-tank and the long wind-break of poplars.

He came to Caraher's place. There was no change here. The saloon had weathered the storm, indispensable to the new as well as to the old regime. The same dusty buggies and buckboards were tied under the shed, and as Presley hurried by he could distinguish Caraher's voice, loud as ever, still proclaiming his creed of annihilation.

Bonneville Presley avoided. He had no associations with the town. He turned aside from the road, and crossing the northwest corner of Los Muertos and the line of the railroad, turned back along the Upper Road till he came to the Long Trestle and Annixter's,—Silence, desolation, abandonment.

A vast stillness, profound, unbroken, brooded low over all the place. No living thing stirred. The rusted wind-mill on the skeleton-like tower of the artesian well was motionless; the great barn empty; the windows of the ranch house, cook house, and dairy boarded up. Nailed upon a tree near the broken gateway was a board, white painted, with stencilled letters, bearing the inscription:

"Warning. ALL PERSONS FOUND TRESPASSING ON THESE PREMISES WILL BE PROSECUTED TO THE FULLEST EXTENT OF THE LAW. By order P. and S. W. R. R."

As he had planned, Presley reached the hills by the head waters of Broderson's Creek late in the afternoon. Toilfully he climbed them, reached the highest crest, and turning about, looked long and for the last time at all the reach of the valley unrolled beneath him. The land of the ranches opened out forever and forever under the stimulus of that measureless range of vision. The whole gigantic sweep of the San Joaquin expanded Titanic before the eye of the mind, flagellated with heat, quivering and shimmering under the sun's red eye. It was the season after the harvest, and the great earth, the mother, after its period of reproduction, its pains of labour, delivered of the fruit of its loins, slept the sleep of exhaustion in the infinite repose of the colossus, benignant, eternal, strong, the nourisher of nations, the feeder of an entire world.

And as Presley looked there came to him strong and true the sense and the significance of all the enigma of growth. He seemed for one instant to touch the explanation of existence. Men were nothings, mere animalculae, mere ephemerides that fluttered and fell and were forgotten between dawn and dusk. Vanamee had said there was no death. But for one second Presley could go one step further. Men were naught, death was naught, life was naught; FORCE only existed—FORCE that brought men into the world, FORCE that crowded them out of it to make way for the succeeding generation, FORCE that made the wheat grow, FORCE that garnered it from the soil to give place to the succeeding crop.

It was the mystery of creation, the stupendous miracle of recreation; the vast rhythm of the seasons, measured, alternative, the sun and the stars keeping time as the eternal symphony of reproduction swung in its tremendous cadences like the colossal pendulum of an almighty machine— primordial energy flung out from the hand of the Lord God himself, immortal, calm, infinitely strong.

But as he stood thus looking down upon the great valley he was aware of the figure of a man, far in the distance, moving steadily towards the Mission of San Juan. The man was hardly more than a dot, but there was something unmistakably familiar in his gait; and besides this, Presley could fancy that he was hatless. He touched his pony with his spur. The man was Vanamee beyond all doubt, and a little later Presley, descending the maze of cow-paths and cattle-trails that led down towards the Broderson Creek, overtook his friend.

Instantly Presley was aware of an immense change. Vanamee's face was still that of an ascetic, still glowed with the rarefied intelligence of a young seer, a half-inspired shepherd-prophet of Hebraic legends; but the shadow of that great sadness which for so long had brooded over him was gone; the grief that once he had fancied deathless was, indeed, dead, or rather swallowed up in a victorious joy that radiated like sunlight at dawn from the deep-set eyes, and the hollow, swarthy cheeks. They talked together till nearly sundown, but to Presley's questions as to the reasons for Vanamee's happiness, the other would say nothing. Once only he allowed himself to touch upon the subject.

"Death and grief are little things," he said. "They are transient. Life must be before death, and joy before grief. Else there are no such things as death or grief. These are only negatives. Life is positive. Death is only the absence of life, just as night is only the absence of day, and if this is so, there is no such thing as death. There is only life, and the suppression of life, that we, foolishly, say is death. 'Suppression,' I say, not extinction. I do not say that life returns. Life never departs. Life simply IS. For certain seasons, it is hidden in the dark, but is that death, extinction, annihilation? I take it, thank God, that it is not. Does the grain of wheat, hidden for certain seasons in the dark, die? The grain we think is dead RESUMES AGAIN; but how? Not as one grain, but as twenty. So all life. Death is only real for all the detritus of the world, for all the sorrow, for all the injustice, for all the grief. Presley, the good never dies; evil dies, cruelty, oppression, selfishness, greed—these die; but nobility, but love, but sacrifice, but generosity, but truth, thank God for it, small as they are, difficult as it is to discover them—these live forever, these are eternal. You are all broken, all cast down by what you have seen in this valley, this hopeless struggle, this apparently hopeless despair. Well, the end is not yet. What is it that remains after all is over, after the dead are buried and the hearts are broken? Look at it all from the vast height of humanity—'the greatest good to the greatest numbers.' What remains? Men perish, men are corrupted, hearts are rent asunder, but what remains untouched, unassailable, undefiled? Try to find that, not only in this, but in every crisis of the world's life, and you will find, if your view be large enough, that it is not evil, but good, that in the end remains."

There was a long pause. Presley, his mind full of new thoughts, held his peace, and Vanamee added at length:

"I believed Angele dead. I wept over her grave; mourned for her as dead in corruption. She has come back to me, more beautiful than ever. Do not ask me any further. To put this story, this idyl, into words, would, for me, be a profanation. This must suffice you. Angele has returned to me, and I am happy. Adios."

He rose suddenly. The friends clasped each other's hands.

"We shall probably never meet again," said Vanamee; "but if these are the last words I ever speak to you, listen to them, and remember them, because I know I speak the truth. Evil is short-lived. Never judge of the whole round of life by the mere segment you can see. The whole is, in the end, perfect."

Abruptly he took himself away. He was gone. Presley, alone, thoughtful, his hands clasped behind him, passed on through the ranches—here teeming with ripened wheat—his face set from them forever.

Not so Vanamee. For hours he roamed the countryside, now through the deserted cluster of buildings that had once been Annixter's home; now through the rustling and, as yet, uncut wheat of Quien Sabe! now treading the slopes of the hills far to the north, and again following the winding courses of the streams. Thus he spent the night.

At length, the day broke, resplendent, cloudless. The night was passed. There was all the sparkle and effervescence of joy in the crystal sunlight as the dawn expanded roseate, and at length flamed dazzling to the zenith when the sun moved over the edge of the world and looked down upon all the earth like the eye of God the Father.

At the moment, Vanamee stood breast-deep in the wheat in a solitary corner of the Quien Sabe rancho. He turned eastward, facing the celestial glory of the day and sent his voiceless call far from him across the golden grain out towards the little valley of flowers.

Swiftly the answer came. It advanced to meet him. The flowers of the Seed ranch were gone, dried and parched by the summer's sun, shedding their seed by handfuls to be sown again and blossom yet another time. The Seed ranch was no longer royal with colour. The roses, the lilies, the carnations, the hyacinths, the poppies, the violets, the mignonette, all these had vanished, the little valley was without colour; where once it had exhaled the most delicious perfume, it was now odourless. Under the blinding light of the day it stretched to its hillsides, bare, brown, unlovely. The romance of the place had vanished, but with it had vanished the Vision.

It was no longer a figment of his imagination, a creature of dreams that advanced to meet Vanamee. It was Reality—it was Angele in the flesh, vital, sane, material, who at last issued forth from the entrance of the little valley. Romance had vanished, but better than romance was here. Not a manifestation, not a dream, but her very self. The night was gone, but the sun had risen; the flowers had disappeared, but strong, vigorous, noble, the wheat had come.

In the wheat he waited for her. He saw her coming. She was simply dressed. No fanciful wreath of tube-roses was about her head now, no strange garment of red and gold enveloped her now. It was no longer an ephemeral illusion of the night, evanescent, mystic, but a simple country girl coming to meet her lover. The vision of the night had been beautiful, but what was it compared to this? Reality was better than Romance. The simple honesty of a loving, trusting heart was better than a legend of flowers, an hallucination of the moonlight. She came nearer. Bathed in sunlight, he saw her face to face, saw her hair hanging in two straight plaits on either side of her face, saw the enchanting fulness of her lips, the strange, balancing movement of her head upon her slender neck. But now she was no longer asleep. The wonderful eyes, violet blue, heavy-lidded, with their perplexing, oriental slant towards the temples, were wide open and fixed upon his.

From out the world of romance, out of the moonlight and the star sheen, out of the faint radiance of the lilies and the still air heavy with perfume, she had at last come to him. The moonlight, the flowers, and the dream were all vanished away. Angele was realised in the Wheat. She stood forth in the sunlight, a fact, and no longer a fancy.

He ran forward to meet her and she held out her arms to him. He caught her to him, and she, turning her face to his, kissed him on the mouth.

"I love you, I love you," she murmured.

Upon descending from his train at Port Costa, S. Behrman asked to be directed at once to where the bark "Swanhilda" was taking on grain. Though he had bought and greatly enlarged his new elevator at this port, he had never seen it. The work had been carried on through agents, S. Behrman having far too many and more pressing occupations to demand his presence and attention. Now, however, he was to see the concrete evidence of his success for the first time.

He picked his way across the railroad tracks to the line of warehouses that bordered the docks, numbered with enormous Roman numerals and full of grain in bags. The sight of these bags of grain put him in mind of the fact that among all the other shippers he was practically alone in his way of handling his wheat. They handled the grain in bags; he, however, preferred it in the bulk. Bags were sometimes four cents apiece, and he had decided to build his elevator and bulk his grain therein, rather than to incur this expense. Only a small part of his wheat—that on Number Three division— had been sacked. All the rest, practically two-thirds of the entire harvest of Los Muertos, now found itself warehoused in his enormous elevator at Port Costa.

To a certain degree it had been the desire of observing the working of his system of handling the wheat in bulk that had drawn S. Behrman to Port Costa. But the more powerful motive had been curiosity, not to say downright sentiment. So long had he planned for this day of triumph, so eagerly had he looked forward to it, that now, when it had come, he wished to enjoy it to its fullest extent, wished to miss no feature of the disposal of the crop. He had watched it harvested, he had watched it hauled to the railway, and now would watch it as it poured into the hold of the ship, would even watch the ship as she cleared and got under way.

He passed through the warehouses and came out upon the dock that ran parallel with the shore of the bay. A great quantity of shipping was in view, barques for the most part, Cape Horners, great, deep sea tramps, whose iron-shod forefeet had parted every ocean the world round from Rangoon to Rio Janeiro, and from Melbourne to Christiania. Some were still in the stream, loaded with wheat to the Plimsoll mark, ready to depart with the next tide. But many others laid their great flanks alongside the docks and at that moment were being filled by derrick and crane with thousands upon thousands of bags of wheat. The scene was brisk; the cranes creaked and swung incessantly with a rattle of chains; stevedores and wharfingers toiled and perspired; boatswains and dock-masters shouted orders, drays rumbled, the water lapped at the piles; a group of sailors, painting the flanks of one of the great ships, raised an occasional chanty; the trade wind sang aeolian in the cordages, filling the air with the nimble taint of salt. All around were the noises of ships and the feel and flavor of the sea.

S. Behrman soon discovered his elevator. It was the largest structure discernible, and upon its red roof, in enormous white letters, was his own name. Thither, between piles of grain bags, halted drays, crates and boxes of merchandise, with an occasional pyramid of salmon cases, S. Behrman took his way. Cabled to the dock, close under his elevator, lay a great ship with lofty masts and great spars. Her stern was toward him as he approached, and upon it, in raised golden letters, he could read the words "Swanhilda — Liverpool."

He went aboard by a very steep gangway and found the mate on the quarter deck. S. Behrman introduced himself.

"Well," he added, "how are you getting on?"

"Very fairly, sir," returned the mate, who was an Englishman. "We'll have her all snugged down tight by this time, day after to-morrow. It's a great saving of time shunting the stuff in her like that, and three men can do the work of seven."

"I'll have a look 'round, I believe," returned S. Behrman.

"Right — oh," answered the mate with a nod.

S. Behrman went forward to the hatch that opened down into the vast hold of the ship. A great iron chute connected this hatch with the elevator, and through it was rushing a veritable cataract of wheat.

It came from some gigantic bin within the elevator itself, rushing down the confines of the chute to plunge into the roomy, gloomy interior of the hold with an incessant, metallic roar, persistent, steady, inevitable. No men were in sight. The place was deserted. No human agency seemed to be back of the movement of the wheat. Rather, the grain seemed impelled with a force of its own, a resistless, huge force, eager, vivid, impatient for the sea.

S. Behrman stood watching, his ears deafened with the roar of the hard grains against the metallic lining of the chute. He put his hand once into the rushing tide, and the contact rasped the flesh of his fingers and like an undertow drew his hand after it in its impetuous dash.

Cautiously he peered down into the hold. A musty odour rose to his nostrils, the vigorous, pungent aroma of the raw cereal. It was dark. He could see nothing; but all about and over the opening of the hatch the air was full of a fine, impalpable dust that blinded the eyes and choked the throat and nostrils.

As his eyes became used to the shadows of the cavern below him, he began to distinguish the grey mass of the wheat, a great expanse, almost liquid in its texture, which, as the cataract from above plunged into it, moved and shifted in long, slow eddies. As he stood there, this cataract on a sudden increased in volume. He turned about, casting his eyes upward toward the elevator to discover the cause. His foot caught in a coil of rope, and he fell headforemost into the hold.

The fall was a long one and he struck the surface of the wheat with the sodden impact of a bundle of damp clothes. For the moment he was stunned. All the breath was driven from his body. He could neither move nor cry out. But, by degrees, his wits steadied themselves and his breath returned to him. He looked about and above him. The daylight in the hold was dimmed and clouded by the thick, chaff-dust thrown off by the pour of grain, and even this dimness dwindled to twilight at a short distance from the opening of the hatch, while the remotest quarters were lost in impenetrable blackness. He got upon his feet only to find that he sunk ankle deep in the loose packed mass underfoot.

"Hell," he muttered, "here's a fix."

Directly underneath the chute, the wheat, as it poured in, raised itself in a conical mound, but from the sides of this mound it shunted away incessantly in thick layers, flowing in all directions with the nimbleness of water. Even as S. Behrman spoke, a wave of grain poured around his legs and rose rapidly to the level of his knees. He stepped quickly back. To stay near the chute would soon bury him to the waist.

No doubt, there was some other exit from the hold, some companion ladder that led up to the deck. He scuffled and waded across the wheat, groping in the dark with outstretched hands. With every inhalation he choked, filling his mouth and nostrils more with dust than with air. At times he could not breathe at all, but gagged and gasped, his lips distended. But search as he would he could find no outlet to the hold, no stairway, no companion ladder. Again and again, staggering along in the black darkness, he bruised his knuckles and forehead against the iron sides of the ship. He gave up the attempt to find any interior means of escape and returned laboriously to the space under the open hatchway. Already he could see that the level of the wheat was raised.

"God," he said, "this isn't going to do at all." He uttered a great shout. "Hello, on deck there, somebody. For God's sake."

The steady, metallic roar of the pouring wheat drowned out his voice. He could scarcely hear it himself above the rush of the cataract. Besides this, he found it impossible to stay under the hatch. The flying grains of wheat, spattering as they fell, stung his face like wind-driven particles of ice. It was a veritable torture; his hands smarted with it. Once he was all but blinded. Furthermore, the succeeding waves of wheat, rolling from the mound under the chute, beat him back, swirling and dashing against his legs and knees, mounting swiftly higher, carrying him off his feet.

Once more he retreated, drawing back from beneath the hatch. He stood still for a moment and shouted again. It was in vain. His voice returned upon him, unable to penetrate the thunder of the chute, and horrified, he discovered that so soon as he stood motionless upon the wheat, he sank into it. Before he knew it, he was knee-deep again, and a long swirl of grain sweeping outward from the ever-breaking, ever-reforming pyramid below the chute, poured around his thighs, immobolising him.

A frenzy of terror suddenly leaped to life within him. The horror of death, the Fear of The Trap, shook him like a dry reed. Shouting, he tore himself free of the wheat and once more scrambled and struggled towards the hatchway. He stumbled as he reached it and fell directly beneath the pour. Like a storm of small shot, mercilessly, pitilessly, the unnumbered multitude of hurtling grains flagellated and beat and tore his flesh. Blood streamed from his forehead and, thickening with the powder-like chaff-dust, blinded his eyes. He struggled to his feet once more. An avalanche from the cone of wheat buried him to his thighs. He was forced back and back and back, beating the air, falling, rising, howling for aid. He could no longer see; his eyes, crammed with dust, smarted as if transfixed with needles whenever he opened them. His mouth was full of the dust, his lips were dry with it; thirst tortured him, while his outcries choked and gagged in his rasped throat.

And all the while without stop, incessantly, inexorably, the wheat, as if moving with a force all its own, shot downward in a prolonged roar, persistent, steady, inevitable.

He retreated to a far corner of the hold and sat down with his back against the iron hull of the ship and tried to collect his thoughts, to calm himself. Surely there must be some way of escape; surely he was not to die like this, die in this dreadful substance that was neither solid nor fluid. What was he to do? How make himself heard?

But even as he thought about this, the cone under the chute broke again and sent a great layer of grain rippling and tumbling toward him. It reached him where he sat and buried his hand and one foot.

He sprang up trembling and made for another corner.

"By God," he cried, "by God, I must think of something pretty quick!"

Once more the level of the wheat rose and the grains began piling deeper about him. Once more he retreated. Once more he crawled staggering to the foot of the cataract, screaming till his ears sang and his eyeballs strained in their sockets, and once more the relentless tide drove him back.

Then began that terrible dance of death; the man dodging, doubling, squirming, hunted from one corner to another, the wheat slowly, inexorably flowing, rising, spreading to every angle, to every nook and cranny. It reached his middle. Furious and with bleeding hands and broken nails, he dug his way out to fall backward, all but exhausted, gasping for breath in the dust-thickened air. Roused again by the slow advance of the tide, he leaped up and stumbled away, blinded with the agony in his eyes, only to crash against the metal hull of the vessel. He turned about, the blood streaming from his face, and paused to collect his senses, and with a rush, another wave swirled about his ankles and knees. Exhaustion grew upon him. To stand still meant to sink; to lie or sit meant to be buried the quicker; and all this in the dark, all this in an air that could scarcely be breathed, all this while he fought an enemy that could not be gripped, toiling in a sea that could not be stayed.

Guided by the sound of the falling wheat, S. Behrman crawled on hands and knees toward the hatchway. Once more he raised his voice in a shout for help. His bleeding throat and raw, parched lips refused to utter but a wheezing moan. Once more he tried to look toward the one patch of faint light above him. His eye-lids, clogged with chaff, could no longer open. The Wheat poured about his waist as he raised himself upon his knees.

Reason fled. Deafened with the roar of the grain, blinded and made dumb with its chaff, he threw himself forward with clutching fingers, rolling upon his back, and lay there, moving feebly, the head rolling from side to side. The Wheat, leaping continuously from the chute, poured around him. It filled the pockets of the coat, it crept up the sleeves and trouser legs, it covered the great, protuberant stomach, it ran at last in rivulets into the distended, gasping mouth. It covered the face. Upon the surface of the Wheat, under the chute, nothing moved but the Wheat itself. There was no sign of life. Then, for an instant, the surface stirred. A hand, fat, with short fingers and swollen veins, reached up, clutching, then fell limp and prone. In another instant it was covered. In the hold of the "Swanhilda" there was no movement but the widening ripples that spread flowing from the ever-breaking, ever-reforming cone; no sound, but the rushing of the Wheat that continued to plunge incessantly from the iron chute in a prolonged roar, persistent, steady, inevitable.

CONCLUSION

The "Swanhilda" cast off from the docks at Port Costa two days after Presley had left Bonneville and the ranches and made her way up to San Francisco, anchoring in the stream off the City front. A few hours after her arrival, Presley, waiting at his club, received a despatch from Cedarquist to the effect that she would clear early the next morning and that he must be aboard of her before midnight.

He sent his trunks aboard and at once hurried to Cedarquist's office to say good-bye. He found the manufacturer in excellent spirits.

"What do you think of Lyman Derrick now, Presley?" he said, when Presley had sat down. "He's in the new politics with a vengeance, isn't he? And our own dear Railroad openly acknowledges him as their candidate. You've heard of his canvass."

"Yes, yes," answered Presley. "Well, he knows his business best."

But Cedarquist was full of another idea: his new venture—the organizing of a line of clipper wheat ships for Pacific and Oriental trade—was prospering.

"The 'Swanhilda' is the mother of the fleet, Pres. I had to buy HER, but the keel of her sister ship will be laid by the time she discharges at Calcutta. We'll carry our wheat into Asia yet. The Anglo-Saxon started from there at the beginning of everything and it's manifest destiny that he must circle the globe and fetch up where he began his march. You are up with procession, Pres, going to India this way in a wheat ship that flies American colours. By the way, do you know where the money is to come from to build the sister ship of the 'Swanhilda'? From the sale of the plant and scrap iron of the Atlas Works. Yes, I've given it up definitely, that business. The people here would not back me up. But I'm working off on this new line now. It may break me, but we'll try it on. You know the 'Million Dollar Fair' was formally opened yesterday. There is," he added with a wink, "a Midway Pleasance in connection with the thing. Mrs. Cedarquist and our friend Hartrath 'got up a subscription' to construct a figure of California—heroic size—out of dried apricots. I assure you," he remarked With prodigious gravity, "it is a real work of art and quite a 'feature' of the Fair. Well, good luck to you, Pres. Write to me from Honolulu, and bon voyage. My respects to the hungry Hindoo. Tell him 'we're coming, Father Abraham, a hundred thousand more.' Tell the men of the East to look out for the men of the West. The irrepressible Yank is knocking at the doors of their temples and he will want to sell 'em carpet-sweepers for their harems and electric light plants for their temple shrines. Good-bye to you."

"Good-bye, sir."

"Get fat yourself while you're about it, Presley," he observed, as the two stood up and shook hands.

"There shouldn't be any lack of food on a wheat ship. Bread enough, surely."

"Little monotonous, though. 'Man cannot live by bread alone.' Well, you're really off. Good-bye."

"Good-bye, sir."

And as Presley issued from the building and stepped out into the street, he was abruptly aware of a great wagon shrouded in white cloth, inside of which a bass drum was being furiously beaten. On the cloth, in great letters, were the words:

"Vote for Lyman Derrick, Regular Republican Nominee for Governor of California."

The "Swanhilda" lifted and rolled slowly, majestically on the ground swell of the Pacific, the water hissing and boiling under her forefoot, her cordage vibrating and droning in the steady rush of the trade winds. It was drawing towards-evening and her lights had just been set. The master passed Presley, who was leaning over the rail smoking a cigarette, and paused long enough to remark:

"The land yonder, if you can make it out, is Point Gordo, and if you were to draw a line from our position now through that point and carry it on about a hundred miles further, it would just about cross Tulare County not very far from where you used to live."

"I see," answered Presley, "I see. Thanks. I am glad to know that."

The master passed on, and Presley, going up to the quarter deck, looked long and earnestly at the faint line of mountains that showed vague and bluish above the waste of tumbling water.

Those were the mountains of the Coast range and beyond them was what once had been his home. Bonneville was there, and Guadalajara and Los Muertos and Quien Sabe, the Mission of San Juan, the Seed ranch, Annixter's desolated home and Dyke's ruined hop-fields.

Well, it was all over now, that terrible drama through which he had lived. Already it was far distant from him; but once again it rose in his memory, portentous, sombre, ineffaceable. He passed it all in review from the day of his first meeting with Vanamee to the day of his parting with Hilma. He saw it all—the great sweep of country opening to view from the summit of the hills at the head waters of Broderson's Creek; the barn dance at Annixter's, the harness room with its jam of furious men; the quiet garden of the Mission; Dyke's house, his flight upon the engine, his brave fight in the chaparral; Lyman Derrick at bay in the dining-room of the ranch house; the rabbit drive; the fight at the irrigating ditch, the shouting mob in the Bonneville Opera House. The drama was over. The fight of Ranch and Railroad had been wrought out to its dreadful close. It was true, as Shelgrim had said, that forces rather than men had locked horns in that struggle, but for all that the men of the Ranch and not the men of the Railroad had suffered. Into the prosperous valley, into the quiet community of farmers, that galloping monster, that terror of steel and steam had burst, shooting athwart the horizons, flinging the echo of its thunder over all the ranches of the valley, leaving blood and destruction in its path.

Yes, the Railroad had prevailed. The ranches had been seized in the tentacles of the octopus; the iniquitous burden of extortionate freight rates had been imposed like a yoke of iron. The monster had killed Harran, had killed Osterman, had killed Broderson, had killed Hooven. It had beggared Magnus and had driven him to a state of semi-insanity after he had wrecked his honour in the vain attempt to do evil that good might come. It had enticed Lyman into its toils to pluck from him his manhood and his honesty, corrupting him and poisoning him beyond redemption; it had hounded Dyke from his legitimate employment and had made of him a highwayman and criminal. It had cast forth Mrs. Hooven to starve to death upon the City streets. It had driven Minna to prostitution. It had slain Annixter at the very moment when painfully and manfully he had at last achieved his own salvation and stood forth resolved to do right, to act unselfishly and to live for others. It had widowed Hilma in the very dawn of her happiness. It had killed the very babe within the mother's womb, strangling life ere yet it had been born, stamping out the spark ordained by God to burn through all eternity.

What then was left? Was there no hope, no outlook for the future, no rift in the black curtain, no glimmer through the night? Was good to be thus overthrown? Was evil thus to be strong and to prevail? Was nothing left?

Then suddenly Vanamee's words came back to his mind. What was the larger view, what contributed the greatest good to the greatest numbers? What was the full round of the circle whose segment only he beheld? In the end, the ultimate, final end of all, what was left? Yes, good issued from this crisis, untouched, unassailable, undefiled.

Men—motes in the sunshine—perished, were shot down in the very noon of life, hearts were broken, little children started in life lamentably handicapped; young girls were brought to a life of shame; old women died in the heart of life for lack of food. In that little, isolated group of human insects, misery, death, and anguish spun like a wheel of fire.

BUT THE WHEAT REMAINED. Untouched, unassailable, undefiled, that mighty world-force, that nourisher of nations, wrapped in Nirvanic calm, indifferent to the human swarm, gigantic, resistless, moved onward in its appointed grooves. Through the welter of blood at the irrigation ditch, through the sham charity and shallow philanthropy of famine relief committees, the great harvest of Los Muertos rolled like a flood from the Sierras to the Himalayas to feed thousands of starving scarecrows on the barren plains of India.

Falseness dies; injustice and oppression in the end of everything fade and vanish away. Greed, cruelty, selfishness, and inhumanity are short-lived; the individual suffers, but the race goes on. Annixter dies, but in a far distant corner of the world a thousand lives are saved. The larger view always and through all shams, all wickednesses, discovers the Truth that will, in the end, prevail, and all things, surely, inevitably, resistlessly work together for good.